# My
# Great-Aunt's
# Diary

## BOOKS BY LAURA SWEENEY

DOVECOTE COTTAGES SERIES

*My Grandmother's Secret*

# My
# Great-Aunt's
# Diary

Laura Sweeney

bookouture

Published by Bookouture in 2025

An imprint of Storyfire Ltd.
Carmelite House
50 Victoria Embankment
London EC4Y 0DZ

www.bookouture.com

The authorised representative in the EEA is Hachette Ireland
8 Castlecourt Centre
Dublin 15 D15 XTP3
Ireland
(email: info@hbgi.ie)

ISBN: 978-1-83618-404-1
eBook ISBN: 978-1-83618-403-4

*For Jo.*

*In Memory of Cpl Arthur Fish ACC.*

# PROLOGUE
## VIOLET

June 1945

I flashed my bravest smile as I walked the length of the trestle table, refilling teacups. Beachfront Road had been decked out in red, white, and blue bunting. The town's children were proudly wearing cloth party hats. We were happy, of course we were. The war was over, and it was a party after all. But, a month since victory had been declared in Europe, some of us were still fearfully waiting for news. My friend, Lily Morrison, placed a delicate hand on my arm and gave it a reassuring squeeze.

'He'll be home soon, Violet,' she said. I blinked back tears.

A train whistled as it pulled into Dovecote station, barely audible above the shrieks and laughter of the children, fuelled by sandwiches and jellies, running up and down the road.

I placed the teapot at the end of the table and turned towards the sea. A gentle breeze ruffled my hair. I pulled a strand that had fallen loose from my bun back behind my ear. Salty spray settled on my lips. I rubbed the band of my engagement ring with my thumb. He was out there, somewhere.

'Still daydreaming, Violet Saunders?' A familiar voice cut through the noise.

I whipped around, not daring to believe it was him. But there he was, at the far end of the table, knapsack in hand, looking dashing in his uniform.

'Hugo?'

My feet barely touched the ground as I ran and flung myself into his arms. Our lingering kiss was met with whistles and whoops from the gathered residents of Dovecote. I couldn't give a fig. My fiancé was alive, he was home.

I couldn't sleep that night. A shaft of silver moonlight on the bed rippled as I slowly peeled back the covers and slipped out. Hugo snuffled in his sleep, and I held my breath for a moment, but he resumed his soft snoring.

Having tiptoed out of the bedroom and down the stairs of Clifftop Cottage, I crossed the sitting room to my ebonised oak Charles Rennie Mackintosh-style writing bureau. Silently I pulled open the top drawer to check that the sketchbook and the brown-leather diary were still in there before closing it again. I turned the key and removed it from the lock.

Lowering the writing shelf, I removed a small panel at the back of the desk revealing a tiny secret compartment. The key just about fit. I replaced the panel and shut the bureau. It was an old piece of furniture, so it was feasible that the key to the locked drawer had been lost decades ago.

I slipped out through the French doors in the kitchen and tiptoed along the path to the old potting shed I'd not long before converted into my art studio. Tucked behind a stack of unused canvases were two paintings, wrapped in brown paper and tied with string. A smile pulled at the corners of my mouth as I ran my fingers over the address on the package: Mrs Z Petherington-Smyth, Sommertown House, Oxford. I'd wrapped them the day after Hugo proposed. It was time to send them to her. They would be a fitting first, and last, reply to her letters.

# ONE

## EMILY

June 2016

Emily Carmichael read the letter for a second time, struggling to understand the words in front of her. She paced the small living room of her girlfriend Maxine's flat, running her fingers through her shoulder-length auburn hair. A wave of guilt churned her stomach, and she chewed the tip of her thumbnail. If she'd known that her great-aunt Violet was going to leave Clifftop Cottage to her in her will, she would have made the effort to go to her funeral and pay her last respects to the woman she hadn't seen in fifteen years.

She rubbed her jaw in disbelief. Why her? Fair enough Violet hadn't had any children to leave the cottage to, but why not leave it to her nephew, Emily's dad? Then again, Paul Carmichael hadn't spoken to anyone in the family for fourteen years, since he'd left Emily's mother and disappeared to the Costa del Sol with his girlfriend.

Emily put the letter down on the kitchen countertop and let out a little squeal. She owned a cottage. No mortgage, no rent. It was hers. There was no way she'd have even dreamt of owning a property at the age of thirty-one. Or ever, considering the ridiculous London property market.

Even though she hadn't visited for fifteen years, she clearly remembered the stone cottage nestled between the edge of the Dovecote Manor estate forest and the cliff that overlooked the south-coast town of Dovecote and the sea. Dovecote was the sort of place Max would hate. She sighed, coming back to reality, and checked the time. Where was Max anyway? She should have been home an hour ago. Her mobile pinged with the answer.

> *Sorry babe, going to be a late one. They've shifted the deadline for this project, so I've loads to do tonight. Be home as soon as I can.*

Another sigh escaped. Max was clearly too busy to even put a kiss at the end of her text. This was the third time in two weeks that Max had worked late. The beginning of a headache throbbed behind Emily's eyes. She needed some air, and something stodgy for dinner. She pulled the front door behind her and headed towards Earl's Court Road. Outside wasn't much better than inside. The stifling summer heat had struck London early, and the evening air was thick and sticky.

As Emily waited at the pedestrian crossing, her heart set on a greasy pizza from the shop across the road, her eyes fell on a table in the window of the pub on the opposite corner. Max's friend Lorna was sitting at the table, her long, blonde hair falling in elegant waves across her bare shoulders. The lowness of her off-the-shoulder top left nothing to the imagination. She was alone but there were two half-drunk glasses of wine on the table in front of her. Her companion returned, tucking her black T-shirt into her jeans and sweeping her dark fringe into her trademark quiff. Lorna smiled, tilted her face upwards, and kissed Max. Emily tried to take a step backwards but tripped over her own trainers, and stumbled back against the window of a fried chicken takeaway. Her heart raced as her vision blurred with tears. How could she have been so stupid?

'I hope you stormed into the pub and threw the wine in her face,' Gio said, refilling Emily's glass. With tears pouring down her face, Emily had run back to the flat, thrown her clothes into whatever bags she could grab, chucked the bags into her car, and driven straight to her best friend's flat. In the ten years Emily had known Gio, since they'd both ended up in the same dingy flat share, he'd been the one she'd turned to when yet another relationship had gone wrong. She'd cried on his shoulder far too many times to count. Gio had cursed Max's name and her family's name, sat Emily down on the expensive sofa in his classily decorated sitting room, and poured them each a large glass of Pinot Grigio. He knew the drill.

'No,' she sniffled. Gio's dark eyes were stormy. 'I can't believe it. She promised me she'd never do it again, after the last time.'

'Darling,' Gio sighed, his beautiful Italian accent drawing the vowels out. 'I don't like to say it, but I *can* believe it. Of course, I'd hoped Max had changed. But some people are trash.' He put his arm around Emily's shoulders, and she sank into his embrace as more tears sprung from her eyes. 'So, what are you going to do now?' he asked. 'You're not going to go back to her, are you?'

Emily picked at a loose thread on her T-shirt. 'No, we're done. A whole year wasted. I may be a softie but even I have my limits, and being cheated on twice is about my limit. Oh God, it hurts though. Why does this always happen to me? Why is everyone I date a nightmare?' She dug her fingers into her hair, pressing the tips hard against her scalp. 'It's me, isn't it? I must deserve to be lied to and cheated on. I'm clearly not worthy of love.'

Gio looked at her for a long moment, a deep frown wrinkling his forehead. 'Drink more wine,' he eventually said. 'You can stay here tonight. Then tomorrow, we will see. And they haven't *all* been nightmares.'

Emily groaned. 'Please don't. Not now.' She did not need to be reminded of the good ones. The ones that got away. That she'd pushed away.

'I'm just saying you can't blame everyone else for your, how shall I put it, disastrous love life.'

Emily scowled at Gio and crossed her arms tightly. 'Don't you have a date tonight that you should be getting ready for?'

He shrugged. 'I can cancel, it's no problem.'

'No, go. I'll be okay here on my own.'

Gio arched an eyebrow. 'And leave you unsupervised with my wine? I don't think so. To be honest, I was looking for a reason to cancel. He's not really my type.'

Emily had to laugh. 'Since when has that stopped you?'

'I am shocked you think that of me,' he said, raising a hand to his chest and faking outrage. 'I have quite strict criteria as to who I'll sleep with.'

'Namely that they have a pulse.'

Emily caught Gio's eye, and they both dissolved into giggles.

'Thanks, Gio,' she said once their laughter had subsided.

He winked and squeezed her hand. 'I love you. And I want you to be happy. But please remember you are a goddess. Anyone who treats you badly does not deserve your tears. You are worthy of love, honesty, and fidelity. You will pick yourself up and dust yourself down. And you will be glorious again.'

Emily's eyes brimmed with fresh tears.

'You soppy thing, Gio,' she said, laughing to hide the wobble in her voice. 'I love you, too.'


The next morning, Emily's head throbbed as Gio refilled her coffee mug. She drew her feet up under herself and sank back against the sofa cushions.

'And you didn't think to tell me last night?' he huffed.

'Well, I had other things on my mind,' Emily replied.

'But an actual cottage, by the sea? Babe, this is exactly what you need.'

Emily frowned. 'Eh?'

Gio rolled his eyes. 'A change of scenery, a new start away from *her*. Away from London. All that fresh sea air. *Perfetto.*'

'I don't know, Gio. I mean, I spent three summers in Dovecote with Violet when I was a teenager and there are some people who might still be there that I don't fancy reuniting with.' Gio was frowning at her. 'It's a long story.'

'Where else are you going to go? Back to your mother's?'

Emily puffed out her cheeks. 'Oh God, no. Anyway, Mum's step-grandkids have moved into my old bedroom, so there's no room.' Even if her bedroom had been vacant, there was no way she could live with her mum again. They got on fine as long as they weren't in each other's pockets. And she could do without her mum's clumsy matchmaking attempts.

There was a glint of satisfaction in Gio's eyes and Emily drummed her fingers on the arm of the sofa. Maybe he had a point. Maybe a new start *was* what she needed. But leaving everyone and everything? On the other hand, what did she have? Gio? For sure, she'd miss him. Her mum? They barely saw each other anyway, now that Julie had her hands full with her step-grandchildren. Max? No, they were done. She could be a self-employed web designer anywhere. And Dovecote was only a two-hour drive from London. But there was still the small matter of what happened that last summer to consider – the broken promise, and the shattered heart. Was it a risk worth taking? Perhaps it was time to confront the shadows of her past.

'Hey.' Gio pinched her arm. 'You okay?'

His question punctured her thoughts. 'Oh, sorry, Gio. I'm fine. I was thinking.'

'Obviously,' he said with a grin. 'So?'

'I might drive down and have a look. I don't have to stay, right? I could go and just check out the cottage?'

'I think that's a very good idea. But can you get on with it and stop lounging about on my sofa?'

Emily threw a cushion at him. 'Alright! Give me a chance to wake up. I have a few things to sort out before I go. I'll need to tell Mum what's happened. She'll probably cry. The letter said to pick up the keys to the cottage from the solicitors in Lewes which is kind of on the way. Oh, and I suppose I should break up with Max.'

Gio kissed her cheek. 'I am so proud of you. You are magnificent. I have to go to work, unfortunately. The bridezillas of London need me to organise their weddings.' He tutted and rolled his eyes, pursing his dark lips. 'I have back-to-back meetings all day.'

'Well, that's what you get for being the hottest wedding planner at one of London's top hotels. Off you go, I'll be fine.'

They hugged each other for a long time and when they let go, they both had tears in their eyes.

'Call me when you get there. And send photos. And let me know when I can come and visit.' Gio sniffled. 'Oh, look at me, crying like a *bambino*.'

'You'll start me off, and I don't think I have any tears left after last night. And, hey, I might be back this evening. The cottage could be a run-down, spider-infested shack.'

Gio hugged her again. 'It won't be. It will be cute and so perfectly *you*. And you'll love it and you'll be free.'

'You will come and visit, won't you?'

Gio winked and blew her a kiss from the doorway. 'Try and stop me.'

At the click of the closing door, Emily drew a deep breath. It was going to be quite a day. Would it end with her coming face-to-face with her past?

# TWO

## VIOLET

June 1940

Balancing my sketchbook on my knee, my pencil flew across the page as I tried to capture the scene in front of me. A steady stream of men in strange uniforms emerged from Brighton train station, hobbling, smoking, or carrying kit bags. They were shepherded into ambulances and vans parked under the wrought-iron and glass canopy at the front of the station by young nurses in starched aprons and perky caps. One of the soldiers said something to a freckled nurse who called to one of her colleagues.

'Lily, there's a man on the train who can't walk.'

Her colleague, a slim woman with blonde curly hair, gestured towards a pair of orderlies who picked up a stretcher and followed her inside.

A few moments later, the blonde nurse and the orderlies reappeared. On the stretcher was a soldier with a bandage around his right thigh. His uniform was soaked with blood, and he looked like he was in a lot of pain. I shivered. Mum would tell me off, say I was too young to be seeing such things. She was probably right, but at fifteen I had no control over what was happening in the world. The war wasn't my fault. And this scene wasn't my fault. But I had the urge to capture it, to put it down on paper so that it wouldn't be forgotten.

A shadow fell across the page of my sketchbook. A silhouette of the squared shoulders of a school blazer and a straw boater.

'That's rather good,' a plummy voice said from behind me. When I turned and looked at her, my breath stalled. She was the most beautiful girl I'd ever seen. Her long golden-blonde plait snaking over her shoulder was tied with a navy ribbon. Her skin was like porcelain, and her green eyes shone like a cat's. She had a dainty upturned nose with a line of pale freckles. They were so perfectly placed that I wouldn't have been surprised to find out they'd been drawn on. 'I'm Zeyla. Zeyla Wythenshawe,' she said, flashing me a smile that showed off a row of perfectly straight teeth.

'Violet Saunders,' I stuttered, wiping the pencil stains off my fingers on my coarse wool skirt. She was one of the girls from the posh school a few miles out of town. The crest on the pocket of her blazer, her navy gymslip, and the matching ribbon around her straw boater were a sure-fire giveaway, if her accent and her ridiculous name hadn't been enough. She looked me up and down, taking in my mended clothes, scuffed shoes, dry auburn hair, too-wide blue eyes, and thin frame. Her eyes lingered on my narrow nose. Did I have a smudge of pencil on it? I shrank back from her gaze.

'Zeyla, come on. We'll miss the train.' A group of girls in matching uniforms shouted and waved to her.

'Must dash. I have to get the train home to Dovecote because Father's driver won't come all the way to Brighton any more.' She rolled her eyes. I immediately envied her problems. 'Say, why don't you come with us? We're spending exeat weekend at mine this term.'

I had no idea what she was talking about. She must have noticed the confusion on my face as she laughed.

'Your parents must not have packed you off to boarding school. It means a weekend of leave at home. It'll be jolly good fun.'

I gave her a shy smile. I had nothing in common with any of these girls. 'Oh, that's very kind, but I have to go to work.'

'Work? Are you not at school still?'

'No, I left when I was fourteen, last year.'

Zeyla's face lit up. 'I say, aren't you the lucky one? I would love to not go to school, it's beastly.'

'I wouldn't say I was lucky,' I huffed, reaching for my shoulder bag and slotting my sketchbook next to my gas mask and a spare pair of stockings. I always managed to snag my stockings carrying boxes from the storeroom to the shop floor at Boland's department store, where I worked. They were more darning than original by now. 'My dad died last year, killed in an explosion at the munitions factory where he worked.' My breath caught in my throat. I missed him so much. 'Mum hasn't been right since, and someone has to keep a roof over our heads.'

Zeyla looked down at her polished shoes, a pink tinge on her cheeks. 'Sorry,' she muttered.

I shrugged. 'It is what it is.'

'Zeyla,' her friends cried.

She gave me a quick half-smile and ran away to join them. As I headed down Queens Road for the half-mile walk to Boland's, I glanced over my shoulder. She was watching me walk away. My skin tingled but I brushed the sensation off. I would never see her again, and even if I did, she probably wasn't like me anyway.

# THREE

## EMILY

June 2016

That afternoon, as she drove south to Dovecote, Emily's mind buzzed with the events of the morning. Her mother had shed happy tears as she loaded Emily's car with bedding and other bits and bobs. As much as her mother embarrassed her sometimes, she'd still miss her. The cold detachment in Max's eyes lingered. She hadn't even apologised, or promised to change, or begged Emily not to leave. A blazing row would have been easier to deal with than apathy. Clearly Max thought so little of Emily that her leaving didn't warrant any sort of emotional outburst. Well, if that was how it was, she was better off out of it. Max had hinted it was fairly serious between her and Lorna. So she would probably have dumped Emily soon. At least this way it had happened on Emily's own terms. But it still hurt enough to make her chest ache.

Having stopped off in Lewes to pick up the keys to Clifftop Cottage, Emily arrived in Dovecote. It had been fifteen years since she'd been in the picturesque seaside town and she couldn't resist a slight detour to see if it had changed. She drove along Blythe Avenue, which ran parallel to the beach, past the back of Dovecote Museum, the empty patch of scrubland next to it, and the wrought-iron gates of Victoria Park. She took a sharp left onto Queen's Parade, which bordered the park, before turning sharply right and ending up alongside The Promenade. She wound down her window. Her car was flooded with the salty tang of sea air laced with sun cream and chips, and the shrill call of circling seagulls. The flowers in the bed separating Queen's Parade from The Promenade were a riot of pink and purple. She smiled to herself as she spotted the hair-dressers on Queen's Parade. The name above the door might have changed but it was unquestionably the place Violet had taken her one summer and allowed her to get her hair crimped like Christina Aguilera. Her mother had been furious.

Navigating the mini roundabout at the end of Queen's Parade, opposite Dovecote train station, Emily turned onto the High Street and headed up the hill towards the turning onto Brighton Road. She flicked off her satnav; she didn't need it now. Harrington's Bookshop was still there on the corner of Blythe Avenue, as was the Royal Oak pub on the opposite corner, and the chip shop across the High Street. Not much had changed at all. At the top of the High Street, on the bridge over the railway line, she glanced in her rearview mirror. The silver sports car behind was far too close to her bumper.

'Back off, you numpty,' she muttered to herself as she passed St. John's Church. Opposite the entrance to Dovecote Primary School, a few yards further down Brighton Road, she pulled over. On her left, high semi-circular railings and gates formed a majestic entrance to the Dovecote Manor estate, on which Clifftop Cottage was situated. The tall stone gateposts were topped with carved lions, glaring imperiously at anyone who dared cross the threshold. The driver of the silver sports car blared his horn before swinging around her and speeding through the gates and up the winding, rhododendron-lined driveway. Could it be...? Emily's grip on the steering wheel tightened.

Immediately inside the gates, there was a fork in the driveway and Emily took the long, twisting road to the left. It was steep and only just wide enough for her car so, occasionally, branches brushed her wing mirrors. Her heart raced as she rounded the last bend, and emerged onto a square, gravel clearing. And there it was – Clifftop Cottage.

The memories came flooding back, and Emily released a slow breath as she pulled up alongside a low, stone wall around the rosebush-filled front garden. Having got out of her car, she placed her hand on the sage-green wooden gate and paused to inhale the scent of rhododendron and oak tree. Climbing roses had grown up the grey stone walls of the cottage, reaching the upper windows and trailing over the pitched roof of the porch. The curtains in the downstairs front window, to the right of the oak front door, were drawn shut. The sun glinted off the slate roof. A sea breeze rustled the grass on the exposed cliff side of the cottage as she walked up the short path to the door. She ran her fingers over the lion's head door knocker and slipped her key into the lock.

Crossing the threshold into the cosy sitting room of Clifftop Cottage was like slipping on a pair of comfy slippers. She stood in the darkened room for a moment, breathing in the familiar scent of old books, well-worn upholstery, and furniture polish. Suddenly fifteen years vanished, and Emily was no longer thirty-one years old; it was 2001 and she was sixteen and relieved to be away from the noise and heat of London's East End.

Emily shook off the warm memories and moved towards the window that looked out at the rose garden and the woods at the front of the cottage. A cloud of dust billowed from the heavy maroon velvet curtains as she pulled them open. With sunlight flooding the room, she took a closer look around. Nothing had changed since she'd last been there. The overstuffed floral sofa and matching pair of armchairs, the oval coffee table, the bookshelves either side of the chimney breast, the red-brick fireplace with its oak mantle, and the heavy wooden door that led out to the back courtyard were all so familiar. Could she even hear the faint peal of Great-Aunt Violet's laugh?

'If you're here, Vi, thank you. But you can go now and rest,' she whispered. No books flew off the shelves and no doors slammed ominously. She puffed out a relieved breath.

'Oh,' she said, crossing the room to the bureau against the opposite wall. 'You're still here too.' She ran her hands over the blackened oak of the Mackintosh-style desk. The silver ring handle of the fold-down writing table jangled as her finger caught in it. Dust had settled on the small stained-glass panels above the desk and Emily wiped the purple rose and green leaf motif with her sleeve.

Moving away from the desk, she pushed open the door into the south-facing kitchen where she was greeted by bright sunlight. The cupboards were the same shade of light blue she remembered, and she ran her hand along the farmhouse table, smiling to herself. She opened the French doors at the far end of the room, stepped out onto a roughly paved path that led through the wood to Dovecote Manor beyond, and drew the cool, salt-tinged breeze deep into her lungs. Her phone rang, shattering the peace and quiet.

'Hi, Gio,' she said, going back inside and sinking into one of the kitchen chairs.

'Emily, you didn't call. I was worried. How are you? Is everything okay?'

Emily had a mental flashback to the silver sports car but pushed it aside. It could have been anyone. She didn't even know who lived at Dovecote Manor these days.

'Everything is great, Gio.'

'And the cottage?'

Emily let out a slow breath. 'It's so weird. It's exactly as I remember it. All the furniture is the same, the décor is the same. It was old fifteen years ago. But it's perfect.'

'So, you won't be back tonight?'

'I don't think so. No, I think I'll stay. For a bit anyway. You won't have a sofa-surfer cramping your style tonight.'

'That is not why I asked. You know I don't mind you staying. Although, I do have a date tonight.'

Emily laughed. 'Of course you do. Gio, honestly, you are outrageous.'

'You're just jealous.'

'Ouch. Kick me while I'm down why don't you?'

'I'm sorry. I didn't mean that.'

'I know you didn't. Actually, I've barely thought about Max.' Two other people had pushed Max out of her mind the moment she'd arrived in Dovecote. One of whom might well have been driving that silver sports car. The knot returned to her stomach.

'Good, she doesn't deserve any space in your head. I have to go. I need time to make myself beautiful before my date.'

'Gio, you are always beautiful. Have fun and be good.'

'You know me, darling. I'm always good, and if I'm not, I'm careful.'

Emily snorted. 'Bye, Gio. Love you.'

'I love you too. Call me. *Ciao.*'

And he was gone. The sudden silence of the cottage caught Emily off guard. She'd never lived alone before. The quiet and the solitude would take some getting used to.

# FOUR

## VIOLET

September 1940

'But you can't,' I cried, grasping Hugo's arm as we walked around the lake in Kemptown's Queen's Park, a few minutes up the hill from Brighton Beach. Two young boys in shorts were dipping a net in the water, trying to catch tadpoles. They reminded me of my brothers. 'You're far too young.'

He grinned back at me, that same mischievous grin he used to flash when he was ten. It was a grin that gave him a dimple in his right cheek. But this time the grin wasn't due to some childish hi-jinks. There was nothing childish about signing up.

'I guess I must look eighteen,' he said, wiggling his dark eyebrows. 'Might try and see if I can get served a pint of beer.'

'Hugo Cooper, this is not funny. You're only seventeen. You *can't* go to war. What shall I do without you?' Even though all I did was work and look after my mum and brothers, Hugo was always there for me to lean on. I might fall over without him holding me up.

He squeezed my hand. 'You'll keep the home fires burning, Vi.'

I sighed. Hugo had been my best friend for most of my life. Ever since my first day of school when he gallantly retrieved my hair ribbon from the puddle a group of bigger children had thrown it in. In all the years I'd known him, he'd never once laughed at me, or taunted me, or picked on me. Even though he was nearly two years older he'd stuck right by me.

He was the only person in the world who knew I didn't care much for boys, but that I found girls fascinating and bewitching. I'd had to tell him, once I'd worked it out for myself at the beginning of the year, as he'd hinted at us stepping out together so many times that it was becoming awkward. He hadn't batted an eyelid. He just hugged me and said that I should always be myself. I hadn't told him about Zeyla Wythenshawe with her perfect freckles and silky voice. I wanted to keep her all for myself.

It was Hugo I ran to on the day of the explosion that killed my dad. He'd held me while I cried myself hoarse. The next day, a delivery of fresh fruit and veg had arrived at our house from his parents' shop. He'd also been the one to get me my job at Boland's, personally recommending me to a friend of his parents who worked there. And although I felt no romantic attraction to him, I loved him. And here he was, on a sunny autumn day, telling me he had enlisted and was leaving that day for army training in Norfolk.

'Is there anything I can say that will make you change your mind?' I asked, fighting back tears. He turned to me, taking my hands in his.

'Tell me you love me and want to marry me.' He was deadly serious.

I had to laugh. 'Oh, Hugo. I do love you, but that's never going to happen.'

'You can't blame a chap for trying.' He kissed me gently on the forehead.

'What time is your train?' I asked.

'Half past four. Just time to say my goodbyes to Ma and Pa. Then off to Norfolk and then, who knows? I might get to see France or Africa or even Asia. Imagine that, Vi. Me, a greengrocer's son from Brighton, travelling the world. And taking out a few Germans along the way.' His eyes sparkled with youthful excitement, and I knew I had to let him go.

'Please be careful, Hugo. Promise me you'll come home.'

He wrapped his strong arms around me and pulled me into his chest. He smelt of Imperial Leather soap.

'I can't make that promise, Vi,' he said into my hair. 'Someone out there probably already has the bullet with my name on it.'

I pulled out of his embrace and wiped the tears from my cheeks.

'Will you at least write?'

'Every day.'

At the far end of the lake, he turned and saluted. How was it possible that the boy with messy hair and permanently scraped knees was going to be a soldier? I could barely see through my tears as he walked away.

The minute I pushed open the front door of my family's terraced house on Hereford Street in Kemptown, I was assaulted by a miniature whirlwind in the shape of my younger brother, John.

'Vi-vi,' John yelled, launching himself at me and wrapping his skinny arms around my neck. He was warm and breathless. His dark hair was plastered against his forehead. He looked like our dad had at his age. 'We've been playing football in the yard. Olly fell over and cut his knee and cried. But he's okay now.'

I envied John his six-year-old innocence. The worst thing that could happen to him was his football going over the wall into the neighbour's yard. I disentangled myself from John's hug and turned to Oliver, who was sitting on the bottom step of the steep, narrow stairs. His pale blue watery eyes were wide, and he hugged his knees to his chest. He was the spitting image of Mum. Just over a year younger than John, Oliver was a quiet boy. He was scared of everything, but I couldn't blame him. The world must be a scary place when you're small.

'Let's see, love.' I smiled, kneeling down to his eye level. There was a deep graze on his knee and bits of gravel amongst the dried blood.

'I washed it,' he said in a voice barely more than a whisper.

'I can see. You did a good job, but I think we need to give it another clean. And put some cream on it. Where's Mummy?'

'In the sitting room,' John said, careering back down the short hallway and into the kitchen. That wasn't a surprise. Mum barely ventured out of the sitting room any more. She mostly sat there on our saggy sofa, day after day, worrying one of Dad's old shirts in her twitching fingers. The doctor said he could give her some pills, but they'd make her sleepy and I worried about how I'd get her out of the house and into a shelter in the event of an air raid. Giving Oliver another reassuring smile, I led him into the kitchen at the back of the house and lifted him onto the worn draining board next to the cracked sink. He whimpered as I cleaned the graze, picking out as much dirt as I could.

'There now,' I said, giving him a kiss on the forehead. 'That's better. I'll nip in and see to Mum and then we'll get some supper.'

I did a mental inventory of what tins we had in the pantry, there was no point looking in the ice box. My stomach growled, but I would have to wait. The boys and Mum needed to be fed first. If there was enough left over, I'd have a bit. It was bad enough being poor at the best of times, but now it was almost unbearable. The boys were pale and thin, they needed fresh fruit and vegetables. But I couldn't stretch the budget that far, even with the help of Hugo's parents and what they could get in at their shop. It was all I could do to keep the four of us alive. I sighed as I pushed open the sitting room door. I sighed a lot.

The small sitting room was bathed in dull twilight. The evenings were drawing in. At least it was still warm enough not to need to light a fire. The evening light reflected off the silver frame of my parents' wedding photograph on the mantlepiece. Michael and Rebecca Saunders frozen in happiness. Sixteen years later, the light was suddenly snuffed out. The world seemed so dark since Dad's death. I pulled the blackout blinds down, checking the whole window was covered, before groping my way along the wall to the light switch.

'Alright, Mum?' I asked, falsely cheery. Her fair hair, once so bouncy and shiny, was dull and hung limply around her shoulders. I'd have to wash it for her one of these days. I hated to see her like this, so broken and lost. But at the same time, I wanted to shake her. I wanted to scream at her that her children needed her. That I couldn't do this. That I was only fifteen and it wasn't fair that I had to be the breadwinner and the house-wife. I swallowed back my bitter tears. I'd let them out later in the darkness of my tiny box bedroom. 'Hugo's joined up,' I added when she didn't reply.

'Oh,' she whispered.

'Do you want a cup of tea?'

She turned her lined, grey face towards me. Her eyes were red raw. She'd been crying again. 'That would be nice.'


Bedtime had been even more trying than usual. Oliver cried because his tummy hurt and John refused to go to bed without his toy Spitfire, which was nowhere to be found. I had sat down to darn another pair of stockings that I'd snagged at work when the air raid siren went off.

'Oh, for crying out loud,' I said.

I had to carry Oliver, still wrapped in his blanket, and drag John by the hand as we ran down the road towards the shelter. Mum followed close behind but dithered at the shelter entrance.

'Come on, Mum,' I said, trying to coax her down the steps into the dank cellar of the pub on the next street over. Most of the houses on our street had gardens with Anderson shelters but those of us with only concrete yards had to run to the cramped public shelter in the pub's damp basement. Quite a few of our neighbours had given up on going to the shelter, preferring to take their chances with the bombs rather than face the rats. Some had decided the best thing to do was to spend all day and night in the pub on the off chance that the siren went off. There were quite a few people in the basement who were a few sheets to the wind. I ushered Mum onto a bench as far away from the drunks as possible and sat next to her, with Oliver on my knee and John squeezed between us. The room quicky filled with weary, anxious people. With any luck, it would be a short one. My stockings wouldn't darn themselves.

A few children screamed at the loud thuds above us. This was a close one and my stomach contracted. I hugged Oliver tighter and grabbed John's hand.

'It'll be over soon, and you'll be back in your beds. Don't worry.'

'I'm not worried,' John said, puffing out his little chest. 'I'm not scared.' Oliver started to cry softly. Mum stared vacantly into the middle distance.

At the all-clear a few hours later, we scrambled back out into the street. Thick smoke hung in the air and flames crackled in the distance. I caught snippets of conversations as the crowd dispersed.

'The Odeon cinema's been hit.'

'The paper shop's gone.'

'Hereford Street's a mess.'

I broke into a run, sweeping John and Oliver up in my arms, Mum clinging to the back of my coat. The minute we turned into Hereford Street I knew. I could see the gap in the terrace. Our home was gone. All that was left was a pile of rubble. I sank to my knees, holding the boys close. Mum screamed and ran towards the smouldering pile. A fireman grabbed her and pulled her back.

'I'm sorry, Miss,' a man in a tin hat said gravely. 'Was anyone in there?'

I shuddered at the thought. 'No, we were all in the shelter.'

The man nodded solemnly. 'Well, that's something. Have you family you can stay with?'

I looked up at him, and shock registered on his face. He must have seen that I was only a child myself. I shook my head, and he placed a gentle hand on my shoulder.

'We'll find you somewhere for the night, and get things sorted in the morning.'

When I was small and had nightmares, Dad used to tell me everything would be alright in the morning. This was one nightmare I wouldn't wake up from, and I didn't hold out much hope for things being better by the light of day.

# FIVE

## EMILY

June 2016

Being woken up by birdsong, rather than police sirens, was something Emily could get used to. The patio at the back of Clifftop Cottage overlooking the sea wasn't a bad place to have a morning coffee either. The salty breeze coming over the top of the cliff mingled with the sweet scent of the blousy peonies and vibrant honeysuckle growing in the flowerbed against the kitchen wall. Emily breathed it in deeply as she watched a couple of seagulls dipping and swooping in the wind.

If she remembered correctly, the path from the gate in the low wall at the end of the patio led to a set of steep steps down the cliff and onto Beachfront Road. The other path, from the French doors in the kitchen, led to Dovecote Manor, passing Violet's old art studio. As a teenager, Emily had been a little intimidated by the studio. She'd been terrified to go inside in case her natural clumsiness led to her knocking something over and ruining one of Violet's paintings. She'd have to investigate what was left in the studio. The only stipulation in Violet's will regarding her paintings was that any works that had been loaned to galleries or museums were to be made permanent gifts, but anything in the cottage was Emily's.

Back inside, Emily was rearranging the contents of the pale-blue kitchen cupboards when she heard a knock at the French doors. It was bound to happen sooner or later. She couldn't hide from the owners of Dovecote Manor forever.

'I wasn't sure if you'd remember us,' Sue Prentice confessed, choosing a chocolate-covered Viennese whirl from the plate of biscuits Emily had placed in the middle of the wrought-iron table on the patio. Her mother had insisted she take the box of fancy biscuits she had stashed in the cupboard in case the neighbours dropped by. 'It's been such a long time. We remember you, though. Don't we, Terry?'

'Of course,' Terry agreed through a mouthful of ginger nut.

'I can't believe it's been fifteen years,' Sue continued. She was just as Emily remembered – robust and sturdy. Although there were a few lines around her blue eyes and a smattering of grey in her fair hair. She could still talk the hind legs off a donkey and dressed as though she was about to set off on a ramble. Terry had aged much more markedly. His face was deeply lined, pale, and gaunt. His dark eyes dull. Emily was sure he'd had a much healthier complexion and been several stone heavier the last time she'd seen him.

'Violet did tell us a few years ago that she was going to leave Clifftop Cottage to you. We sold it to Violet and Hugo not long after we first bought the manor back in 1987. You wouldn't remember Hugo of course; he died when you were only small.'

Emily nodded. She'd never met Violet's husband, but she'd heard snippets about him.

Sue barely paused for breath. 'It was such a shame she and Hugo never had children of their own. You were the closest thing she had.' Sue reached over and patted Emily's hand. 'It did her good, you coming to see her those summers. She'd been quite down since Hugo died. Your visits brought her back to life.'

'I'm so sorry I couldn't come down for her funeral.' The tips of her ears burned, and she fiddled with her teaspoon.

Terry shook his head slowly. 'That's alright, love. She knew you had your own life to be living and getting on with. She talked about you a lot though.'

'She kept painting, right up until a few months before she died. She'd stopped about ten years after she started teaching at the art school in Brighton in the sixties. I think she was a bit discouraged after she tried some new styles which didn't sell very well. After she retired, she took it up again. For the love of it really. She wasn't bothered about trying to sell anything by then. She was marvellous. Our Will, you remember him, has a few of her paintings in his London apartment.'

Emily's stomach knotted itself into a tight ball. She remembered Will alright.

'Oh, Will lives in London?' There was a false lightness to her question.

'Yes, he's been there for a few years. He was in New York for a while before then. He's got a lovely penthouse apartment near the City, which is a short commute to the investment company he works for. Don't ask me what he does, though, I don't understand it at all. I zone out when he starts talking about hedge funds and investment strategies and market fluctuations and all that malarkey.'

'He's done alright for himself, that boy,' Terry said sagely, reaching for another biscuit. Sue gave him the sort of look you'd give a child caught rummaging in the sweet jar. He withdrew his hand, empty.

'Do you see him often?'

'Not as often as I'd like. He pops down occasionally. He was here yesterday, but I expect you were busy settling in. It's shame you missed him.'

Emily forced a polite smile. So, it *had* been him tailgating her in his fancy sports car. She should have known.

'Our Harrison still lives at home. He's at work today. He's got his own veterinary practice in town now. But he's often out and about on farm visits and whatnot.'

'He's a vet? I wouldn't have seen that coming,' Emily said with a laugh.

'I know,' Sue agreed. 'I had him down as a becoming a librarian or an accountant. But one day he decided he wanted to be a vet. And fair play to him, he's seen it through. Quite handy seeing as we have a few dogs of our own. I'm sure he'll swing by and say hello when he gets a moment.'

Or maybe Harrison was as nervous at seeing her again after that summer as she was of seeing him.

'Right, we'd better leave you in peace. I'm sure you have a lot to be getting on with.' Sue stood and reached out a hand for Terry as he hoisted himself up from the chair. He reached for his walking stick with the other hand and swayed slightly.

'I'll tell you one thing, Emily,' he said, as he righted himself and tentatively took a step. 'Getting old is no joke. I'd put it off for as long as possible if I were you.'

'One minor heart attack and he thinks he's ready for the scrap heap,' Sue said, rolling her eyes.

Emily flashed Terry a sympathetic smile. That explained his complexion and fragility.

Sue wrapped her arm around Terry's. 'Come on, you old fool. It's so lovely to see you again, Emily, and I do hope you'll stay in the cottage for a while. But I suppose you have your own life in London and would probably miss your friends and family.'

Emily drew a deep breath. 'We'll see,' she said. There were

so many factors that would influence her decision whether to stay in Dovecote, not least the Prentice boys.

# SIX

## VIOLET

September 1940

I hadn't slept a wink. Kemptown's church hall had been crowded and noisy. Children, and a few adults, cried all night. Thankfully Oliver and John had curled up and slept, but even John was subdued in the morning. It was hard for them to understand that we didn't have a home to go to.

The housing officer was apologetic but the best they could offer us was a room in a shared house in a small town a few miles down the coast. I'd heard of Dovecote. A few of the families in our street had been there for days out before the war. Dad had promised us he'd take us one day. And now we *were* going, whether we liked it or not.

My nerves were frayed and the bumping and jolting of the bus along the twisty country road out of Brighton did nothing to lift my spirits. Oliver wouldn't stop sobbing. John was sulky and prone to lashing out with his feet and fists. Mum sat quietly, clutching the photograph of her and Dad on their wedding day. I'd managed to salvage a few bits from the pile of rubble that had once been our home – my sketchbook and pencils, Oliver's stuffed rabbit, John's model aeroplane, and the photograph. The silver frame was dented, and the glass had fallen out, but Mum held it as though it was the most precious thing in the world. I held my brothers in the same way. Thankfully, I'd grabbed my handbag on the way out to the shelter, so I had all our papers, and our ration books and coupons.

At last we arrived in Dovecote, approaching the town via a bridge over the railway line. It did seem like a pretty little place and was, unlike Brighton, devoid of wrecked houses and cratered roads. My heart leapt a fraction at the sight of a book-shop on the High Street.

'Look, boys,' I said, as we turned into Blythe Avenue, a long road lined with terraced two-up-two-down houses on the left, and double-fronted three-storey townhouses on the right. 'There's a park you can play in.'

'I want to go to the beach,' John huffed.

I ruffed his hair. 'I'm sorry, John, but the beach is closed, like in Brighton.'

He kicked the back of the seat in front of him. An elderly man turned around and tutted loudly. I offered an apologetic smile. The bus pulled up outside one of the white stucco-fronted townhouses.

'Violet Saunders and family,' the bus driver yelled, and we gathered our meagre belongings and stepped down onto the pavement outside 24 Blythe Avenue. A tall, square woman wearing a tweed suit and sturdy shoes approached. Her eyes were beady, and her thin lips were tightly pursed.

'I'm Mrs Marshall. This way,' she barked, like a drill sergeant, as she led us up the front steps and into a bright, but chilly hallway. She thrust a key at me. 'You're on the second floor. Bathroom's at the end of the corridor. Front door is locked at ten p.m. sharp. No overnight visitors.' She eyed me hawkishly as she said that, clearly marking me as a wayward girl who couldn't be trusted. 'Towels and bedding have been provided.

Make sure they're kept clean and returned in the same manner as you've been given them.'

Then and there I was determined to save up enough coupons and money to buy our own bedding and towels. Mrs Marshall could shove hers where the sun didn't shine. I just had to work out how I was going to get the money. Boland's had been heavily bombed too, so not only had I lost my home, but I'd also lost my job. I could have used one of Hugo's bearhugs.

The room was actually rather nice. I'd hoped for a view of the sea but instead the only window looked out onto another house. There were two single beds and one double, a little kitchenette with a stove and an ice box, and a small dining table with four chairs. There was even some tea and a jug of milk. The room was clean and dry, and I'd been assured it was only temporary.

We had been there barely an hour when there was a sharp rap at the door. Mrs Marshall swept into the room with a waft of soap and laundry powder. She ushered in a small, wiry woman with close-cropped hair and reading glasses on a chain around her neck.

'Miss Evans is from the Women's Voluntary Service and would like to discuss the matter of the children,' Mrs Marshall boomed, before closing the door with a loud bang that made everyone jump. Miss Evans consulted her notebook.

'Mrs Saunders?' She looked at Mum who was sitting at the kitchen table, the photograph still in her hands.

'I'm sorry, Miss Evans. Mum's not well, can I help? I'm her daughter, Violet. Can I get you a cup of tea?'

'Thank you.'

We sat at the table, Mum barely registering that we had company.

'How can I help, Miss Evans?' I asked, my hand shaking slightly as I poured the tea. The teapot dripped and I longed for our good one at home. The tea service had been a wedding present to my parents, and *that* teapot never dripped.

Miss Evans shot a scathing look at the boys, who were sitting on the double bed scribbling on a page I'd torn from my sketchbook. That was those pencils ruined.

'Your brothers were not evacuated?' she asked, a thin eyebrow twitching slightly.

'No!' The venom in Mum's voice startled us and Miss Evans sloshed some tea onto her saucer. 'You're not taking my babies.'

I reached across the table and took Mum's hand in mine. 'Shush, Mum. It's alright.' I turned to Miss Evans. 'Mum wouldn't let them go,' I explained. 'After our father died, she wanted the family kept together.'

Miss Evans tutted. 'But surely the safety of the children must be placed ahead of sentimentality, Miss Saunders?'

My stomach jolted. Of course she was right, but how could I let them go? They were so small.

'There is a train leaving for York tomorrow. There is space for two more. I would recommend that your brothers are on that train. For their own safety. Do you think that yesterday's raid will be the last we see in these parts? John and Oliver will be much safer in Yorkshire.'

I closed my eyes for a moment and listened to the sensible voice in my head. She was right. There would be more raids. We had been lucky that we'd not all been killed. And ultimately, they would be better cared for, and better fed, with another family. I took a deep breath.

'But isn't there a list of things that evacuees need to take with them? Look around, Miss Evans, what you see is what we have. The boys are still in their pyjamas. They don't even have any shoes.' My face burned with shame. To my surprise, a soft smile cracked Miss Evans's hard face.

'In exceptional circumstances, we can provide everything a

child needs, Miss Saunders. And you and your family are certainly an exceptional circumstance.' She turned to Mum. 'Mrs Saunders, I believe your daughter has agreed that John and Oliver would be better off if they were evacuated, but I do need your approval, as their mother.'

I squeezed Mum's hand. 'Please, Mum. I know it's hard but it's for the best.'

She nodded slowly and I released a long breath.

Miss Evans made a note in her book. 'I'll drop by with the things for the boys later.'

'Thank you,' I said, holding back my tears until she had left the flat. How was I going to explain it to my brothers?

The platform at Dovecote's pretty grey stone train station was thronged with parents and children of all ages, hugging and crying. Some children boarded the train with enthusiasm, as though they were going on holiday. Perhaps that was what their parents had told them. Others clung to their mothers like limpets, having to be peeled off by exasperated evacuation officers, members of the Women's Voluntary Service, and teachers. I crouched down to look Oliver and John in their eyes. Mum had said her goodbyes at the flat.

'Now,' I said, straightening the collar of John's shirt. It was at least two sizes too big on him, but at least he no longer looked like a street urchin. I'd given them both a thorough scrub in the bath the night before. I had some pride. 'You both have to be brave, alright? And be good and do exactly what Mr and Mrs Carmichael tell you. You're going to have lots of fun on their farm. Oh, Oliver, don't cry.' I bit my lip to stop my own tears from spilling over. I placed Oliver's hand in John's. 'Now you look after each other. And I'll see you soon.' I ushered them onto the train and into the hands of one of the teachers from Dovecote Primary School, who was making the journey with some of her own pupils. 'I love you,' I called, as the door was slammed shut and the train's whistle blew. It was the saddest sound I'd ever heard.

As the train chugged out of the station and disappeared around the curve in the track, the platform echoed with the sobs of broken-hearted mothers. I sank down on a stone bench outside the station and wept.

# SEVEN

## EMILY

June 2016

A couple of days after Terry and Sue's visit, Emily had connected her laptop to the cottage's Wi-Fi and was back working on a few web design projects. Harrison still hadn't made an appearance, but she couldn't stay holed up in Clifftop Cottage forever. Cabin fever was starting to set in. Coming face-to-face with him in the middle of the High Street wouldn't be ideal, but that was a chance she was going to have to take.

The path from the patio *did* lead along the top of the cliff to a set of steep steps zigzagging down towards the beach below. The wind whipped her hair as she descended, and she held onto the handrail for dear life. Now would not be a good time to trip over her own feet. At the bottom of the cliff, the path curved sharply to the left, the end gated with a large 'Private' sign. Emily stepped through the gate onto the end of Beachfront Road. Here the beach was a thin strip of pebbles, and at high tide the waves slapped the stone wall that ran along the road. There were three pretty whitewashed cottages along the road, all with different coloured pastels on the gates, window frames, and front doors. They all had sea-themed names: Seaspray Cottage, Seafoam Cottage, and Seaglass Cottage. Being so close to the sea must be lovely, but Emily liked that Clifftop Cottage was nestled against the forest. And the climb up the cliff was worth it for the bird's-eye view of the whole town.

Reaching the post box at the end of the road, near the train station, Emily turned down the steps that lead to the beach. Stones crunched underfoot as she made her way down to the edge of the sea. The waves washed the pebbles with a rhythmic fizz. She bent and let a wave tickle her fingers. The water of the English Channel was still cold enough to turn your skin blue. The stone wall carried on along the beach with The Promenade behind it, the turquoise railings shimmering in the sunshine.

Emily sat down on a stone bench against the wall and looked out over the sea to the lighthouse on the headland. She breathed in time to the swish of the waves, the salt drying on her lips, and closed her eyes.

'So, you're back.'

Her eyes flew open, and she looked up at the man leaning against the wall, his hands tucked into the pockets of his summer jacket. The designer stubble and the earring were new, and he was slim rather than scrawny, but the blue eyes that looked at her with curiosity, and a touch of suspicion, were the same as they'd been fifteen years before.

'Hi, Harrison,' she said, moving down the bench to give him space to sit down if he wanted to. He didn't. His blond hair, the same ashy shade as his mother's, hung in a long fringe swept over one eye. 'Yes, I'm back.'

Harrison puffed out his cheeks and turned away to look at the sea. 'Are you planning on hanging around this time?'

His words cut deep.

'I'm not sure. I've not decided.' The road out of Dovecote and back to London was looking rather tempting.

He glanced at her. 'Well, don't forget to say goodbye.'

They locked eyes for the briefest of moments before Harrison turned and walked away. Emily waited, her heart pounding. Having given Harrison a good head start she made her way off the beach and scurried back to the safety of Clifftop Cottage.

Later that day Clifftop Cottage was shrouded in darkness, and Emily was putting the finishing touches to a website for an organic cosmetics company when there was a knock at the door.

'I come with a peace offering,' Harrison said, running his fingers through his fringe and giving Emily an apologetic smile. He held up a bottle of champagne. 'I raided Mum's wine fridge, so it's cold.'

'In that case, you'd better come in,' Emily chuckled.

Harrison handed her the bottle as he stepped into the cottage and looked around.

'I can't believe Violet's gone,' he said, following Emily into the kitchen. 'But I suppose ninety-one's a pretty decent age.'

'Were you still close to her?' Emily asked, searching the cupboards for champagne flutes. Violet was the sort of person to have some, somewhere.

'Yeah, I guess. We lost touch while I was studying in Bristol, but when I came back to Dovecote, I used to visit a couple of times a week to keep an eye on her. Not that she needed it; she was in better shape than some people half her age.' He ran his hand over the back of one of the kitchen chairs. 'I guess that's why it was such a shock when she died. We all thought she'd live forever.'

Emily popped the cork from the bottle and poured two glasses. She passed one to Harrison and led him out into the courtyard. It was too warm to waste the evening indoors. Below, the lights of Dovecote twinkled in the dark and the lighthouse's beam swept over the inky sea.

'Cheers,' he said. 'To Violet, for bringing you back to Dove-cote, finally.'

Emily couldn't think of what to say to that, so clinked her glass against his and took a large gulp. The bubbles fizzed against her tongue. It had been a while since she'd had proper champagne, not since Max's birthday almost a year ago. She brushed that memory aside. Max was banned from her consciousness. Harrison set his glass down heavily on the wrought-iron table.

'Look, I'm sorry about earlier. It was a surprise to see you. Mum told me you were back but all the same...' He gave her a shy smile. 'It *is* nice to see you again. I wondered if I ever would.'

'Yeah, same.'

'You left without saying goodbye.'

'I know.' Emily's voice was thick, and she took another gulp of champagne.

'You promised you'd come back.'

'And I didn't. I'm sorry.' The sadness in his eyes made Emily's chest ache.

'You said you didn't want to go back to London.'

He remembered more than Emily did. 'Harrison, I was sixteen. Going home meant going back to school, and what teenager wants to do that?'

He picked up his glass and took a long swig. 'I thought... never mind,' he said, swirling the glass between his finger and thumb.

Emily gave him a little prod on the shin with her foot. 'They were three good summers though. We did have some fun.' He didn't return her weak smile.

'Why?'

'Huh?'

'Why didn't you come back after the summer of 2001? I

thought we were friends. I needed you. You knew how much I needed you, and why.'

Emily ran her fingers through her auburn hair and let out a long breath. Somewhere in the grass, a cricket chirped. 'I know. I felt terrible letting you down, but I couldn't come back.' She held up her hand when Harrison opened his mouth. 'Please don't ask me why. Please trust me when I say I had my reasons, okay?'

Harrison shrugged. 'Sure,' he said. 'You know, I blamed myself for pushing you away. I thought that after I'd told you I was gay, you didn't like me any more.'

Emily's hand flew to her mouth. In all the intervening years, she'd presumed he'd be angry at her for breaking her promise, but never expected that he would have thought it was his fault.

'Oh Harrison, I'm so sorry. That was definitely *not* the reason.' She bit her lip. Harrison's bottom lip was trembling too, and when their eyes met, neither of them could hold back the tears that sprung up. She wrapped her arms around his shoulders and pulled him in tight, like she had on that day in 2001 when he'd tearfully come out to her, sitting on her bed upstairs in this same cottage. He wrapped his thin arms around her waist.

After a long, tight hug, Emily sat back on her chair wiping her eyes. 'No one gives hugs like yours,' she said.

'It is good to see you again,' he replied. 'Buddies?'

'If you'll forgive me.'

'How could I not after a hug like that?'

Emily grinned. 'Buddies,' she said with a chuckle. Harrison drained his glass and picked up the bottle to refill them.

'You're right, they were good times. Except when Will was around, making a nuisance of himself.'

Emily grimaced. It was only natural that Harrison would mention his brother. But Emily wasn't ready to talk about Will yet, and certainly not to tell Harrison what happened the night before she fled back to London, never to return to Dovecote.

'It was all attention seeking.'

'What?' Emily asked, brought back to the present by Harrison's comment.

'Will. The way he was back then. He was like it all the time, always doing something for attention. Whether it was having to be first or best at everything, or throwing a tantrum to get his own way, or bullying others, it was all about attention. He couldn't stand to not be top dog.'

'Has he changed?' The way he drove his sports car made her think not.

'I suppose we all have. You've changed.'

The half-bottle of champagne blurred the normally sharp edges of Emily's mind. 'Have I?'

'Yeah. In a good way though.' Harrison reached across the table and poked her gently on the arm. 'You're not geeky any more. You were a proper nerd.'

'Oy, cheeky,' Emily said with a laugh. 'That's rich coming from the guy who had a full replica *Star Trek* uniform.'

Harrison tossed his head. 'In my defence, I looked pretty good in Lycra.'

It was good to hear his laugh again. She'd missed him, and Dovecote, more than she realised.

# EIGHT

## EMILY

It was the half-bottle of champagne that made Emily agree to Harrison's suggestion of nipping to the pub in town to meet some of his friends.

The Royal Oak, on the corner of the High Street and Blythe Avenue was comfortably lively. Harrison steered Emily over to a round table by the frosted front window where two women were deep in conversation. They both looked up as Harrison approached and beamed at him.

'Harrison. How lovely to see you.' The woman with long brown wavy hair got up and gave him a hug.

'Hey, Molly. Alright?'

'Come here, you,' the other woman said in a broad Irish accent, and Harrison leant over the table to give her a hug. Having extracted himself from her embrace, he turned to Emily.

'Emily, this is Molly and Aoife. Aoife owns the hair salon on Queen's Parade and Molly runs Harrington's Bookshop across the road. This is Emily. She's Violet's great-niece and has inherited Clifftop Cottage.' He gave her a sideways look. 'She's not sure whether she's staying for good, or just visiting.'

'Hi,' Emily said, giving the two women a small wave. They smiled back.

'What's everyone on, then?' Harrison asked, looking at the glasses on the table. 'I'll go up while Declan doesn't have a queue.'

'G and T for me, please,' replied Molly.

'Vodka and diet coke, ta,' added Aoife.

'Emily?'

'I'd better stick to the grape. A white wine please.' Emily sat down. 'We've already polished off a bottle of Sue's champagne.'

Molly and Aoife laughed.

'Sounds about right for Harrison,' Molly said with a grin. 'So how do you know him? I'm guessing you've not only just met.'

Emily laughed. 'No, we used to know each other when we were kids. I spent a few summers at Clifftop Cottage with Violet when I was a teenager, and Harrison and I used to hang out. But we've not seen each other in years.'

'Ah, it's lovely you've met up again,' Aoife said, shaking her head. 'I'm going to miss Violet. She was a scream. Like, every time she came into the salon, she'd have me roaring with her stories.'

'She was a regular at the bookshop too. She was a big fan of anything a bit spicy. She loved a good bodice-ripper.' Molly wiggled her eyebrows.

'Oh, God. Really?' Emily laughed. 'I didn't spot any on the bookshelves, maybe they're stashed away. I'm not adverse to a saucy book myself.'

'Well, if you find her collection, you'll have plenty to read.' Molly beamed, with a sparkle in her eye.

'So,' Aoife said, glancing over her shoulder at Harrison who was chatting with the baby-faced barman. 'Considering that summer hadn't got going, Declan had either been away on holiday or been on a sunbed. 'I guess you know Harrison's brother, Will?'

'Good grief, Aoife. You're *obsessed* with Will Prentice,' Molly groaned, rolling her eyes.

'I am not,' Aoife said, with a mock sulk.

Molly turned to Emily. 'She is, though. She's been trying to get into his pants for years.'

'Molly,' Aoife shrieked. 'Give away all my secrets, why don't you?' There was a laugh in her voice. 'You're jealous because you're all loved up and spoken for and you don't get to have as much fun as us single girls. Isn't that right, Emily?'

'Oh. Um...'

Aoife's hand went to her mouth. 'God, sorry. I kind of presumed seeing as you're in Dovecote on your own that you're single. Are you not?'

Emily sighed. 'I am single. I've only just broken up with...' she hesitated. There was always this moment of doubt, of trepidation. The girls seemed nice, but you could never tell. She drew a breath. 'I've not long broken up with my girlfriend. That's part of the reason I came down to Dovecote.'

Molly reached out a hand and patted Emily's arm. 'Sorry to hear that, Emily. I hope you're okay.'

'Who's okay?' Harrison said, placing a tray of drinks on the table and handing them out.

'Emily was telling us she's recently broken up with her girlfriend. The girlfriend's loss, if you ask me, like.' Aoife took a long swig of her vodka and diet coke and missed the look that Harrison gave Emily.

'Girlfriend?' Harrison asked, sitting down next to Emily.

Aoife's face went an even paler shade of white. 'Oh, God, have I put my foot in it? Emily, I'm sorry. I'm such an idiot. I presumed Harrison knew you were a lesbian.'

'I'm not—'

'Sorry I'm late. Veronica Rutherford wouldn't stop chatting. Honestly, it's taking me twice as long to finish her kitchen. She talks non-stop to me all day.' The tall man with long, ginger hair tied up in a bun and a thick ginger beard, leant over and gave Molly a kiss.

'No bother, Jez. I've just got a round in,' Harrison said. 'This is Emily. She's inherited Clifftop Cottage. Emily, this is Jez, Molly's fiancé.'

Jez flashed Emily a smile. 'Hi. Nice to meet you. I'm dying for a beer. Back in a tick.' Molly got up and followed Jez to the bar. He wrapped his arm around her shoulders as they waited for Declan to finish serving another couple.

Aoife stared awkwardly into her drink, her pink cheeks clashing with her flame-red hair. Harrison was giving Emily a searching look and there was a soft smirk on his lips. She probably should have told him about Max earlier. He was about to say something when a small, wiry woman with tight, dark curls launched herself at him, wrapping her arms around his neck in a tight hug.

'Hey, H,' she said, giving him a kiss on the cheek. 'Long time, no see. Hey, Aoife.'

'Heather,' Harrison said. 'I'm always around, you're always working.'

'That is true. Oh, hello,' Heather said, turning to Emily. 'I'm Heather.'

'Hi, Heather. I'm Emily.'

'Emily is Violet's great-niece,' Harrison explained.

Heather's smile sank a fraction. 'Oh. We all miss Violet so much. Although she refused to come and live at Bayview, she used to pop in every so often. Or one of us would check in on her at Clifftop Cottage. She was such a lovely lady.'

'Heather is one of the carers at Bayview Care Home, up on the hill at the top of town, before you go over the railway bridge.

She and the other carers basically look after everyone in Dovecote who's getting on a bit.' Harrison smiled.

'I love my old dears,' Heather said with a grin. 'And it's sad
when they leave us, but we try and make sure they go well and
have had a good life. Violet didn't need care, as such. I think she
liked the company, and to chat to people her own age.'

'Thank you for looking after her,' Emily said. 'I'm glad she
had friends and a community around her. I kind of lost touch
with her over the years. The more I hear about her, the more I
wish I'd remained in contact.'

'Don't beat yourself up over it,' Heather said softly, placing
a warm hand on Emily's arm. 'It happens.'

'Hiya, Heather.' Molly came back to the table and handed
Heather a glass of red wine. 'We heard you come in.'

'Molly, you're an absolute legend. Cheers.'

It was cosy around the table. But Emily could sense that
Harrison desperately wanted to talk to her alone. She'd explain
on their walk home.


An hour or so later, Declan had told them to leave so he could
close up, and Emily's head was buzzing with the life stories and
histories of Harrison's group of friends. She'd never remember it
all. Molly and Jez were getting married in July. They were
having their reception in the grounds of Dovecote Manor. They
had two children, both from previous relationships. Toby,
Molly's son, was six and his dad had upped and left the moment
Molly told him she was pregnant. Jez's wife had died five years
ago when their daughter, Zoe, was only two. Aoife was a
confirmed singleton who was living her best life doing whatever
she wanted with whoever she wanted. From what Emily could
gather, Aoife had dated pretty much every bloke in Dovecote at
some stage. Heather was far too busy looking after her old dears

to have much of a social life, but she was happy with her two cats, Rodney and Del Boy, and her budgie, Malcolm.

Harrison and Emily waved the rest of the gang off and walked up the High Street and over the railway bridge.

'So, you've only been back in Dovecote a couple of years, then?' Emily asked. Mentioning Max would only spoil what had been a great evening.

'About five. I left for uni, and I stayed in Bristol after graduating. But seriously, are we going to talk about my career when Aoife let slip that you're gay?'

They had reached the gates of Dovecote Manor and Harrison crossed his arms and leant against one of the gateposts. Emily scuffed at the dusty tarmac with the toe of her trainer.

'I'm not.'

'Well, now I'm disappointed.'

'Will you let me finish?' Emily smiled. She was safe with him, like he'd been safe with her all those years ago. 'I'm not gay. I'm bisexual.'

'I mean, you could have told me.' There was a glint in his eye as he nudged her with his elbow. Emily blushed. 'Well, there's not much of a scene in Dovecote, but Brighton's only down the road and there's plenty going on there.'

Emily wrinkled her nose. 'I've never been one for the scene. I'm not a fan of nightclubs or rammed bars. And anyway, I've barely been single for a week. This battered old heart needs time to heal.'

Harrison looped his arm around her shoulders as they staggered up the sloping driveway to Clifftop Cottage. In the warm yellow glow of the storm lantern porch light, he hugged her.

'How about a nightcap and you can tell me all about it?' he said gently. 'This time *I'll* listen, and you can cry into *my* shoulder.'

Emily rubbed her wet eyes. It might have taken fifteen

years, but they had come full circle. It was her turn to confide in Harrison.

# NINE

## VIOLET

April 1943

I was rearranging the fiction section of Harrington's Bookshop, where I'd been working for almost three years. I tried not to dwell on the passing of time, or how long this war was going on. Instead, I kept myself busy with the bookshop and some war work now I was eighteen, and just tried to get Mum and I through each day as best I could.

It had been a quiet day with only a handful of people stopping by, including Lily Morrison and her daughter who was the cutest little thing. Lily and I had chatted a few times. She was the closest thing I had to a friend. I really missed Hugo.

My boss, Joanna Harrington, stood by the window, her beady eyes sweeping the street, her thin fingers laced together at the small of her back. She reminded me of a sparrow.

'It never used to be like this,' she muttered, turning to me as if requiring a response.

'No?' I noticed the Cs were not in alphabetical order.

'Before the war, on a sunny day like this we'd be overrun.

The till wouldn't stop ringing. And now look.' She gestured towards the High Street. 'Not a soul.'

'Well, sadly I suppose people have more pressing priorities than books,' I said, reaching up to a high shelf to retrieve a misplaced Agatha Christie.

'It's a real shame. Even the paperbacks have gone up in price.' Mrs Harrington huffed. Sometimes I wondered whether things were any better in Brighton, and if Boland's had ever reopened. I didn't harbour any desire to go back. There were too many sad memories.

'Am I alright to finish up a little early? I need to pick up Mum's glasses from Crawford's before they close.' Mum had tripped up the stairs a few weeks before and bent the frames. Mr Crawford had very kindly offered to repair them without charge. That was what our experience of Dovecote had been for the last three years: little moments of kindness.

'Oh, very well, if you must.'

I thanked her, picked up my shopping basket, and closed the door to Harrington's behind me. As I crossed the High Street my thoughts turned, as they often did, to my brothers. I missed them terribly. When they were first evacuated, we used to get letters from Beryl and Arthur Carmichael, who they were living with on their farm. But as time had gone on, they'd become less frequent. The boys were both in school now. They might have developed Yorkshire accents.

The bell above the door of Crawford's Opticians tinkled as I stepped inside. Mr Crawford looked up from the pair of spectacles he was polishing and gave me a warm smile, deepening the wrinkles around his eyes.

'Afternoon, Miss Saunders. How's life treating you?'

I smiled back. 'Oh, you know how it is, Mr Crawford. One thing after another.'

He chuckled. 'Well, there's some truth in that. You on duty tonight?'

'Yes, I'm fire watching tonight. I don't mind it now it's getting bit warmer. But even in the cold, I think I'd rather be up on the roof looking out for incendiary bombs than stuck indoors packing relief boxes like I was last week. It wasn't much fun being bossed around by Mrs Marshall. It's bad enough having her as a landlady.' I grimaced and Mr Crawford nodded knowingly.

'I'm in awe of all of you in the Volunteer Fire Service. I prefer to stay firmly on the ground for my Civil Defence duties. Well, I'll pray for a quiet one for you.' He handed me Mum's glasses. 'Here you go, love. I'm sure they could find space at Bayview for your mum. If it gets too much, looking after her, I mean.'

I couldn't lie, I'd considered that myself on more than one occasion. Mum's low mood had got worse since the boys had been evacuated and she'd become sullen and angry, lashing out if the mood took her. She rarely left our, supposedly temporary, one-room flat in Blythe Avenue where we were *still* living, and barely spoke a word. If it wasn't for my job at Harrington's, and the chance for little chats like this, I'd probably go out of my mind. But she was my mother, and I couldn't put her in an institution, not even one as nice and friendly as Bayview. A few of the nurses would pop into the bookshop on their way to or from the train station, or on their lunch breaks. There was a red-haired, freckled nurse called Dilys who, when she came in, would send me scuttling to the storeroom for fear of blushing and giving away that I found her intolerably attractive. I'd heard her talking about a fiancé, though, so she wasn't of my persuasion.

'Miss Saunders?' Mr Crawford's question brought me out of my daydream.

'Oh, sorry, I was miles away.'

He laughed. 'I would be too if I could. I was saying it's a

shame that you young people are stuck in quiet Dovecote. I'm sure you'd rather be somewhere with theatres and cinemas and suchlike. How old are you now?'

'Eighteen. But I don't mind. I like it here. I like the quiet.' I thought back to our street in Brighton where drunks would stumble against our front door, and we were privy to every argument between our next-door neighbours. There had never been a quiet moment on that street, what with the constant rumble of the trains behind, and the buses, not to mention the delivery boys cycling around in groups hollering at each other. I'd take the quiet of Dovecote any day.

'You'll be on the lookout for a husband soon. Not many options for that around here.' Mr Crawford was looking at me with a curious intensity. Why did everyone assume I was in the market for a husband? The memory of the pretty nurse's smile flashed in my head. If only. 'Oh, now there's no need to blush, dear. Even *I* was young once.'

'I think potential husbands are in short supply all over the country, what with most of the chaps away. But I'm in no rush.' My thoughts went straight to Hugo. In his last letter, he'd sounded frustrated and bored. Three years of being cooped up in a training camp in Norfolk wasn't quite what he'd signed up for. At least I knew he was relatively safe where he was. The idea of him over in Europe on the front line made my stomach hurt.

'Good for you. Plenty of time for that sort of thing.'

I put Mum's glasses into my basket. 'I'd better be off. I need to pick up a few bits on the way home.'

'Right ho. Give my regards to your mum.'

'Bye, Mr Crawford.'

'Bye, love.'

As the door of the shop closed behind me, I scolded myself. I'd forgotten to ask if there was any news from his son, Alf. The

last they'd heard he was about to go into Burma. It was frightening that all these young men were so far away, facing who
knew what sort of horrors. The jungle sounded petrifying. I
needed to stop disappearing into my own little world and pay
more attention to those around me. I wasn't a child any more
and it was about time I began to return some of the kindness the
residents of Dovecote had shown me and Mum.

I was still berating myself as I crossed the High Street when
the shrill whine of the air raid siren punctured my thoughts.

'Oh blast,' I muttered. I was too far from home to run for it.
It would have to be the cellar of The Royal Oak, which had
been set up as Dovecote's main public air raid shelter, much to
the annoyance of the landlord, Derek. Mum would be alright;
Dora in the next flat along would chivvy her into the basement
of 24 Blythe Avenue.

'Here we are again,' I said to Derek, as I joined the line of
people traipsing down the steps to his cellar.

'Hopefully a short one today,' he replied with a wink and a
nod of his bald head. With his shirt sleeves rolled up to his
elbows as he held the hatch open with one hand, and chain-
smoked Woodbines with the other, the faded outlines of Royal
Navy tattoos were visible on his arms. A veteran of the last war.
'I better not get a delivery while you're all down there.'

'We'll help you unload,' a voice called from the murky
depths.

'Yeah, and do a stocktake,' someone else said, to much
amusement from the gathered Dovecote residents who'd had
their early-evening plans disrupted.

'Move along, you lot. There's a few more. Evening, ladies.'
And with that, Derek shut us in to wait for the 'all-clear', or
whatever fate awaited us. He never came down to the shelter.
He said if the pub was going down, he'd go down with it.

I had settled into a space on the bench in the far corner of
the cellar when a high-pitched laugh made me look up. It had

been three years, but I recognised her instantly. The last time I'd seen her, her blonde hair had been tied in a long plait. Now it was shorter, in a fashionable bob. Her slightly upturned nose was still sprinkled with freckles and her green eyes sparkled despite the dull muted light of the shelter. She wouldn't remember me. To people like her, people like me were invisible. She was with another girl, probably a friend from her school days. Whoever the girl was, she was obviously a riot. Zeyla Wythenshawe laughed at everything she said. My eyes narrowed and I forced myself to look away. A small girl, curled up on her mother's knee started to cry softly. The siren was still going so we weren't getting out anytime soon. I pulled my sketchbook and pencils out of my bag and tried to concentrate on the drawing I was doing of Brighton Beach, how I remembered it before the war – full of happy children and people enjoying an ice cream in peace.

'Oh, hello. I remember you. I saw you outside Brighton station, drawing.'

My heart thudded as I looked up. I hadn't noticed Zeyla shuffling along the bench, so she was now directly opposite me. 'Oh, yes. Hello.'

'Isn't this ghastly? The first time Mother and Father have let me out for an evening since I finished school, and we end up in the cellar of a pub. Mother would have one of her funny turns if she knew.'

The sound of the all-clear and Derek's welcome appearance at the door of the shelter stopped me from replying.

'Right, out of my cellar!' Derek called out as the light of a weak evening sun poured down into the shelter.

'Oh hurrah,' Zeyla cried. 'Come on, Lottie, if we hurry we can still make the start of the show. We're off to the pictures in Brighton,' she added, turning back to me. 'Told Mother I'd come home after but we're going to say we got caught in a raid and go to a girls-only dance club instead.' She flashed me a mischievous smile which turned my insides to liquid. She took Lottie's hand in hers as they climbed the steps. I followed, fighting a rising jealously that this other girl got to touch Zeyla's skin. At the top, Zeyla turned and looked me dead in the eyes. 'I hope to see you again, Violet,' she said, her voice low and husky. She remembered my name. My knees nearly went from under me.

# TEN

## EMILY

June 2016

The following Saturday was a glorious summer's day and a hoard of day trippers from London flooded out of Dovecote train station and onto the beach. Emily's heart skipped a beat when a silver sports car roared down the High Street. Sue had said they didn't see their eldest son enough but judging by how many times Emily had seen Will's car around town in the ten days she'd been there, he was in Dovecote more than he was in London. Before she could get too tied up thinking about Will, Gio emerged from the station, a picture of cool elegance.

'Emily,' he cried enveloping her in a tight hug. 'You look wonderful. You have colour back in your cheeks.'

'Gio, it's so good to see you.' It really was. Although she'd been spending time with Harrison, and he'd been so kind to her the night she'd bawled her eyes out over Max, he was no replacement for Gio. The spectre of Will lurked in every conversation with Harrison, and it was only a matter of time before he brought up the summer of 2001 again. 'Why aren't you staying over?'

'I have brunch with a bodybuilder tomorrow.' There was a familiar glint in Gio's eyes and Emily shook her head.

'I dread to think what you're getting up to without me around to keep an eye on you. Well, I'm honoured you could fit me in between your assignations. Come on, I'll show you around. There's the cutest café down by the beach. I've booked a table for lunch at Las Gaviotas, a tapas place I've been dying to try. And then we'll pop into The Royal Oak for a drink.' Emily wrapped her arm around Gio's and led him towards The Promenade, aware that he was attracting quite a lot of attention. It happened everywhere he went. He pretended not to notice but that didn't fool her. He loved it really.

Halfway along The Promenade, they stopped and leant against the turquoise railings looking out over the beach and the sea. Seagulls circled overhead waiting for the opportunity to divebomb an unsuspecting child and steal their chips. At the water's edge, a couple of children ran in and out of the cold waves, their parents keeping watch from a safe distance. The occasional shriek punctuated the air as swimsuits and exposed skin got splashed.

'This is a charming place, Emily,' Gio said. 'I think it suits you.'

Emily ran her fingers through her hair as she gazed at the sea. 'Yes, it is. But I'm not making any decisions yet, it's only been just over a week.'

'Have you heard from Max?'

Emily scrunched up her nose. 'No, not a word. I miss her sometimes.'

'That's normal, I guess. I don't know, I've never been in a relationship long enough to miss someone when it's over.'

'Gio, you've never been in a relationship that's lasted longer than a bank holiday weekend.'

'That's not true,' he said with a laugh. 'What about Scott?'

'Scott? The art gallery guy? Oh, come on. That wasn't a relationship, that was a situation.'

'Okay, I'll admit that.' He paused and glanced behind Emily. 'Oh, hello there.' Gio stepped around Emily and walked over to a tiny dog that looked like a teddy bear, sitting by the edge of the flowerbed, yapping. The dog was completely white and had luxurious fur and big brown eyes that were looking up dolefully at Gio as he approached. He leant down and the dog let him stroke her head and give her a scratch behind her ears. When he withdrew his hand, she started yapping again.

'Where has she come from?' Gio asked as Emily looked around for the dog's owners but couldn't see anyone obviously searching for a lost pet. 'Maybe she's lost.'

Emily eyed the tiny dog suspiciously. 'She looks too well-groomed to be a stray.'

'I think she's a Maltese, but she must only be a puppy. They have long hair when they get older. Do you think we should take her somewhere? She's so small. She might get hurt wandering around by herself.'

Emily's plan of visiting The Seaside Café evaporated with the look Gio gave her. He may not have been the type of person to lose his heart over someone, but he was a complete sucker for a pair of puppy eyes.

'Honestly, Gio, I've never known anyone to be so soppy over dogs. Alright,' she relented, with a huff. 'We'll take her up to Harrison's vet surgery. Maybe she's got a chip or something and they can find her owners. Harrison's bound to know who owns her anyway. I think he's the only vet around, so he probably knows every dog and cat in Dovecote.'

The little dog allowed Gio to pick her up. She glared malevolently at Emily who narrowed her eyes at the lump of fluff. The dog had prevented her from having a sticky bun; a crime that would not be easily forgiven.

. . .

The dog had to be examined by the vet before they could leave her. As they sat in the waiting room, Gio fussed and cooed over his new best friend.

'Who's a good girl? Yes, you are. Oh, you're so cute.'

'For goodness' sake, Gio. It's a dog.'

Gio placed his hands gently over the dog's ears and her tongue lolled out of her mouth. 'Don't you listen to the mean lady.'

Emily stuck her tongue out at him. The dog growled and bared her teeth.

'Emily?'

Emily turned at Harrison's voice. 'Hey. Look, we found this dog. We think she's lost. Can you take her off our hands so we can go for lunch?'

Harrison glanced at the dog and then at Gio. He didn't look back at the dog.

'This is my friend Gio,' Emily said.

'Hi,' Harrison said, his voice strangely constrained.

'Hello,' Gio replied. Gio was far too cool to let his jaw drop, but there was a certain look in his eyes.

'Harrison, the dog,' Emily barked, making the dog growl again.

'Oh, yeah, sorry. Do you want to bring her in and we'll have a look?'

As he led the way to the consulting room, Emily snuck a look at Gio. He looked as lost as the dog. She groaned. That was all she needed.


Later that afternoon, after a delicious lunch of *gambas al pil pil, chorizo frito, patatas bravas,* and *croquetas,* Emily bundled Gio on to the train back to London. With a bottle of red inside him, it was too risky to introduce him to everyone, particularly after the way he'd looked at Harrison. Her life was uncertain enough without any entanglements, romantic or otherwise, complicating things further. Someone would get hurt, and she'd be caught in the middle. It wouldn't be the first time.

With a few hours spare and having not been in the mood to help Gio with the bottle of wine, she took the opportunity to drive to the big DIY shop on the road to Brighton that Molly had recommended to pick up some paint and decorating supplies. Clifftop Cottage was delightful, but it could do with a refresh.

By the time she was on her way back to Dovecote, the sun had dipped below the treeline and flashed occasionally through the branches making Emily squint. It was right in her eyes when something squat and solid darted out into the road right in front of her.

She screamed as she slammed on the brakes. The badger was getting closer and now stood in the middle of the road, paralysed by the oncoming car. In a microsecond, her subconscious chose to swerve sharply towards the verge rather than across the road, which turned blindly right. She held her breath and closed her eyes as the front of her car lurched forwards and downwards.

She forced her eyes open. There was no way she was getting out of this ditch. Grabbing her phone, she scrambled out of the car. She mustn't have hit anything too solid seeing as the airbag hadn't gone off. She released a long, slow breath. A chunky grey backside trotted merrily across the road and through the hedge beyond.

'You little...' she muttered. Luckily, apart from being stuck nose-first in a ditch, her lime green Volkswagen Polo looked as though it was in one piece, as was she.

Emily stood by the ditch, staring at her car until the sun had set and a bluish twilight bathed the road and surrounding fields and hedgerows. The ditch didn't look all that deep, but there was no way the car was coming out of there without assistance.

She glanced up and down the road a few times, and then back down at her phone in her hand. Did she have any roadside assistance cover? She must have. Didn't she? There was a number for a breakdown company saved to her contacts. Her finger was poised over the call icon when a car drove up slowly and pulled over. The driver was clearly smarter than her as they pulled over onto a piece of solid ground, not into a sodding ditch. But then, they hadn't nearly hit a sodding badger. The phone in her hand was vibrating and she looked at it in confusion. There were no incoming calls. It wasn't her phone that was shaking, it was her hand.

A shadowy figure emerged from the car into the completely dark road. Great. She'd survived a potentially serious car accident only to be attacked by some crazed lunatic in the middle of nowhere. She should have been tucked up safe and warm in Max's flat in Earl's Court. This was all Max's fault. If Max had been able to keep her hands to herself, Emily wouldn't have had to move to Dovecote, wouldn't have been driving down winding country roads, wouldn't have come face-to-face with a badger, and wouldn't be about to be brutally murdered. The figure stepped into the beam of their car headlights and Emily's heart, which was already doing double time, sank. Of all the people who could have come to her rescue, why did it have to be him? Why did it have to be Will Prentice?

# ELEVEN

## VIOLET

May 1943

When the bell rang above the door of Harrington's, I cursed softly. It was five minutes to closing time, and inevitably anyone who came into the shop that close to the end of the day was a browser. And they probably wouldn't buy anything either. My heart leapt into my throat when our eyes met.

'Hello, Violet,' Zeyla said, in that same low, husky voice she'd bid me farewell with at The Royal Oak two weeks previously.

'Zeyla,' I managed to utter as she came towards the dark-wooden counter at the back of the shop. My cheeks were warm enough to toast a teacake on.

'I wonder if you can help me?'

My heart sank. She was here looking for a book, not to see me.

'Of course. Was there something in particular you were looking for?'

'I was hoping you might have a copy of *Orlando* by Virginia Woolf?' Zeyla twirled a lock of hair around her finger. I would have given anything in that moment to press that fingertip against my lips. There was something else in her question. She wasn't really asking about the book.

'Um, yes. I think we do. It will be over here.' I stepped from behind the counter, suddenly conscious of the darn in my grey utility skirt. At least my blouse was new and, so far, devoid of marks of repair. Zeyla didn't seem to have been affected by clothing rations or reduced to utility garments. Her blue silk summer dress skimmed her knees, and she wore a matching headscarf tied in a fashionable bow on the top of her head. I led her past the low shelf units in the middle of the shop and over to the fiction section, which ran along the right-hand-side wall. The Ws were right at the end, by the window. I picked the book off the shelf and handed it to her. My fingers grazed hers as she took it and regarded the orange and cream banded cover.

'Have you read it?' Her green cat-like eyes fixed on me. Again, a question within a question.

'Yes,' I said, not entirely sure whether the word actually left my mouth.

Zeyla's ruby lips parted in a broad smile; her eyes sparkled. There was that mischievous glint that made my stomach flutter.

'What I would really like...' She paused and leant closer to me. Her perfume was mellow and lightly floral, with a hint of vanilla. 'Is a copy of *The Well of Loneliness*,' she whispered with a coy giggle. 'Have you heard of it?'

I most certainly had. The book, about the relationship between two women, had been famously labelled obscene and banned in Britian in 1928. I looked away, my cheeks burning.

'But, seeing as some boring old men have decided it's not suitable, I shall have to make do with Ms Woolf. Can you put it on Father's account?'

I nodded. Zeyla's complete and utter shamelessness robbed me of my ability to speak *and* raised my temperature.

'And then perhaps we could take a walk?'

I tried to swallow, only to find my mouth completely dry.

Having pulled down the blinds and checked all the lights were off, I turned the key in the front door of Harrington's Bookshop. The late afternoon sun warmed my shoulders. Zeyla slipped her arm through mine, as though we were old pals.

'I must say, it is lovely to be out and about.'

'I don't see you around Dovecote much,' I said. It was true. Apart from that time in the air raid shelter, I hadn't seen her in town.

She blew a sharp breath out between her teeth as we walked down the High Street, aiming for Victoria Park.

'I wish I could get out more. Ever since I came home from school, Mother and Father seem to think I need to be protected. I'm kept at home mostly. Of course, if there wasn't a war on, I'd be at finishing school in Switzerland, before being presented at Court. Mother is trying to replicate finishing school at home. I don't know why. It's not as if I shall have a coming out season. No one is now.' She let out a short sharp laugh. 'I'm not sorry about that. I think it's all a load of nonsense, all that preening and prancing about. Mind you, I wouldn't say no to a couple of new frocks.'

I nodded as if I had any idea of what she was talking about. I had seen pictures of debutantes being presented to the King and Queen at Buckingham Palace in the picture papers, of course. The idea that I'd ever meet anyone who moved in those circles had never entered my mind.

'It's all about getting young girls married off, of course. That's the only reason for the balls and the dinners and the opera trips. The girls are being paraded, like prize cows, to attract the highest bidder.'

'Don't you want a husband?' I asked quietly, as we crossed the threshold of Victoria Park. Most of the lawn was dug over and planted with rows of vegetables. It must have been quite lovely before the war.

'No, I do not.' Zeyla laughed. 'And, judging by the way you blushed when I mentioned *The Well of Loneliness*, I don't think you do either.'

My cheeks burned. 'I... Um. Oh.' She had taken my hand in hers. Her skin against mine sent ripples through my body. I glanced around.

'Don't look so panicked. Girls hold hands all the time.'

'Maybe the sort of girls you know. Maybe that's how it works at boarding school.' I tried to pull my hand away, but she gripped it tighter. I wasn't trying very hard to break free.

'Violet, we are not schoolgirls. I'm trying to tell you that I like you.'

I very nearly passed out. 'What about that girl you were with in the air raid shelter?'

'Lottie? Oh, we're just pals. Well, I think she had a bit of a pash on me.'

'A pash?'

'A passing fancy. Surely you had a pash at school?'

I rolled my eyes. How different our lives were. 'Zeyla, I think our experiences of school may have differed somewhat.'

'I'm sorry, I do forget.' She squeezed my hand a little tighter, sending a shockwave up my arm.

'That's alright.'

We reached the bench by the bandstand, which had a spectacular view of the pebbly beach, the white-tipped waves out at sea, and the lighthouse in the distance. We sat down, our knees touching, and our fingers still intertwined.

'So,' she said, a question in her eyes.

'So?'

'Well, now you know that I like you, don't you think you ought to tell me whether you like me too?'

How could I put it into words? How could I tell her how my

pulse raced when she looked into my eyes? How could I explain the desire I had to hold her face in my hands and gaze at her for hours? How could I say how afraid these feelings made me? How sitting here with her was thrilling and terrifying in equal measure?

'I do,' I finally whispered.

The sun was low in the sky, casting long shadows across the park, when her lips touched mine. For a brief moment, I was falling. Then it hit me – I was kissing another woman. In public. I drew back suddenly, tears pricking my eyes.

'I have to go,' I said. And I ran away.

# TWELVE

## EMILY

June 2016

'Hi. Are you okay?' Will asked. It was the first time Emily had heard his voice in years; how dare it still make her knees soften. It must be the shock of the accident. Where his brother had inherited their mother's fair colouring, Will had dark features like Terry. His silhouette in the car headlights was broad-shouldered, and he'd always been tall. His chestnut brown hair was neatly cut.

'Fine.'

He was next to her now, looking at her with an expression of concern and disbelief in his eyes. Emily had never met anyone else with irises like his – latte brown speckled with gold flecks.

'Are you sure? How did your car end up in a ditch? Are you hurt?'

How dare he show concern? He never used to. Why was he being kind to her now? He hadn't before. She fought against a very strong urge to copy the badger and run without looking across the road, so as not to be stood next to Will Prentice. Yet a part of her was glad someone was there.

'It's my own fault. There was a badger in the road, and I swerved.' She gave him a half-smile. 'Next thing I knew, I was stuck in there.' She jerked her head towards her stricken car.

'But you're okay?'

Emily nodded slowly. She didn't want to think about whether the slight ache across her breastbone was due to Will's proximity or the impact of her seatbelt.

'You're going to need a tow truck to get that out of there,' Will added. 'Have you called someone?'

'Yes.' Emily tried to keep a touch of impatience out of her voice, she wasn't a complete moron. She paused and looked down at her phone. She remembered looking up the number. 'I mean, I was about to.'

He gave her a look which might have been sympathy, or indulgence. As she dialled and waited for someone to answer, she watched Will walk to the front of her car. He stood, hands on hips, surveying the scene. He scratched his head. Then he went back to his car and rummaged around in the boot.

'Sorry?' she said, realising the woman on the phone had asked her a question.

'Where exactly are you? I'm having trouble picking up your location.'

'The middle of nowhere, I think. Hang on. Will?' His name was awkward in her mouth. He turned and straightened at the same time, narrowly avoiding hitting his head on the boot. 'Where am I?'

He half-jogged back towards her, his long legs covering the distance quickly. 'On Brighton Road, about a mile and a half west of Dovecote,' he said with a grin. Emily relayed the information to the woman on the phone.

'They'll be about half an hour,' Emily said to Will after she'd hung up.

'Here.' He handed her a blanket he'd retrieved from his car. 'You're a bit shaky.'

A small, stubborn part of Emily wanted to refuse, but she was trembling so accepted the blanket with as much grace as she could muster and wrapped it around her shoulders.

'So,' Will said after a moment. 'You're back.'

'Apparently so.'

'I heard about what happened with... what's his name? Max? Sounds pretty awful.'

'Her.'

'Sorry?'

'Her. Max is Maxine.'

'Oh. Right.'

Emily pulled the blanket tighter around her shoulders. Despite the warmth of the summer evening, she was still trembling. The adrenaline from the accident was wearing off and the pain in her chest was getting worse. Not that she'd let on to Will that she was in any way injured. She'd learnt a long time ago not to reveal any sort of weakness to him. Will was looking down at his folded arms. A couple of cars passed by. The drivers turning to look as they went past. She, heroically, resisted the urge to stick her tongue out at them, or give them the finger.

'What happened?'

'With Max?'

'With you.' The intensity in his look made her insides quiver slightly.

'Me?' she stuttered, dying to look away but finding herself as caught in his gaze as the badger had been in her headlights.

'One day you were here all fine, and then you were gone without saying anything. And we never saw you again. What happened?'

The loud engine of the breakdown truck, accompanied by flashing orange lights, gave her an excuse not to answer.

'Breakdown truck is here,' she said, rather redundantly.

'Apparently so,' Will replied, flicking his eyebrows and pursing his lips. 'I'll get out of your way.'

Emily didn't reply as he walked away. How could he not remember?

The breakdown truck had taken Emily's car to a local garage at the far end of Dovecote, near the caravan holiday park on the cliff behind the lighthouse, after the accident. The next morning Emily walked along The Promenade, past The Seaside Café and Dovecote Museum, and onto a cobbled street. There was a row of whitewashed cottages that looked even older than the ones on Beachfront Road. Rob, the mechanic, passed her car safe to drive. Miraculously, the paint tins in her boot had remained sealed and undamaged.

That afternoon, with her car safely back outside Clifftop Cottage, Emily stood in the sitting room with an unopened tin of Meadow White paint at her feet and a roller in her hand. Whether the uneven surfaces of the walls were beyond her limited decorating experience, would remain to be seen. She frowned, the bureau had proven annoyingly difficult to shift and remained stubbornly against the wall. The ebonised oak desk wasn't particularly heavy, just awkward, and when she tried to manoeuvre it, the antique wood groaned in complaint. The last thing she wanted was for it to fall apart on her, or for one of the stained-glass panels to get broken.

She was considering her options when there was a knock at the front door. The wind was taken completely out of her sails when she opened it to find Will on the step.

'Hi,' he said, flashing her a somewhat shy smile. 'Hope you don't mind me dropping by. I wanted to see how you were after yesterday.'

Emily automatically touched her breastbone. The bruise from the impact of the seatbelt had turned a very interesting shade of purple. And it still hurt like hell. She probably should have gone to hospital and got herself checked over yesterday. But it wasn't as if she'd banged her head, or lost consciousness. She didn't fancy spending hours in A&E, only to be told it was just a bruise. Instead, she'd laid a bag of frozen peas wrapped in a tea towel on her chest.

'I'm fine, thanks,' she said.

As he ran his hand through his chestnut hair, Emily caught a glimpse of a crisp white shirt collar under his summer jacket. The curve of his neck and the line of his jaw was infuriating. Why couldn't she take her eyes off his skin? This was Will, the guy who derailed her entire life. The thumping from behind the bruise refused to be stilled.

'Did Rob at the garage manage to repair your car okay?' he asked.

'Yeah.'

'Oh. That's good. Well, I'd better be—'

'Will, hang on.' Emily reached behind her and picked up his blanket. Once she'd stopped stroking the incredibly soft cashmere, she'd folded it and draped it over the back of the sofa. As he took it from her, his fingers brushed against hers for the tiniest fraction of time. It was enough to trigger a flood of memories that Emily saw in a flash. Will taunting her, laughing at her clothes, her hair, her figure, her accent. A summer evening full of laughter and excitement. The rustling of branches, the creak of the door of a summer house. A churchyard drenched in soft rain. He was looking at her with a curious intensity and she banished the memories to the far depths of her mind.

He glanced behind her. 'Decorating?'

'Oh. Um, yeah. Just a lick of paint, to freshen it up a bit.'

'Do you want a hand?'

Emily raised an eyebrow. 'From you? I wouldn't have had you down as the practical type.'

Will tilted his head slightly. 'No, that's fair. I'm more of a "pay someone else to do it" kind of guy.'

'Yeah, I figured.' His silver sports car was parked next to her, now even more, dented lime green VW Polo. 'Actually, there is something you can do, if you have a minute?' Even as she said the words, her brain screamed at her. What was she doing?

'Yeah, sure.'

'I've tried to move Violet's bureau but it's not shifting.'

Will stepped across the threshold and glanced around the sitting room. 'Not been in here for a good few decades,' he said, shaking his head. 'It's just as I remember.' His hand trailed along the back of an armchair as he followed Emily over to the desk. 'Is it heavy?'

'Not especially. I've emptied all the drawers, except that one.' She pointed at the top drawer. 'It's locked and I've not been able to find the key.'

'Ooh, a locked drawer. How mysterious. I wonder what's in there?'

Emily had to laugh. 'It's probably nothing more exciting than Violet's passport and bank statements.'

'And here's me thinking you were the romantic sort,' Will said with a chuckle. 'Right, where do you want to move it to?'

'Just into the middle of the room, so I can paint behind it. It's a bit awkward, there's nowhere to get a good grip on it.'

'Do you think if we opened the fold-down desk it might help?'

'Worth a try.' If it worked, he was going to be so smug about it. Emily groaned inwardly. And she'd owe him two favours. That grated.

The desk complained as they lifted it off the ground. Emily's grip slipped, and it tilted forward. A small panel of wood at the back of the desk fell out, and a key slid onto the surface of the desk. Will caught Emily's eye as they put the bureau back down a few feet away from the wall.

'It looks like you might get your answer,' he said, reaching for the key.

# THIRTEEN

## EMILY

June 2016

Emily's heart gave a little flutter. Despite her outward nonchalance, she'd been intrigued by the locked drawer. The key slotted into the lock smoothly and clicked satisfyingly. The drawer creaked as she pulled it open.

'Anything interesting?' Will asked, peering over Emily's shoulder. She reached into the drawer, and pulled out a sketch-pad, yellowed with age, and a dark-brown leather covered book. She tucked the leather-bound book under her arm and flicked through the sketchbook.

'Oh,' she breathed softly. 'It's Violet's sketchbook.' She leafed through pages of hands, faces, buildings, and landscapes. At one page, she paused. This page was covered in studies of two small children, all drawn from behind. She turned to Will. 'By the time I was old enough to know Violet, she'd retired from the art school in Brighton and wasn't producing much commercially successful work. But Mum used to tell me about the time when Violet was very well known.'

Will raised an eyebrow. 'Yes, in the 1960s and '70s. She

even had a couple of exhibitions in London in the mid-sixties, I think.'

'Yeah, it was mostly of her landscapes and beach scenes.'

Will nodded. 'We have a couple of her beach scenes up at the manor. And I have two of her later pieces at home in London.'

'Have you noticed the pair of young boys in the beach paintings?'

Will shook his head.

'Have a closer look.' She turned the sketchbook so Will could see the drawings. 'In Violet's beach paintings that she produced in the twenty years after the Second World War, there are always two small boys somewhere in the background. When my mum and dad met in the late seventies and Dad introduced Mum to his family, Violet and Mum became friends. Mum noticed the two boys in Violet's paintings and asked Violet about them. Apparently, she was quite shy about it, but eventually confessed that they are her brothers, John and Oliver. They were evacuated during the war but were adopted by their host family. Violet never talked about why they never came home.'

'Oh, that's sad.'

'They did eventually reunite, but not until the mid-seventies, I think. So not long before my parents met. Oliver was my grandfather.'

'So was Violet's maiden name Carmichael, then?'

'No, she was Saunders, as were Oliver and John. When the boys were adopted, their new parents changed their name to theirs – Carmichael. That's who I get my surname from. Grandad lived up in Yorkshire until he died a couple of years ago, but I'd not seen him in years. When Dad ran off with his bit on the side in 2002, Mum and I kind of lost contact with his side of the family, including Violet. I only knew Violet as Violet Cooper, which she became when she married Hugo. It was the name everyone knew her by, including the art world.' Will looked away for a moment and Emily turned the page of the sketchbook over. She gasped.

'What?' Will returned his attention to her and leant closer to look at the sketchbook. Emily caught a waft of his aftershave. It was spicy and woody. Probably some designer brand that cost hundreds of pounds a bottle.

'Okay, how well did you know Violet?'

He pursed his lips. 'Not that well. Harrison was the one who was friendlier with her.' He looked down at the floor. 'I wasn't here much.'

'So, as we know, Violet was quite famous for her landscapes, but there were rumours.'

'Rumours?' Will raised a sceptical eyebrow.

'Going around when her style fell out of fashion and she stopped painting commercially in the late seventies, so Dad said. It was rumoured that she also painted portraits. Nude portraits. Allegedly there's a set of portraits somewhere that she painted during the war of her lovers. Dad used to go on about them when I was little. He thought they might be valuable. According to Mum, Violet used to laugh it off if he brought it up around her. She'd say it was all nonsense, and that people were getting her confused with some other artist. No evidence has ever been found that she drew, never mind painted, portraits. Until now.' She flipped open the sketchbook so Will could see.

'Oh,' he said, looking at the page. 'I reckon that's a young Hugo.'

'Really?'

Will took the book and looked closer at the man's face. 'Yeah. I mean I only knew him as a much older man. He and Violet would have been in their sixties when Mum and Dad bought Dovecote Manor in the eighties and sold Clifftop Cottage to them. But I remember he had very kind eyes.'

Emily peered at the drawing. Will was right – the eyes were kind and gentle.

'I wouldn't know about the rest, obviously,' Will added, raising both eyebrows.

In the sketch, Hugo was naked, lounging on a couch or something similar. There was only a hint of a potential background. His kind eyes were heavy-lidded and sleepy, a cigarette dangled from his lips. His torso and limbs were unfinished. Violet had been focusing on studying his face, and other areas.

'The question is, are these preliminary studies for a portrait?' Emily asked, taking back the book and flicking over the page to reveal another nude of Hugo, this time standing at a window, looking back over his shoulder at Violet. The lines of his buttocks had been drawn and redrawn several times. 'And if they are, what happened to the portraits? And what about the other ones? The rumours Dad was so obsessed with in the eighties hinted at multiple subjects.' She turned the page again and the wind was knocked out of her lungs. It was more drawings, but not of Hugo. These were of a woman.

# FOURTEEN

## VIOLET

May 1943

It had been three weeks since that kiss, and I'd managed to avoid Zeyla. She hadn't come back to Harrington's Bookshop. On the one hand, it was a relief, but I was kicking myself for having blown it. Why had I run? The question had plagued me nightly and was still on my mind as I climbed the steep, winding driveway to Bayview Convalescent Home. The answer was as plain as the nose on my face. I was scared. Scared of what I was, of the things I wanted to do. It wasn't natural, people said. What would Mrs Harrington say, or my mother? I nearly dropped the bag of clothes I was carrying. Could I lose my job? Could Mrs Marshall evict us? It would probably finish my mother off.

The formidable twin red-bricked, bay-fronted buildings of Bayview glowered at me as I approached. Mr Crawford had again suggested that it might be a good idea for Mum to move into the convalescent home. I had a sneaking suspicion that Mr Crawford had me lined up as a potential wife for his son, Alf, and thought I'd be more amenable to the idea if I didn't have to

look after Mum. If Alf came home, of course. That was the
problem with being in the middle of a war – it was terribly difficult to make long-term arrangements. It was a moot point
anyway. Mum was not going anywhere. I couldn't bear to have
no one. A sudden bubble of sadness burst in my chest. I missed
Dad. I missed the boys. I missed Hugo.

The clothing drive donation station was in the building on
the right, according to the handwritten sign pinned to the large
sycamore tree at the edge of the front lawn. A couple of nurses
were eating their sandwiches on the bench under the tree. The
clothing collection was in aid of the injured soldiers conva-
lescing at the home and for bombed-out families. Inside, underneath an impressive oak staircase, a tall, thin nun manned the
desk. There were four or five women ahead of me. I joined the
queue and waited my turn. The presence of the nun, in her
habit and wimple, made me even more ashamed of what had
happened between Zeyla and me. But if it was wrong, why had
it felt so right?

The queue moved slowly, each woman seemingly as eager
for a chat as they were to donate the clothes their children had
outgrown, or the men's clothing that had been hanging in the
wardrobe with no one at home to wear it. In Bayview's men's
house, injured soldiers were being clothed by the people of
Dovecote. A cold shiver ran down my spine. These clothes
belonged to men who may never need them again. I closed my
eyes for a moment and mouthed a silent plea for Hugo's safe
return. A familiar voice from behind made me jump.

'Fancy seeing you here.'

No one else I knew had a cut-glass accent like that.

'Zeyla,' I said, my heart thudding against my ribs.

'Can we talk?'

'I... I don't know,' I stuttered.

'Just talk,' Zeyla said softly, touching the tips of her fingers
to my bare forearm. A white-hot heat flared across my skin.

'Alright.'

The edges of her ruby-red lips curled upwards, and her eyes sparkled. I was a lost cause.

I handed over the bundle of children's clothing without hearing anything the nun was saying. Of course, the clothes weren't from us, they were from the families we shared 24 Blythe Avenue with. All the clothes that were too small for Oliver, having already been worn by John, were amongst the rubble that had been cleared from Hereford Street. I had gone back, a month or so after the bombing. The gap in the terrace, like a missing tooth, had been like a punch in the stomach. I hadn't been back since.

Having passed over the clothes, I loitered outside for Zeyla.

'Charles is going to be furious,' she said, emerging from Bayview with a wicked grin on her face. 'He loved that coat.'

'Who's Charles?' I asked, falling into step with her as we wound our way down the steep driveway.

'Charles is a constant thorn in my side. My older brother. Darling of London society, apple of my mother's eye, light of my father's life, and total swine. Why all my friends adore him, I have no idea. I only hope he doesn't end up marrying one of them, then I shall be stuck with him forever. I'm rather hoping he'll do the decent thing and marry a rich American, then he can sod off across the Atlantic. Although, I doubt he will. He'll inherit Dovecote Manor, of course.'

She must have seen the look on my face.

'Oh. Sorry, Vi. I forget.'

I shrugged. 'It's fine.'

We were at the top of the High Street and without thinking I led Zeyla down the hill, towards the beach. A spring sea breeze ruffled my hair, although there wasn't a cloud in the cornflower-blue sky. If it stayed clear, we'd be sitting ducks for another bombing raid.

'You don't have any brothers, do you?' she asked. She moved

as though to wrap her hand around my elbow but stopped herself.

'Yes, I have two.'

'Oh.'

'They're much younger than me. John is eight, nine in September, and Oliver is seven, eight in November. I've not seen them in years. They were evacuated to Yorkshire. I miss them.'

'Must have been hard to let them go, but I suppose it *is* safer up there. We do seem to be a bit of a target of late.' Zeyla elbowed me in the ribs. 'I say, you don't think I could arrange for Charles to be evacuated, do you? Although at twenty-two he's probably a little too old.'

'Is he not in the forces?'

'Charles? Doing the honourable thing and serving his country? Don't be ridiculous. No, Charles is far too weaselly for that. He landed himself a job as private secretary to a Member of Parliament straight out of university. Spends most of his time in a secure office deep underground writing letters, as far as I can tell.'

At the bottom of the slope of the High Street, we turned onto The Promenade. There was a sharp wind blowing in off the sea. The seagulls were having a jolly time. I let out a long sigh, I hadn't heard from Hugo in a few weeks. They say no news is good news, but not when your best friend is in the middle of it all.

We found ourselves outside The Seaside Café. The morning sun glinted off the pink-framed windows and the smell of fresh coffee wafted from the open door.

'Shall we?' Zeyla asked, inclining her head towards the café. 'My treat.'

If I'd *had* a spare fivepence I would have argued that she didn't have to treat me, and that I could buy my own tea and toasted teacake. But I didn't.

. . .

'Vi, I'm sorry about the other week.'

I glanced around nervously as I spread the butter and margarine mix on my toasted teacake.

'I never should have done that, not in public. I...' She put her cup down on the saucer. 'I really like you, Vi.' Her voice was low but there was so much chatter in the café that I doubted anyone could have heard her. 'And, well, I was quite hoping that if you felt the same way, then maybe we could—'

'What? Step out together? Like girls and chaps do? I don't know, Zeyla. I'm sorry too that I ran away from you that day in Victoria Park. You scared me. I scared myself a bit. I do like you, I like you very much. But what if we get caught? What if someone sees? We can't go about holding hands and suchlike.' I leant closer to her. 'I could lose my job if it got out that I'm... of that persuasion. It's alright for you, you have the security of social status and money. I'm sure what you're suggesting is rife amongst boarding school chums. But I can't risk it. Not even for you.'

'What if I found somewhere secret we could meet?'

My blood rushed in my ears. It was so tempting. Even here, in the café, I wanted to stroke her porcelain skin, to run the tip of my finger along her red lips. I wanted her like I'd never wanted anyone or anything before. And it was driving me crazy.

'Where?'

Under the table, her knee pressed against mine, the heat of her skin penetrating the thin fabric of my summer dress.

'There's a cottage on the estate. It used to be where the head gardener lived, but we don't have our own gardener now; a company comes in to do it. The cottage is empty and has been since the start of the war. It's hidden from the house, right on the edge of the forest.'

'I don't know, Zeyla.' This was tearing me apart. 'If your parents saw us.'

'They won't.'

'But...'

'Just come and see.'

I drew a deep breath. Once I stepped onto this path, there would be no turning back. I desperately wanted to take that step. But I was so scared.

'Alright,' I agreed. I hoped my leap off the cliff wouldn't end with me being dashed against the rocks.

# FIFTEEN
## EMILY

Will had left abruptly and without explanation after Emily showed him the sketch of the naked woman. His loss. The rest of the book was filled with intimate sketches of the same woman, whoever she was. Emily couldn't help but stare at the drawings. It was the woman's eyes. Whereas Hugo's were kind and gentle, hers were full of fire, desire, and longing. They were heavy-lidded and tapered almost to a point, like the eyes of a cat.

Emily dropped heavily onto the sofa and puffed out a long breath. Who was this woman? A friend? No, friends didn't pose nude. An anonymous subject for a life drawing class? No, it was obvious Violet must have known this woman, been close to her. Even in the rough sketches, the chemistry between the artist and the subject jumped off the page. A lover, then? Emily closed the sketchbook and carefully placed it down on the sofa cushion. She brought her hands to her face, chin resting in her palms, and raised her eyes to the ceiling. Did Great-Aunt Violet have a love affair with a woman? A prickle of excitement ran down Emily's spine and a smile slowly spread across her lips.

'Well, Violet Cooper, you just keep surprising me,' she whispered. Was that why Violet had left her Clifftop Cottage? Had she sensed a kindred spirit in Emily, even before Emily had worked it out for herself?

She brushed the cover of the sketchbook idly, a frown replacing her smile. There was something else though, something darker. Why was the sketchbook hidden away in a locked drawer? Had Violet been ashamed of her relationship, if that was what it had been, with this woman? But if that was the case then why keep it at all? Why not burn it? There was something here, something that needed to be unveiled and brought from the dark into the light.

'The portraits!' Emily jumped off the sofa, sending the sketchbook and the leather-bound book tumbling to the floor.

She pushed open the French doors from the kitchen and stepped out into bright sunshine. Violet's art studio was little more than an old potting shed. The grey brickwork crumbled as Emily ran her fingers across it. A few of the red tiles were missing from the roof which had been overrun by the ivy growing up the gables. Dark green paint was peeling from the door and the frame around the little window. Remarkably, the light still worked when Emily flicked it on.

She surveyed the room. It was much the same as the last time she'd stood at the threshold, fifteen years before, just peering in the door petrified of going in and causing some sort of catastrophe. At least now Violet couldn't tell her off, but all the same she gingerly stepped inside, keeping her arms stuck to her sides.

The studio wasn't large, no more than ten-foot square at Emily's estimation, which may or may not have been accurate – distance comprehension wasn't one of her strongest skills.

Thankfully she wasn't afraid of spiders as the ceiling was criss-crossed with gossamer cobwebs. The workbench underneath the window groaned with paints and brushes. In the middle of the room, standing in a spotlight of sunshine that poured through the window, was an easel. And on it, a canvas. Emily raised a hand and touched the unfinished painting. It looked like it was going to be the view from the top of the cliff, down over Dovecote and the headlands beyond. She traced the curve of the shoreline with her finger. About halfway along the beach, Violet had added the two boys – her brothers, Oliver and John. Emily's grandfather and great-uncle. Even before Violet had finished the sea, or the sky, or the white chalky cliffs, the boys had been placed where they belonged – their toes being tickled by the swishing waves for all eternity.

Was it odd to miss someone you'd never been close to? Maybe there'd been a subconscious link between the old lady with a colourful past and the restless teenager on the cusp of understanding herself.

'I'm sorry, Auntie Vi,' Emily said to the painting. 'I should have kept in touch.'

Pressing her lips together against the tightening of her throat, she turned away from the painting on the easel. She walked over to the far wall where rows of canvases stood stacked against each other. Emily flicked through each one. There were several landscapes, some experimental blocks of bright colours, and a couple of canvases covered in Jackson Pollock-esque abstract splodges and drips. Tucked down the side of a tall cupboard, were two paintings covered with an old sheet. Emily carefully lifted them out of their hiding place and gently unwrapped them. Hugo, in all his youthful glory, stared back at her.

. . .

Back in Clifftop Cottage, with Hugo's portraits balanced on the mantlepiece, Emily sat down on the sofa, all desire to paint the room gone. She picked up her phone but put it down again when she couldn't find anyone in her contacts who could help. Ironically, the person who would have been most interested in the portraits, and who had the expertise to critically assess them, was Lorna. But there was no way she was tracking down Max's girlfriend, even if she did work at the National Portrait Gallery. A tear dripped down Emily's cheek. Where had that come from? From thinking about Max, obviously. Emily wiped it away. She inhaled for four seconds, held it in for four, and breathed it out for four.

'Chin up, chest out, shoulders back,' she said to herself. 'Remember, *she's* not crying over you.'

As she sat on the edge of the sofa, hands on her knees, willing her broken heart away, the corner of the leather-bound book poking out from under the sofa caught her eye.

'Oh, hello,' she said as she fanned the pages with her thumb. It wasn't a book; it was a diary. From 1943. It fell open on 4 May 1943. The writing was neat but pretty, clearly the hand of an educated young woman.

> *Dash and blast, I've gone and blown it. Kissing her beside the bandstand in Victoria Park was an idiotic thing to do. Think I've scared her off. Never seen someone run away that fast. Oh, but it was delicious. So much nicer than the others. Probably because she means so much more to me than they do. But I'm all quite a dither, don't quite know what to do with myself. Might invite L down for the weekend.*

Emily closed the diary and sat staring into the middle distance for a long moment, her heart pounding. Could this be Violet's diary? She wiped the cover with her sleeve. There was a gold 'Z' embossed on the top right-hand corner of the diary, and on the front page there was an inscription: *Property of Z*. Her heart sank a little. It wasn't Violet's diary. So who wrote it? And how had it come to be hidden in a locked drawer with Violet's sketchbook? Her phone rang, bringing her back to earth with a bump. It was the organic cosmetics company. Work had to come first. The diary would have to wait.

# SIXTEEN

## EMILY

June 2016

It wasn't until Harrison knocked on the door of Clifftop Cottage that evening that Emily remembered she'd arranged to go to the pub with him. After a long phone call with the organic cosmetics company, she was desperate to get back to the diary. Who on earth was this Z? And who was the woman she kissed so openly in the park? Could it have been Violet? Why was the diary at Clifftop Cottage? And where were the other portraits? She had so many questions. But the minute she sat down on the sofa her eyes closed, and it took Harrison banging on the door to wake her from her unscheduled nap.

'I hear you've been reacquainted with my brother,' Harrison said as they walked down the driveway and turned right onto Brighton Road towards the centre of Dovecote.

'He stopped by this afternoon to check how I was after yesterday.' She didn't want to talk about Will. The memories their brief touch had unleashed still lingered.

'Chucking your car into a ditch is a pretty dramatic way to

reunite with him. You could have popped up to the house for a cuppa.'

Emily rolled her eyes at him.

'Are you alright, though?'

'Yeah, I'm fine. Bit of bruising, but other than that, no damage done.' She tapped him on the arm. 'Did you tell him about Max?' Will had heard it from somewhere, and his brother was the likely culprit. 'I don't mind if you did.'

'Not directly,' Harrison said. They had reached the end of Brighton Road and were walking over the railway bridge. A train pulled into the station to their right and the platform was crowded with people waiting to board. 'I think he might have overheard me telling Mum.'

'He presumed Max was male.'

'Heteronormativity strikes again. Sorry, Will is very straight.'

Emily shrugged. 'I corrected him.'

'Good, he needs educating.'

She paused outside The Royal Oak. They were meeting his friends again, so she might not get another chance to ask him tonight. 'Do you get on okay now, you and Will? You didn't used to.'

Harrison smiled. 'Yeah, we do. A lot has changed since 2001, Emily. None of us are the same people we were back then. I mean, we were kids. But you're right, there were a few years where Will and I did not get on. I think we were growing up into very different people. He was the sporty, athletic, popular one. And he was developing that arrogance that comes with being popular. I, as you will remember, was none of those things, and it was only after we went to uni that we both had the space to grow into what we needed to be.'

'I remember you were shy and quiet around people. But when it was just us, you never shut up.'

'That's because I was comfortable with you.'

'I'm going to have to say it again; I'm sorry I let you down.'

He took her hand in his and gave it a squeeze. 'I'm glad you came back.'

'Me too.'


Being greeted by Aoife, Molly, and Heather as a friend of theirs in her own right warmed Emily's core. Dovecote was starting to exert a grip on her. The road out of town was looking less enticing, and not just because she now knew it was frequented by badgers with a death wish.

'I'm sorry I've not had a chance to pop round,' Molly said, stirring her drink with a straw. The ice clinked against the glass. 'Toby's had a niggly cough and Zoe's been doing my head in lately.' She took a long drink. 'I'm very glad to get out and leave them both for Jez to sort out. Honestly, I love Toby and Zoe but, God, kids wreck you.'

'I'm sure you're doing a fine job, Molly.' Emily chuckled as Harrison handed her a glass of white wine. 'But if you need a break, or to sit in a quiet house with some tea and biscuits, I'm home most of the time.'

'Sounds like heaven. I'll definitely take you up on that. God, a cup of tea I actually get to finish. There's a rarity.'

Harrison nudged Emily's elbow. 'Come over here a sec, there's a couple of people I want you to meet.'

He led her to a table on the other side of the bar, past the huge open fireplace. It looked like it would be a very cosy spot in winter. Terry was sat at the table, along with two men Emily didn't recognise. One of the strangers was Terry's age, maybe a touch older, with a rounded face and a full head of greying hair. The other had to be his son – they had the same shaped face.

'Hey,' Harrison said as they approached the table. 'I want you to meet Emily. She's moved into Clifftop Cottage.'

'Hi,' Emily said, slightly awkwardly.

'Emily, you know Dad. But you've not met Gordon and James Rutherford. Gordon has recently taken over managing Dovecote Museum.'

'Hi,' James said, pushing his black-rimmed glasses back up his nose and sweeping his floppy dark fringe off his forehead. Gordon looked at her curiously, his dark eyes slightly narrowed. Emily didn't have any more idea of what was going on than he apparently did.

'Emily is a web designer,' Harrison added.

Gordon's face lit up with a smile that touched his eyes. 'A web designer? You could be the answer to our prayers.'

Emily raised an eyebrow at Harrison, but he grinned enigmatically back.

'Dad's right,' James said. 'The museum website is ancient, and awful. We could do with a new one, but we have no idea where to start. Any chance we could get you on board?'

'Of course.' Emily flashed Harrison a grateful smile. 'If you have a look at my website, you'll see examples of the kinds of sites I've created before, but I can work to whatever you want.'

'Are your prices on there too? I'll need to check the budget before we sign up to anything,' Terry added, earning a tut from Gordon. 'These two don't like when I bang on about the purse strings, but that's what treasurers do, I'm afraid.'

'Yes they are, Terry. I presume the museum has charity status?' Emily asked.

Gordon and James nodded their matching heads in unison.

'Good. Well, we can talk about costs once you've decided what sort of thing you want,' she said. The contract she'd signed with a big pet food brand earlier in the week would keep her in bottles of Merlot for a while, so she could probably do mates-rates for the museum. They were nice blokes, doing a good thing keeping a small, local museum going.

'We'll leave you to your *planning meeting*,' Harrison said, glancing at the empty pint glasses on the table.

'Cheeky sod,' Terry said with a snort. 'We think better when we're hydrated.'

'Yeah, alright Dad. I'll tell Mum you said that.'

'You'll tell her nothing.' Terry laughed.

'Nice to meet you. Drop me an email or whatever.' Emily gave them a small wave.

'They'll insist on paying full price for the web design,' Harrison whispered into Emily's ear as they walked away.

'I know. That's why I won't ask them to,' she replied with a wink. 'What are they planning? Anything exciting?'

'That depends on your definition of exciting. Gordon's had the idea of expanding Dovecote Museum. Not sure if you've had a chance to pop in? It's pretty good. The museum has owned the patch of disused land next to the museum building behind The Seaside Café for years, but never done anything with it. Now Gordon's taken over and roped Dad in, they want to reconstruct Dovecote's World War Two air raid shelter on it. Apparently, people used to shelter in the cellar of this pub during air raids, and Gordon thinks it would be good for school children to learn what it was like by visiting a replica at the museum. They're trying to fundraise for it, so a decent website would really help.'

'Makes sense.'

As they neared their table, Harrison paused. He looked down at the maroon carpet.

'So, um, how's Gio?'

He was blushing, and Emily suppressed a sigh. She'd received a text from Gio as she was quickly getting ready to come out, asking if she'd seen Harrison and how he was. It was looking as if her two worlds were about to collide, whether she liked it or not.

# SEVENTEEN

## VIOLET

May 1943

Zeyla kept a discreet distance from me as we left The Seaside Café and walked through Dovecote. I steered her across the High Street before we came to Harrington's Bookshop – I didn't need Mrs Harrington asking questions that I couldn't answer truthfully. My jaw dropped when I first saw the grand, sweeping entrance to the Dovecote Manor estate and the driveway lined with rhododendrons.

The carved lions atop the gateposts seemed to be judging me. I wanted to ask Zeyla how they'd been allowed to keep their wrought-iron gates and railings when all over town walls were lined with stumps of metal and wooden gates had been erected in place of iron ones. But she'd hinted that her father, Randolph Wythenshawe, had something to do with the government, so I held my tongue. She took my hand as she led me up the winding path that forked away from the main driveway to Dovecote Manor. This time, I didn't pull away. Here, hidden from the world by rhododendron bushes and oak trees, I was safe. Her skin was so soft.

We came to a clearing where the path widened, and there in front of us was the most beautiful, chocolate box cottage I had ever seen. The rose garden beyond the sage-green wooden gate was overgrown. Weeds grew as high as the rose bushes, which were spindly and bent. We'd had a garden once, before we moved to Hereford Street. Dad had loved his rose bushes. The memory of him bringing me a freshly cut rose made my bones ache. The curtains in the window to the right of the front door were closed. Upstairs, there were two smaller windows. Zeyla had marched on ahead of me, up the stone path, and was standing by the oak door covered in peeling sage-green paint under a storm lantern hanging from the pitched roof of the porch.

'It's lovely,' I whispered, reaching her. 'I want to paint it.'

'There's an even better view from the back. Let's go in.'

'Are you sure it's alright, that there's no one living here?' My stomach clenched.

Zeyla rolled her eyes. 'I'm sure. Do you trust me?'

Now there was a question. I looked into her green eyes.

'Yes,' I breathed.

She rubbed the lion's head door knocker and pulled a key from her pocket.

'I swiped this from the spare key drawer this morning.' The mischievous glint was back in her eyes, and for a moment I was reminded of Hugo. They had a similar spirit. Was I doomed to always be the sensible one? Considering what I'd been through in the past four years, it wasn't surprising.

'Won't someone realise it's missing?'

'I shouldn't think so. Why would they?' She shrugged casually.

The key clicked in the lock and the door swung open. It was immediately clear that no one had lived in the house for a while. There was a thick layer of dust on everything – the armchairs, the oak mantlepiece above the red-brick fireplace, and the dark-wood writing desk against the far wall. I crossed the room to the desk and ran my hand across the purple stained-glass roses in the glass panels above the slope of the closed writing surface. My fingers left a trail in the dust. I crossed the room again, Zeyla watching my every step, and reached for one of the heavy, dark red curtains, releasing a plume of dust into the air.

'No, wait,' Zeyla said, pulling it shut again. She took my hands in hers and drew me closer to her. Our bodies touched, igniting my every nerve. She placed one of my hands against her face and softly kissed the base of my thumb. 'We are completely alone. No one knows where we are. No one can see us. We are safe.'

This time, when she kissed me, I allowed myself to freefall.


'I found some coffee in the cupboard,' Zeyla said, stepping out into the courtyard at the back of the cottage and handing me a mug.

We'd stopped kissing long enough to explore the rest of the downstairs of the cottage. It didn't take long; there was only the cosy sitting room and a large kitchen with a long farmhouse table. The kitchen cupboards needed a lick of paint, the brown wood made the room seem dark and oppressive. We'd not ventured upstairs yet, partially because I was a little afraid of what we might end up doing if we did.

'I hope it's alright,' Zeyla added, interrupting my musings on the bedroom situation. 'There's no milk of course, but the ice box is cold and the stove works. I guess Father must still be paying the electricity bill.'

'He won't come down here?' I was hit with a blind panic, imagining Randolph using Clifftop Cottage as his own private bolthole.

'Father wouldn't descend to visiting the staff quarters,' Zeyla said, in her haughtiest voice. Then she wrinkled her freckle-dappled nose. 'This coffee is awful. I'll pinch some from the kitchen.'

I took a tentative sip. It was hot, but bitter and tasted slightly of mould.

'I think I'd prefer tea,' I said with a smile. I inhaled a lungful of sea-scented air. The sun-drenched courtyard had the most magnificent view of Dovecote below. The town stretched out to the left and the sea to the right, the stony beach a grey no man's land between the two. Chalky cliffs topped with green petered away to the horizon opposite. The only sounds were the birds in the trees behind us, and the distant crash of waves on the rocks below. It was the closest to paradise I had ever been. I yearned for my paintbox, buried like so many precious things in the rubble of Hereford Street. I had tried to save up to replace it, but there wasn't enough money. I only had my sketchbook and a few pencils in my bag.

Zeyla reached for my hand across the small white wrought-iron table. She brought my fingers to her lips and kissed each one in turn. My breathing shallowed as she looked at me from under heavy eyelids. The shrill wail of the air raid siren shattered the peace.

'Oh, hell,' Zeyla cursed.

'What shall we do?' I asked. 'You must have a shelter at the manor?'

'We use the wine cellar. But I don't want to go. I hate being in confined quarters with Mother and Father. They'll ask too many questions. And I shan't be able to sit next to you for hours without kissing you. Let's stay here.'

'But if we get hit...' My stomach lurched at the memory of the pile of rubble that had been our house. 'We'll be killed. What if the windows get blown in? What if the roof collapses?'

Zeyla dragged me back into the house, closing the sturdy oak door behind us. The heavy velvet curtains were still drawn across the sitting room window. The siren was dulled by the thick stone walls. She pulled me down onto the rug in front of the fireplace, and we leant against the sofa.

'We'll be fine,' she said softly, stroking my hair. She drew a finger across my lips. 'I can think of several ways to take our minds off it.'

The distant thud of bombs was drowned out by the thumping of my heart.

I woke a few hours later, before Zeyla, and scrabbled around in the dark for my clothes. All was quiet now, the all-clear had sounded as we'd drifted off to sleep, wrapped in each other's arms. I slowly peeled back the curtain from the window. After-noon had bled into evening and the setting sun was casting long shadows across the driveway. I perched on the edge of an armchair and reached for my sketchbook. Zeyla was the singu-larly most beautiful creature on earth, lying there naked on the threadbare rug, eyes closed, one arm flung up over her head, her lips slightly parted.

I put my pencil down when I lost the light. Lying down on the rug next to her, I gently kissed her and her eyes fluttered open.

'Oh, gosh. Is it late?' she mumbled. Her voice was heavy with sleep.

'Yes, it's getting late. I'd better go.'

'Must you?'

I resisted the urge to run my finger down her long neck and along her collarbone. There were other places I longed to touch, but I had to resist.

'Yes, Mum will be worried. I need to make supper for her. And I'm on fire watch tonight. If you look closely out of your window, you might even be able to see me on the roof of our building.'

Zeyla drew a deep breath and sat up. 'Alright. I suppose I

ought to make an appearance at dinner or else my parents will send out a search party.'

I watched from my perch on the arm of the sofa as she dressed, her graceful body slipping easily into her fine clothes.

'When can we meet again?' she asked, standing over me and kissing me gently on the forehead. I placed my hands around her waist and pulled her close, until my face was buried in her chest.

'Soon.'

She took a step back and I reluctantly let her escape my grasp. She cupped my face.

'My bedroom window is the farthest one on the right of the upper floor as you face the manor. When I'm home, I generally confine myself to my room. I'm sure you can throw a bit of gravel that far.'

I laughed. 'Are you suggesting I walk up the manor and start throwing stones at your window? Sounds like the quickest way to get the dogs set on me or get arrested.'

'The dogs would most probably lick you to death. But no, maybe you're right. It's a bit risky. We'll think of something. Come on, we'd best be going.'

Having locked the front door, Zeyla handed me the key.

'Why don't you keep hold of this? That way, if you ever need somewhere to go, you'll be able to get in. Anyway, it's best if it's not found in my possession.'

I turned the key over in my hand before slipping it into my pocket.

'Be careful walking in the dark,' Zeyla said.

'I will.'

Our parting kiss was bitter from our separating and sweet with the promise of meeting again. I watched her nip around the cottage towards the path that led to the manor. It was entirely possible that I was in love.

# EIGHTEEN

## EMILY

In the week since meeting Gordon and James Rutherford, Emily had finally painted the sitting room (enlisting Harrison's help to move Violet's bureau back against the wall), finished the pet food website, and had become thoroughly engrossed in the diary.

For the first three months of 1943, Z had been away at boarding school. The diary was full of secret late-night meetings with various girls, and kisses snatched between library stacks. These giddy stories gave way to panic at approaching final exams. Having arrived home in April, the entries became odes to boredom. Z was bored of the war, of her mother, of not getting to be a debutante, of having to wear last summer's dresses again. Only the occasional weekend visit by a girl, named only as L, seemed to cheer her up. Although, she seemed frustrated at L's lack of willingness to progress the physical aspect of their relationship beyond kissing. The line '*L won't even let me touch her Bristols*' had Emily searching a rhyming slang dictionary on Google.

With a cup of coffee in hand, Emily flicked to the next entry.

*25 April 1943*

*I never want to see L again. I had hoped that taking her to the women's only dance club in Brighton might loosen her up a bit. And it did, but not towards me. I turned my back for one moment and she was all over someone else. I left them to it.*

Emily took a sip of coffee. The mental image of Max kissing Lorna made it hard to swallow.

'Oh, Z. I feel your pain.' Emily drew a deep breath and pushed Max out of her mind, turning back to the diary.

*But on the upside, I saw V. The siren went off as L and I were heading to the station, so we had to duck into the shelter under The Royal Oak, and there she was. Although it's nearly three years since I last saw her, I recognised her immediately. Still got a pencil in her hand. Her eyes are a more dazzling shade of blue than I remembered. Was almost sorry when the all-clear sounded and we had to leave. She blushed when she saw me. God, I hope she's one of us.*

Emily put down the diary, and her coffee cup. Her hand was shaking so much she was liable to drop it. Her pulse thundered in her ears. It was as though she'd been handed a jigsaw puzzle without a picture and been told that some of the pieces were missing. Each entry led to more questions. Was Z a Dovecote local? Could V be Violet? Emily turned the diary over in her hand. Violet had grown up in Brighton, but Emily had no idea when she'd come to Dovecote. And what was Z's diary doing locked in a drawer of Great-Aunt Violet's writing desk?

· · ·

Her phone buzzed with a message from Harrison.

*Meet you at the main gate in five.*

Emily grabbed the bunch of roses and peonies she'd picked from the garden and headed down the driveway.

Harrison was waiting, leaning casually against the gatepost, his slicked back fringe making him look like a blond James Dean. The dog Gio and Emily had found was sat at his feet and growled and bared her teeth as Emily approached. As the puppy was a six-inch-tall ball of white fluff the effect was more comical than menacing.

'That dog is quite the diva,' Emily said, giving Harrison a peck on the cheek.

He grinned. 'Why do you think we named her Cher?'

'We?'

A pink tinge spread over the tips of Harrison's ears. 'Me and Gio.'

'Hmm,' Emily murmured. 'Gio did say something about adopting her if she wasn't claimed.' He had also begged Emily to take her in seeing as he wasn't allowed pets in his London flat. Emily's reply had been a sharp, firm refusal. 'I'm guessing no one's come forward?'

'No,' Harrison sighed sadly. 'And I don't know why. She's a very sweet little thing.' As if on cue Cher began yapping ferociously until Harrison picked her up and gave her a scratch behind her ear. The dog glared malevolently at Emily.

'If you say so,' Emily said, raising a dubious eyebrow.

As they crossed Brighton Road opposite the school and walked the few yards to St. John's Church, Emily nudged Harrison. 'You know, if you were to look after her at the manor for Gio, it would give you an excuse to call him.' Harrison's cheeks flared and Emily grinned to herself. He'd been well and truly caught by Gio's charm. And who could blame him, many others had been before. She just hoped he wasn't looking for anything long term. Serious relationships were not Gio's style.

'I guess I could do that. I'd have to see how she got on with the other dogs.' Harrison's forehead had furrowed into a deep frown. 'She's snack-sized for some of them. And Margo, for one, has a tendency to chase after small, furry things. Margo is a Border Collie. She's a sheepdog without a flock of sheep to roundup. She tends to try to round up squirrels and small children instead. Gerry is the other Collie; he's a bit more chilled out. And then there's Bernie, a mad Irish Setter.'

They passed under the lychgate and took the path around the church towards the graveyard behind.

'Thanks for coming with me,' Emily said, following Harrison up the path between the lines of graves.

'Not a problem. Those flowers are pretty.'

Emily looked down at the bunch. 'I thought Violet might like something from her garden. Did Will tell you we found Violet's old sketchbook and a diary?'

'No, he failed to mention that. Honestly, he never tells me anything useful.'

'They were locked in a drawer. Looking at the sketches, I think I can understand why it was hidden. It was full of sketches of a nude Hugo.'

'OMG!' Harrison spluttered.

'And a nude woman.'

'O.M. double G.'

'I think Violet might have had a love affair with a woman, possibly before she met Hugo.'

'So was Violet bisexual?'

Emily ran a hand through her hair. Was she making it all into something it wasn't to create some sort of link between her and Violet? Or had she really found someone in her family like her?

'It's possible. But we can't know how Violet would have self-identified, and I'm not comfortable attaching labels to people. Did she ever talk to you about it?'

Harrison shook his head. 'No. I'd drop in for a cup of tea and a slice of cake or, when I was old enough, a martini and some smoked salmon blinis. Violet mixed a mean martini. But she never mentioned anything about her past. She was more interested in what I was up to. But I think she was quite good friends with Janice, who runs The Seaside Café. Maybe you could have a chat with her, see what she knows?'

'The more I learn about Violet, the more I like her. And the more I wish I'd made the effort to keep in touch with her.'

Harrison led Emily through the cemetery. Some of the graves were very old and clearly untended, the names barely legible on the weathered stone. Others had fresh flowers and clean, bright headstones. The ones with multiple names drew a mixed bag of emotions. All graves were sad. Death was sad. But seeing people reunited in death, lying together for eternity, their bodies nutrifying the same soil, drew a strange sort of soft satisfaction. It was okay that they had died because they were together again.

Harrison stopped and gestured to the second grave in from the path.

'There she is, with Hugo. I'll give you a moment with her. Come on Cher, let's keep walking. You need all the exercise you can get, you're a little on the tubby side.'

Emily snort-laughed before stepping off the path. The gravestone was grey marble, with simple white engraved lettering.

## HUGO THOMAS COOPER

### 1922-1993
*Beloved husband and friend. His garden is his legacy.*

## VIOLET REBECCA COOPER

1925-2016
*Beloved wife, sister, and friend. She lives on in her art.*

A bunch of blue forget-me-nots with their bright yellow centres had grown up at the edge of the grave. They were the perfect reminder to not forget those who had gone. It was right that they grew in a place so full of memories.

'I'm learning more and more about you, Aunt Vi,' Emily sniffed, giving in to tears, as she placed the roses next to the headstone. 'I wish I could have talked to you about who you really were. I think we could have talked for hours. Maybe that's why I'm here, to tell the world about you, and to find out things about myself too.'

Harrison was talking to a woman when Emily caught up with him at the far side of the cemetery. The graves here were rather close to the train tracks. The residents probably didn't mind. The woman's straight brown hair, and long brown cardigan with fluffy cuffs made her look a little like the Afghan hound sitting obediently at the other end of the lead she was holding. Harrison was keeping Cher at arm's length from the much bigger dog. Cher was making her displeasure known, loudly.

'Keep putting the drops in her eyes twice a day and it will soon clear up,' Harrison was saying to the woman, who gave Emily a shy smile as she approached.

'I will do. Thanks,' the woman said, blushing slightly as she turned and walked away, her dog strutting alongside and Cher yapping after them.

'I don't think Cher likes you talking to other women,' Emily said. 'And I'm pretty sure that woman has a thing for you.'

Harrison scrunched up his nose. 'Daphne? Nah, she's happily married, with a son. And it's common knowledge around here that I'm gay.'

'Fair enough. So, we got distracted by my bisexuality the other day and you never told me why you ended up back in Dovecote? Bristol too exciting for you?' she asked, giving him a nudge with her elbow as they crossed back over Brighton Road and walked through the Dovecote Manor gates.

'Not quite. I loved the practice there. I had a great time.' He looked down at his feet. 'I even met someone.' When he looked up, Emily could see the shadow of pain in his blue eyes. 'His name was Lev. We were planning on getting married.' He drew a slightly wobbly breath. 'But then one day, he was involved in a head-on collision with a drunk driver. He didn't make it.'

'Oh, Harrison. That's awful. I'm so sorry.'

He gave her a weak smile. 'After that, I couldn't stay, so I came home. It was around the time Dad started to have problems with his heart, so Mum was glad to have me around. That was five years ago, and I've been here ever since. I do still miss Lev, but now I tend to remember the happy times we had together.' He blinked a couple of times, then drew a steadying breath and pulled his shoulders back. 'I guess it's true that grief never really leaves you, you just get better at living with it.'

They were back outside Clifftop Cottage. Harrison picked up Cher again.

'Come on, little lady, let's see how you get on with the others. And no shouting your head off at them, okay?' He gave Emily a hug, which she returned. 'It's good to have you back. I've missed you,' he said, before turning away.

'Harrison,' Emily called out, and he turned. 'Losing Lev hasn't put you off?'

He raised his eyebrows. 'Put me off what? Love?'

Emily nodded.

'Not at all. In fact, now that I know how good it can be, I'm definitely up for it.'

'Even if it means you might get hurt?'

'I think it's worth the risk. See you on Friday.'

Inside Clifftop Cottage, Emily threw herself down on the sofa. She needed to have a word with Gio, she couldn't have him breaking Harrison's heart. She reached for the diary. Visiting Violet's grave, and Harrison's question about Violet's sexuality, made her even more desperate to read on. The pages of the diary whispered with intrigue and the promise of revelation.

# NINETEEN

## EMILY

July 2016

*25 May 1943*

*I have died and gone to heaven. Today, during an air raid of all things, V and I became lovers. It seems awfully prudish to write it like that. But the names we used for it at school are too vulgar to describe something so beautiful. When she touched me, it was like emerging from a dark tunnel into bright light. And the way her body responded to my touch made me feel as though I possessed a special kind of magic. I want to hold her neat little body in my arms forever. Oh, listen to me, you must think I have lost my mind, dear diary. And perhaps I have. Or perhaps I am in love.*

Emily put Z's diary down and puffed out a breath.

'Well,' she said. That was quite the entry. It was beginning to become clear why the diary had been locked away. But presuming V *was* Violet, how did she end up with it? What happened to Z? Who was she? The buzz of her phone interrupted her thoughts.

*Hey, you ready? Heading out now. Meet you at the gate H x*

Declan had invested in a karaoke machine for The Royal Oak, and tonight was its first outing. Harrison had cajoled until Emily gave in, if only to shut him up. It was not her idea of a fun way to spend a Friday evening. Not when the diary was starting to get really interesting.


'Just to warn you,' Harrison said, pushing open the door of the pub. 'Will's girlfriend is going to be here.'

Emily raised an eyebrow. 'Will has a girlfriend?'

'Everyone hates her. Including Mum and Dad.'

'Oh, that's not awkward at all.'

'Tell me about it. Thankfully, she doesn't come down often.'

'Why doesn't anyone like her?'

'You'll see.'

There was a decent crowd in The Royal Oak, and Harrison led Emily to a table by the fireplace. Declan had set up a little stage over to the left of the bar, and Aoife and Molly had sensibly chosen a table as far away from it as possible. A glass of white wine was waiting for her. Aoife and Molly had remembered her favourite drink.

Harrison elbowed Emily in the ribs and flicked his head over his right shoulder. In the booth behind them, by the front window to the right of the door, sat Will and a couple of his friends. Some of them were vaguely familiar and Emily had a flashback to the summer of 2001. She pushed it away. Now was not the time. And then she saw *her*. Of course, Will's girlfriend would be stunning. Her long, blonde wavy hair was draped over her slim shoulders. Thick eyelashes framed her beguiling hazel eyes, and her dark pink lips pouted seductively.

'So that's...' Emily whispered to Harrison.

'That's Tabitha. Her friends call her Tabby, apparently. Spoiler alert, no one around here calls her Tabby.'

'She doesn't look like she's enjoying herself.' There was a sulky undertone to Tabitha's beauty, and boredom in her eyes.

'She always looks like that when Will drags her to Dovecote. Mum would never say so to him, but she'd rather he left Tabitha at home.'

'I'm guessing it's pretty serious if they live together?' Not that she cared. Will's relationship status was none of her business.

'That's the worry. I've not said anything to Mum and Dad, but I have a sneaking suspicion that he's going to pop the question sometime soon.'

'Oh God, really? Surely he knows she's not liked, especially by your parents. Can't your dad have a word, man to man?'

'Mum and Dad let us live our own lives and make our own mistakes. They always have. It's something I love about them. As long as Will's happy, they won't say a word.'

Emily considered her glass of wine for a long moment, stealing occasional glances at Will and Tabitha. She was right; despite his actions the night of her car crash, Harrison's words made it clear Will was still as selfish, self-absorbed, and egotistical as he had been as a teenager. The silver sports car, the designer clothes, the cashmere blanket causally chucked in his car, the beautiful girlfriend was all proof that Will was still someone who put himself on a pedestal and looked down his nose at anyone who wasn't like him. Well, Tabitha was welcome to him. Emily had been there fifteen years ago and had suffered for allowing herself to get close to Will Prentice. The passing years hadn't dulled the pain.

Emily downed her wine and tried to focus on the conversation going on around her. Aoife was telling everyone about her latest one-night stand who hadn't delivered quite what he'd promised in the bedroom department. The peals of laughter washed over Emily as her mind wandered back to the diary waiting on the coffee table. What had she learnt so far? That Z was a woman, of that Emily was certain. That she lived in Dovecote but had been away at boarding school. Which meant she was probably from one of Dovecote's wealthier families. Could she have even lived at the manor? Emily knew so little of Dovecote's history and about the people who lived there. Harrison had said that Terry and Sue bought Dovecote Manor in the 1980s and then sold Clifftop Cottage to Hugo and Violet, but where had Hugo and Violet lived before then? When, and why, had Violet come to live in Dovecote? Where had she met Hugo? And if Violet *was* the V in Z's diary, how did Hugo fit in with her love affair with Z?

Some of the answers *had* to be in the diary. But she was stuck listening to a rotund, middle-aged man with thinning hair and a beer-reddened face, mutilating Johnny Cash's 'Ring of Fire'.

'Hey, you okay?' Harrison's question pulled her out of her daydream and back into the pub. 'You don't seem yourself.'

'I'm fine. A little tired.'

'You sure? We can go if you want.'

Emily patted his arm. 'You stay. I think I'll head off. Get an early night.'

'Ah, you're not going, are you?' Aoife asked. 'I'm going to do Madonna's "Like a Virgin" in a bit.'

'Really?' Molly spluttered. 'I'm surprised you can remember what that's like.'

'Ah, give over,' Aoife replied with a grin.

'Sorry, Aoife, but I'm a bit tired. I'll be fine after an early night.'

'Are you coming to the Victoria Park fair tomorrow? It's the annual highlight of the Dovecote social calendar.' Molly laughed.

'I was planning on it. It sounds like great fun. I think I remember going when I came down for those summers.'

Harrison snorted. 'We went the first year you were here, but the next two years we thought we were too cool. It has got a lot better in the last fifteen years.'

Emily shook her head. 'What were we thinking? Neither of us have ever been cool.'

Aoife laughed. 'Come along, sure. It's a grand excuse for a bit of day drinking.'

'Well, that seals it.' Emily laughed. 'Gio's coming down for the weekend, but I doubt he'll take much convincing.' She glanced at Harrison out of the corner of her eye. He was giving his drink his full attention, but the tip of his ear had gone pink.

Molly beamed. 'The kids are so excited, they love it. Jez is mostly looking forward to the beer tent.'

'Well at least you'll know where to find him. I'll see you tomorrow.'

'Hang on, Emily. I'll walk with you,' Harrison said, suddenly getting up from the table, leaving half a Malibu and coke behind. Emily glanced one last time at Will's table. He hadn't even noticed her.

'You didn't have to leave on my account,' Emily said as she and Harrison made their way up the High Street.

'I wasn't in the mood either. And I've heard Aoife's Madonna impression before. It's *not* an experience I wish to repeat.'

'Poor Aoife. I like her.'

'Yeah, she's great. She's got a heart of gold too. So, um, Gio's coming down for the weekend?' Harrison didn't look at her as he spoke, and Emily supressed a laugh.

'Yeah, he has a rare weekend off. I think he's probably more interested in seeing Cher than me though. He did ask if you were around.'

'He did?' Harrison's eyes lit up and he cleared his throat. 'I mean, oh, right. Yeah, sure.'

At the fork in the Dovecote Manor driveway, Emily placed a hand on Harrison's arm.

'I think you quite like him.'

'Gio?'

'Yeah. And I can see why. He's drop-dead gorgeous and that smile of his has snagged many an admirer. And he's a good guy.'

'I sense there's a "but" coming.'

Emily scrunched up her nose. 'Gio's a bit like Aoife. Long-term, serious relationships aren't his thing.'

'Oh, right.'

'You're big enough and old enough to look after yourself, Harrison, but be careful. I wouldn't like to see you get hurt.'

'Isn't he your best friend?'

'Yeah, he is, and I love him dearly. And nothing would make me happier than for him to meet someone nice like you. But Gio is Gio, and I can't see that changing.'

'He's probably not interested in me anyway.'

'I don't know, Harrison. Considering the number of times he's asked after you, I wouldn't be surprised if it wasn't only Cher he was keen to see again.'


Once back in the cottage and tucked up in bed, Emily opened Z's diary again, hungry for the next part of the story.

# TWENTY

## VIOLET

May 1943

There was an odd sort of atmosphere as I walked through Dovecote in the fading evening light, as though something had happened and I was the only one who didn't know about it. I was anxious that Mum would ask me where I'd been all day, since I'd only popped out to quickly drop off some clothes at Bayview. That, and the lingering warm glow from what Zeyla and I had done that afternoon, took up all of my thoughts. If Mum did ask, I could say I'd been at the bookshop, working. But I didn't want to lie to her. I wanted to tell her. I wanted her to know that I was in love, and that the woman I loved might love me too. I wanted her to know I had experienced something wonderful, and beautiful, and magical. I wanted her to be happy for me, to still love me. Most of all, I wanted her not to pity me or to see me as something broken, or deviant. But I didn't know how she'd react if I told her.

Since Dad's accident Mum and I had become strangers as she'd retreated into herself, shut away from the world. I knew so little of her feelings, her opinions, her passions that I couldn't even guess as to what her reaction would be to finding out her daughter was a lesbian. I wanted to shout from the rooftops that I was a lesbian, and I was happy. But the very idea was laughable. I'd probably be arrested.

I turned into Blythe Avenue and came to a cordon by the wooden-gated entrance to Victoria Park. The road beyond was full of men in tin hats with flashlights. It was also full of rubble and smoke and flames. I ducked under the rope, ignoring the bursts from a policeman's whistle. It was just like that night in Hereford Street.

'Please, God, no. Please,' I whispered to myself as I sprinted past Victoria Park, the trees and shrubs dark shadows against the rising moon.

A hand grabbed my arm, and I turned to see Mrs Marshall, tears streaming down her face. And I knew. I wrenched my arm free and ran towards number 24. I needn't have run. There was nothing to see. Number 24 Blythe Avenue was gone, the whole block of fine townhouses was gone. Just like our house in Hereford Street. Except this time I didn't have my arms around my family.

'Mum,' I screamed. I ran towards the men in tin hats who swarmed the rubble, smoke rising from beneath their feet. 'Where's my mum?'

One of the men turned and looked at me blankly.

'You alright, Miss?'

Was he stupid? Of course I wasn't alright.

'My mum was in there. Where is she?' My voice was thick with fear and hot tears ran down my face. 'Where's Mum?' I cried. I was smothered in a tight hug. I vaguely recognised the scent of Mrs Marshall's soap and laundry powder.

'Calm down, Violet. We took a direct hit, love,' she said, in a soft voice that I never imagined could have come from her. 'Brighton got a pounding, and we caught a stray one. There wasn't time to get your mum into the basement. We tried, me and Dora, we did.'

'Is she...?' I asked into the dust coating Mrs Marshall's housecoat.

'They pulled her out of the rubble about an hour ago, pet. She wasn't in a good way. They took her up to the triage station at Bayview.'

I lifted my head and looked at Mrs Marshall. She was trying to comfort me through her own pain. She'd lost her home. My heart went out to her. I knew how much that hurt.

'Thank you,' I said, pulling out of her embrace.

I looked over my shoulder as I ran back down Blythe Avenue. Mrs Marshall was ordering the men in the rubble to look out for anything they could salvage. My stomach churned as I ran up the hill towards Bayview. This was my fault. I'd committed a sin. My love for Zeyla was wrong, and this was my punishment. My mum might die, and it would be my fault.

The driveway of Bayview Convalescent Home was a hive of activity. Ambulances were parked at odd angles and their crews bustled back and forth between their vehicles and the buildings. Of course, other people must have been injured in the bombing too. A man was being carried out of Bayview on a stretcher and loaded into the back of an ambulance. The bandage around his head was soaked with blood.

'Anyone else we can take to the hospital while we're going?' one of the ambulance crew shouted. A tall, thin nun appeared in the doorway. It was the same woman who had taken the clothing donation from me. Had that only been this morning? So much had happened, so much had changed, including me, since then.

'No, that's the last. Thank you. We can take care of the rest. God bless,' the nun said, raising her hand in either farewell or blessing. I approached her nervously. Could she see the marks of sin on me?

'Excuse me?'

'Hello, dear.'

'I think my mum is here. Um, Rebecca Saunders. From 24 Blythe Avenue.' I wiped my clammy hands on my dress and pinched my bottom lip between my teeth to stop it trembling. Mrs Marshall said Mum had been in a bad way. What if I was too late? The nun looked at me, her beady eyes softening.

'You must be Violet. I'm Sister Margaret. Yes, your mum is here. She's resting. Come on in and I'll take you to see her.'

I breathed normally. It was alright, I wasn't too late. Mum was still alive. I followed Sister Margaret through the hallway I'd stood in that morning. The table had been pushed back right under the stairs. There was a pile of boxes stacked neatly next to it, donations waiting to be distributed to those in need. Once again, I was homeless. Once again, I carried everything I owned in my handbag. Once again, I would have to start over. But I would do it. Mum and I would do it. We'd be alright. We were survivors.

Sister Margaret led me into a large room. Perhaps in peacetime it had been a day room, where residents could enjoy the sun, read a book, or listen to the wireless. Now it was a makeshift ward. The soft sofas and armchairs had been replaced by two straight rows of six beds. All occupied by women with bandaged heads, arms, and legs, covered in soot and smoke stains, grief and exhaustion etched on their faces. And there was Mum, in the bed by the window.

I ran to her, carefully wrapping my arms around her shoulders and hugging her gently.

'Mrs Saunders hasn't said a word since she was brought in,' Sister Margaret said. 'There's no medical reason why. Perhaps...'

'Mum doesn't speak much,' I said gripping Mum's hand. 'Do you, Mum?'

She looked at me with wide, doleful eyes and a tendril of guilt wrapped itself around my gut. I should have been there. I shouldn't have left her on her own. I'd failed her. Sister Margaret bowed her head and moved away.

'I'm sorry, Mum. I'm so sorry I left you. I won't leave you on your own again, I promise.'

'Violet?'

'Yes, Mum.'

'I'm tired.'

'Alright, Mum. Why don't you get some sleep? You're a bit bruised and battered by the look of you. You'll be better after some rest. I'll be right here if you need anything.'

A cloud drifted over Mum's eyes. 'No, I'm tired. Of everything. Of bombings. Of grief and pain. Of every day being shrouded in darkness.'

It was the most I'd heard her say since Dad died, and I held my breath waiting for more.

'I miss John and Oliver.'

'I miss them too, Mum. We can get them home if you want?'

She shook her head so slightly it was barely a movement. 'No. They are safe.'

'Alright.'

She turned away from me towards the dark window. There was a slight pink tinge to the sky; the glow from the fires still burning on Blythe Avenue.

'I miss Michael. I want to see him.'

'Oh Mum,' I said, gulping back tears. 'I miss Dad so much too.'

'You've been a good girl, Violet. You've looked after me and your brothers. I asked too much of you, but you managed. I'm proud of you.'

I broke. The tears flowed freely down my cheeks. If only she knew. If only she knew that I wasn't the good girl she thought I was. That I was something that people said was wicked, unnatural. How could I tell her when she had suffered and been injured for what I'd done? She should be ashamed of me, not proud. She turned her head back from the window and squeezed my hand very slightly. The movement must have hurt as she let out a soft gasp of pain.

'Violet?'

'Yes, Mum?'

'You can be whatever you want to be and no matter what you do, no matter who you are, who you become, I will always love you and be proud of you. I think it's time I was reunited with my husband. I can hear him. He's calling me home to him.'

'No. Mum. No. Don't go. Please! I *need* you.' I was sobbing now, my tears dripping onto the bedsheets. Her chest rose slowly, and then fell for the last time.

# TWENTY-ONE
## EMILY

July 2016

Summer had peaked in time for the Victoria Park fair. The park was filled with stalls selling everything from fudge to locally made gin. The sweet, sugary smell of ice cream and candy floss mingled with the sea air, and seagulls stalked the path picking at dropped chips. Children ran between the coconut shy, hook-a-duck, and the ring toss, and expended their energy on a bouncy castle, occasionally breaking off to check in with parents relaxing on the grass. A brass band played on the bandstand.

In the beer tent, Emily fanned herself with a flyer advertising guided tours of the brewery sponsoring the tent on behalf of The Royal Oak. It wasn't making any difference to the stifling heat. What also wasn't helping was Gio, who kept looking around every two minutes. From the moment they'd met at the train station, he'd been jumpy. It was almost as if he was nervous.

'Will you sit still, Gio? God, you're making me all hot and bothered.'

'He's definitely coming, right?'

Emily laughed and rolled her eyes. 'Yes, he's coming. And he's bringing Cher.' She gave him a playful slap on the knee. 'You like him, don't you?'

Gio sighed. 'I don't know what's happened to me. Ever since that day, I have not been sleeping properly, not eating properly. Look,' he pinched his thigh, 'I am skin and bones.'

'Oh, Gio, you crack me up.'

'I am not joking, Emily. When he sends me a text message about Cher, my heart does a little dance to see his name on my phone.'

'So why did it take you so long to come back down? You could have visited anytime.'

The excited smile slipped from Gio's handsome face. 'I think maybe I was a little scared. I don't know. It is all very new.'

'Oh, Gio.' She gave his knee a quick squeeze. 'You're in love.'

'Oh, *Santo Cielo!*'

Harrison chose that moment to enter the tent, his arrival announced by Cher yapping her head off as usual. Gio muttered something else in Italian and puffed out his cheeks.

'Don't worry, he's looking forward to seeing you too,' Emily whispered.

'Hey,' Harrison called as he came towards the table.

'Hey, you,' Emily replied.

Gio coughed. 'Hi.'

Harrison picked Cher up and handed her to Gio. A broad grin cracked Gio's face as Cher wagged her stumpy tail and licked him.

'Oh, I have missed you, my little *bambina*. Look at you, so pretty. Who's a good girl?'

'He didn't tell *me* he'd missed me,' Emily said raising an eyebrow at Harrison. 'Or that I was pretty.'

'But I have talked to you on the phone,' Gio said.

'You mean Cher hasn't FaceTimed you?' Emily grinned.

'Oh, I never thought of that. What a great idea. We'll definitely have to do that.'

'I was joking, Harrison.'

'I'm not, it's a great idea.' Harrison turned to Gio. 'So, um, we could take her for a walk, if you wanted? Um, there's a Pride stand, if that's your thing.'

'Oh, yeah sure. But Emily...'

Emily could have quite happily banged their heads together. Instead, she gave Gio a look.

'I'll be fine. Aoife and the others will be here any minute. Go on you two. Get out of here and have fun.'

Gio gave her a peck on one cheek, while Harrison did the same on the other. Cupid had nothing on her.


There was a half-price offer on bottles of prosecco and Emily bought two from Declan behind the bar. Aoife could be relied on to help. The wind had picked up a little and it drifted through the tent, lifting the heavy stickiness and giving the air a salty tang. It also brought with it the smell of frying onions from the hot dog stand that made her mouth water.

'Hello, gorgeous,' Aoife called, waving frantically. She air-kissed Emily and plopped down in the chair next to her.

Emily reached for the bottle and an empty glass. 'Prosecco?'

'Ah yeah, go on. I won't say no, like.' She picked up the flyer and fanned herself. 'It's far too hot. I'm not made for it.' She took a gulp of prosecco. 'That's better. Be grand after a few of these. So, I saw Harrison. He was with a fine-looking fella I've never seen before.'

'That will be Giovanni. My friend from London. They met when we found that little madam of a dog and took her to Harrison at the vets. You should have been there, Aoife.

Honestly, I've never seen two people so instantly attracted to each other. I mean you could see the sparks.'

'Ah here, that's lovely. It's about time Harrison found someone nice. And what about yourself? Anything going on?'

'Nah. To be honest, Aoife, I'm not that bothered.'

'And sure, that's grand. As long as you're happy, like. Ah, here's Molly and the kids. Will you have a prosecco, Molly?'

'Hiya. Oh, yes please, that would be lovely.' Molly turned to the young girl with ginger hair beside her. 'Zoe, go and tell Daddy that I don't need a drink, please.'

'Mummy, can I have an ice cream?' The little boy with brown hair and serious eyes tugged at Molly's arm.

'In a bit, Toby. Let me sit down for a minute, would you? And say hello to Aoife and Emily.'

'Hi,' he whispered, shyly looking down at the grass.

Jez arrived with glasses of juice for the kids and a pint for himself. 'Hello all,' he said. 'Nice day for it.'

'Daddy, I wanted pink juice. This is red juice.'

'It looks pink to me, Zoe. It's the one you asked for.' He raised an eyebrow, and any further protestation was silenced.

'Here Molly, listen—' Aoife began.

'Mummy. I *want* an ice cream,' Toby interrupted.

'I said in a minute, Toby. Sorry, Aoife.' She flashed an apologetic smile.

'Mummy?'

Aoife bristled. Kids were kids and they were the centre of their own universes. And when you're six, getting an ice cream is *really* important. Emily caught the look Molly gave Jez. He drained his pint.

'Come on, you two. Let's get out of Mummy's way. Give her five minutes' peace. Who wants to go on the bouncy castle?'

'Yay,' Toby and Zoe cried in unison, and Molly let out a long breath.

'Seriously I'm going to snap one of these days. All I hear

every day is "Mummy, Mummy, Mummy". Any chance of a top-up?'

Emily reached for the bottle and refilled all their glasses.

'Sweet holy mother,' Aoife breathed, and Emily followed her gaze. She involuntarily drew a sharp breath. Even by Will's standards, he looked good, as much as it was painful to admit it. Aoife was practically drooling as Will removed his sunglasses and tossed his dark hair. But her face fell when Tabitha appeared at his side. 'Ah, for feck's sake. He's only gone and brought *her*.'

'What is the deal with Tabitha?' Emily asked.

'She's a money-grabbing little madam. She's got her eyes on Dovecote Manor, I'm sure of it,' Molly said, leaning closer to whisper. 'She'd have it sold to a hotel chain in a heartbeat.'

'What does he see in her, though? Apart from the obvious.'

Molly's lip curled. 'I guess she fits the brand.'

Will had spotted them and was coming over. Tabitha was trailing behind him, scrolling on her phone. Emily supressed a groan.

'Hi, Will,' Aoife purred. 'Tabitha,' she added icily.

Tabitha looked up from her phone and scanned the table. Her eyes hovered on Emily, no doubt judging her charity-shop bargain pinafore dress. Tabitha was a picture of effortless, cool elegance in a cream cotton summer dress that accentuated her tiny waist. Emily had to begrudgingly admire Tabitha's confidence – if she'd worn something that colour, it would have been covered with marks and stains before she'd even left the house. The designer handbag swinging from Tabitha's petite arm probably cost more than Emily's car. If she had any notion of vying for Will's affection, there would be no point. How could she compare? And where had that come from anyway? She was *not* interested in Will Prentice. Absolutely not.

'Do you mind if we join you?' Will asked. 'I was looking for Mum and Dad, but I can't see them.'

'Not at all,' Aoife said, patting the chair next to her. 'The more the merrier.'

'Is that champagne?' Tabitha asked, her nasally voice grating against Emily's ears.

'Prosecco,' Molly said, lifting the second bottle out of the ice bucket.

Tabitha scrunched up her nose. 'Oh. No, thank you. I don't drink cheap rubbish.'

'I do,' said Aoife cheerily. 'Fill us up, Mol.'

'Me too,' Emily added passing her glass across the table. If she was going to have to put up with little-miss-up-herself and mister-designer-sunglasses, she was going to have to get roaring drunk.

Tabitha looked up from her phone. 'Will, I'm bored. Can we go now? You said we'd only stay for five minutes, and it's been, like, forever.'

She was worse than Molly and Jez's kids. Before Will had a chance to reply, there was a commotion at the entrance of the tent and Sue and Terry staggered in, Terry leaning heavily on Sue. Will jumped up from his chair and helped Sue guide Terry into it.

'Stop fussing, I'm alright,' Terry grumbled. He looked far from alright. His face was almost purple, and his breathing was erratic. 'I'm just a bit warm.'

Molly ran to the bar and came back with a pint of water, and Aoife fanned Terry with the leaflet as Sue undid the top button of his shirt. Emily put her arm around Sue's shoulder.

'He nearly keeled over,' Sue said. She was shaking slightly, and Emily sat her down in Molly's chair. 'One minute he was walking along fine, the next he sort of folded over. Do you think we should call an ambulance?'

'You'll do no such thing, Sue,' Terry snapped. But then his face softened, and he reached for Sue's hand. 'I'm fine, love. Stop fretting.'

'You're supposed to be taking it easy, Dad.' Will's face was pale, and his brow knitted with worry. Maybe he did have some redeeming qualities, after all. He clearly adored his parents. Emily gave Sue's arm a squeeze. Terry really didn't look well.

'Will?' Tabitha's grating moan made Emily shudder. 'Can we go? I *need* to get to Harvey Nichols before they close.'

'Tabby, just wait, okay?' Will's tone was only marginally more patient than Molly's had been at Toby's repeated requests for ice cream. The difference was that Toby was six years old.

'But Will.'

He turned away from Terry and placed a hand on Tabitha's elbow, escorting her gently, but firmly, out of the tent. Emily glanced at Aoife who had a satisfied smirk on her lips. They couldn't hear what Will was saying but it was clearly getting heated. Emily spotted James Rutherford, hand-in-hand with a woman with golden-blonde hair, and a young boy, who was clearly James's son. There were strong genes in the Rutherford family. James was steering them well away from Will and Tabitha's argument.

'Trouble in paradise?' Emily whispered, and Aoife's smirk widened.

'Oh, ouch,' Aoife snorted, as Will pulled his car keys out of his pocket and handed them to Tabitha. He had a face like thunder when he came back to the table, but it softened as he placed a protective hand on Terry's shoulder. That was one tally mark in the 'maybe-he's-not-all-that-bad' column. There were still plenty of tallies in the 'he's-a-self-absorbed-tosser' column though. In the distance, the roar of a sports car engine faded into the sea air.

'Come on, Mum,' Will said, not making eye contact with anyone. 'Give me your car keys, let's get Dad home, at least. Then we can call someone out to check him over.'

'I'd better go and find Jez and the kids,' Molly said quietly, after the Prentices had left.

'Yeah, I think I'll call it a day,' Aoife added. 'It shakes everyone up to see Terry unwell. He's a good guy and does a lot for the town. I mean, like, the work he and Sue have done on the manor. Apparently, it was quite run down when they bought it. And now the grounds are one of the top wedding reception venues around. It's good for us all, like. I definitely get an increase in bookings at the salon when there's a wedding on.'

There was a message from Gio on Emily's phone.

*Going out in Brighton with Harrison and some of the guys from the Pride committee. Don't wait up x*

She smiled and typed back.

*Nice one. Have a fab night. I've only had a couple of small glasses of prosecco, so call if you need picking up later xx*

She flashed Aoife a smile. 'Sounds like things are going well between Gio and Harrison. I've been told not to wait up.'

'Wow, Gio's a faster mover than I am,' she laughed. 'Fair play.'

'A long bath and a good book for me tonight, then. Oh, Aoife?'

They had reached the gates of Victoria Park.

'Yeah?'

'I don't suppose you know of anyone in Dovecote whose first name begins with Z, do you?'

Aoife scrunched up her nose. 'Can't say that I do. Why?'

'I found a diary the other day, along with one of Aunt Violet's sketchbooks. It belongs to someone with the initial Z.'

'If it's old, I'd say you'd want to ask Janice. She's lived in Dovecote all her life.'

Emily glanced over her shoulder. The roof of The Seaside Café was visible behind the hot dog stand and bouncy castle.

'Yeah, that's what Harrison said. I might pop into the café tomorrow, have a chat with her.'

'If you do, make sure you get one of her sticky buns. They're the business.'

Emily chuckled. 'Thanks Aoife, I will do.'

She opted for the shortcut, along Beachfront Road and up the steep steps. At the top, she turned and looked back down at the town that was seemingly determined to become her new home. London felt like a lifetime ago. She could live with that.

# TWENTY-TWO

## VIOLET

May 1943

I was a homeless orphan. That dawned on me, sickeningly, as the sun rose over the chalk cliffs to the east of Dovecote and shone on the bench in Victoria Park where I'd been sitting for most of the night. Sister Margaret had given me a heavily sweetened tea and said I wasn't to worry, that she'd get in touch with Reverend Douglas and make all the necessary arrangements. I'd declined her offer to stay overnight at Bayview; the idea made me shiver. Instead, I'd wandered down the hill and ended up in Victoria Park, clutching the bag of clothes and other essentials Sister Margaret had given me from the donation boxes. I'd gone from donor to beneficiary in one day. Fresh tears poured from my eyes. I'd have to write to Beryl and Arthur Carmichael and tell them, so they could break the news to John and Oliver. My heart ached for my brothers.

Standing up from the bench that overlooked the mined beach surrounded with barbed wire, I slipped my hand into my dress pocket and my fingers closed around the key to Clifftop Cottage. The idea of hiding in the cottage, sneaking around and avoiding the owners, filled me with dread. Did I want to spend my life looking over my shoulder? Maybe Zeyla's parents would accept a token rent. A token would be all I could pay. And then there were the electricity bills, and coal or wood for the fire, and groceries. Tears pricked at my eyes again, but I blinked them away. I'd kept four people alive on my Boland's wages, I could keep myself alive on my wages from Harrington's. There was a war on – nobody had two brass farthings to rub together. I was no worse off than a lot of people. The future was a long way off and could be dealt with when the sting of grief had passed. For now, I needed a friend. I needed Zeyla.

The sun was barely poking over the top of the rhododendron bushes as I made my way slowly up the driveway of Dovecote Manor. Ahead, the grey stone gothic manor house was like something from a Daphne du Maurier book in the early morning light, the sun rising behind it, trapping it in its own shadow. The dark mullioned windows were blank, eerie eyes and the grey sloping roof a heavy brow. The house was judging me. A shiver ran down my spine. I looked up at the last window on the right of the upper floor. I could see, now that I was closer, that the windows weren't dark and empty, they were covered with blackout fabric.

I bent down and picked up a few small bits of gravel from the driveway and took a deep breath. My first attempt missed the glass and hit the stone windowsill. The second hit, but there was no movement of the blackout blind. Zeyla was probably still asleep. One more try and if I had no luck I'd go to Clifftop Cottage alone and come back later. The tiny pebble hit the middle of the left-hand pane of glass. A moment later, the blind was pulled back to reveal Zeyla's startled face. She pointed to the right-hand side corner of the manor, where a narrow path skirted the grey wall.

Around the corner, past a large bay window, was an unobtrusive door. I waited until I heard faint footsteps on the other side. I held my breath as a key turned in the lock. I had no excuse planned if it was anyone other than Zeyla.

'Vi?' Zeyla hissed at me. She had wrapped herself in a silk dressing gown, but I could see her white nightgown underneath. Her feet were encased in delicate slippers. 'What on earth? You look a mess. What's happened?'

'A bomb. Yesterday afternoon. Mum's dead.' The words came out disjointed and staccato, the rise of tears preventing me from forming full sentences. Zeyla took my hand in hers. It was still warm from sleep.

'Oh, Vi. I'm so sorry.' She squeezed my hand and wiped a soft thumb across my wet cheek. 'Come on. You're filthy. You need a hot bath.'

She put a finger to her lips as she led me into a dark hallway with stairs leading up and down from it.

'Quick,' she whispered, pulling me through a narrow door in the wall. She glanced around the large high-ceilinged room we had entered before leading me across it, my shoes squeaking softly against the wooden floor. I'd never seen an actual ballroom before. I glanced up at the crystal chandelier hanging from the middle of the frescoed ceiling and covered my mouth with my hand as I gasped.

'Shush,' Zeyla whispered. 'Mother and Father aren't up yet but the staff will be lurking.'

The double door creaked as Zeyla pulled one of them open.

'Oh damnation,' she cursed. 'Come on, we need to be quick up the stairs before Mallory goes up to Mother.'

Was Mallory one of the staff? It didn't seem the right time to ask. The mahogany stairs that swept up and around the oak-panelled hall were carpeted with thick, light-green carpet, so our feet made no sound as we dashed upstairs. Zeyla was clearly well-versed in the art of sneaking around unheard. It must be a boarding school thing. All those midnight feasts and suchlike. At the top of the stairs, Zeyla pointed to a door.

'That's Mother's room,' she mouthed, before putting a finger to her lips once more. Despite the sharp stab of jealousy at Zeyla still having a mother when I'd lost mine, I had the sudden urge to grab hold of her finger and kiss the tip of it. Even though I was filthy dirty and had missed a night's sleep, Zeyla had the power to bewitch me. The fact that her dressing gown had slipped open was not helping.

She guided me along the gallery overlooking the stairs and across a wide landing and pushed open a door on the right where the landing became a narrow hallway leading to the left. She exhaled in relief as she closed her bedroom door behind us.

'Made it. I was sure we were going to run into Mallory, or worse, Baxter.'

'Who?'

'Mallory is Mother's lady's maid and Baxter is Father's valet. They both despise me and will take any opportunity to catch me doing something I shouldn't. The first weekend I was home from school and Lottie came to stay, Baxter caught me sneaking out of her bedroom across the landing at three in the morning. We'd been drinking gin.' Zeyla lifted her hand as if to stroke my cheek but left it hovering half an inch from my skin. 'Oh, Vi, I want to hug you and kiss you, but I'll end up looking as much like a chimney sweep as you do.'

I managed a weak smile, and Zeyla brought my hand to her mouth and softly kissed the base of my thumb. She took my bag of handouts and flung it on her bed.

'Come on, I'll run you a bath.'

I glanced around Zeyla's bedroom. How many times had I tried to picture it in my imagination? Now all I could focus on was the high double bed and how much I longed to sink between the luxurious covers and be comforted by Zeyla's touch. Tearing my eyes and thoughts away from the bed, I followed Zeyla into the bathroom. The idea of a private bathroom adjoining her bedroom made my head spin. There was no need to be dashing across the hallway, or worse the yard, on a cold winter's morning at Dovecote Manor. She had already begun to fill the rolltop bath and the air was steamy and scented with lavender. She had instant hot water? I opened my mouth to say something but found myself unable to speak. I tried to undo my dress, but my fingers fumbled with the zip.

'Come here,' Zeyla said softly. 'Let me.'

I surrendered to her hands. She undressed me, even unbuckling my shoes and rolling my stockings off. She held my hand as I stepped into the bath. The water was hot and full of bubbles. It was luxury like I had never dreamt of. Zeyla took hold of a sponge and very gently began to wash me as silent tears flowed down my cheeks.

'It's all my fault,' I said, speaking to the bubbles that gathered around my toes.

'What is?' Zeyla's voice was soft and soothing.

'Mum dying. It's punishment for who I am.'

Zeyla moved the sponge in circles on my back. 'You know that's not true, Vi. There is nothing wrong with what we are, you and I. Or what we do.'

'People say it's unnatural, sinful.'

'Nonsense. People say a lot of ridiculous things. Like Mother and Father's friends who say we should make an agreement with Hitler and let him take over England. Some people spout utter rubbish, and we have to ignore them.' She cupped my face in her hand and titled it towards hers. She looked me straight in the eyes. 'There is nothing wrong with you. We are not sinning. You are not being punished. You are not something that *needs* to be punished. A stray bomb falling on Dovecote is plain bad luck. I am so sorry about your mum but Violet, please, you cannot blame yourself. This was not your fault.'

'I should have been there.'

'And been killed too?' She moved closer to me, and her lips brushed mine. 'I would have cried for years and years if you'd been killed,' she whispered. 'I love you, Violet Saunders. And dash it all, I think you love me too.'

I bit my bottom lip. 'Yes, I think I do.'

In her kiss, I unfurled like a daisy in the morning sunlight.


I turned onto my side and draped my leg over Zeyla's. We were back at Clifftop Cottage, in the soft double bed in the front bedroom, like a proper couple. The afternoon sun peeked around the edges of the brown curtains. I smiled to myself as I traced a line with my finger down her neck, along her collarbone, around and under her shoulder. She flinched as I brushed the delicate skin of her underarm.

'That tickles,' she giggled.

'Tell me about them.'

'Who?'

'Your parents. My new landlords.' How Zeyla had managed to concoct a story that convinced her parents to let me rent Clifftop Cottage from them in the space of a few hours was beyond me. She must have laid it on quite thick and been overwhelmingly complimentary. They hadn't even requested to meet me. I suspected she was well able to turn on the charm with Randolph and Venetia Wythenshawe when required. When I asked her what she'd said to them, she smiled enigmatically, kissed me, and led me up the stairs to my new bedroom. Maybe it was for the best that I didn't know.

Zeyla drew a deep breath and turned onto her side, facing me. She propped herself up on her elbow, cradling her head in her hand.

'Mother and Father both come from a long line of landed aristocracy. Theirs was not a love match, but a financial one. I suppose they have come to love each other in some form or another, but, well, they've had separate bedrooms for as long as I can remember. They are not good people, Vi. It breaks my heart to say it, but they're not. I see the stories of families bombed out in London and here we are in a massive manor house, that could provide a safe haven for dozens of children. Mother refused to take in any evacuees, and Father managed to pull some strings to avoid being made to. As I'm sure you saw, even our railings haven't been taken for the war effort. They've done *nothing* for the good of the country. I'm ashamed of them.'

I raised my head and kissed her. Her lips were salty with tears she didn't seem to realise she'd shed.

'And I'm no better, Vi. You've done your bit. Fire watching, sticking to your rations, obeying the rules.'

I laughed. 'Oh, believe me, Zeyla. If I'd had any money, I would have used it to get my hands on some proper food for my brothers, even if it meant using the black market. The poor things, they were hungry all the time. We *all* were. And you've done your bit today, rehousing a bombed-out evacuee.'

'I just wanted my girlfriend close by.'

A tingle of excitement fluttered through my stomach. We were girlfriends, and not in a chummy way.

'Do they know?'

'No. And I don't know how to tell them.'

'I think Mum knew. The last thing she said to me was that whatever I was, whatever I became, she would always love me and be proud of me.' My voice cracked. Her final words to me, along with what Zeyla had said that morning as she washed me, wrapped themselves around my heart like a warm blanket.

'That's beautiful. I don't think my parents would say the same.' A single tear dripped down her cheek.

I laid back down and curled my arm around Zeyla's bare shoulders, drawing her into me. She laid her head on my chest.

'We'll go away. After the war,' I whispered, stroking her soft skin. 'America, Ireland, Canada, Australia. Anywhere you want, we'll go. I shall paint, and you will sit around being beautiful. We'll eat fresh fruit and vegetables every day. We'll have bread that isn't soggy in the middle, with real butter and proper strawberry jam, and all the chocolate we could ever want. And we'll get fat and old and live happily ever after.'

'That sounds wonderful,' she said as sleep claimed her.

I stared at the ceiling for a long time until evening fell and the room was bathed in a silvery-blue light. I would always carry some guilt over Mum's death; I really should have been there. But Zeyla was right, if I had been maybe I wouldn't be here now in this perfect moment. My heart was broken but Zeyla's warm breaths against my skin were the stitches beginning to bind it back together.

# TWENTY-THREE

## EMILY

July 2016

*3 July 1943*

*We've settled into quite a routine now, V and I. I watch as she descends the cliff side steps for a day at Harrington's Bookshop. I then spend the day reading or in the garden. Mother is still trying to finish me, but I fear in her eyes I am a lost cause. She is still living in the pre-war years, trying desperately to hang on to the old ways. When V and I run away, I shall get a job. I shall be something useful and not merely a domestic decoration. I do quite fancy working in a factory, but V says I would hate it. Perhaps she's right, perhaps I could get work as a gardener instead. I've come to love pottering about deadheading things and pulling up weeds. V insists I wear gloves; she says she doesn't want my hands to become hardened. Bless her heart, she really is a born carer. I think she misses her mother, although she rarely speaks of what happened.*

*The evenings are my favourite time of day, when I sneak down to Clifftop Cottage. V makes supper from whatever she*

*has been able to get and from what I've been able to pinch
from the kitchen. We make love and then she spends hours
drawing me. I do enjoy being watched by her. Her eyes caress
my bare skin. Some days it becomes too much to bear, and I
can't resist pulling her back into an embrace. She laughs
when I do this, saying I'm interrupting her creative flow. The
way her fingers move across my skin feels like she is still
drawing me. Then I go home. I long for the days when I can
spend the whole night with her. I do wish I could see the
morning sun on her sleeping face. Mother thinks I'm
teaching V how to be a lady. Father doesn't even notice I'm
not home.*

Emily put Z's diary down on her bedside table and peeled back
the duvet cover. The wooden floor was cold against her bare
feet. For the first couple of nights at Clifftop Cottage, Emily had
slept in the small bedroom, the same room where she'd happily
slept for those three summers. The idea of sleeping in Violet's
bed made her uneasy. But the pull of the big double bed ended
up being too much and she'd moved into Violet's bedroom at the
front. The window looked out onto a tangle of rhododendrons
and oaks but the birds in the branches were a soothing morning
soundtrack. In the distance, the bells of St. John's chimed for
morning prayer.

She checked her phone. Gio had sent her a message at half
past midnight.

*Still alive.*

She'd been fast asleep when he'd sent it. That fact that he
hadn't come home wasn't surprising. In the years they'd shared
a flat, Emily had learnt to stop waiting up for him, pacing the
floor, worrying if he was okay. He always turned up eventually,
tired but glowing after a night of tousling someone's bedsheets.

As long as he'd not done anything to upset Harrison, everything would be okay.

It was another beautiful summer Sunday and, despite looming deadlines, the beach was calling.

Having taken the long way round, down the woodland driveway, over the stone railway bridge, and into the bustling High Street, Emily took the chance to finally visit Harrington's Bookshop.

'Hiya, Molly.' A bell tinkled softly as she pushed open the door. The shop was small and cosy, with dark shelves lining the walls and two low shelf units in the middle of the floor. Fiction on the left. Non-fiction on the right. The shelves in the children's section, along the back wall to the right of the counter, had been painted bright yellow and an orange bean bag sat nearby.

Molly was leaning on the dark-wooden counter, typing on her phone.

'Hey, Emily. Lovely to see you.'

'I thought I'd better pop in. I can't believe I've been in Dovecote for almost a month and haven't stopped by yet.'

'Well, I suppose there's plenty of books in the cottage to keep you busy. Did you ever find Violet's stash of spicy romance books?'

Emily laughed. 'I did actually. They were in a box under her bed. There are some brilliant titles amongst them, and a lot of half-naked men on the covers. I'm beginning to get the impression that Violet was more than just a sweet, old lady. I think she had quite a spark to her. I found a diary locked in a drawer. It's not hers though. It belonged to someone with the initial Z, and, well, it's enlightening.'

Molly's eyebrow arched. 'It sounds intriguing. If your diarist was a friend of Violet's, then the best person to speak to would be—'

'Janice. Yes, Harrison and Aoife have suggested that. I'm on my way down to the café now.'

Emily looked out of the window as a familiar face looked in. Will's brown eyes met hers and her shoulders drooped as he stepped inside. Typical of him to be the cloud across the sun of her day.

'Will.' Molly greeted him with a smile, while Emily turned back to the shelf of new releases under the window. 'How nice to see you. Normally I get a fleeting glimpse of your car as you whiz past.'

'Driving too fast and making a racket with that noisy engine,' Emily muttered to herself. She watched Will's reflection in the window as he ran his fingers through his hair. Her stomach contracted a fraction. What was it about rolled-up shirt sleeves and exposed forearms that sent her temperature rocketing? No, this was Will. Just no.

'Hi, Molly. Well, I thought I'd drop in on my way to the station. Getting the train back since Tabitha took my car yesterday.'

Emily bowed her head to hide the smirk that pulled on her lips. Served him right. Yet he had chosen Terry over Tabitha. She *could* cut him a little slack. Maybe.

'How is Terry?' Molly asked, diplomatically glossing over why Will's girlfriend had driven off into the sunset in his sports car.

'Better today, thanks. We think he had a bit too much sun yesterday. He's under strict orders to stay indoors today. Thankfully there's a test match on the TV so that will keep him occupied.'

'Ah, bless him. Sue's order has come in, so I'll pop up after I close and drop it off.'

'Thanks Molly. She'll be thrilled.' He had wandered back in the direction of the door but took a step to the left and was

almost at Emily's side. She turned away and intensely inspected
a row of World War Two books.

'Hi, Emily.'

She glanced at him briefly and gave him a weak smile. 'Hi.'

'So, um. Found any more racy sketchbooks hidden away in
Violet's cottage?' There was the hint of a smirk on his lips. The
light coming through the window illuminated the gold in his
eyes. Was he flirting with her? She rolled her eyes.

'No, and it's *my* cottage.'

He moved as if backing away from a snarling dog. 'Oh.
Yeah. Course. Right, well, see you around. Bye, Molly.'

'Bye, Will. See you next weekend.'

Emily watched out of the corner of her eye as Will walked
past the shop window. He glanced in at her and she quickly
turned her head away. When she looked back out of the
window, he was gone. Molly was smiling impishly at her.

'What?' Emily asked, placing a copy of *Brighton at War*
down on the counter. It couldn't hurt to do a bit of reading
about what was going on at the same time the mysterious Z was
writing her diary.

Molly shook her head but kept smirking as she scanned the
book, and Emily entered her PIN into the card machine. 'Nothing.' She handed Emily the book. 'Is there history between you
and Will?'

Emily glanced over her shoulder. 'Why do you ask?' Her
stomach knotted itself.

'I don't know. There's a bit of an atmosphere.'

'Yeah, I suppose you could say there's history. But it was all
a long time ago. We were just kids.'

'Uh-huh. I thought there was some chemistry there alright.'

Emily shook her head vigorously. 'Oh no, nothing like that.'

'Oh God, sorry. Of course. Stupid thing to say to a lesbian.
Sorry.'

'It's okay,' Emily chuckled. 'And I'm not a lesbian, I'm bi.

But there has never been, nor will there ever be, anything between me and Will Prentice. He's got the lovely Tabitha, don't forget.'

Molly made a retching sound and screwed up her nose. 'I'm *so* happy she's not coming to our wedding next weekend. Honestly, I think I'd have called the whole thing off if she'd accepted.'

'You invited her?'

'Yeah, we kind of had to. You're coming, aren't you?'

'Of course, thank you so much for inviting me. I know last-minute additions are annoying.'

Molly waved her hand. 'It's only a relaxed, informal thing. The kids will be running riot no doubt. And I couldn't have my wedding reception practically on your doorstep and not invite you. How rude would that have been?' She reached across the counter and placed a hand on Emily's arm. 'There was an empty space anyway.'

Emily blinked back an unexpected tear. 'Violet?'

'Violet.'

'I'll do my best to fill her place.'

'You'll be knocking back martinis and leading the singsong, then? Violet made the strongest martinis; they could blow your head off. We all got properly trolleyed on them after her funeral. Harrison made them according to her recipe. I was not okay the next day. And she loved a good singsong. She was a fabulous lady.'

'I love that she had so many friends. I don't think anyone wants to hear my singing, but I'll have a few martinis in her honour.'

'I think I'll join you.'

Emily said goodbye to Molly and stood outside the shop, looking down the hill at the sea for a long moment.

'I'm going to find out the truth about you, Aunt Violet,' she said, into the salty sea breeze. 'You and Z.'

. . .

At the bottom of the High Street, Emily crossed the road by the station as a train pulled in. She laughed as a pair of exhausted-looking men emerged behind the stream of day-tripping families with picnic blankets and all manner of beach paraphernalia. Gio and Harrison looked like two people who hadn't been to bed, either that or they had but hadn't got any sleep. And they were holding hands.

'Don't tell me you two dirty stop-outs have been partying all night?' she asked, grinning at them. Gio and Harrison glanced at each other as if wondering how much to tell her. That told her everything she needed to know.

'We missed the last train,' Harrison confessed, blushing slightly. 'So, we crashed with one of the Pride committee guys.'

'I'm heading down for a coffee and a sticky bun at The Seaside Café. I want to ask Janice about our mysterious Z. Coming?'

Gio looked from her to Harrison and back again. 'Actually, I could do with a shower and some sleep.'

Emily fished in her handbag and threw him the keys to Clifftop Cottage. 'Go on up, then. I'll see you later.' She winked over her shoulder at Gio as she walked away. She'd take her time over her tea and bun.


There was quite a crowd on The Promenade and the beach was packed with families and people enjoying the sunshine. The scent of sun cream mingled with the smell of the sea, and the air was punctuated with excited squeals and bursts of laughter. The soft thwack of leather on willow drifted down from the cricket pitch in Victoria Park. In the distance, the lighthouse shimmered in the heat haze. Emily pushed up the sleeves of her shirt. It was going to be another scorcher.

The wrought-iron tables under the pink awning of The Seaside Café were occupied, but there were plenty of lace tablecloth-covered tables inside.

'Hello,' said the woman behind the counter. She had a distinct grey bob and reading glasses hung on a chain around her neck. She was frothing milk in a stainless-steel jug. 'Won't be a minute, love.'

Emily browsed the cakes under the glass domes as the woman poured the hot, frothy milk into two cups with a flourish, before delivering them to two dads with young babies on their laps. The men looked like they needed the caffeine.

'So, what can I get you?' she asked, returning to the counter.

'A latte and one of your sticky buns, please.' The chocolate cake and the lemon tart had been tempting, but everyone said the buns were amazing. She claimed the small, round table by the window. The sun coming through the lace curtain cast an intricate shadow over the table.

'Here you go, love. I'm Janice, and I'm guessing you're Emily. I've been wondering when you'd be in to see me,' Janice said, placing Emily's coffee and bun down on the table.

Emily blinked a few times and stuttered her confirmation, a little stunned that she knew who she was. Janice beamed back.

'Sue's been telling me all about you. How are you getting on? Settling in alright?'

'Yes, thanks, Janice. Everyone has been so lovely and welcoming. I feel like I'm part of the gang now.'

'Well, any family of Violet's will always be family in Dovecote. She loved it when you came down to visit. She'd give me a running countdown to your arrival. "Two weeks until Emily" she'd say, or "only a couple of days now". She missed you when you stopped coming.'

'That's what Sue said.' Emily gave Janice a sad, half-smile. 'I wish I could tell her I'm sorry.'

Janice shook her head and her silver dangly earrings

jangled. 'Oh, she understood. A teenage girl with a choice between the bright lights of London, or a small town like Dovecote, is *always* going to choose London.'

'No, that wasn't it. I loved coming down for the summer. It was nice to get away from the dirt and the noise. August in London is horrific. It was just that after the last summer, I couldn't come back.' Emily shoved the memory away. 'Janice?'

'Yes, love.'

'Lots of people have told me you're the person to speak to about Great-Aunt Violet. Were you two close?'

'I suppose so. Yes, she was a good friend. Why?'

'You might be able to shed some light on something for me. While I was decorating the cottage, I found an old diary. It belonged to someone with the initial Z. I don't suppose you have any idea who that might be, do you?'

Janice knitted her fingers together, checked that there was no one at the counter, and sat down next to Emily.

'Emily, I'm not sure how much you know about Violet. There are some things about her that not everyone knows. It's not that it's a secret; she wasn't ashamed of it or anything. It was more that it wasn't relevant, I suppose.'

'I've worked out from the diary that Z was a woman and that she and someone only referred to as V, had a love affair.'

Janice chewed her lip for a moment. 'All I know is that her name was Zeyla and, during the war, she and Violet were very much in love.'

# TWENTY-FOUR

## EMILY

July 2016

Finally, she had a name. Zeyla. Such a unique name. Now she had to find out more about her. What happened to her relationship with Violet? And where did Hugo fit into all of this? These questions flew around Emily's head as she walked back along The Promenade, down Beachfront Road, and up the steep steps to the top of the cliff.

There were no signs of life at Clifftop Cottage and Emily picked up the handwritten note tucked into the frame of the French doors.

*Gone up to Dovecote Manor. Gio xx*

Emily raised her eyebrows. Harrison was introducing Gio to Terry and Sue already? They were moving fast. Gio must have been bricking it. For Harrison's sake, Emily hoped it didn't scare Gio off.

. . .

Dovecote Manor loomed out from behind a rhododendron bush as Emily rounded the corner of the path from the cottage. The severity of the grey stone walls was softened by the window boxes full of yellow and orange flowers. The mullioned windows reflected the sun from under gothic arches and the oak front door was bedecked in a wreath of candy-coloured wild-flowers. There was no doubt the house was imposing, and even a little forbidding, but the brightness of these touches gave it the softness of a normal family home.

She was only a little less intimidated by the manor than she had been as a teenager. Back then, she hadn't even considered coming anywhere near, no matter how many times Harrison tried to get her to. She'd preferred to hang out with him in the garden of Clifftop Cottage, or down on the beach, or anywhere they could avoid Will and his obnoxious mates.

The two Border Collies lounging on the front step added to the magazine-cover perfection. The crunch of gravel under Emily's feet roused the dogs and they got up, stretched, yawned, and trotted over to her. No vicious guard dogs for the Prentice family.

'Now,' Emily said, stroking each of the dogs. 'Which one of you is Margo and which is Gerry?'

'The one on your right, with the brown splodge across her back, is Margo.' Emily looked up to see Harrison in the door-way, glass of champagne in hand. 'You're just in time for a drink. Mum's opened the bubbly.'

She probably wouldn't get a better chance to get him alone.

'Harrison?'

'Yeah?'

'Look, you and Gio. I can't believe he agreed to meeting your parents already. You've been on one date. This is very unlike him, and I don't want either of you to get hurt. I don't know, maybe slow down a little?'

Harrison leant back against the door frame and drained his champagne. He chewed his top lip for a moment.

'It was Gio's idea, coming over.'

Emily's eyes widened. 'Really? Harrison, I don't think Gio has ever met the parents of anyone he's dated. He hasn't even met most of their housemates. What's going on between you two?'

'When I met Lev, I knew instantly that it was something special. Don't ask how I knew, I just did. The closest thing I can compare it to is when you get through your front door after being away for ages. Like you're stepping into something familiar, comfortable, somewhere you belong. The minute I first saw Gio, when you brought Cher in, I had that same feeling. Was it love at first sight? If that's a thing then, yeah, I guess it was. Gio and I didn't end up in a club last night. We walked up and down Brighton seafront just talking. Then we sat on the beach under the stars, still talking. He's told me all about his love life. He's also told me that he's tired of all that, that he's ready to try something serious, something that will last. I'm going into this with my eyes wide open, Emily. And I trust him. Somehow this feels right. Haven't you ever felt like that about someone?'

Emily flinched. 'Yes, I have.'

'Then you know that sometimes you have to take that leap of faith.'

'Actually, all I learnt is that when you open up to someone, they throw it back at you. I made that leap once, and I ended up being dashed against the rocks at the bottom of the cliff.'

Harrison enveloped her in a tight hug. Her tears soaked into the cotton of his T-shirt.

He released her and placed his hands on her arms. He bent his head to look her in the eyes. 'I'd like to have a word with the person who did that to you.'

Emily turned her head to avoid his searching look. 'You've

plenty of opportunity... he's your brother.' She sniffed and pulled out of his grasp. 'I don't want to talk about it, okay?'

'Emily, I don't know what to say.'

'It was a long time ago.' She wiped her eyes. 'It's fine. Hi, Sue.'

Harrison turned as Sue came out of the front door.

'Hello, Emily. I'd wondered where you'd got to, Harrison.' She looked from Harrison to Emily. 'Is everything okay?'

'Fine, Mum.'

'Fine,' Emily said, forcing a smile. 'Harrison was... we were just talking about him and Gio. I got a bit emotional.'

'Me too,' Sue said, taking Emily by the arm and leading her into the house. 'Oh, Gio's *so* lovely, Emily. I adore him so much already. At least one of my sons has good taste in partners.'

They walked into a high-ceilinged, oak-panelled room and Emily gasped. The parquet floor was partially covered with a deep-red carpet. Long-dead aristocrats peered imperiously from their dark portraits in gilded frames covering the walls. A heavy-looking brass corona chandelier hung from the ceiling, and coats of arms decorated the space between the top of the oak panels and the carved cornices. There was a huge stone fireplace on the end wall and sunlight flowed in through leaded mullioned windows, the stained panels scattering colourful diamonds across the floor.

'Goodness. This room is stunning,' she said, her eyes darting around, trying to take it all in.

'Oh, thank you,' Sue said, beaming. 'It's at its best this time of day, when the sun comes in through the windows. It can be cold in the winter though. Come on through, we're out on the terrace.'

Emily followed Sue and Harrison through a set of double doors, into an oak-panelled hallway dominated by an imposing, green-carpeted mahogany staircase. Sue pushed open another set of double doors at the foot of the stairs.

'We have far too many huge rooms in this house,' Sue said with a grin. Emily could only nod. 'Although all the space is handy on the rare occasions when we throw a party.'

'Do you hire out the house as a venue as well as the grounds?' Emily asked.

'We've thought about it, but with the house being Grade II listed, it gets complicated in terms of fire safety, toilets, and all that malarkey. Not to mention the cost of repairs if something were to get damaged. So, no, we stick to hiring out the bottom half of the west lawn. That way any revellers are far enough away from the house so as not to wander in accidentally.'

'You have an actual ballroom?' Emily whispered to Harrison. She looked up and gasped again as they passed underneath a crystal chandelier hanging from an ornate ceiling rose, flanked by painted cherubs. 'A full-size grand piano too.' She let out a low whistle. 'This is like *Beauty and the Beast*. Please tell me you have a library as well?'

'Through that door,' Harrison said with a wink.

'You're not even kidding, are you?'

Harrison shook his head.

'Blimey,' Emily breathed.

They stepped through a set of French doors and out onto the terrace. Chairs were arranged around a glass and wrought-iron circular table, groaning under the weight of an ice bucket with two bottles of champagne in it, several glasses, and a full charcuterie board. Emily went over to Gio and hugged him. He looked at her closely.

'You okay?' he whispered in her ear.

'Fine. You?'

'I am happier than I have ever been in my life.'

'Stop, you'll set me off crying again.' She disentangled herself from his embrace and Terry handed her a glass of champagne.

'How are you doing, Terry? You gave us quite the scare yesterday at the fair.'

He chuckled. 'I'm grand, love, thanks. Sue's been fussing over me.' He flashed a grin at his wife. There were dark circles under Sue's eyes.

Emily sat down next to Gio. Beyond a low wall, the wide lawn sloped gently and then disappeared at the edge of the cliff. There was nothing to see except a huge expanse of sparkling sea and the sharp line of the horizon. It was a view you could look at for days, years even, and not get bored.

'That is some view,' she said.

'It's not always that pretty,' Terry said. 'It's a bit bleak in the middle of winter.'

'Oh, Terry, you always see the negative in everything,' Sue admonished, giving her husband a light slap on the arm.

'Ems, did you speak to Janice?' Harrison asked, picking a piece of serrano ham off the charcuterie board.

'I did.'

'And?' Harrison asked through a mouthful of ham.

'Janice said the diary probably belonged to someone called Zeyla. She knows nothing about her, only that during the war she and Aunt Violet were very much in love. And from the diary, it sounds like much of their love affair was conducted in secret, at Clifftop Cottage.'

'Zeyla, Zeyla,' Sue whispered. 'I don't know why, but that name does sound familiar.'

'You're right, Mum. It does. You don't think she was connected to Dovecote Manor, do you?'

Emily tilted her head. 'I think she might have been. In the diary, she writes about watching Violet, and there's quite a few mentions of her parents.'

Terry frowned. 'So, we bought the manor in what, 1987 was it?'

'Yes, that would be right. Will was a toddler, and Harrison

was only a baby.' Sue turned to Emily. 'We wanted to raise the boys somewhere safe by the sea. We'd had a few issues with crime where we lived in London. When this place came up for sale, we grabbed our chance to get out of the rat race.'

Terry grunted. 'It was a complete wreck, needed a lot of work doing to it. Anyway, what was I saying. Oh, yes. We bought it from a Charles Wythenshawe. It had been in his family for generations, but his father had died, and he didn't want the cost of the upkeep. I think he was going off to America to invest in Silicon Valley or somewhere. He was the sole owner. There was no mention of a Zeyla.'

'Still though, I think it's worth us having a look through the archives,' Harrison pondered, spearing an olive. 'They left everything in the house. Family photographs, books, accounts, papers, *everything*. It's all in the cupboards in the library.'

'Good idea. I'll have a dig about during the week and let you know if I find anything, Emily.'

'That would be great, thanks Sue. I want to know everything about her and try to work out where Hugo fits into all of this.'

Terry nodded. 'Well, Hugo was the head gardener here for years. He'd been looking after the grounds since he came back from the war. He was in the army. 30 Corps, I believe. He was on Gold Beach on D-Day and then went on to liberate Belgium. He was of retirement age when we bought the manor. The gardens were the only part that were in good nick. He said he'd keep on working but he wasn't physically up for it. We needed to recoup some of the purchase cost, to put into the repairs, so we sold Clifftop Cottage and the land that side of the driveway to Hugo and Violet. They were thrilled to finally be able to call it their own. They'd been paying rent to the Wythenshawe family for decades.' Terry sat back in his chair. He still looked a bit tired. Wasn't he supposed to be staying out of the sun?

Emily rubbed her nose. 'Judging by Zeyla's diary, Violet was living in the cottage in 1943. So, if she was paying rent then, it was forty-four years.'

'They probably could have bought the cottage a few times over,' Harrison said.

'There's something else about Zeyla that intrigues me,' Emily added. 'You know that sketchbook that Will and I found along with the diary? Well, I had a rummage in Violet's studio, and I found two portraits of Hugo.'

'Will did mention something about missing portraits,' Sue said, looking confused.

'The thing is, I think there might be more. Judging by the sketchbook, and the way Zeyla talks about Violet drawing her in the diary, I think Violet may have also created portraits of Zeyla. The question is, where are they?'

'Ooh, I love a good mystery.' Sue giggled.

'What *are* you going to do with Violet's artwork, Emily?' Harrison asked. 'I'm sure there'd be people interested in buying it.'

Emily finished her champagne and put her glass on the table. 'I've been thinking about that. And I have an idea.'

'Oh?' The other four around the table breathed.

'Terry, you and Gordon and James Rutherford have plans for the museum, don't you?'

'The air raid shelter project, you mean?'

'Yeah. Harrison mentioned you were looking to do some fundraising, as well as getting the website redone. What would you think about us putting on an exhibition of Violet's paintings, including the fabled "missing portraits"?'

Terry rubbed his chin thoughtfully. 'I think that's a fantastic idea. I'll have to run it past Gordon and James, but I'd say they'd be up for it. It could be a good money-spinner, that's for sure.'

'And if we find Zeyla's portraits...' Gio said, raising an eyebrow.

'That's what I was thinking, Gio. But first we have to find Zeyla, or her descendants.'

'I'll start in the archives,' Sue said rubbing her hands together. 'Oh, this is rather exciting. Like some sort of treasure hunt, or an episode of *Who Do You Think You Are?*'

'I might go and speak to the vicar. If there was a Zeyla living at the manor, then she'll probably show up in the parish records,' Emily added.

'Reverend Clive will be delighted to help, I'm sure.'

Sue had refilled Emily's champagne glass, and she took a long sip. If someone had told her that one day she'd be drinking champagne on the terrace of a stunning manor house with two of her best friends who were at the start of a, hopefully, long-lasting relationship, she'd have laughed at them. But here she was and, thrillingly, she was close to discovering the truth about Great-Aunt Violet's past. She smiled inwardly. She was on the verge of working out where she belonged.

# TWENTY-FIVE

## EMILY

July 2016

The following Saturday dawned bright and clear. Emily spent the morning working on a website for a small chain of hairdressers. The money was coming in, so relocating to the seaside had made zero difference to her business. On Monday, she was due to meet Gordon Rutherford to discuss Dovecote Museum's website, so she'd been playing around with possible colour palettes, and setting out ideas around the layout. That was what she loved most about her job, the creative bit. With a famous artist in the family, maybe that shouldn't have been a surprise.

Pushing work out of her mind, she stood at her wardrobe trying to find an outfit for Molly and Jez's wedding. She'd left it to the last minute, until it was too late to buy anything new. She had nothing appropriate to wear. All her dresses were more suited to a night out in London than a country wedding, and were a touch too low-cut. The last thing she needed was to give some old duffer an eyeful.

Running out of time and patience, she pulled open Violet's wardrobe. It had been on her mind to clear it out, but like a lot of things on her to-do list, like washing her car, or painting her toenails, it hadn't happened. She glided her hand along the soft fabrics. There was proper vintage stuff in there, and all pristine. She paused over a baby-blue tea dress, covered in little dots which, after a closer look, were actually tiny daisies. She slipped it on over her head, holding her breath as her arms found the short, puffed sleeves. The zip glided up the side. It fitted perfectly. She dug under her bed for her butter-yellow Mary Jane shoes and grabbed a matching yellow cardigan from her drawer. Molly had said it wasn't a hat-type of wedding, so Emily slipped a pearl comb into her auburn hair, leaving it long over her shoulders. The sun had lightened it, and the red strands glowed almost gold. It was too hot for a full face of make-up, so she'd kept it simple: a dusting of bronzer to give the illusion of cheekbones on her heart-shaped face, a swipe of mascara to make her blue eyes bigger, and a hint of tinted gloss on her Cupid's bow lips. She smiled at herself in the mirrored door of Violet's wardrobe.

'Not too shabby, Ems.' Her reflection winked back at her.


Sue had admitted it was ridiculous that they were driving across the road to the church, but Terry still wasn't at his best. Accepting the offer of a lift was a no-brainer. What was the point of risking a twisted ankle when you could hop in a car?

'Oh, Emily,' Sue cried as Emily came out from behind the rhododendron bush. 'You look lovely. New dress?'

Emily laughed. 'I suspect it's actually very old. I found it in Violet's wardrobe. I don't think she'd have minded.'

'She would have been delighted. Oh, here are the boys.'

Emily's breath hitched. Of course, Will was going to look devastatingly gorgeous in a suit. Especially in one that had clearly been tailored to fit him perfectly. And he wore it with such effortless ease. It was probably one of several he had in his walk-in wardrobe in his London penthouse apartment.

'You scrub up alright,' Harrison laughed, giving Emily a quick peck on the cheek.

'I could say the same about you.'

Harrison groaned and tugged at the collar of his shirt. 'Give me a set of scrubs any day,' he joked. 'I don't know how you wear this stuff every day, Will.'

Will winked at his brother. 'Some of us have natural class, H. You do look very nice, Emily.'

'Thanks,' Emily said, cringing inwardly. He was such a creep.

'You get in the front, Emily,' Terry said. 'We'll squeeze in the back.'

Clearly Will was driving.

'Are you sure? I don't...' she started, but Sue was already shuffling into the middle seat, one hand on the hem of her green shift dress to stop it catching on the leather seats of Terry's Range Rover. Reluctantly she got in the front next to Will and glanced at him. His tie was baby-blue with tiny white polka dots. And he had a matching pocket square.

'What?' he said, clearly noticing the look of horror on her face.

'Your tie,' she groaned. 'We look like we're matching.'

He looked down and laughed. 'So, we do. Well, I don't have time to go and change,' he said, turning the key in the ignition. 'As long as no one thinks we're a couple, eh?'

Emily bit her tongue to stop herself from commenting that if people did, they'd probably be delighted he'd ditched Tabitha. Their accidental co-ordination gave her an excuse to avoid him throughout the day as much as she could.

. . .

The wedding was beautiful. Jez cried through his vows. Then everyone cried. Toby conducted himself with solemnity and Zoe relished her role as flower girl. Back in the grounds of Dovecote Manor, the marquee on the west lawn was bedecked in fairy lights, the champagne was flowing, and the evening was warm. Everyone cried again during Molly and Jez's first dance, and then laughed when Toby cut in and demanded a dance with his mum. The menagerie of children had commandeered the dance floor and were strutting their stuff to tunes that were older than their parents.

Emily had settled down in a chair at a table near enough to the bar to ensure a steady supply of beverages, but far enough away from the disco that conversation was possible. It was incredibly relaxing knowing that she only had to cross the driveway to fall into her bed.

'Hey, you, having a nice time?' Molly appeared at her shoulder.

'Molly, you look amazing. It's been a perfect day.'

Molly sighed happily and looked around at her gathered friends and family. There was the hint of a tear in her eye. 'It has, hasn't it? I love your dress, by the way.'

'Thanks.' Emily smiled. 'It's actually Violet's. I found it in her wardrobe.'

'Aw, that's so sweet. She is here in spirit.'

'I'm pretty sure she is.'

'Cute that it matches Will's tie. Oh, sorry, better go. Looks like my Auntie Joan has captured my cousin Josh. Best go and rescue him.'

Emily put her head in her hands. If Molly had noticed, everyone else would have too.

'What's up with you?'

'Hey, Harrison. Nothing, I'm alright.'

'Is this about Will's tie matching your dress?'

'Oh, for goodness' sake.'

'I'm winding you up. No one has noticed.'

'Molly has.'

'Not until I pointed it out.'

Emily punched the top of his arm. 'You little...' She laughed. 'I suppose it *is* pretty funny. I wonder what Tabitha would think.'

'Who cares?'

'Fair point.'

'Drink?'

'I won't say no.'

As Harrison got up and went to the bar, Emily glanced around and caught sight of Aoife. She looked stunning in her emerald-green bridesmaid dress that perfectly complemented her fiery hair and porcelain-white skin. And she wasn't the only one to have their eye caught. Will was practically drooling as Aoife made eyes at him. The way Aoife was tracing the rim of her glass with her finger was blatant flirting and he was lapping it up. Emily's lip curled. He was a piece of work. As much as Emily wasn't a fan of the obnoxious Tabitha, no one deserved to have their other half drooling over someone else the moment they were out of sight. Aoife placed a hand on Will's forearm and Emily stood up suddenly, almost knocking her chair over. She'd seen enough. She detoured to the bar and tapped Harrison on the shoulder.

'I'm calling it a night. And you might want to remind your brother that he's not in London. Everyone can see what he's doing.'

'What? Emily, wait.'

Emily waved at him without turning around. She huffed. Not only was Will an egotistical, selfish snob, but he was a cheat too. It wound her up to find out he was just like her father, and Max. But considering everything she knew about Will Prentice, should she have expected anything different? She slid her key into the door of Clifftop Cottage. Probably not.

# TWENTY-SIX

## VIOLET

December 1943

I stood in the moonlit kitchen staring at the two teacups on the counter. I'd done it again – made a cup of tea for Mum. I'd found myself doing that sometimes out of habit. I wasn't used to not having to look after her yet, even though it had been seven months since she died. The French doors creaked open, and Zeyla stumbled into the dark room.

'Gracious, Violet, darling. What are you doing standing in the dark?' she asked as she flicked on the light and hurriedly pulled the blackout blinds over the window above the sink and the French doors. She kissed my cheek, the soft caress of her lips pulling me out of my trance. I pushed the teacups away.

'I wasn't expecting to see you this evening,' I said.

'The dinner got cancelled,' Zeyla called over her shoulder, as she went into the sitting room and flounced down on the sofa. 'The Petherington-Smyths had a problem with their car.' She looked up from the magazine she was flicking through. 'Can't say I'm sorry about it.'

'You've been busy lately,' I said, sitting in the armchair

nearest Zeyla and picking up a pair of stockings that needed darning. Some things never changed. 'What with that shopping trip, and tea with Reverend Douglas and his wife, and supper with your brother.' She didn't reply and I sighed. 'And yet we never go anywhere together.'

We lapsed into silence, my thoughts momentarily distracted by the pile of post on the writing desk – that was what I'd been doing before I made the tea. I'd been looking through the pile for a letter from Yorkshire. I'd not heard from Beryl and Arthur Carmichael since the short, but kind, letter they wrote in response to my letter about Mum. There'd been nothing from Hugo for a while, either. All I could do was hope he was alright. While Zeyla had been a social butterfly, I'd kept myself busy in the evenings after work doing up the cottage. The tin of green paint I'd found in the potting shed next to the house had been just enough to cover the oppressive brown the sitting room had been painted in. I'd considered throwing away the threadbare rug but couldn't bear to be parted with it. It was on it that Zeyla and I had first declared our love in touches and caresses. That rug was like the ravens at the Tower of London. If it ever left the cottage we would crumble and fall.

The flick of Zeyla's magazine pages brought my thoughts back to her. I put down my sewing. The low light was hurting my eyes.

'Zeyla?' I asked, with some trepidation.

'Yes, darling.' She turned her green eyes on me and for a moment I lost my nerve.

'Are you ashamed of me?'

She put down her *Woman's Weekly* and reached out a hand. I took it, entwining my fingers between her long, slender ones.

'Goodness, Vi. Of course not. What makes you ask such a ridiculous question?'

I shrugged. 'It feels as though you don't want to be seen out with me. That I'm not good enough to be seen with you. I know I don't wear the latest fashions or have clothes made of expensive fabrics. But I can't help where I come from, who I am. I'm a working-class woman, not an aristocratic lady.' Tears brimmed in my eyes. Had I been a fool to think that such things wouldn't matter, that she could still love me even though I was from a world so alien to her? Zeyla roused herself from the sofa and perched on the arm of my chair.

'Oh, poor darling. You really are out of sorts tonight, aren't you?' She stroked my hair. 'Do you want to know the truth?'

'Yes, please.' I couldn't look at her.

'I love you. I love your spirit, your complete inability to ever admit that you're beaten. I love your auburn hair, your big blue eyes. And I love the parts of your body that only I have touched. What I don't love are all the tiresome social events I am forced to attend. If I had my way, I would stay here in this cottage with just you for all eternity. I know you would like to go out sometimes, but I'm tired. When I get the chance to see you, I want to be with you. Just the two of us, like the old married couple that we are. I'm selfish, Vi. I don't want to share you with the world, I want to keep you for myself.'

'Oh.' It was a pretty speech, and I had no riposte to it.

'And I don't want anyone else making eyes at you either. I've been burnt before.'

I folded my arms tightly. 'I'm not Lottie, Zeyla.'

She kissed my forehead, the velvety softness of her lips forcing away the creases of my frown.

'I know. I'm sorry, that was a silly thing to say.' Her delicate fingers crept around my jaw and tilted my face to hers. The remnants of my sulk dissolved in her green eyes. A slow smile spread across her lips. 'Alright, if you really want to go out, then we shall. There is a ladies-only tea dance at the Brighton Dome tomorrow afternoon. How does that sound?'

'Wonderful, except I have nothing to wear to a tea dance,' I sighed.

'Then I shall give you a dress and take you out dancing.'

I giggled. 'Like an old-fashioned beau.'

'Milady,' she whispered. 'May I be permitted to kiss you?'

'Oh, good sir. You scandalise me.'

We dissolved into laughter. My giggles died when she looked deep into my eyes with a burning intensity. My heart pounded and my breaths came short and sharp as she guided me down onto the rug in front of the fire. It was like the start of our love affair all over again.

The next afternoon, Zeyla was sitting on my bed watching me look at myself in the mirrored wardrobe. Her long, olive-green dress fanned out across my sheets.

'Zeyla, are you sure you want me to have this? I can wear it today and then you can have it back.'

She fell back on the bed. 'Vi, I have a dozen dresses like that. And, yes, I want you to have it because it is the perfect colour to complement your blue eyes. It clashes with mine.'

I ran my hands over the silky fabric of the classic tea dress. It skimmed my knees as though it had been made for me, and the slightly puffed sleeves balanced out my skinny shoulders. The baby-blue did bring out my eyes. The white dots all over the dress were actually very tiny daisies, with little yellow centres.

'You're beautiful, Violet Saunders,' Zeyla whispered, appearing over my shoulder. I turned my head and lightly kissed the freckles across the bridge of her nose.

'As are you, Zeyla Wythenshawe.'

Her hands reached around my waist and crept slowly upwards.

'We should be going.'

Zeyla groaned. 'I shall be thinking of getting you out of that dress all day.'

The dance was already in progress when we entered the Brighton Dome, and the all-lady band were in full flow. I tried not to stare at the pairs of women dancing together. Zeyla led me to an empty table, and we shed our winter coats. Despite growing up a stone's throw from the Dome, I'd never been inside. I'd not had the money or the connections to go to any of the events held in the building itself. The pictures I'd seen in the papers didn't do the ballroom justice. It was simply magnificent, and I pinched myself to make sure I wasn't dreaming.

'Are they all...?' I whispered.

'I wouldn't think so. Some are, no doubt. Others are women who are missing their men but are missing dancing more.' She flashed me a smile. 'The point is, there's no telling who is and who isn't. Isn't that marvellous?'

I squealed slightly. Zeyla stood and offered her hand.

'May I have this dance?'

I giggled. 'You may.'

I let out a contented sigh as Zeyla took me in her arms and placed her soft cheek against mine.

'Am I leading? Or are you?' she asked.

'You. You're a fraction taller. And you're bossier than me.'

Her laugh was like a tinkling bell in my ear. I would never have believed I could hold her in my arms in public. I thought back to the first time she kissed me and I'd bolted. Obviously, we still couldn't kiss, not even in this ballroom. But being able to hold her body close to mine, with nobody batting an eyelid, was intoxicating. If only our whole lives could be lived in this room.

# TWENTY-SEVEN

## EMILY

July 2016

*31 December 1943*

*Well, dearest diary, we have survived another year. And what a year. The end of school, hurrah. Mother's continued attempt to turn me into a version of herself, tiresome. And the arrival of V into my life. And how much better she has made it, but also how much more difficult. For half the year, I have been living a double life. At home, I'm the dutiful, modest, young lady I am expected to be. At Clifftop Cottage, I make love to a beautiful woman, often on an old rug in front of the fire. But it cannot last, one of these personas is going to have to win out. All I can do is pray for the war to end soon. V has said we will run away together once it's all over. I shan't be sorry to leave Mother and Father, and I don't care where we go. I'd quite happily journey to hell for her. But if the war goes on, then I fear for the future. R is being annoyingly persistent, and Mother's encouragement is not helping. It may come to a head soon, and it breaks my heart that I shall have to tell V. I can only hope she will want to continue to see me in secret should the worst happen.*

Emily closed Zeyla's diary. She had been hoping to find out what happened between Zeyla and Violet. Something must have happened, Violet married Hugo after all. But it seemed that at the end of 1943, Violet and Zeyla were still very much together. Whoever 'R' was, they sounded like trouble.

Her head ached slightly from the champagne at Jez and Molly's wedding the day before. She dragged herself out of bed and into the bathroom and turned on the shower. The answers were out there, as were the portraits. It would take bit of luck to find them.

And why couldn't she get Will and Aoife out of her head? Every second they were in her thoughts made her grind her teeth. Why should she care if Will cheated on Tabitha? She couldn't care less about that stuck-up little madam. A small part of her had hoped Will was better than that. That the concern he'd shown for her after her car accident, and that he'd shown for Terry when he fell ill, was an indication that she was wrong about him and that he wasn't the entitled bully he had once been. But, as is so often the case, her gut instinct had been correct. He hadn't changed. Why did that make her heart feel like it was shrinking?

The sight of Will's silver sports car outside the door of Dovecote Manor creased her forehead in a deep frown. She was not in the mood for him. She'd go in, chat through the initial design ideas and costs for the museum website with Terry as planned, and leave. No hanging around, no conversations, and definitely *no* Will. God alone knew what would come out of her mouth if she found herself in his company; it wouldn't be complimentary.

Emily gave Margo a quick scratch behind her ears and

pushed open the front door which had been left ajar. She paused a minute to look around the hall, marvelling at its grandeur. The sun would be on the terrace, and she'd put money on Terry being out there, ignoring doctor's orders yet again. As she pulled open the door to the inner hall, she could hear the faint strains of a piano coming from the ballroom. Beethoven's 'Moonlight Sonata', if she wasn't mistaken. One of Great-Aunt Violet's favourites. A soft smile pulled at her lips at the memory of Violet humming along to the radio in her studio. If only she'd stopped to talk to her properly, rather than rushing out to hang around The Promenade with Harrison. How much could Violet have taught her about music, and art, and love?

She could see the grand piano through the gap between the ballroom's double doors. As she stepped into the room, she did a double take. Will glanced up and his fingers tripped over the notes. He frowned and lifted his hands from the keys.

'I'm sorry. I distracted you,' Emily said softly, forgetting that she was furious at him.

He shook his head. 'No, I'm very rusty. It's been years since I played. Kind of hard to practise when you live in an apartment, even if it is a penthouse,' he said. 'If you were looking for Harrison, I've not seen him.'

His casual shrug reignited the rage inside her and she stepped towards the door.

'Emily?' Will called after her, and she turned around with a huff.

'What?' she snapped, giving him her best hard stare. 'I'm not talking to you after what you've done.'

He looked at her blankly.

'I saw what you were up to at the wedding reception,' she said, biting her bottom lip when it started to wobble. 'I don't even know why I care. I *don't* care. Just like you don't care about anyone but yourself.'

Will's head dropped and his fingers found the piano keys

again. This time it wasn't Beethoven. It took Emily a second to recognise the tune. Elton John's 'Goodbye Yellow Brick Road'.

'Okay, I admit it wasn't my finest hour.'

That was putting it mildly. Emily folded her arms. 'Really? That's all you have to say for yourself after you've cheated on your girlfriend. And with Aoife? Talk about going after low-hanging fruit.'

The slamming of the piano lid made Emily jump. Will's shoulders drooped, and he ran his hands through his hair. There was pain in his eyes when he looked up and Emily's rage cooled, just a fraction.

'Aoife's been after me for years, and I've been fending her off for years. I had a bit too much to drink and let my guard down. I'm not proud of it. But I didn't cheat on Tabitha. I'm not like that.'

Emily narrowed her eyes. 'And exactly how do you figure that?'

Will let out a very deep sigh. 'Tabitha and I broke up last weekend, after what happened at the fair. I mean the whole of Dovecote saw the argument.'

'Oh.' That explained the pain in his dark brown eyes.

Will opened up the piano lid again. 'Yeah.'

Emily was about to say she was sorry when he spoke again.

'Seemingly, by asking her to come down to Dovecote once in a while, *I* was being unreasonable and ignoring *her* needs. I'm a selfish, self-absorbed, insensitive bully, apparently.'

'Yikes. I'm sorry, Will,' Emily said, guilt churning her stomach. She'd called him all those things too, albeit only in her head. Walking around the piano and standing next to him, she almost reached out and put her hand on his shoulder. He took a deep breath and squared his shoulders.

'So that's the end of that.' He played the chorus of the Elton John song again, his fingers flying across the keys. He stopped and looked up at Emily. 'In all honesty, I think it might be for the best anyway.'

'Really? I thought you were mad about her.'

'Oh, I was. Bought the ring and everything.'

Harrison had been right. Whatever that said about his priorities, knowing Tabitha hadn't been liked by his family, Emily still thawed a fraction.

'But if I think about it, and I've thought about nothing else for the past week, I don't think it was good for me. Don't get me wrong, it was great in that being with the most beautiful, popular woman I could find was great for my image, and my ego.' He huffed. 'All my life I've worked hard to be the best at everything, and Tabitha was another example of that. But I got it wrong, which is hard for me to admit.'

Emily gave him a gentle smile, despite the part of her brain railing against showing him any kindness or sympathy. It was a rare thing to find a man willing to admit he'd been wrong.

Will looked back down at his fingers resting lightly on the piano keys. 'I mean, she is popular and undeniably beautiful, but it's all fake. Her beauty is only skin deep. Underneath she can be nasty and manipulative. And her popularity is based on Instagram likes and friends that would drop her in an instant if it served their own purposes. No, I got it badly wrong. I did something I vowed never to do – I failed.' He didn't look up at Emily, instead he ran a finger along the lip of the music rack.

'You didn't fail. The only thing you're guilty of is seeing the best in her. And we've all been there. I think you're being very hard on yourself. It sounds to me like you've dodged a bullet, if you don't mind me saying. And anyway, regardless of her, look at everything else you've achieved.'

Will scratched his temple.

'You're an incredibly successful whatever-it-is-you-actually-do, and you've got a family that love you dearly. That's not failure, that looks like a pretty decent success to me.' This time,

Emily didn't hesitate and placed a hand on Will's shoulder. The softness of his cashmere jumper tickled her palm. 'And hey, there's not many people who can pull off both Beethoven and Elton John.'

Will's face relaxed and he gave Emily a weak smile.

'Thanks. I guess I'll survive. Maybe there are other parts of my life that could use a shake up.'

'Thirty-one's a bit young for a mid-life crisis.'

'I'm nearly thirty-two. But maybe you're right. How about an existential crisis?'

Emily titled her head. 'Yeah, that works.'

His laugh creased the edges of his eyes, and a swarm of butterflies took off inside Emily's stomach as their eyes met. She looked away, her cheeks warming a fraction, and gave the cream wallpaper on the opposite wall her full attention.

'I better go and find your dad. I've had some ideas for the museum website, and I want him to okay it before I start coding,' she said, her voice oddly high-pitched.

'Emily?' Will called and she turned, halfway through the door. 'Have you found out anything else about Zeyla or the portraits?'

Emily shook her head, not daring to speak. He turned his attention back to the keys and, as Emily closed the door behind her, began to play Elton John's 'The One'. She let out a long breath and headed down the corridor to the kitchen. What the hell had just happened?

By following the smell of freshly brewed coffee through an archway beneath the stairs and down a winding stone staircase, she found Terry in the kitchen.

'Hi, Terry, how are you doing?'

'Hello, Emily. I'm alright thanks, love. Still here at any rate.'

'Glad to hear. I've got some ideas for the website, if you wanted to have a look?'

Terry sighed heavily. 'I'm beginning to wonder if it's worth it. We've had the quote through from the builders and it's going to be a big ask. And that's even with the grant and the funding. Your exhibition could be the difference between getting the extension built or not.'

'I've been thinking about that, mostly in the early hours when the enormity of organising an art exhibition plays on my mind. I agree it would make a huge difference if we can find the other portraits. Since Violet died, the rumours about the portraits seem to have been popping up on social media and in art forums again. If she'd thought that everyone had forgotten about her when she stopped selling paintings, she was wrong. Did Sue have any luck with the archives?'

'Did I hear my name?' Sue came into the kitchen and dropped a bag of groceries on the polished marble countertop. 'Sorry, I've not had time to check the archives, what with the wedding and everything. We're getting a bit old to be running a business like this. It's pretty stressful. I can't believe we've been doing it for twenty years. Don't get me wrong, Molly and Jez were lovely to deal with, but they aren't all like that. Some can be quite a challenge.'

Emily laughed. 'Oh, I know. Gio has some stories. I remember one about a bride and her mother who fell out over the size of the ribbon on the cake stand. Don't worry, I'm meeting with Reverend Clive this afternoon; he's been rummaging in the parish records. I'll let you know if he's come up with anything.'

Terry had been looking at Emily's website plans. 'This all looks lovely to me, Emily. Why don't you go ahead with what you think is best? You're the expert.'

'I will do, Terry. I'll drop James and Gordon some screenshots by email too. And we need to start to think about what we can do for the exhibition, with or without the missing portraits. I reckon we could still draw a sizeable crowd.'

'Right you are.' He stifled a yawn. 'Let me know if you need me to do anything.'

Emily glanced at Sue who frowned at her husband. There was a lot of worry on her face. Emily tried to offer a comforting smile but failed. He wasn't getting any better. If anything he was looking worse.

# TWENTY-EIGHT

## EMILY

July 2016

Emily stepped under the gothic stone arch of St. John's Church and pushed open the heavy oak door. Inside, the church was a cool, shaded sanctuary from the heat and bright sunshine outside. The mullioned windows along the south aisle offered framed snapshots of Dovecote beyond.

'Reverend Clive?'

The door of the vestry creaked open, and Clive emerged, a bundle of papers in his arms.

'Ah, hello Emily. Gosh, it's another warm one today.' He wiped a bead of sweat off his forehead with a white handkerchief. 'The sun shines right into the vestry all day. It's like a sauna in there.'

'I hope you weren't sweltering in there going through parish records for me,' Emily said, a coil of guilt squeezing her stomach.

Clive shook his bald head. 'Nothing as diverting, I'm afraid. Service rotas. We have more rotas than I know what to do with. Usually the Church Wardens do the majority of it, but they are both away on holiday. No doubt I shall have done it all wrong. But I can only do my best.' He sat down on the front pew and motioned for her to join him.

She cast a glance at the altar as she sat down. For a church in a small town, it was remarkably ornate. Clive spread the papers out on the pew between them.

'Right then, let's see. Ah yes, you were looking for mentions of someone by the name of Zeyla, round about the Second World War.'

'I think she was linked to Dovecote Manor in some way. I know she had a connection with Great-Aunt Violet.'

'She was definitely connected to the Wythenshawe family at the manor.' He passed her an A4 sheet of paper. Sue was right, this was like an episode of *Who Do You Think You Are?*

'That is a copy of the baptismal record of one Zeyla Wythenshawe, daughter of Randolph and Venetia Wythenshawe of Dovecote Manor.'

'March 1925. So, she was the same age, roughly, as Violet.'

'The next record I found was this.' He handed her another photocopy. 'In June 1944, Zeyla married a Rupert Petherington-Smyth. He was the son of a barrister from Oxford.'

'That's only six months after the end of her diary. At the end of 1943, she and Violet were very much still seeing each other. Sorry, that's probably inappropriate to discuss in here.'

Clive waved away her protestations. 'Not at all. Love is love, and we celebrate it in all its forms at St. John's.'

'I think they were in love. At least, judging by Zeyla's diary, she was very much in love with Violet. But the final entry, from New Year's Eve 1943, mentioned an "R" who was being persistent about something. I can only presume that "R" was Rupert, and that the "something" was marriage.' The muscles in Emily's neck tightened. How had Zeyla's marriage affected Violet? It must have been crushing. 'Anything else?'

'No, that's it for Zeyla. Seeing as Rupert was from Oxford, I can only assume she moved there with him after they married. There aren't any more mentions of the Wythenshawe family, but I believe they moved away after the war, only visiting Dovecote occasionally.'

'Thank you so much for this. I had hoped to be able to track down Zeyla, or her descendants, considering her age, and knowing her married name will help enormously. I'm also hoping that Sue can unearth some clues in the archives of the manor.'

'I did come across a few other records which I thought might be of interest.' He passed her yet another sheet of paper. 'The marriage record of Violet Saunders and Hugo Cooper.'

Emily squinted at the photocopied image; the handwriting was almost illegible.

'February 1946?'

Clive nodded.

'Terry said Hugo was in the army up until 1945 before becoming the head gardener at Dovecote Manor. I wonder how and when he met Violet?'

'And then there was this.'

Clive's cheery smile had faltered, and Emily took the paper nervously.

'Oh.' She looked up at Clive who nodded sadly.

'An all-too-common occurrence, unfortunately.'

Emily folded the paper and tucked it into her handbag. The other records she would share with Gio and the Prentices. The last one she would keep secret for the time being.

Stepping out of the cool church into the heat of the summer sun, Emily needed to feel the salty breeze from the sea on her skin. Leaning against the turquoise railings of The Promenade, the swish of the sea and the squawking of the gulls filling her ears, she glanced up at the cliff to her right. When the wind got up and rustled the trees, the chimney pots of Dovecote Manor were visible between the branches.

The view must have been much the same in Violet's time. Had she stood here watching the waves bubbling over the pebbles while thinking about Zeyla and Rupert? It must have come as such a shock, the likes of which Emily couldn't fathom. But then where did Hugo come into the story? Before or after Rupert? And that last photocopy Clive had given her! Emily's vision blurred, and not from the wind coming in off the sea. She pushed herself away from the balustrade and wandered towards Beachfront Road, focusing on the large glass of wine she'd pour when she got home.

She shielded her eyes from the sun as she drew close to two familiar figures outside one of the fishermen's cottages on Beachfront Road.

'I see. That's how it's going to be, is it?' she called out and Harrison turned sharply. Gio opened his mouth but then shut it again. 'You come down to see Harrison, and don't even tell me? Well, at least now I know where I stand.'

'Emily. Darling. It was a last-minute thing. I was going to call you.'

She had to laugh at the panic on his face. She kissed his cheek. 'I'm only kidding. You do whatever you want. Don't forget about your poor, neglected, single friend. Either of you.' She gave Harrison a light slap on the arm. 'What are you doing hanging around outside someone's house?' she asked, giving the cottage a once over. The front garden was a bit overgrown with weeds but the pastel-pink paint on the front door and around the windows looked fresh. There was a hand-painted sign on the whitewashed wall by the front door and Emily squinted at it. 'Seaglass Cottage. Cute.'

'It's about to go up for sale. The owner, Betty Jones, moved into Bayview Care Home a few years ago and died recently. I've had my eye on these cottages for ages,' Harrison said, his eyes sparkling. 'I have this urge to live in one of them.'

'Why? You've got a massive manor house to live in.'

'I'm thirty years old, Emily. I don't want to live with my parents forever. Even if it is in the manor. The estate agent knew I was interested and came down to show me around.'

'On a Sunday?'

'I saved his daughter's pet gerbil's life. He owed me.'

Emily laughed. 'Fair enough. And why are you here?' She poked Gio in the arm. 'Not thinking of moving in together, are you? You've only been together a week. Meeting his parents is one thing, Gio. I draw the line at co-habitation this early on.'

Gio blushed. 'No, I just...'

'I wanted a second pair of eyes,' Harrison interjected. 'That's all.'

'And there was no one else you could have asked?' Emily pouted and pretended to be hurt.

Harrison rolled his eyes, realising she was having him on. 'Oh, get over it,' he said.

'So?'

'What?' Harrison asked.

'The cottage.'

'I like it. Good sized reception rooms, a lovely kitchen, three bedrooms, and there's a nice garden for Cher. I'm pretty sure James Rutherford lives next door.' He looked at Gio who raised his eyebrows and then reached for Harrison's hand. 'I think I'm going to go for it.'

'Do your mum and dad know?'

'Not yet, I'll break it to them gently. After they've had a few glasses of wine. Are you heading back up?'

'Yeah, I needed a bit of a walk.'

'Is everything okay?' Gio asked, and Emily nodded to disguise her deep intake of breath.

'Fine, Gio. All fine.' At least, she would be once she'd tracked down Zeyla and discovered whether Violet or Zeyla had been the one to suffer a broken heart.

# TWENTY-NINE

## EMILY

July 2016

'Zeyla Wythenshawe became Zeyla Petherington-Smyth? That's a bit of a mouthful,' Harrison chuckled as Sue handed him a glass of wine. The weather had turned, and dark clouds were tumbling in from the sea, so that evening they'd all retreated to the sitting room of Dovecote Manor. Like the main hall, the room was dominated by a huge stone fireplace. There was also a large bay window with a seat covered in red velvet cushions. It was a cosy room with dark green walls, a pair of overstuffed deep-red and gold sofas, and two matching armchairs. Every available surface was crammed with pot plants, vases of flowers, and collections of photo frames. It was a room that could have been lifted straight out of a period drama. Gerry and Margo, who had come in from their post at the front door, were lounging on the rug in front of the fireplace which only added to the *Downton Abbey* aesthetic.

'It certainly is,' Sue pondered, settling back into the sofa. Bernie, who had followed Sue and the plate of smoked salmon and brown bread up from the kitchen, placed her snout on Sue's lap. Sue rolled her eyes and fed Bernie a sliver of salmon. Terry had gone upstairs for a nap.

'And Clive didn't know where she went after she got married?' Harrison asked.

'No. We can only assume, seeing as Rupert was from Oxford, that's where she went.'

'I wonder if there's anything online about her?' Gio asked, pulling his phone from his pocket. This slight movement earned him a grunt from Cher who was snoozing on his knees.

'Good thinking, Gio. Maybe a death notice in a newspaper?' Sue suggested.

Emily sighed. 'I suppose that's what we'd be looking for. She would be over ninety, if she's still alive.'

They all looked up when the sitting room door creaked open. Even the dogs raised their heads, except Bernie who was completely focused on the coffee table, hoping for another bit of smoked salmon.

'Hey, Mum.' Will was looking at a piece of paper in his hand and only looked up when he'd closed the door behind himself. 'Oh. Sorry, I didn't know you were all in here. Hi. How was the house viewing, H?'

Sue's head whipped around so fast she almost gave herself whiplash. She shot Harrison a questioning look.

'I'll tell you later, Mum.' Harrison pursed his lips at Will who grimaced and mouthed 'sorry'.

Will nudged Bernie out of the way and sat down on the sofa next to Sue. He stretched across the coffee table and handed Emily the piece of paper.

'I was having a quick look in the library and found this in a box with some other letters belonging to Venetia Wythenshawe.'

Emily took the letter. The paper was thin and crinkly, and

yellowed with age. In some spots, the ink was smudged with what might have been tears. Gio put down his phone as Emily began to read.

'*Mother. No doubt by now you will have heard that I have left Rupert. I have held out in a loveless marriage for as long as I could, and now that Philip and George are grown up, I feel I have done my duty. I do not expect you to understand, but nevertheless I shall explain. I have never loved Rupert and have spent the past twenty years regretting that I allowed you and Father to determine my life's path. I should have stood up for myself a long time ago.*'

Emily swallowed the lump in her throat and glanced around the room. Wide eyes looked back at her. She turned her gaze back to the letter.

'*The truth is that I could never love any man. I am, and always have been, a lesbian. It is about time I embraced the truth of who I am. I intend to move to the west coast of Ireland and live the rest of my life by my rules, not yours. I do not expect, nor do I wish, to receive a reply. Zeyla. Dated June* 1964.'

A chorus of exhaled breaths filled the room.

'Gosh,' puffed Sue. 'That's quite the letter.'

'Poor Zeyla having to come out by a letter. That must have been hard. I'm very glad I didn't have to do that.' Harrison gave Sue a soft smile which she returned.

'For sure, but sometimes it's the safer option. It certainly was for me,' Gio said, with a raised eyebrow. Emily squeezed his knee. The day Gio's father had called him after receiving Gio's letter was seared into her memory. It had been the only time she'd seen Gio cry. Harrison rested his head on Gio's shoulder and Sue nodded sympathetically.

'She says so much in quite a short letter. And not expecting or wanting a reply from her own mother. That's so sad.' Emily handed the letter back to Will. The paper shook slightly in her hand. It was all so much to take in. Zeyla's words bounced around in her head. To have to go through life pretending to be someone you're not, and to be forced to be with someone you felt nothing for. That was painful to read. Of course there was the matter of Violet, not mentioned in Zeyla's letter. Had they been in contact at all after Zeyla got married?

'So, Zeyla went to live in Ireland,' Gio said, interrupting Emily's thoughts.

'I presume the Philip and George in the letter are her sons?' Will asked, folding the letter carefully and putting it down on the coffee table, out of Bernie's reach. She had given up on the smoked salmon and was curled up at his feet. 'Maybe we should focus on trying to find them?'

'Sounds like they were adults by 1964. Zeyla and Rupert got married in June 1944, so must have had their children pretty quickly,' Sue pointed out. 'It wouldn't have been unusual at the time, I suppose.'

'Considering Zeyla's lack of attraction to Rupert, and her sexuality, I'm surprised they had any children at all,' Emily added. 'Poor Zeyla, what an awful situation to be in. It doesn't bear thinking about.'

'I wonder if her mother ever replied?' Will asked. 'Or is this the last piece of communication between them? I'll keep looking in the library and see if I can find anything else.'

Emily nodded and gave Will a half-smile. 'I would love to meet her, if she's still alive obviously. I kind of want to give her a hug.'

Gio was tapping on his phone again, and a smile spread slowly across his lips. 'Emily, I think you might be in luck.'

He passed his phone to her. She looked down at the screen which displayed a newspaper article from *Killarney Today*. The photo was of a thin, elderly lady with a grey bob and dazzling green eyes wearing a bright yellow and turquoise kaftan. She was holding a children's book and smiling at a sea of small children sitting on a carpet in a semicircle around her. Emily read out the caption.

'*Ms Zeyla Wythenshawe (91) reads to children from Glencaragh National School as part of a nationwide scheme to combat isolation in elderly people.* It's from last week.'

'Good gracious,' Sue exclaimed. 'She's still alive.'

Emily's hand was shaking as she passed Gio back his phone. 'I can't believe it,' she whispered.

'Emily, you have to go and meet her,' Harrison said. 'She might have the portraits.' His eyes flashed with excitement.

Emily deflated like a week-old balloon. 'I'd love to, Harrison. But, well, cash is a bit tight at the moment. I'll contact the newspaper though and see if they can put me in touch with her.'

'I'll pay for the trip, if I can tag along.'

Emily's head whipped up at Will's words. She searched his face for traces of laughter but could find none. He was serious.

'There you go, Emily. You and Will can both go.' Sue's matter-of-fact tone sent a ripple of fear through Emily's body. There was no way in the world she was going to Ireland with Will. The mere idea made her queasy.

'That's very kind, Will,' Emily eventually stammered. 'But I couldn't possibly...'

'Who couldn't possibly what?' Terry asked, coming into the room and lowering himself into one of the armchairs. 'What have I missed?' Gerry trotted over and sat at Terry's feet, his head on Terry's lap.

'We've found Zeyla, Terry,' Sue gushed. 'She's alive, can you believe it? And she's living in Ireland. Will has said he'll pay for him and Emily to go and find her.'

'Splendid,' Terry said. 'Marvellous idea.'

The look that passed between Terry and Sue made Emily shudder. They couldn't possibly think that something might happen between her and Will. Could they? Emily's palms were

slick with sweat. She glanced at Gio who was watching her
closely.

'I think it's best if I just contact the newspaper. For now,'
she added, at the look of disappointment on Sue's face. 'Thank
you, Will, but I'm sure you have better things to do with your
time.'

He shrugged. 'Not really. I've got two weeks of annual leave
I have to use by the end of August or lose. And anyway, Tabitha
is still in the apartment, so I'd rather be anywhere but there
right now.'

Sue visibly tensed at the mention of Tabitha's name.

'No,' Emily said, a little too forcefully. 'I mean, it's okay,
Will. Let's see how we get on with contacting the newspaper.'

Terry leant forward in his chair. 'Emily, I've had an email
from Gordon. The builders have upped their quote. The land
survey has revealed that where we're building the extension for
Dovecote Museum will need a complete archaeological excava-
tion. Apparently, there used to be houses there that were
destroyed by a stray bomb during the Brighton Blitz and the
builders are worried about unexploded bombs now. It's going to
cost an extra couple of thousand.' He paused. 'We could do
with those portraits.'

Four pairs of expectant eyes stared at her. A fifth, Gio's
brown eyes, had a trace of concern in them. She stood up.

'If I don't have any luck contacting Zeyla via the newspaper,
then we'll see. I have to go, excuse me.'

Outside the manor, she leant against the cold stone wall and
took a few deep breaths. Her heart was beating way too fast.
Gio appeared at her side, concern in his dark eyes.

'I think it's time you told me what's really going on.'

Tears pricked at Emily's eyes as Gio took hold of her hand.

·   ·   ·

At the weathered pine kitchen table in Clifftop Cottage, Emily cradled the mug of tea Gio had made for her.

'So now you know why I can't go to Ireland with him.'

'Yes, I understand. I'm sorry, darling, I should never have encouraged you to come back to Dovecote. We can pack up your things now and go back to London, my sofa is always available to you.'

Emily wiped her sleeve across her face. 'I thought I'd be okay as long as he stayed in London. But since I've been back, he's here *all* the time. The thing is, I love it here. If only *he* wasn't here so much.'

He kissed her forehead. 'Do you want me to stay?'

'No, I'll be alright. Thanks, Gio. You'd better go back. And please don't tell anyone, not even Harrison. *Especially* not Harrison.'

'Of course not. Are you sure you'll be alright?'

Emily drew a deep breath and tucked her hair back behind her ears as she and Gio walked to the front door. 'Yeah, I'll be fine.'

'It's a shame. I know you wanted to meet Zeyla. She could tell you a lot about your Aunt Violet. And if she did have the portraits, it would mean so much to a lot of people.'

'I know. If there was some other way, then I would take it. I don't suppose you fancy a little trip to Ireland?'

'Emily, I would sell a kidney to give you anything you wanted, but time off in August? I have more chance of getting a date with Tom Hardy than getting time off in August. Which reminds me, I have an eight o'clock meeting tomorrow morning with a bride who wants to know if she can have a pond with live swans in the hotel's ballroom.' He threw up his hands. 'Swans? These people are ridiculous.'

'You better go and catch your train, then. Thank you, Gio. Love you.'

'Love you too.'

The gate of Clifftop Cottage banged shut, and Emily was alone. She looked at the portraits of Hugo on the mantlepiece. The one of Hugo at a window reminded her of Duncan Grant's portrait *Paul Roche, Opening Curtain*. Moody and yet tender at the same time. Full of longing and desire. Violet and Hugo had clearly been in love. Did the portraits of Zeyla have the same slightly tense, but electrifying, intimate energy to them? There was only one way to find out, even if it meant facing Will Prentice head-on.

# THIRTY

## VIOLET

January 1944

It was a grey, drizzly Saturday in late January and the Dovecote Manor ballroom was full to bursting. The Wythenshawe family, and their assorted friends, gathered beneath the glittering splendour of the crystal chandelier to celebrate Zeyla's nineteenth birthday. The room buzzed with excited chatter and laughter. I would rather have stayed at home in Clifftop Cottage than subject myself to scrutiny. I had no issue with strangers seeing Zeyla and I together, but her friends and family were a different prospect entirely. I'd avoided Christmas with the Wythenshawes, but Zeyla had begged me to come to her party. I couldn't say no when she flashed her best puppy-dog eyes.

Due to the inconvenience of the blackout, it was an afternoon party, but everyone was still getting stuck into the abundant champagne. I didn't want to think too much about how Zeyla's father had manged to obtain *real* champagne, and in such quantities. There may have been a decent stockpile in the wine cellar of Dovecote Manor before the war, but in case it was all from the black market, I wouldn't be touching it or the smoked salmon and caviar that was being washed down by it. The idea of the abuse of regulations for unnecessary luxuries turned my stomach, which was already constricted in one of Zeyla's old ankle-length dresses.

Unlike the tea dress I had worn to the dance in the Brighton Dome that glorious day, just a month previously, this gown was a little tight in all the wrong places. The judgemental stares from Zeyla's friends made it quite clear that they recognised the dress as one of Zeyla's from a previous season. Mustard-yellow wouldn't have been my first choice of colour with my complexion, and the high neck gave me the look of a rather sickly giraffe. But beggars can't be choosers. Zeyla had been gifted a new dress, all the way from New York. The plum lace brought out her eyes and the delicate chiffon off-the-shoulder neckline revealed her porcelain skin and made me want to bury my head in her cleavage.

Zeyla finally introduced me to her parents. I was beginning to think she was purposefully keeping me away from them. I took the opportunity to thank them for allowing me to rent Clifftop Cottage. I was about to apologise that I couldn't pay them more, but Venetia made some condescending comment about it being their duty to help those in need. I got the distinct impression that being invited to Zeyla's party was taking duty a step too far.

'Hallo, you must be Violet,' a plummy voice said from behind me. How she managed to sneak up on me, I don't know. I had my back so close to the wall, I feared I would make an imprint on the ballroom wallpaper.

'Hello. Yes, I am,' I replied. The woman was rather horsey looking with large teeth. Her raven-black hair was quite pretty though.

'The gals were saying we don't remember you from school.'

Wonderful. Not only was I a topic of conversation, but I was clearly so unremarkable that, while they all presumed I'd been at school with them, none of them could remember me. I should have stuck to my guns and refused to come. I'd known I wouldn't fit in with her glamorous friends. And it wasn't as if I was being introduced as Zeyla's girlfriend. To everyone in the room, I was the poor girl the Wythenshawes had benevolently rented a small cottage on their estate to. I was the charity case. The 'good deed'. The proof they were 'doing their bit'. In the Brighton Dome ballroom, we'd been equals. In this ballroom, I was being reminded of how different we were. It hurt.

Zeyla had barely even glanced in my direction for the last hour. Horse-face was blinking at me, waiting for an answer, even though she'd not actually asked a question.

'That will be because I didn't go to school with you or Zeyla.'

'Oh, golly. I didn't think Zeyla was allowed to fraternise with the locals. Old Randy and Ven Wythenshawe must be going soft in their old age.' Even her laugh was a horse-like whinny. If only she knew the level of our fraternising. Hugo's voice popped into my head, urging me to tell her or to make some smutty comment. But I just smiled faintly until she walked away.

I was rummaging in my handbag, pretending to look for a handkerchief when a conversation a few feet away caught my attention. The fair-haired man in full morning dress had been pointed out to me on arrival as Charles, Zeyla's 'swine' of an older brother. As for the darker-haired man he was talking to, I had no idea.

'Charles, wonderful to see you, old chap. How's life and this blasted war treating you?'

'Oh, you know how it is, Rupert. One gets on with it and is thankful that a damned fine meal can still be had at the Savoy Grill. You still at Oxford?'

'I am. Tried to sign up, quite fancied doing my bit. Duty calls and all that. But was refused. Told I had stay and study.'

Whoever this Rupert was, he'd clearly been born with a silver spoon in his mouth.

'Well, we need doctors on the home front as well, old boy.'

'Yes, I know. But not quite the same, is it? Sitting on the roof with a book watching for bombs that never fall gets a bit tiresome after a while. Well, it can't be helped, I suppose.' Rupert ran his fingers through his hair. He wasn't a bad-looking chap, if that pinched upper-class look was what you called attractive.

My stomach clenched at his mention of bombs. I blinked away the tears that threatened to break through when I thought of Mum. Clearly Oxford was having a better time of it than Brighton or Dovecote. Maybe it was true what people were saying – that Hitler wanted Oxford to be his capital city if he ever took Britain. Fat chance of that, not when good men like Hugo were fighting back to save us. Oh, Hugo. I missed him so much. I'd not had a letter from him for a few weeks. I hoped he was alright. I turned my attention back to the conversation between Charles and Rupert.

'Going to do it tonight, actually,' Rupert was saying. I leant in a fraction closer. They paid me no more attention than they did the staff refilling the champagne flutes. That was where I belonged, downstairs with the staff.

Charles gave Rupert a hearty slap on his shoulder. 'Good luck, old bean. Not that you need it. I'm quite sure she'll say yes. If you'll excuse me, Mitsy Bancroft is looking rather splendid and she's on her third glass of champagne.'

Rupert chuckled as Charles made a beeline for a pretty redhead in a bias-cut navy gown that clung to her curves in exactly the right places. I had to admire his taste. Rupert put down his empty glass and straightened his tie. There was a distinctly nervous energy about him. My heart nearly leapt clean out of my chest when he went over to Zeyla, placing a hand on her forearm. That was a bit intimate. She smiled at him. Perhaps they were childhood friends. Rupert and her

brother certainly seemed to be old chums. He whispered something in her ear, and she glanced quickly over her shoulder at
me. I was momentarily distracted by someone cackling loudly at
the grand piano and when I looked back, I saw Rupert guiding
Zeyla out of the room, his arm around her waist.

More guests arrived out of nowhere and it took me several
minutes to push my way through the crowd and into the inner
hallway. The door to the room next to the ballroom was slightly
ajar, so I put my eye to the gap and peered into the library. I
stifled a gasp as Rupert put his arms around Zeyla. Then he
kissed her, and she kissed him back. Zeyla placed a hand on
Rupert's shoulder and the new diamond on her ring finger
sparkled in the light.

# THIRTY-ONE

## EMILY

August 2016

Twelve days after Will's offer to fund the Zeyla-finding trip to Ireland, Emily found herself sitting in Cork airport chewing her thumb cuticle as Will collected the keys to the car he'd hired. She now owed him three favours – rescuing her from the accident, helping her move Violet's writing desk, and now this. The flight from Gatwick to Cork had been smooth, but was there turbulence ahead? The only thing that would make being in close proximity to Will bearable would be finding Zeyla and the portraits. Emily's thoughts about the woman in the yellow kaftan were interrupted by Will's return.

'I hope you're not too upset that I've not got you down as a named driver. Only, I've seen your car nose-down in a ditch,' he said, leading her out into the car park.

Emily scowled. 'That was the first accident I've had in thirteen years.'

'And all the other dents and scratches?' Will asked, raising an eyebrow and Emily's temperature at the same time.

'Minor dings.'

'My point exactly. Here we are.'

Okay, it was fair enough he didn't want her driving his expensive rental car.

'Do you ever stop showing off?'

They were spending three days in County Kerry on the west coast of Ireland, not swanning around Monte Carlo. Hiring a convertible BMW was macho posturing. She wouldn't be swayed by it.

He flashed her a lopsided grin. 'Hey, I'm on holiday. I thought we'd have a bit of fun. You like it?'

'It's alright, I suppose.' Emily fought hard to feign nonchalance. The car was a stunning shade of midnight blue.

'You're hard to impress,' Will said, putting her suitcase into the boot.

'I don't know why you're even trying,' she replied, climbing into the passenger seat and giving the dashboard a quick stroke before he saw.

'I'm not. If I was, you'd know about it.' He grinned as he got in beside her and fiddled with the car, connecting his phone to the Bluetooth and adjusting the seat for his long legs. The minute he switched on the ignition, the stereo blared into life, pumping out Elton John's 'Crocodile Rock'. Emily only managed to half-stifle her giggle.

Will shrugged. 'What can I say, Elton is my guilty pleasure. You can put something else on, if you want?'

'No, it's fine. I like a bit of Elton. I had you down as more of a... actually, I don't know what I would have put you down as a fan of. Maybe opera, or something posh like that.'

'I guess there's quite a lot we don't know about each other,' Will said, as they pulled out of the airport car park. If Emily had her way, that was how it would stay.

·  ·  ·

They passed through Killarney and Emily giddily pointed out the horse-drawn carriages waiting to take tourists on a trip around nearby Killarney National Park and Lough Leane. Beyond the town, the landscape opened up and Will turned off the stereo. It was a good call; the scenery deserved their full attention. Green fields dotted with white sheep were interspersed with heather-sprinkled peatbogs and gorse-covered hills, as the road twisted and turned through the increasingly wild countryside. Gurgling streams passed under the road and occasional single-storey farmhouses slipped by. In the distance, the dragon-toothed silhouettes of dark mountains shimmered purple in the heat haze coming up off the tarmac. Through gaps in the hedgerows, Emily caught glimpses of rocky coves and bays in the distance, the sea silvery in the sun. It was a glorious day, with unbroken sunshine but a pleasant breeze. Surprisingly, the silence was comfortable as Will concentrated on the road and Emily let the beauty of the scenery imprint itself on her memory.

'Glencaragh is about another mile down the road,' Will said, turning into a narrow road with thick forest on either side. 'But all the hotels in town were booked up. I think you'll like this one though.'

They turned off the road at a modest gate. The pillars were only half the height of the ones marking the entrance to Dovecote Manor. A dark green sign standing in a small, neat flowerbed to the right of the gate had *Loughnacran House* painted on it in looping gold lettering. The tree-lined driveway ended in a sweeping curve and, as Will steered into the car park, Emily caught a glimpse of the hotel. She bit the inside of her cheek to stop herself gasping out loud.

The house was long, low, and gabled with casement windows set in stone mullions. The higgledy-piggledy warm brown sandstone had flecks of red and green throughout that flashed in the sunshine. Tall chimneys reached up into the blue sky from a green-grey slate roof. The flowerbeds leading up to the arched oak entrance door were bursting with vibrant orange and fiery red flowers. Beyond the hotel building, Emily could make out manicured grounds leading down to a shimmering lake.

'Thought you'd like it,' Will said, as they climbed out of the car. Emily jolted back to reality. More showing off. Their stay here was not going to be cheap. He was enjoying this.

'It's lovely, but you didn't have to.'

Will shook his head. 'Like I said, everywhere else was booked up.'


They collected their keys from the reception desk in the oak-panelled, flagstone-floored entrance hall. At the top of the wide, olive-green-carpeted oak staircase, Emily and Will went in separate directions. Will, naturally, looked quite at home amongst the Arts and Crafts-style décor that didn't differ much from that of Dovecote Manor. Emily carefully picked her way along the corridor, avoiding touching anything or knocking the wall with her suitcase, suddenly nostalgic for the faded homeliness of Clifftop Cottage.

She stepped into her room.

'Oh, for goodness' sake,' she muttered. A four-poster bed? Seriously? She sat down gingerly on the immaculate bedsheets. The light-blue walls, dark-wood furniture, black fireplace, and deep-pile cream carpet were spectacular, but what stole the breath from her lungs was the view. Beyond the small panes of the leaded window was a narrow strip of lawn, a low stone wall, a flower bed, and Lough Caragh. A single fishing boat bobbed around in the rippling, shimmering water. The far side of the sun-bathed lake was dotted with pine trees, beyond which the mountains rose majestically.

The buzz of her mobile disturbed her gazing.

*Drinks on the terrace at six. Dinner at seven.*

Thankfully she'd taken Harrison's advice and packed something nice to wear.

After a soak in the roll top bath in the tastefully decorated bathroom, Emily was dressed in a pale pink sundress and down at the edge of the lake well before six o'clock. The gentle breeze coming over the water tickled her bare arms, and she breathed in the heady scent of pine and honeysuckle. The soft tread of feet on grass and a waft of sandalwood announced Will's arrival.

'This is all very normal to you, isn't it?' she asked as he drew up next to her. Thankfully he wasn't wearing a tie that matched her dress this time. His crisp shirt and tailored jacket were enough to make him look like he'd stepped out of the pages of a magazine. Emily envied anyone who could look that effortlessly elegant.

'What?'

'All of this. Convertible rental cars, luxury hotels, drinks before dinner.'

'I wouldn't say normal. It's a long weekend away. It's nice to make it special.'

'Why?'

He took a sip of champagne. The glass he'd handed Emily was still untouched in her hand. 'Why what?'

'We're here to find Zeyla and try to convince her to lend us the portraits for the exhibition, if they exist. Why the need to make it special? Do you enjoy showing off?'

'Emily, listen.' Will scratched his temple. He did that a lot. 'Okay, fine. Yes, I may have gone a little bit overboard with the car. And this place, well, I just liked the look of it. It kind of reminded me of home. But I work hard, too hard. And I don't see anything wrong with enjoying the benefits of that. And I'm not showing off or trying to make you uncomfortable in any way. I... let me do things my way, okay? Think of it as a treat and enjoy it.'

Emily drew a deep breath. He was infuriating. She had no choice but to accept what he'd arranged with as much grace as she could. Even if it rankled that she'd never be able to repay him, either financially or in returned favours. 'Thank you.'

'You're welcome,' Will said with a grin. 'And I'm not keeping score of favours.'

'*I* am,' she said. He wasn't fooling her; he was definitely keeping track.

It was Will's turn to inhale deeply. 'Whatever. One day I'm going to crack that tough shell of yours. You're a softy underneath it, aren't you?'

Emily laughed dryly. It wasn't a shell; it was armour, and it would not be moved. 'Nope. I'm solid rock, all the way to my core.'

'Shall we go in for dinner? I'm starving.'

That was one thing she could not disagree with.


The dining room was small and intimate, and subtly decorated in pale sage green, so as not to distract from the view. The large bay window overlooked the lake, framed by tall trees. The evening sun glinted off the water. It was a scene Emily could stare at for eternity and never get bored.

'I keep thinking about what your dad said. It makes my blood run cold knowing the museum was built on land where houses were bombed during the war,' Emily said, while they waited for their starters.

'Yeah, we learnt about it at school, I think.'

'I mean, I'm from the East End of London. Nowhere was more badly bombed than there. But somehow finding it happened in a pretty, quiet little town like Dovecote is just more horrifying.'

Will nodded slowly. 'Let's change the subject. Tell me more about Zeyla. You probably know her better than anyone, having read her diary,' he said, spreading some of his warm chicken mousse on a sourdough cracker. Emily broke open her filo pastry parcel and the baked goat's cheese inside oozed out, mingling with a warm chutney sauce. Her mind flicked to the leather-bound book currently resting on the table next to her four-poster bed. How could she sum up the woman whose words she'd inhaled?

'Zeyla didn't like her family much. She was particularly scathing in parts about her older brother, Charles. It's clear she was a bit stifled. She says that the moments she shared with Violet were the only times she could be herself. Don't get me wrong, I don't think she was intending to turn her back on the trappings of wealth and privilege and there's no mention of her doing any war work. It's hard to explain, but it's like she never felt she belonged anywhere, except when she was with Violet.'

'I don't know much about it, but I imagine it wasn't easy for them. Back then, I mean.'

Emily put her knife and fork down and reached for her wine glass. A discussion about the challenges of being a queer person was not something she wanted to have with Will, of all people.

'No, I don't suppose it was. From what Zeyla wrote, their relationship was very much conducted in secret. Although they did go to a tea dance together.'

'A tea dance?' Will chuckled, finishing his last morsel of chicken mousse.

'Yeah. I looked it up online. During the war, there were a lot of women around and, obviously, not many young men. So a few of the hotels and venues in Brighton held women-only tea dances. I don't think it was a lesbian thing, more of a make-the-best-of-what-we-have thing. According to Zeyla, it was quite thrilling being able to dance with Violet, to have that level of intimacy in public.'

'How did they meet?'

'From what I can gather, they met in an air raid shelter and got talking. Zeyla's diary doesn't go into much detail, but it sounds like she made the first move which didn't go well. Then Violet moved into Clifftop Cottage for some reason and their relationship blossomed. I wish I'd known about Zeyla before, so I could have asked Aunt Violet about her.'

Will's half-smile gave him a dimple in his cheek. She remembered the dimple now. She brushed aside thoughts of long-ago days when that dimple made her knees go weak. It wasn't a warm memory.

'We'll have to make sure we find Zeyla, and she can give us the whole story,' he said.

'Indeed. I'm dying to know what happened between them.'

'Do you think they got found out?'

Emily bit her lip. 'I hadn't thought of that. Oh, God. What if it was all traumatic and awful? Maybe Zeyla won't want to talk about it. I've been so caught up in wanting to know more about Violet's past, that I didn't stop to think it might be painful for those involved. I'm such an idiot.'

Will laughed. 'You're not an idiot. Whatever happened, it was a long time ago. I'm sure Zeyla will be over it.'

Their main courses arrived before Emily could make a comment about how sometimes people don't get over things that happened in the past, or the way people treated them.

They were too full for dessert but went into the hotel's cosy lounge to finish their bottle of wine. Despite herself, Emily was enjoying Will's company. But the shadows of the past still lurked at the fringes of her mind, keeping her slightly on edge. It didn't help that the lounge was suspiciously empty, most of the other guests having decamped to the terrace outside after dinner. They sank into a dark red Chesterfield sofa beside the large stone fireplace.

'This is nice,' she said, reaching for her glass of wine. 'The room I mean,' she hastily added. She would not inflate his ego by making him think it was his company she was compliment-ing. 'You probably don't think it's anything special.'

'I do, actually,' he replied, raising an eyebrow at her. 'I don't take it for granted. I do realise how lucky I am to have had the childhood I had and to grow up where I did.'

They were getting dangerously close to discussing *those* summers, and Emily took a large gulp of wine. How much did he remember? She wanted to know, but she would never ask. She trawled her wine-soaked brain for a safe subject of conver-sation. He beat her to it.

'Harrison and Gio seem to be getting on well,' Will said, leaning back into the sofa and stretching out his long legs, crossing his ankles and revealing dark red socks. His jacket lay, discarded, across the arm of the couch. Effortless elegance or pompous posing? Definitely the latter.

'Yes, they are,' she replied, resisting the urge to kick off her shoes and tuck her legs up under her. 'And to think it started with a tiny, yappy dog.'

Will laughed. 'The way to Harrison's heart is with animals, for sure.'

'Gio's the same. He falls in love with dogs more than people.'

Will raised an eyebrow at her.

'I mean he's not been one for long-term, serious relation-ships before, that's all.' What a stupid thing to say to Harrison's brother. Now Will would think that Gio wasn't to be trusted. Emily put down her half-drunk glass of wine. Losing the ability to engage her brain before opening her mouth was a sure sign she'd had enough alcohol. 'But he's definitely serious about Harrison, I'm sure he is.' No, that was making it worse. She needed to stop digging.

'Hmm,' Will murmured, pursing his lips. Emily tried to focus on smoothing her dress, but her gaze somehow found its way back to Will's face. Their eyes met and Emily was catapulted back to *that* summer evening. She could almost hear the gentle swish of the breeze through the long grass in the field, the pop and fizz of opened beer bottles, the laughter. Could almost feel the warmth of his touch on her sun-kissed skin that had made her heart thud against her ribs, the velvety softness of his lips against hers. She remembered the messy pile of discarded clothes, the fiery glint of gold in his brown eyes.

She forced herself back to the present and tore her eyes away from his, grabbing her handbag and getting to her feet.

'Emily?' Will asked, reaching for her. She backed away. 'What's wrong?'

'Nothing. I, um, I think I should... Night.' She turned away and walked out of the room, desperately trying to conceal her trembling hands. Once safely out of sight, she bolted, running up the stairs and down the corridor. She slammed the bedroom door behind her and leant against it, breathing heavily. That had been too close.

# THIRTY-TWO

## EMILY

August 2016

Glencaragh village could have been plucked straight from the Irish Tourism Office's website. The footpath through the forest from Loughnacran House that Emily and Will followed the next morning led them along the side of a graveyard and ended where a low stone wall met the wrought-iron gates of a church. The church sat on a small hill overlooking the rest of the village.

'We've missed daily Mass,' Will said, reading the notice board beside the church gates. 'I wonder whether Zeyla would have been here?'

'How should I know?' Emily grunted. It wasn't just the residual hangover from the previous night's wine that was making her grouchy. She was scared at how close she'd come to letting Will charm his way back into her good books. She'd let that happen once, and she still carried the scars. It would not happen again.

They were standing at a T-junction without much of a plan, but with a vague hope of bumping into Zeyla. With the church behind them, directly across the road was a two-storey hotel and pub. The top half was painted white, the bottom half exposed stone, and ivy grew across the gabled porch above the door. In the small, paved area at the front of the pub, black parasols optimistically shaded picnic bench tables. The sky was covered in light-grey cloud. But there was a stiff wind blowing in off the sea, and on the horizon a chink of blue was valiantly trying to break through. Similar to Dovecote, the weather on the Wild Atlantic Way could best be described as 'changeable'.

The rest of the buildings in the village were low, white-washed cottages or two-storey buildings painted in bright colours. The post office, which doubled-up as a convenience store, was buttercup yellow with emerald-green window frames. A second pub, next to the post office, was fuchsia pink with black woodwork. A little way down the main road, Emily could make out the roof of a petrol station.

'A church, two pubs, and a post office,' Emily said with a slight laugh. 'We could stand here all day, and we'd probably see Zeyla.'

Will rolled his eyes. 'You're in a right grump this morning. I know what you need. Follow me.'

'I am not in a grump,' Emily protested, but all it earned her was a cheeky grin and another flash of that dimple. With a low grunt, she followed Will across the road and past the post office, the pub, and a trio of white cottages with overflowing hanging baskets. He turned into a narrow lane beside the last cottage, ducking underneath low-hanging wisteria.

'You can go around by the road, but I found this shortcut on Google Maps,' Will said, glancing over his shoulder at Emily. Clearly, he'd done more preparation for the trip than she had, which made her stomach roll painfully. Stepping out of the lane, a gust of sea wind caught her off guard and nearly knocked her sideways into Will. Having regained her balance, her eyes widened.

'Oh, wow,' she whispered. They were standing in a wide,

sweeping bay. Arms of dark green hills embraced the sea, almost meeting at the horizon, and sheltered a long curve of sandy beach. The sun chose that moment to break through the grey cloud, throwing sparkles across the steel-blue water. A photograph could never capture the scale and beauty of the scene. It needed to be painted. It was the sort of place Violet might have loved.

To the left, a row of brightly painted cottages lined the road, and to the right, beyond a coffee shop and a car park, field after field stretched away to the base of the hills on the headland. Somewhere, beyond the bay, the Atlantic Ocean thrashed its wild foam against rocks and cliffs. But the bay was calm and small waves gently lapped the sandy shoreline.

'Okay, so Google Street View does not do this place justice,' Will said, with a deep inhale of sea air. Emily barely heard him she was so lost in the view. He elbowed her gently and nodded towards the café on the corner. The neon pink sign above the door said 'Sandy's'. 'Coffee?'


Emily stirred a lump of sugar into her latte as they sat outside Sandy's. A green and white-striped parasol sheltered them from the sun, which was now blazing above them. Irritating though it was, Will had been right; a blast of sea air and the gorgeous sandy beach had perked her up. She couldn't stay in a mood surrounded by a view like the one before her.

'So, how do we find her?' she asked, tapping her fingers on the table. It was as much a question to herself, as it was to Will.

Will raised an eyebrow above the frame of his designer sunglasses. 'Well, we can either sit here all day in the hope that she walks past, and that we recognise her, or we start asking questions.'

Emily chewed her bottom lip for a moment. 'Yeah, but it's not the done thing, is it? Rocking up somewhere asking strangers if they know of an old woman called Zeyla. It makes me a bit uncomfortable. I was hoping the newspaper might have done the hard work and put me in touch with her.'

'They could have at least acknowledged your email and replied, even if they didn't want to help. Remember why we're doing this.' Will paused and caught Emily's eye. 'It's for the greater good. Getting that museum extension built is looking pretty far off, unless we can raise more money, and to do that we need those portraits. Gio was right, they'd be a real crowd-puller.'

'*And* because I'm nosy and want to know about my great-aunt's wartime love affair.'

Will flashed her a grin. 'That too. Anyway, why don't we start... oh hell.' He stood suddenly, banging against the table, and ran towards the car park where an ice cream van was parked up. At the same time, an ear-splitting scream and a blaring car horn shattered the quiet. By the time Emily turned around, Will was standing in the middle of the road holding a small child in his arms, the boy's ice cream dripping onto Will's shirt. Not a sight she'd ever expected to see.

'Oh my God,' a blonde woman in large sunglasses cried, reaching out for the boy. 'Thank you so much.' Tears streamed down the woman's cheeks as Will led her to the table where Emily had mopped up Will's espresso which had gone flying when he knocked it.

'Come and sit down for a minute,' he said.

'What happened?' Emily asked, pulling up a spare chair.

'I saw this little runaway venture out into the road as that car was reversing out of a parking space,' Will said, sitting back down and handing the woman, presumably the boy's mother, a tissue. A black SUV drove past the café, the driver not even checking to see if the child they'd almost hit was alright. Emily puffed out a short, sharp breath.

The woman pushed her sunglasses up onto her head and

wiped her eyes, sitting the boy on her knee. 'I'm so sorry. I'm Caroline, and this is my son, Freddie.' There was an American lilt to Caroline's voice. She wiped Freddie's blond fringe out of his eyes. He was so engrossed in what was left of his ice cream that he didn't look up and seemed to be totally oblivious of the stress he'd caused. 'He's only three,' she added by way of an explanation as to why he had zero road sense. 'I only took my eyes of him for a second to pay for his ice cream. The next thing I know, he's walked off and is in the road. If it hadn't been for you, anything might have happened.'

'I'm sure that car would have stopped in time.' There was a dubious tone to Will's voice and the frown creasing his forehead was a touch endearing. No doubt when they returned to Dove-cote, he'd be insufferable, telling everyone he'd saved a small child's life. Emily would let him boast though, it was a pretty big deal. 'I'm Will and this is my friend Emily.' Will reached for a napkin and dabbed at the ice cream stain on his light-blue shirt.

'Hi,' Caroline said, her green eyes glancing between Emily and Will. 'I'm so sorry, did he get ice cream on you?'

Will's frown deepened for an instant, but he hastily rearranged his features at the panic in Caroline's eyes. 'Only a little bit. It'll wash out.'

Emily nearly choked on a mouthful of latte. How could he be so blasé about something probably eye-wateringly expensive? Caroline seemed to be having trouble tearing her eyes away from Will, and Emily supressed a groan.

'Can I get you a coffee?' Will asked. 'You're a bit shaky.'

Caroline laughed. 'Only if you're sure I'm not interrupting?' She placed her hand lightly on Will's forearm. It was like Aoife all over again. 'I'd love a latte.'

'Sure,' Will replied, getting up.

'I'm not usually such a bag of nerves,' Caroline said, ruffling Freddie's hair, when Will had gone inside. 'It's this little guy's fault. Ever since we got to Ireland, he's refused to get in his stroller. I'm a nervous wreck. You sure do need to have eyes in the back of your head with kids, right?'

'I wouldn't know,' Emily said, more frostily than she'd intended.

'So, are you guys here on vacation?' Caroline asked, clearly fishing for information on Will.

'Kind of.' Why was this woman winding her up so easily? She needed to get over herself. She forced a smile. 'You?'

'Yeah, kind of. I'm visiting my grandmother. It's a long story but my father and her fell out years ago and I never knew her. After I split up from my husband, I had the urge to track her down.'

'Track who down?' Will asked, placing a latte and another espresso down on the table. He hadn't got Emily a refill. She scooped out the foam with her spoon and pushed her empty cup away. He didn't notice.

'I was just saying I traced my grandmother to Glencaragh earlier this year,' Caroline continued, pulling Freddie into her shoulder. He was starting to drop off to sleep. 'I'd never met her because of a family falling-out years ago. After my messy divorce, I needed a change of scenery, so I figured I'd take a trip. And it's been awesome to meet her.'

'Oh. Sorry to hear you've been having a tough time,' Will said. 'Funnily enough, we've tracked someone to Glencaragh too.'

Caroline glanced from Will to Emily. 'Well, ain't that a coincidence. Who are you looking for? I've met quite a few folks around the village. Maybe I can help?'

Emily opened her mouth to protest, she didn't need this woman getting involved in her family's history, but Will gave her a look.

She took a deep breath.

'We're looking for an old friend of my great-aunt's. I've

recently inherited my great-aunt Violet's cottage in a little town on the south coast of England called Dovecote. We found a diary there belonging to someone she used to know way back during the war.'

Caroline squealed. The sound went right through Emily. 'Oh my God, that's incredible.'

'Yeah, we think that this friend grew up in the house where my parents now live, and where my brother and I grew up,' Will added.

'Wow. That is *so* cool. What's her name?'

'Zeyla,' Emily said. 'Zeyla Wythenshawe.'

Caroline's green eyes widened, and she put her coffee cup down slowly. 'Well then, I sure am excited I bumped into you. My father is Philip Petherington-Smyth and his mother's maiden name was Wythenshawe. Zeyla is my grandmother.'

# THIRTY-THREE

## EMILY

August 2016

The rest of the morning whizzed by in a blur. Emily barely tasted her lunchtime crab and rocket sandwich, unable to concentrate on anything but Caroline's revelation. She'd actually done it. She'd found Zeyla. Well, Will had. Kind of. In a roundabout way. Another favour to add to the list.

'I sent Mum a message,' Will said, as he ushered Emily through the door of the pub opposite the church later that afternoon. The inside of the pub was bright and airy with distressed wooden tables and a French grey panelled bar topped with reclaimed driftwood. Chalk menu boards and storm-lantern candles were accompanied by the malty aroma of Guinness. 'She's thrilled that we're going to meet Zeyla.'

'No doubt you told her how we came to meet Caroline,' Emily snapped. Their imminent meeting with the woman who had been in love with her great-aunt was fraying her nerves. It could all go horribly wrong.

Will ran a hand through his hair. 'I didn't actually.'

Emily snorted. 'I wouldn't have thought you'd pass up an opportunity to blow your own trumpet.'

Will sighed but didn't respond. His phone beeped, fanning the embers of annoyance that had been lit in Emily earlier that day when Caroline had given her number to Will rather than her. Why did it bother her so much to see women throwing themselves at him? Because they reminded her of herself, all those years ago, that was why. It riled her up because every time she witnessed it, the door to the room where she kept those memories locked away was forced open a fraction, and scenes she didn't want to relive crawled back into her consciousness.

'They'll be here in a couple of minutes. Caroline said it takes her grandmother a little while to get in and out of the car these days. And Freddie's fallen asleep, so she needs to get him into his pushchair.'

Even the way he said Caroline's name made her skin crawl. It was only when the pub door opened, and the personification of sunshine walked in, did the weight lift from Emily's shoulders.

Zeyla was tiny, shrunk in her old age, but every head turned in her direction when she swept into the bar leaning slightly on a bright pink walking stick, her orange kaftan billowing in her wake. She had a string of oversized electric-blue beads around her neck and matching earrings dangled underneath her grey bob. There was a sort of regal elegance to her; she must have been stunning in her youth. Her eyes were brilliant emeralds and tapered like a cat's. As Zeyla glanced at Emily, she did a double take. Emily's breath caught in her throat. People had often commented that she looked like Violet's side of the family.

When introductions had been made and drinks bought by Caroline, who insisted on repaying Will's earlier gallantry, Zeyla turned her attention to Will.

'So, old Dovecote Manor is still standing, then?' She had a rich, plummy voice. A real old-fashioned BBC radio voice. Emily could have listened to her speak for hours. Had Violet also been captivated by it? Emily shifted in her seat, waiting for the right moment to introduce Violet to the conversation.

Will chuckled. 'It is indeed. The house was a bit of a wreck when Mum and Dad bought it.'

'Well, Mother and Father used it as a summer house after the war for a few decades. Then they stopped visiting altogether,' Zeyla said with a slight shrug.

Will flashed one of his charming smiles. 'We did wonder if that might have been the case. Mum and Dad did a lot of work to restore it. If you walked in tomorrow, you'd probably recognise most of it. They even had the original chandelier in the ballroom restored.'

'Oh gracious, that thing? I always thought it was rather ridiculous.' Zeyla laughed. 'There used to be a grand piano in that room. I messed about on it, but never got the hang of playing properly.'

'It's still there. I learnt on it.' Will blushed slightly and Emily averted her eyes. Their conversation by that piano still confused her.

'Wow, guys, this is all so exciting,' Caroline gushed. 'You'll have to go back and see it, Grandma. If that would be okay with you, Will? And your parents, of course.'

Emily fought back a rising tide of bile. It was one thing to be gooey over Will Prentice but another to be so shameless about it.

'You'd be very welcome anytime, Zeyla. When were you last there?'

Zeyla fingered the beads of her necklace. 'The sixth of June 1944.'

'D-Day,' Will said, at the same moment Emily said, 'Your wedding day.'

Zeyla smiled. 'You are both correct. Completely coinciden-
tal. Had I known Churchill and Eisenhower were planning on
launching the invasion that day, I would never have tried to
upstage them with my wedding. But yes, D-Day was the second
most important thing to happen on that day. I became Mrs
Rupert Petherington-Smyth, and thousands of allied forces
began to liberate Europe. A momentous day all round. I am glad
to hear you remembered some of your schooling, young man,'
she said to Will, before turning to Emily. 'But how did you
know it was my wedding day?'

'The incumbent vicar at St. John's very kindly searched the
parish records for me. We wanted to know who you were.'

'Hmm,' Zeyla murmured. 'Now I am intrigued. What is it
about this ancient ruin that's had you two youngsters hotfooting
it over to this little corner of the world?'

Emily glanced at Will who gave her a slight nod.

'As no doubt Caroline has told you, I recently inherited, and
moved into, Clifftop Cottage on the Dovecote Manor estate. I
think you knew the previous resident.' Emily drew a breath to
disguise the trembling in her voice and looked into Zeyla's green
eyes. 'My great-aunt, Violet Cooper. You would have known
her as Violet Saunders.'

Emily searched Zeyla's face for some trace of recognition,
but it was expressionless. She would be a great poker player.
Either that or Emily had got it all wrong and the V in the diary
wasn't Violet, or the diarist wasn't Zeyla. It was only when
Emily took the diary out of her bag and placed it on the table
that Zeyla's expression altered. And it was thunderous. Zeyla's
eyes darkened and then flashed, her mouth became a thin line,
and pink spots appeared on her hollow cheeks. Without a word,
she got to her feet, reached for her walking stick, and stormed
out of the pub with a speed and determination that belied her
age. Caroline stood frozen to the spot for a moment before

turning back to Emily and Will. Will rose to his feet but Emily was stuck in her chair, paralysed.

'I didn't tell her about you, Emily, or your great-aunt. I only mentioned Will and Dovecote Manor.' She placed a hand on Will's forearm. 'Gee, I'm so sorry.' She grabbed the handles of Freddie's pushchair and ran out of the pub to catch Zeyla.

Will slumped back into his seat and he and Emily briefly stared at each other before they both downed their drinks.

'Well, that could have gone better,' Will said, dryly.

'You don't say.' After all the anticipation and planning she'd blown it. Now she may never know what had happened all those decades ago. She could have cried.

# THIRTY-FOUR

## VIOLET

January 1944

My mind raced as I fled from Dovecote Manor as quickly as I could in Zeyla's tight yellow dress and launched myself through the French doors of Clifftop Cottage. Had I seen what I thought I'd seen? It couldn't be real. I must have imagined it. But as I stood in the sitting room, the fading early-evening light casting shadows on the walls, I knew I hadn't. I had seen *my* Zeyla kissing that Rupert chap. And the ring? My knees buckled. I stumbled up the stairs and threw myself onto my bed, ignoring the ripping of the dress's seams. Tears streamed down my face as I broke down in loud, gulping sobs.

It was completely dark by the time I pulled myself together enough to change out of her dress, which now had a long rip along the seam of the bodice, and into my usual outfit of a wool skirt and brown cardigan. That dress wasn't me *at all*. I pulled the blackout curtains across the sitting room window but didn't turn on the light. Instead, I lit the fire and curled up in the armchair, watching the flames. How long had it been going on? For the past few months, even before our outing to the tea dance, Zeyla had been spending less time at Clifftop Cottage. She said it was all the social meetings her mother was making her attend, but what if that had been a lie? What if she'd been meeting Rupert? How many lies had Zeyla told?

I didn't turn my head away from the fire when the lock of the front door clicked.

'What are you doing sitting here in the dark?' Zeyla asked as she flicked on the light. I forced myself to look at her, fighting back more tears. She was still in her beautiful plum lace and chiffon dress. I glanced at her hand; the ring was gone. She swept across the sitting room and perched on the arm of the chair. I tried not to flinch and pull away. 'I'm sorry I didn't get a chance to talk to you much. It's so tiresome hosting parties where one is obliged to talk to everyone. I finally got a moment and was looking for you, but you must have left by then. I'm sorry, were you terribly bored?'

I shrugged. 'A little.' My ribs ached from the effort of keeping what I'd seen in. I wanted to hold on to what we had a little longer. I clenched my fists around the fabric of my skirt to stop my hands reaching for Zeyla. I wanted to put my arms around her and hold her close. I wanted to breathe in her perfume, to caress her soft skin. I wanted to taste the champagne on her lips. I bit down hard on my own bottom lip, but I couldn't prevent the tears from seeping out. I turned away and stared into the fire for a moment. I couldn't deny what had to be said.

'You've taken it off,' I whispered.

'What, darling?'

I turned back to face her. There wasn't a mark of shame or guilt on her face. In an instant, the sadness morphed into anger. How dare she sit there and look at me with those beautiful green eyes without a shred of discomfort?

'Rupert's ring,' I said, the strength returning to my voice. 'You've taken off Rupert's ring. He won't like that.'

Zeyla glanced down at her hands. When she raised her head, she couldn't meet my stare. Finally, a hint of guilt clouded those shining eyes. I got up from the armchair which rocked slightly at the loss of counterbalance to the weight of Zeyla on the arm.

'I *saw* you. I saw you and him in the library, Zeyla. I watched you kiss him.' My voice wavered and fresh tears streamed from my eyes. I wiped them away.

'Vi, please don't cry. It doesn't mean anything, I promise.' She got up and came over to me. She tried to wrap her arms around me, but I ducked out of her reach.

'It doesn't mean anything? How can you say that? You're marrying him, aren't you?' I was shouting now, which was most unbecoming, but I didn't care. My voice cracked again. 'You said you were the same as me, that you didn't like men. And now I find that not only have you been seeing someone else behind my back, but it's a man.' I put my hands to my head, I wanted to rip my hair out. 'Zeyla how could you do this? I thought you loved me.'

'Violet, please stop shouting.'

'No, I won't. How long has this been going on for, Zeyla? Don't you love me any more? Am I not good enough for you, is that it?'

'Violet, please. Calm down and let me explain.'

'How can you possibly explain this?'

'Violet,' Zeyla yelled. 'Listen to me.' She grabbed my wrists, yanking my hands out of my hair which fell in loose strands onto my shoulders. 'I love you.'

I let out a short, sharp laugh. Did she expect me to believe that?

She shook my wrists. 'I love you, Violet. But I have to marry Rupert.'

A sob broke through. I couldn't look at her. 'Why?'

'Because Mother and Father have said so.'

There was such sadness in her words that I made myself look into her eyes. They were wide and pleading. She led me to the couch and pulled me down beside her. Her intake of breath was shaky.

'I was introduced to Rupert in October. He is a medical student at Oxford. Our fathers have known each other for some time. Anyway, that's not important. Rupert was keen, but I tried to put him off. I couldn't tell him the truth, obviously, but I kept my distance as much as I could. He's been very persistent these last three months.' She kept her eyes fixed on her hands folded in her lap. Her pale skin almost glowing against the deep plum-coloured lace. 'Mother sat me down suddenly this morning and instructed me to stop playing games. She said Rupert was a good match, and that he had asked Father for his permission to ask me to marry him. She made it very clear that if I didn't say yes there would be consequences. Not just for me, but for the family. I had no choice.' She reached for my hand and I allowed her to take it. 'I don't want to marry him, Vi. I can't tell you how sick it makes me to think about what I will have to do. He shall expect me to have his children.'

'You didn't seem to have any issues with kissing him in the library.' I couldn't help the sarcasm that dripped from my words.

'Would you believe me if I said that I ran to my bathroom and threw up afterwards?'

I pulled my hand out of her grasp with a loud sigh. 'The problem is, Zeyla, I don't know what to believe now. You had no intention of telling me you were engaged when you came here tonight, did you?'

She had the grace to shake her head at that.

'You were going to carry on letting me believe that you loved me.'

'I *do* love you.'

I got up and started pacing the sitting room. 'Letting me believe that we had a future together, then. We had plans. What happened to us running away when this stupid war is over? What happened to our dream of spending the rest of our lives together?'

'It could never have happened, Vi.'

'What do you mean? Of course it could. You said it yourself. You said you could give up all of this.' I waved my hand in the general direction of Dovecote Manor. 'For me. For us.'

She got up and placed a hand on my shoulder, I shrugged it off.

'That's the thing, Vi, I can't. I can't give up Dovecote Manor because it's not mine to give up. Charles will get everything, so unless I marry, I'll have nothing.'

'You'd have *me*,' I said, my voice wavering as more tears brimmed in my eyes. 'But I guess I can't compete with champagne, and caviar, and new dresses, and parties, and diamonds. I'm sorry that my love isn't enough for you, Zeyla. But it's all I have to offer. So, I guess you need to decide what matters to you more.'

I reached for my coat and pulled it on. I lifted my handbag from the hook by the door.

'Where are you going?' Zeyla asked. There were tears on her cheeks now. I brushed them away with my thumb.

'I'm going out for a walk. I can't bear to be in the same room as you right now, I'm sorry.'

'Vi, please don't go. Please hold me, kiss me. I need you.'

I shook my head slowly. 'No, darling, you need to decide who you are.'

# THIRTY-FIVE

## EMILY

August 2016

Emily and Will barely exchanged a handful of words as they traipsed along the woodland path back to Loughnacran House. Emily made a beeline for the picnic bench at the edge of the lake. Will disappeared inside. The water lapped the muddy shore as Emily rested her chin in the palm of her hand. There was a flash of electric blue and orange in the corner of her eye; a kingfisher rested for a moment on a tree branch that stretched out over the lake before flying away.

She hadn't planned to reveal the diary so quickly. That was a stupid mistake. A stranger suddenly revealing they'd read a year's worth of her most intimate and private secrets must have given Zeyla quite a fright. She groaned softly. At least her reaction proved Zeyla was the diarist. Cautiously, as though it might burn her fingers, Emily pulled the brown-leather bound diary from her bag, opening it at a random page.

*25 September 1943*

*I shall never be happier than I am now. This love that we share,*
*it's like a warm fire on a cold day, or the shade of a tree in the*
*height of summer. It's, oh, it's so perfectly wonderful. I am in*
*love, and it is magical. C has gone back to his bunker, thank*
*goodness. I do so hate when he is home. He treats me like a*
*child. But never mind, I would put up with a thousand days of*
*C, for one hour of V.*

How had it all gone wrong? How had Zeyla Wythenshawe
and Violet Saunders, who seemed to share such a deep love, end
up as Mrs Rupert Petherington-Smyth and Mrs Hugo Cooper
respectively? Considering Zeyla's reaction to seeing the diary, it
was likely that Emily would never know. And she could also
kiss goodbye to finding out if Violet ever painted Zeyla's
portrait, never mind get to see any paintings.

The sun was beginning to dip below the mountains that
bordered the lake when Emily heard the crunch of gravel under
foot and turned, expecting to see Will. Caroline stepped off the
driveway and onto the pine needle-carpeted path that led down
to the lake edge. She pushed her ridiculous sunglasses up into
her hair as she walked. Emily rubbed her brow; this was all she
needed.

'Hey, Emily.'

Emily forced herself to return Caroline's smile and wave.
The woman might be nauseating around Will, but she was also
the only way Emily could access Zeyla.

'Honey, I'm so glad I caught you. I wanted to apologise for
my grandma.'

Emily motioned for Caroline to join her at the table. 'You
don't need to apologise, seeing her diary must have been a
shock.'

'I'll say.' Caroline reached across the table and put her hand
on Emily's. Her nails were manicured and painted a deep red.

Emily fought the urge to flinch. 'She's told me a little bit about Violet and how they were close once.'

'Did she say *how* close?'

Caroline blushed slightly. 'Yes. She also said she didn't want to talk to you, or anyone, about what happened. I think Grandma might be a bit ashamed. Not of her and Violet's relationship, please don't get me wrong. No, I think there's something about the way it ended that she doesn't want to be reminded of.' Caroline shook her head, tousling her long blonde hair. There were flecks of red in it that glistened in the evening sun.

'I was hoping she would be able to tell me what happened between them, I'm curious.'

There was the hint of a smile on Caroline's lips as she leant across the table. 'Me too,' she whispered. Okay, so maybe Caroline wasn't that bad. Emily nodded towards the hotel.

'Drink?'

'Sure. Grandma's minding Freddie so I don't need to rush back.'

Emily returned to a table tucked in the corner of the dark green hotel bar with a bottle of Merlot and two large glasses.

'Is everything okay?' Caroline asked, her eyebrows raised.

Emily relaxed her face to smooth out her frown. 'Sorry, yes, fine. The, um, woman behind the bar reminds me a bit of my ex.' Maybe it was the barmaid's short dark hair, styled into an Elvis-style quiff, or her tight black T-shirt tucked into her black jeans. Emily hadn't seen the woman's feet, but she'd put money on her wearing a pair of Doc Martens. The resemblance to Max had thrown Emily off-kilter. Emily could practically see the lightbulb go off in Caroline's head as she made an 'O' shape with her mouth.

'So, you and Will aren't...?'

Emily shook her head vigorously. 'No.'

'Oh, okay. I wasn't sure. There seemed to be a vibe between you. Just friends, then?'

'Hardly even that.'

'Right.'

They both looked into their glasses for a moment.

'Caroline?'

'Uh-huh.'

'Tell me more about Zeyla. I've read quite a lot about her and Violet in the diary, but what happened between her and your grandad, Rupert?'

'Oh, sure. Well, Grandma left him in the mid-sixties, I think.'

'Will found a letter in the archives at Dovecote Manor that Zeyla wrote to her mother in 1963, telling her she'd left Rupert and was moving away.'

'Did I hear my name?'

Emily and Caroline looked up in unison at Will standing next to the table.

'Hey, Will,' Caroline said, shuffling over on the bench seat. 'Grab another glass and come join us.'

Emily shrugged when Will glanced at her.

'Sorry, I interrupted,' he said after he'd returned with a glass, filled it from the bottle in the middle of the table, and sat down next to Caroline.

'Yes, you did,' Emily said, forcing a tight smile. 'You were saying about Zeyla and Rupert, Caroline.'

'Oh, yeah. My father, Philip, who is Zeyla and Rupert's youngest son, was still at medical school when Grandma left Grandad. Apparently, he came home for summer vacation one year, and she'd gone.'

'Ouch,' Will said.

'Dad never saw Zeyla again after that,' Caroline added. 'He moved to the US right after college, met my mom, and the rest is history. He kept in touch with his dad, and we occasionally went to Oxford on vacation when I was a small kid. But Grandad remarried and Dad didn't get on with his stepmom, Iris. Both Grandad and Iris have passed away now.' She drew a breath. 'Dad's older brother, George, is also a doctor and stayed in Oxford. He still lives there. Dad and Uncle George exchange Christmas and birthday cards, but they haven't seen each other since Rupert's funeral. We never had any contact with the Wythenshawe family. I'm pretty sure Grandma isn't in touch with George.'

Emily twirled her wine glass between her finger and thumb. 'I can understand that. After my mum and dad split up in 2002, Mum and I lost touch with all of Dad's relatives, including Great-Aunt Violet. My grandad, Violet's youngest brother, Oliver, would send cards and presents at birthdays and Christmas, but Mum and I never saw him after the divorce.'

'Oh, honey, that's so sad.' Caroline gave Emily's arm a friendly pat. 'Wait, so you weren't in contact with your aunt? But she still left her cottage to you? Wow. When was the last time you saw her?'

Emily averted her eyes down towards the table. She did not want to be talking about the summers of 1999 to 2001 with Caroline.

'Fifteen years ago.' She couldn't raise her eyes to look at Will.

'Oh, well, okay.'

Emily breathed a sigh of relief when Caroline didn't press for more information. It was the one time she didn't mind a woman turning her full attention on Will.

'So, Will,' Caroline said, her voice suddenly dripping with the sweetness of honey. 'I totally adore London. I'd love to visit more. Do you live close to the centre of the city?'

Emily's wine glass was empty and so was the bottle.

'I need another drink,' she said, getting up from the table

and grabbing the empty bottle. Caroline didn't take her eyes off Will who flashed Emily a half-smile.

'I'll be with you there now in just a sec,' the barmaid said. Did her glance linger a fraction longer than normal?

'Same again?' she asked, approaching Emily.

Emily handed her the empty bottle. 'Thanks.'

'So, are ya bored yet?' She placed a fresh bottle of Merlot on the bar.

'Sorry?'

'Of being the third wheel with the pair of them. I've been keeping an eye.'

Emily blushed a little. 'You have?'

'I like to know what's going on, like. Sure, you wouldn't believe the number of times I've had to step in when some pushy fecker doesn't take no for an answer.'

When she smiled, she had the same creases at the sides of her nose as Max. Emily looked over her shoulder. The inches between Caroline and Will seemed smaller from this distance. She turned back and glanced at the barmaid's name tag. No, she wasn't going to even try to say 'Órfhlaith'. She'd struggle sober, and she'd had half a bottle of wine.

'It's pronounced Orla,' the barmaid said, locking eyes with Emily. 'And look, you're more than welcome to sit up here at the bar with me, if you want to give those two some privacy.'

Emily held Órfhlaith's gaze. 'I might do that,' she said.

'You stay there. I'll take over the bottle, and we'll leave them to it.'

Órfhlaith refilled Emily's glass and stepped out from behind the bar. She *was* wearing Docs.


By the time Emily reached the bottom of her glass of wine, Caroline and Will had left without a word. She didn't like to think about where they had probably gone, but she was glad she wasn't in the room next door to Will's. The wine sat heavily in her stomach; she probably should have eaten. Órfhlaith was wiping down the bar and she leant close to Emily's ear.

'I'll be closing up in half an hour, if you wanted to hang around?' The invitation sparkled in Órfhlaith's brown eyes.

Emily's pulse quickened. 'Yeah, alright.'

Órfhlaith winked. Just like Max. Why should Will have all the fun? Not that Emily wanted anything like that from him. She would *not* be going all gooey eyed over him ever again. Caroline was welcome to him. But it had been a while since she'd been chatted up by someone. There was no harm in her ego getting a little boost, while at the same time proving to Will Prentice that he wasn't the only one who could turn heads.

# THIRTY-SIX

## VIOLET

January 1944

It was bitterly cold and pitch black as I made my way down the winding driveway from Clifftop Cottage. At first, I stopped every couple of feet and looked back, but then I gave up expecting Zeyla to come running after me. How was it possible to survive this much pain? I could have quite happily laid down in the ditch running alongside the road into Dovecote and let nature take its course.

Beneath the crushing sadness, I was angry. How dare Zeyla treat me this way? I may have been poorer than a church mouse, but I still didn't deserve this. To be cast aside the minute a man with money appeared and took an interest made my blood boil. I wasn't even that badly off. I'd managed to keep my job at Harrington's Bookshop, and I had saved up enough to get Zeyla and I out of Dovecote. But this had forced my old insecurity to resurface – I wasn't good enough for her.

As I crossed Dovecote's railway bridge, I paused and looked over the side, keeping my torch shielded with the sleeve of my coat. The station was deserted, even though it wasn't that late and there were still a few trains shuttling to Brighton before the last one of the night. People were finding fewer reasons to venture out these days. It was almost as if everyone was too tired to keep their spirits up any more. The morsels of good news filtering through from the rest of Europe were mere crumbs, and not enough to nourish and provide encouragement.

The High Street was looking rather sorry for itself too. Every second shop had a sign in the window letting customers know what they didn't have, and warning that only registered customers were allowed to queue. I knew the queues well and frequently watched them grow from the bookshop window, only to see the housewives of Dovecote disperse, disappointment etched on their tired faces, as word filtered down the line that whatever they were queuing for had run out. At Harrington's, we were also struggling to meet demand. The paper shortage meant that fewer new books were being published, and they were selling out quicker. A popular book could sell out within a couple of days. But Mrs Harrington's idea to branch out into second-hand books was proving to be inspired. I was glad that we were the only shop in town that people enjoyed coming to. More than one customer had recently remarked to me that as long as they had a good book, they could get through the dark winter evenings.

On the opposite corner of Blythe Avenue to Harrington's Bookshop was The Royal Oak. I shivered as another gust of cold sea wind stung my cheeks. I'd never ventured into a pub on my own. I'd been into a pub in Brighton with Hugo once but as soon as the landlord realised we were underage, he'd turfed us out. The closest I'd been to the inside of The Royal Oak was the air raid shelter in the cellar. My stomach flipped over. The air raid shelter where I'd first properly met Zeyla. Stuffing my hands into my pockets to stop them freezing, I fumbled a few loose coins as I crossed the High Street. I avoided glancing down Blythe Avenue and being reminded of the evening it had been filled with smoke and flame. Maybe a tot of sherry would help keep out the cold and the memories.

I changed my mind several times as I navigated the unfamiliar system of external and internal doors, designed for the blackout of course. I had expected to find the pub full of people but, apart from Derek behind the bar, there were only a few old men at a table in the corner, a man and a woman in mended clothes huddled together by the roaring fire, and one man in uniform at the bar.

I approached the bar gingerly. Only when Derek gave me a nod of his bald head did I manage to exhale.

'Hello, Violet,' Derek said, stubbing out his cigarette and lighting a replacement. 'What brings you in here? We don't usually see you unless the siren's blaring. Need something to warm you up?' There was a hint of concern in his eyes, and I remembered I'd come out without washing my face after all that crying. I must have looked quite a state.

I nodded. 'Small sherry, please, Derek. Thanks.'

I was vaguely aware of the man in uniform turning towards me and I caught a faint smell of Imperial Leather soap. I was about to move away when he spoke.

'Violet?'

I'd not heard that voice in years.

'Hugo?'

He grabbed me in a bear hug and held on tight for a long time, while I sobbed into his shoulder. He laughed into my hair. It was the loveliest sound in the world. Eventually he let go and took a step backwards, his hands still on my arms.

'Let me look at you,' he said, shaking his head. 'I didn't think it would be possible but you're more beautiful than I remember.'

'Oh, I have missed you so much,' I said, wiping my eyes and trying to steady my breath. The pink scar above his left eyebrow was new and his dark hair was far more tamed than it had ever been. 'I can't quite believe it's you. All grown up and in uniform. Where's my Hugo with the mismatched socks and grazed knees? And what are you doing in Dovecote, anyway?'

He drew a deep breath, and a dark shadow passed across his face. The tiredness in his eyes aged him. He nodded towards a table, and we sat down.

He lit a cigarette. His hand was shaking slightly. 'Something big is coming, Vi. I don't know what and I don't know when. They're sending us on strange training camps, and there's a peculiar atmosphere around.' His voice was low, and I leant in to hear him. 'They've got us training in water and all sorts. And next month, we're being moved down to the south coast. There must be something on the horizon.' He rubbed his eyes. 'There was an accident at one of the training camps, Vi. One of my chaps died. He was from Dovecote. I've just been to visit his parents and return his personal things to them.' His voice cracked and I reached across the table and took his hand in mine. When I squeezed his hand, he gave me a small smile. 'But let's not dwell on that. God, Vi, it's so good to see you. Letters aren't the same.'

'I have to say, Hugo, your timing is impeccable.'

'I figured something must be up for you to be hanging around a boozer.' He squeezed my hand this time. 'Tell me all about it.'

And I did. I told him all the sad things I hadn't put in my letters because I hadn't wanted him to be upset or worried on my behalf. I told him about Hereford Street, about the boys being evacuated, about Blythe Avenue, and Mum dying. I was getting to Zeyla when Derek politely, but firmly, told us it was time to go.

I shivered as we stepped out into the dark street. A pale moon provided just enough light that we could see each other.

'Oops,' I said, tripping over the edge of the pavement. Luckily Hugo grabbed me before I tumbled into the gutter.

'I think I'd better hold on to you,' he said. I could just about see his grin in the gloom. 'That sherry's gone right to your head.'

I drew a deep breath of salty air, which made my head spin. 'Hmm, you may be right. Where are we going?'

'I think I should take you home,' he said.

I groaned. 'No, not there. Oh Hugo, there's so much more I need to tell you. Let's go to Victoria Park.'

Hugo wrapped his thick army coat around himself a little tighter as he glanced back at the pub. 'Alright, but I'd only go wandering about in the cold and dark for you, Vi.'

The wooden gate of Victoria Park creaked as I opened it. The effects of the sherry were wearing off in the cold of the night. But as my head cleared, the ache in my heart grew. I led Hugo around the allotments and past the bandstand. Why had I come to the place where Zeyla kissed me for the first time? I stood at the bench but couldn't sit down.

'You're right. Hugo, it's too cold.'

He put his arms around me. 'Look, I wouldn't normally suggest this to a lady but why don't you come back to my room. I'm staying at The Royal Oak.'

I was too weary to be shocked by his suggestion; I simply nodded, and Hugo took my hand and led me back the way we'd come.

In his warm, cosy room above the pub, Hugo removed the tops off two bottles of beer he'd wheedled out of Derek, as I crept unseen up the stairs, and handed me one. I curled up on the narrow bed, my feet tucked under me and leant against the wall. I drew a deep breath and told him all about Zeyla.

By the time I stopped speaking, the beer bottles were empty, and we were lying on the bed, my head on Hugo's chest and his arm around my shoulders. It was nice to be held. It occurred to me that Zeyla had never held me when we'd lain together. It had always been me with my arm around her while she rested her head on me. I needed to be the one being held tonight.

'You know the worst of it all, Hugo?'

'What's that, Vi?'

'I blame myself.' I raised my head to look at Hugo. He was frowning. 'Not for what she's done, I don't think I could have done anything that would have prevented that. But for believing that we would be together forever. For thinking that it didn't matter that we were from different worlds, that our love could erase our differences, or overcome whatever obstacles life put in our path. I blame myself for thinking I was good enough for her.'

Hugo sat up and looked me right in the eyes. 'I'm not having that, Vi. Not for one second. You listen to me.' He put a hand gently to my cheek. I leant into his touch. 'You are an amazing woman. You're strong, capable, a fighter, and a survivor. You're independent and so, so brave. But more than that, you are smart, and caring, and kind, and honest, and devastatingly beautiful. And all of that is worth a thousand new dresses or bottles of black-market champagne. You're not equal to Zeyla, you're better than her. There are many men, and women, who would give their right arm to have the love of a woman like you, me included. If Zeyla can't see that, then she's a fool.'

I tried to tear my eyes away, but I couldn't. I stared back at him. I put my hand over his, suddenly needing to touch him. Before I could second-guess what every fibre of my being was begging me to do, I kissed him.

# THIRTY-SEVEN

## EMILY

August 2016

The early morning sea breeze on Glencaragh's sandy beach whipped Emily's hair around her face and made her eyes water. At least she could claim it was the wind and not tears of frustration and self-pity. It had been going well with Órfhlaith the night before, until Emily blurted out how much she reminded her of Max and then promptly burst out ugly crying. Poor Órfhlaith, all she could do was pat Emily on the back, lie her down in the bed, and slip quietly out the door. It was a good job Emily couldn't afford to stay in Loughnacran House; at least she'd never have to see Órfhlaith again. Órfhlaith was probably just as relieved about that.

Once again, the morning was cloudy, but there were already blue cracks appearing in the fluffy blanket across the sky. By lunchtime, the sun would be splitting the pavements. By three o'clock she'd be back in the ridiculous convertible heading to the airport, the long weekend over. And she was no closer to finding out what happened to Violet's love affair or seeing any portraits.

The shrieks of the circling seagulls echoed mockingly off

the hills. At least Will would have fond memories of his weekend. That was if he remembered his one-night stands at all. Her stomach churned. Maybe he forgot their names the minute he snuck from their beds. And if that was the case, how could she expect him to remember the night they shared fifteen years ago?

Emily was standing, arms folded, looking out over the undulating water to the horizon. The force of the Atlantic was evident in the white tips of the distant waves. The sound of a throat being cleared made her turn around.

'Here you are,' Will said, pushing up the sleeves of this navy summer jumper. Emily looked away from the sight of his bare forearms. 'I've been looking all over for you. I got your bag from reception and put it in the car, is that okay?'

Emily shrugged, looking back out to sea.

'Fine. Emily, I have been trying to get through to you ever since you turned up again in Dovecote. And yet no matter what I do, I'm getting nothing but hostility back. I get the impression you don't like me very much, but I'll be damned if I can work out why. Seriously, what have I done to upset you? Is this about Aoife, still?'

Emily dragged her eyes away from the grey horizon and slowly turned towards Will.

'You have to ask?'

'Well, yes, because I'm stumped. And I don't want it to be like this, I'd like us to be friends. I don't see why we can't.'

Emily raised an eyebrow.

'Clearly there is a reason, then. You're going to have to spell it out for me, Emily, because I don't have the first clue about what is going on here.'

'Alright, I'll spell it out for you. You've disappointed me.'

'How?'

'I'd hoped you might have grown out of using women to get what you want before ditching them. I guess when you're so used to getting your own way, you don't want to change.'

'This *is* about Aoife.' He rolled his eyes.

'It's not about Aoife, or Caroline.'

Will scrunched up his face in confusion. 'Wait, what?'

'This is about you and me, Will. You, me, and the summer of 2001.' Her voice was a whisper on the wind. Had she even said the words out loud?

'Hang on. All of this,' he gestured towards her, sweeping his hand around in a wide circle, 'is about something that happened fifteen years ago?'

The words bubbled up inside Emily, finally sensing an opportunity to break free from the prison in which she'd been keeping them. Once she started, she wouldn't be able to stop, but the urge to let it all out was too great.

'For three summers, I worshipped you while you laughed at me, taunted me, downright bullied me, and your brother for good measure. And then suddenly it changed. One day you were nice to me. You invited me to hang out with you and your friends.'

Will crossed his arms but didn't say anything. He had the look of someone who knew that the safest thing to do was to keep quiet.

'And I thought all my Christmases had come at once. Will Prentice, the most popular boy in town, wanted to spend time with *me*. Could he actually *like* me? I was madly in love with him and finally he was being nice to me. Do you have any idea how confused yet elated that made me feel?'

Again, Will remained silent. He tilted his head slightly to one side as though recognising it was a rhetorical question.

'And then a miracle happened. Not only did you like me, you *liked* me. Or so I thought.' Her voice cracked. She would not cry in front of him. She'd cried over him many, many times, but she would never let him see her tears. 'I know you remember that night. I can see it in your face that you remember the summer house, and what we did there. But do you remember the following day, when you asked me to meet you in the graveyard behind the church? Do you remember that it was raining? Do you remember what you said to me?'

Will unfolded his arms and stuffed his hands into his pockets. 'Not exactly. I think I said something about how you were nice, and I liked you, but we weren't going to be seeing each other again until the following summer so...' His voice faded out as Emily shook her head.

'If only you had been that eloquent at almost seventeen years old. I was never a confident child, and that lack of self-confidence only magnified as a teenager. What you said to me that day tore apart what little shred of self-esteem I had. I wasn't good enough for you. I would never be good enough for anyone. I waited for hours for you and when you finally turned up with all your mates you laughed at me and said I was "a nobody from a council estate".' The dam broke, and half a lifetime of hurt and pain gushed out in sobs. 'That was what you called me. And I have been hearing your voice in my head saying it over and over for fifteen years,' she croaked through the tears. She dropped her eyes. 'I loved you. And you broke not only my heart, but my spirit.'

He stood there, on the beach, frowning and blinking at her. She wiped her eyes and walked away down the beach. She heard a faint sound. It might have been 'I'm sorry'. Or it might have been the moan of the wind through the dunes. She didn't look back.

# THIRTY-EIGHT

## EMILY

August 2016

Will was not going to come after her. Emily had been sitting on the sand amongst the marram grass for long enough to make that painfully obvious. The sand in her shoes was gritty and abrasive against her skin as she clambered down the landward side of the dunes towards the car park.

'Emily?'

Her head jerked up at the call of her name and she looked around for the source. She found it sitting at a shaded table outside Sandy's café. Today's kaftan was the same neon pink colour as the café's sign, printed with giant orange and yellow daisies. Zeyla was wearing matching orange daisy earrings. Her lipstick was the same shade as her dress. It was a glorious outfit and Emily smiled at herself. She was going to get old like Zeyla: loudly and colourfully.

'Join me,' Zeyla said, nodding to the empty chair on the opposite side of the table. It was more of an order than an invitation, and Emily sat down. Zeyla eyed Emily's handbag as she put it down by her feet. The diary would stay in there for now.

'I watched that young man of yours stomping off the beach and into town. He didn't look very happy. In fact, he looked rather shell-shocked. Had a row?'

'I suppose you could call it a row, although I didn't give him the chance to say much. He's not my young man, Zeyla. Once upon a time, I had wanted him to be, but let's just say things were said many years ago that made it quite clear I wasn't good enough for him. It would have been nice to know that before... never mind.'

Zeyla gave Emily a hawk-like look over the top of her teacup that made her bristle slightly.

'No need to be coy with me, dear. I may be old, but I was young once. Shame, he seemed like such a nice chap. We had a lovely chat when he walked Caroline home yesterday evening.'

Emily's mouth dried up. 'He walked Caroline home?'

'Yes. Of course, he's used to places like London and such, where there's a lot more danger. But he insisted on seeing her back safely which was rather kind of him. Don't you think?'

Emily chewed her bottom lip to stop herself from grimacing. But, on the other hand, it had been a natural assumption to make. After all, she'd been right about Aoife.

'Anyway, he came in for a cup of tea and we had a nice chat about Dovecote and the manor. He was quite put out when I explained that when Charles sold the estate, I didn't get a penny. I'd lost touch with the family by then. I hadn't even known they'd died, my own parents. Imagine that. Charles neglected to tell me. Instead, he liquidated everything and took off with the cash. He always was a swine. But he's dead now too. I don't even know if he left a widow or any children. Funny, isn't it, how you can completely lose touch with people? I do seem to make rather a habit of it.'

'Caroline told us what happened with Rupert and how you lost touch with your sons, Philip and George. That must be so hard for you.'

Zeyla laughed. It was a joyously filthy sound. 'Oh, my dear, Caroline told you what *she* knows. There are things I didn't tell her, because I didn't want to upset her or cause any conflict between her and her father. He'll be about seventy-one now. Both Philip and George adored their father, Rupert. And even as small boys they were so like him, serious and fastidious. They both went on to study medicine and became doctors, just like Rupert. I had hoped that at least one of my children might have been a hell-raiser, that would have been quite good fun. But sadly, I got two very well-behaved boys who never got up to even the smallest amount of mischief. Did I love them? Of course, all mothers love their children. I just didn't like them very much.'

She paused, running her finger along the handle of her teacup. 'But perhaps it was the situation I didn't like. I was rather unhappy. Our house can't have been much fun to grow up in. Rupert and I barely spoke to each other, and marital relations weren't exactly, how shall I put it, frequent. Rupert, naturally, had a mistress. And I can't say I blame him. Apparently, they were very much in love. She never married; she was waiting for him to leave me. Once the boys were of an age when they no longer needed their mother, I got out of their way. I made a decision I should have made twenty years earlier.' Zeyla looked at Emily who was caught in her sparkling green eyes. 'You have read the diary, I take it?'

'Yes.'

'Well, then you must understand.'

'Actually, no, I don't. Your diary only goes up to the end of 1943, and from what you wrote then, it seemed that you and Violet were still together, and you were happy. I don't understand what happened between you. How did it end?'

Zeyla put down her teacup and looked around. 'Come back to my house, Emily. Caroline has taken Freddie to see the puffins on Valentia Island. We can talk more freely there.' She raised an eyebrow and tilted her head towards the woman behind the counter. 'Bridget hears everything and is as much good at keeping things to herself as a colander is at holding water.'

It was Emily's turn to laugh. 'Ah yes, sounds like Janice who owns one of the cafés in Dovecote. She's a public broadcast system of her own.'

Zeyla wrapped her hand around Emily's elbow as they walked slowly down the road towards the brightly painted stone cottages along the seafront.

'I do apologise for walking out so abruptly yesterday, Emily. You must forgive me. It was quite a shock to see my diary again after so many years.'

'No, I should be the one apologising. I shouldn't have shown it to you like that, not without some sort of warning.'

'It's a good job I've got a very strong heart.'

If only Emily could say the same. Her heart seemed to have an uncanny ability to fracture easily and stay broken for years.

# THIRTY-NINE
## VIOLET

January 1944

It was late in the morning. There was a pinprick hole in the blackout blind that covered the small window in the room above The Royal Oak. It allowed a thin shaft of weak winter sunlight to fall across the bed. I laid still, trying not to breathe too loudly for fear of waking Hugo. The narrowness of the bed forced us close together. His arm was draped over my waist and our bare legs were tangled. The heat from his body more than made up for the chill in the room. I sighed softly, the weight of his arm rising and falling with my breath. There was no way I could slip from the bed without waking him. I wanted to stay, but I had to leave.

'Don't go.'

I turned from the mirror in which I was desperately trying to do something with my hair, without the aid of a brush or comb.

'How long have you been watching me?' I asked. It was impossible to be angry at him, especially when his hair was adorably tousled. 'I have to go, Hugo.'

'I'm sorry, Vi. I should never, we should never have...' His sleep-thickened voice faded away and he rubbed his eyes.

I drew a deep breath and sat down on the bed. The sheet slipped, revealing more than just his broad chest, and I looked away. He ran his finger down my arm, his warmth penetrating the sleeve of my cardigan. I looked up at him again.

'I'm not sorry,' I said. And I meant it.

He frowned, but it was a confused frown, not an angry one. 'But I thought you didn't...'

'So did I.'

'Oh.'

I sighed. 'I don't know what it means, Hugo.' I gave him a weak smile. 'I'm as confused as you are, believe me. Which is why I need to go. I need time and space to think.'

Hugo nodded. 'I understand. I meant what I said last night. When I said I love you.'

I bit my lip. 'I know you do.' I stood and picked up my coat from the back of the chair. 'How long are you around for?'

'A week. Then the regiment are moving down to Portsmouth for more training.' He reached out a hand. I took it. 'Come with me. Mum and Dad have decamped to my grandmother's place in Aberdeen, so I'm going to bed down in their flat for the week. Come back home to Brighton with me.'

'I can't, Hugo. For many reasons.'

He kissed my hand. 'I'll be getting the two o'clock train if you change your mind.'

'Be careful, please. I couldn't bear to lose you.'

He winked, and I crossed the room and let myself out.


Out in the High Street, I pulled my coat around me and headed for The Promenade. I was so confused. I never thought I would do that. But I had, and I'd liked it. It was different, of course, to how it was with Zeyla, but still.

'Oh God,' I muttered to myself. 'Why me? Why can't life be straightforward?' The sea wind took my questions and flung them out over the dark, choppy water. The only response came in the form of a squawk from a circling seagull. My stomach was a writhing mass as I walked down Beachfront Road and climbed the steep steps up the cliff towards Clifftop Cottage. How was I going to explain it to her, when I didn't understand it myself?

It threw me off guard to find Zeyla standing at the bookshelves by the fireplace in the sitting room of Clifftop Cottage. Her hand was resting on my copy of *Orlando*.

'Goodness.' I exclaimed. 'You startled me.'

Zeyla was still wearing her party dress, although it was creased and crumpled, presumably from where she'd fallen asleep on the couch. Her hair was in disarray. She ran to me and grabbed my arms.

'Where have you been all night? I've been worried sick.'

I avoided her gaze. 'I stayed with a friend.' A half-truth was better than a lie.

She stroked my face. 'I'm glad you're back. Funny, isn't it? The first time I've stayed all night at Clifftop Cottage, and you weren't here.' She ran a finger across my lips, and I fought against the desire that rose from deep in my belly. 'Would it help if I said again that I'm sorry?'

I let out a deep sigh full of frustration, sadness, and longing. 'I know you are, and I do understand. But I wish you'd been honest with me from the start. I wish you'd told me this was how it would end.'

'But it doesn't have to end, Vi,' Zeyla said, cupping my chin in her fingers. 'I've been thinking, and I have an idea.'

I raised my eyebrows but held my tongue.

'What if you came to live with me?'

'What on earth are you talking about?' I asked.

'As a married woman, I shall need a household, and you could be part of it. Just think, we could see each other every day and Rupert will be working long hours. When he's not there...'

I jerked my head out of her grasp and stared at her. Then from nowhere I started laughing.

'You cannot be serious?'

'Why not, Vi? It would be so lovely to have you around.'

'To clean and tidy your house, or wash your clothes, all while being your dirty little secret. Is this something all rich people dream of? Having a love affair with one of the servants?' My laughter died. 'Go to hell, Zeyla.'

'Vi,' she gasped, her hand flying to her heaving chest.

'I mean it, Zeyla. I am not going to be anyone's secret. I am worth more than that. I am deserving of respect and care and love, and I will not be anyone's bit on the side.'

She started to cry. If only I could believe her tears were genuine.

'But I shall hate every minute of being with him. I will do what I must as a wife, but I will need you. I'll need you to love me, to touch me the way you do, to care about me, to make me happy. You know what *he's* going to want to do to me, don't you?'

Oh, I knew.

'Maybe you'll find it's not so bad. You might even enjoy it.'

'How can you say that? It's revolting. The thought of it. I can't even bear to think about it.' She turned away and paced the rug in front of the fire. It was terribly threadbare, perhaps it was time to throw it away. 'I know there are some people who can quite happily be with men or women, and that's jolly good for them, but I'm not one of them. I don't even want other women. I only want *you*.'

Could that be it? Was I one of *those* people? What if I was? But what did it mean? I couldn't think with Zeyla pacing the sitting room.

'Oh Zeyla, if that were true then you'd choose me, wouldn't you?' My bottom lip started to tremble. It was coming to an end. 'But you won't choose me. And you never will.' The tears that came were soft and silent as the truth shone as brightly as the sun.

'I love you,' Zeyla whimpered.

I crossed the room and gave her a soft kiss on the forehead. Our tears mingled and I leant my head against hers.

'No, Zeyla. You love being the centre of someone's attention. Go and be Rupert's. Have your grand house in Oxford, be an upstanding doctor's wife, a pillar of the community, and all-round good egg. And you never know, maybe it won't be as bad as you think.'

'It shall be horrid.'

I drew a deep breath; it was time to tell her. Not because I wanted to hurt her, but because I wasn't ashamed of what I'd done. And I wanted her to know that life can have a funny way of surprising you sometimes.

'I can tell you from experience, Zeyla. It's not. It can actually be rather wonderful and lovely.'

She pulled away sharply. 'But you've not...' She stared at me, aghast, and horrified. I blushed. 'Oh, Violet. How could you?'

'The same way you could, Zeyla. Except, I am being honest with myself. I know what I want, and that is to be someone's choice. I want to be with someone who has the courage to be their true self, and who never makes me feel like I'm not good enough.'

The clock on the wall chimed one o'clock, and I knew what I had to do.

'I'm going to go away for a while, Zeyla. Just a week. To get my head clear and decide what I want my future to be. Don't wait for me. Do what you have to do; what you *want* to do. Make your choice.' But she already had, it was written on her face. She was choosing the easy path. What was I choosing? I kissed her cheek and led her to the door.

'Clifftop Cottage will still be here for you, I'll make sure of it,' Zeyla said, her eyes shining.

'Thank you.'

'I shall think of you all the time,' she said, turning back one last time.

'And I shall never forget you.'

I leant against the closed door and let the tears flow freely down my cheeks. It had been a glorious love affair, and I loved her so much. But it was time for me to love myself too.


I ran down the High Street, my case banging against my leg. It was nearly two o'clock, I *had* to make the train. I threw myself through the station entrance and onto the platform, nearly losing my hat. He turned as I was about to call his name.

'Violet? What are you doing here?'

'I changed my mind. I'm not saying I want to start a love affair with you, Hugo. I can't promise what the next week will bring in that regard. But I need to get away, I need to think. I need to be with my best friend. I need you.'

He took hold of my hand. 'And you will always have me.'

# FORTY

## EMILY

August 2016

'Here we are,' Zeyla said, and they stopped outside the middle cottage. The bright pink and purple of the flowers in the window boxes popped against the yellow walls. Lace curtains hung at the four small windows and the red roof tiles glistened in the sun. A small plaque by the door had *Cois Farraige* inscribed in Celtic script.

'What a pretty cottage,' Emily said, as Zeyla fumbled her key in the front door.

'The name means "Seaside". The original owners obviously took a long time to come up with that. It's old and small, like me.' Zeyla chuckled, eventually managing to turn the key and push open the door. 'When I first saw these houses, they reminded me of the fishermen's cottages along the seafront in Dovecote. They're probably gone now, replaced by luxury flats or something.' She led Emily into a small kitchen. It looked like it had last been decorated in the 1970s. Zeyla even had a free-standing cooker with a grill over the top of the hob. Emily hadn't seen one of those since her Home Economics classes at school.

'They're still there. Will's brother, Harrison, is thinking of buying one of them.'

'Oh, how lovely.' Zeyla paused and then shook her head. 'I'm trying to remember who lived in those cottages back when I lived at the manor. But my memory of it has gone.'

'Can I give you a hand?' Emily asked, as Zeyla fussed around the kitchen.

Zeyla waved away Emily's offer. 'Not at all, dear. I might be...' she paused, holding the lid of the teapot in mid-air, 'ninety-one years of age, but I'm perfectly capable of making a pot of tea.'

'If I may, Zeyla, you look a great deal younger.'

Zeyla glanced over her shoulder. 'Fifty years of sea air and singledom, Emily. That's how to stay young. Avoid men, that would be my advice.'

With a pot of tea and a plate of biscuits on the round table covered with a lace tablecloth, Zeyla settled back in her chair.

'Well, as I'm getting on a bit, I suppose it's about time I told someone my story. And seeing as your great-aunt is the best part of it, I shall tell you. You already know some of it anyway.' She drew a breath. 'I knew from an early age that I was not like other girls. They were always going on about the male film stars they fancied, or about how they were going to get married and have babies. The very idea made me sick. Back in those days, things tended to happen between girls at boarding school; it was a bit of a rite of passage to have the odd fumble or what have you. The others said it was practising for when they found a man. I was not practising for anything. And then, the summer after I left school I met Violet.' Zeyla's eyes misted over, and Emily held her breath.

'I'd met her once, a few years earlier. She'd been drawing outside Brighton train station. I invited her back home for the weekend, as I had a few other girls staying, but she refused. She had to work. She worked hard and from such a young age. Her father had been killed and her mother, I believe, was quite affected mentally so it was left to Violet to keep a roof over their heads. I remember thinking how sad it was that such a beautiful young woman was being trodden on so harshly by the world. Anyway, I digress. You'll have to forgive me, my dear. At my age, rambling does tend to occur.'

Emily smiled softly. 'I don't mind in the slightest, I want to hear everything.'

'It took a while to crack Violet. She was terribly worried about people finding out about her and me. It was only when I had the idea of us meeting at Clifftop Cottage that she let down her guard and let me kiss her. It was the best idea I've ever had. She moved into the cottage after she was bombed out a second time. Her home in Brighton had been destroyed a few years earlier, which was how she ended up in Dovecote in the first place. But a stray bomb during the Brighton Blitz of 1943 landed on Blythe Avenue, where she and her mother were living. Her younger brothers had been evacuated before then. Her mother was tragically killed.'

Emily's stomach contracted, remembering what Terry had said about the worries over unexploded bombs. Was the extension being built where Emily's great-grandmother had been killed? A shiver ran down her spine.

'Violet was only spared because she'd been at Clifftop Cottage, making love to me all afternoon.'

There was a slight pink tinge to Zeyla's cheeks and Emily failed to supress a grin.

'Yes, alright, you can stop grinning at me. We were young and we fancied each other, what did you expect us to be doing? Playing tiddlywinks?'

Emily snorted. 'Zeyla, I barely know you, but I do love you already.'

'Anyway, 1943 you know about from my diary. All the

wonderful times Violet and I spent together. I probably wrote about the tea dance, didn't I?'

'Yes, you did.'

'That was a magical day. If only our whole lives could have been like that. It makes me so happy when I see gay people out and about, openly holding hands. It wasn't like that in those days. Sex between men was illegal, and between women it was hushed up, swept under the carpet. The general approach was that it was best not to mention it, otherwise all the women would leave their husbands and shack-up with their female friends. It was because of that attitude that I couldn't tell my parents I was a lesbian at the time. And because they didn't know, they expected me to marry.'

Zeyla picked up a ginger nut biscuit and put it down on her saucer. Emily kept still and quiet so as not to derail Zeyla's train of thought.

'So, Rupert enters the story. Our fathers were old acquaintances. Even before Rupert and I met, Mother had decided he was the one she'd offload me on. Unfortunately, Rupert took rather a liking to me. I tried to put him off. But Mother was having none of it. My parents threw a party for my nineteenth birthday in January 1944. We were in the middle of the war; it was ridiculous, and preposterous. I was embarrassed by the whole fuss, but I was also a vain, young creature. When I look back, I can see how much I loved being the centre of attention and having a fuss made of me. Of course, what I should have been happy with was being the centre of Violet's attention, but I was also stupid.' She shook her head sadly.

'That day, Mother presented me with a new ballgown. I should have known something was afoot then. While she was doing my hair, she said that Rupert was going to ask me to marry him, and if I knew what was good for me, and for the family, I would say yes. The other thing I was, besides vain and stupid, was a coward. I loved Violet; I knew I did. I told myself that I would do anything to be with her, but when push came to shove, I didn't. I folded and accepted Rupert's proposal.

'I had intended to keep it secret from Violet, to break it to her gently, but she unfortunately witnessed the moment I said yes. And that was when I lost her. We had a row, there were lots of tears, and she stormed out of the cottage. She was gone all night. I sat there, trying to think of a way that I could marry Rupert without having to give up Violet.

'The next morning when Violet came home, there was something different about her. She was glowing. She looked strong and certain, like she'd blossomed overnight. I tried to convince her that we could still see each other in secret. I even suggested she come to Oxford with me as a member of my household so we could keep seeing each other. That did not go down well.'

'No, I can imagine. No one likes being reminded that they're from a different social class to the person they love.' Emily's chest ached as Will's words to her on that rainy day fifteen years ago reverberated in her head.

Zeyla looked down at her wrinkled hands. 'I know, and I made such a mess of it. Violet often asked whether I was ashamed of her being a working-class woman. I said I wasn't, but a part of me must have been. I was certainly afraid of losing the lifestyle I had. Vain, selfish, and stupid I chose Rupert's money over Violet's love. I was a coward when I should have stood up for myself and the woman I loved.'

'Oh Zeyla, you were stuck in a difficult situation. At that time, did you really have a choice as a young woman?'

'One thing I have learnt in all my years is that you *always* have a choice. It may not be an easy one, it may look like you don't, but you do.'

'So, what happened?'

'Violet said she was going away for a week. She hinted that she had met someone, a man, that night. I don't know whether she was going away with him, or on her own. I didn't ask. Part of me didn't want to know. The thought of being married to Rupert, and what that would entail, filled me with such dread and horror. I couldn't allow myself to think that Violet might be attracted to men, may enjoy doing things with them. That she might be what we'd refer to today as bisexual.'

There was too much going on in Emily's head for her to be able to say anything, so she didn't. But, there was a slight shift, as though something heavy had been lifted from her shoulders. The pieces of the puzzle were finally beginning to fit and reveal the full picture.

'She tried to tell me I shouldn't worry and that things with Rupert might not be as bad as I feared. But anyway, she went away leaving me to decide for once and for all what I wanted my life to be. She went away for a week but didn't come back for over four months. The next time I saw her, she was standing at the bottom of the driveway up to Clifftop Cottage and I was in the back of Father's motor car being driven to the church to marry Rupert. She looked more beautiful than ever that day. She caught my eye, but I had to look away. It hurt too much to look at her.' She pulled a cotton handkerchief from the pocket of her kaftan and wiped her eyes. 'Gosh, look at me, even after all these years, I still get emotional over it. I don't ever cry when I think about Rupert.'

'That's because you never loved him. Like you said in the letter you sent to your mother.'

'Oh Lord, I'd forgotten about that letter.'

'Did she ever reply?'

Zeyla shook her head, and her daisy earrings jangled. 'No, she never did. I didn't hear from any of them again.'

Emily scrunched up her nose. 'But she kept your letter. Will found it in a box that had been left in the library archives at Dovecote Manor. It's marked with what look like tear stains.'

Zeyla laughed loudly. 'My mother? Crying? Over me? I doubt it.'

'I wouldn't be so sure. She must have loved you, and probably missed you,' Emily said with a reassuring smile. 'There's one thing I don't understand. How did your diary end up at Clifftop Cottage?'

'I hid it there. Once I'd committed to marrying Rupert, I couldn't risk him or my mother finding the diary in which I'd written so much about Violet. I could have burned it, I suppose, but there was too much beauty in it.'

'I'm rather glad you didn't.'

'I snuck home that night, after the row, and retrieved it. I slipped it onto the bookshelf beside the fireplace. I think I wanted Violet to find it and read it so she would know that I *did* love her. I wonder if she ever did.'

'Oh, I think so. Will and I found it locked in the drawer of her writing desk.'

'Not the old Mackintosh-style desk?'

Emily smiled. 'Yes.'

'I loved that desk. Violet did too.'

'She must have found your diary at some point and put it in the desk drawer. There was also a sketchbook with it.'

Zeyla locked her eyes on Emily. It was an intense stare, and a slight shudder worked its way down her back. Emily reached for her bag and pulled out the sketchbook. Zeyla didn't look at it.

'I know she drew you, Zeyla. You wrote about it in your diary.'

'She never showed me what she drew,' Zeyla whispered, finally breaking the unnerving eye contact and looking at the book. Emily opened it at the first page of the sketches of Zeyla and handed it over. Zeyla said nothing as she traced a bony finger across the page.

'Good God, I was so young,' she breathed.

Emily held her breath as Zeyla turned over the page.

'Oh, my.'

'That's Hugo, Zeyla. That's the man Violet married and lived very happily with for nearly fifty years.'

'Did you know him?'

'No, he'd died a few years before I started spending summer holidays in Dovecote with Violet.'

'Even *I* can appreciate he was a handsome chap.' Zeyla laughed. 'Oh Emily, I am glad she was happy.'

'I'm sure she would have wanted you to be happy too.'

'I was, eventually. Once I grew a backbone and decided to stand up for myself, and to live as me.'

'Violet turned those sketches of Hugo into portraits. I found them in her studio, the little shed next to Clifftop Cottage. Did she turn the drawings of you into paintings too?'

Zeyla glanced down at the floor, a pink tinge rising on her pale cheeks. When she looked back up, there was steel in her green eyes.

'Not that I know of.'

Emily pursed her lips. Did she believe her? Absolutely not. But what could she do?

'There's a small museum in Dovecote, that opened in the seventies. The people who run it want to expand it and build a replica of the World War Two air raid shelter that was in the basement of the pub, The Royal Oak.'

There was a flicker of recognition in Zeyla's eyes.

'But they need money. Violet became quite an accomplished artist and moderately well known. There was a lot of buzz around her work in the sixties and seventies, and a long-standing rumour surfaced in the late seventies that there were some never-before-seen portraits she painted. We're holding an exhibition of her work to raise money for the building project. I found the portraits of Hugo. If there *were* others, they would be hugely helpful at generating interest in the exhibition, and in turn, funds for the museum.'

'The air raid shelter?' Zeyla's voice was barely a whisper. 'I remember.'

'Are you sure Violet didn't paint your portrait, Zeyla?'

The clock on the wall chimed three o'clock.

'I have to go, Zeyla. You know my address, if there is anything you want to send me.' Emily drew a breath and softened. 'Thank you,' she said, placing a hand on Zeyla's. 'Thank you for telling me all about you and Violet, and for not burning your diary. I can't tell you how much it means to me to hear that she loved you; how important it is to me that she was who she was, that she loved who she loved. Because it means she was like me. And we all want to know there are people like us, don't we?'

Zeyla squeezed Emily's hand. 'Did you ever tell her that you're bi?'

'No, I didn't work it out until I was older, and by then my parents had split up and I'd lost contact with her. It seems I have a habit of doing that too.'

'I'm sure she would be proud of you.'

'I hope so.'

Zeyla got up and wrapped Emily in a hug. Emily hugged back, careful not to apply too much pressure to the woman's old bones.

'I'm glad I met you, Emily. Maybe we'll see each other again some time?'

'I'd like that,' Emily said, sniffing back the tears that gathered in her eyes. 'In the meantime, I have some awkward hours ahead.'

'With Will?'

'Yeah.' Emily's stomach twisted itself into a knot.

'Be what I wasn't, Emily. Be brave. And be honest. With him, but most importantly with yourself.'

. . .

As Emily approached the hotel, her stomach sank, Will's hire car was gone. She stepped into the entrance hall.

The raven-haired receptionist gave her a wave. 'Ah, there you are, Miss Carmichael. I was about to give you a ring. Mr Prentice has asked me to pass on his apologies, but he's had to get the earlier flight. He's paid for a taxi to take you to the airport. It'll be here any minute. Go on in and sit down at the bar, I'll give you a shout when it's here.'

Emily glanced into the bar. Órfhlaith was on duty.

'Um, thanks. I think I'd rather enjoy my last few minutes in your garden.'

The woman smiled pleasantly. 'Grand. That's no bother at all, sure. You'll be able to see the taxi from out there anyway.'

Emily left her suitcase by the hotel door and made her way down the springy path to the edge of the lake, her head buzzing with everything she'd learnt. Violet had loved Zeyla *and* Hugo. Zeyla had broken Violet's heart, but Emily couldn't hold that against her, not after hearing what Zeyla had been through. That Violet allowed herself to fall in love again was proof of her resilience and bravery. Would Emily ever be that brave? Will entered her mind, but she brushed the thought of him away. He'd rather run away than face up to what he'd done. Allowing even a shred of feeling for him to creep into her heart wasn't bravery. It was stupidity.

# FORTY-ONE
## VIOLET

January 1944

I had never seen Brighton so busy, not even the previous month when Zeyla and I came for the tea dance. My heart fluttered at the memory. Hugo and I had to fight our way through a throng of uniforms to get out of the train station.

'See, Vi,' Hugo said, taking my hand and leading me away from the crowd. 'Something's coming. Why else would there be so many troops around?' He grinned, nodding at a group of young men horsing around under the glass and cast-iron canopy at the station entrance. 'The Americans are here.'

I glanced over my shoulder as one of the American soldiers looked at us and caught my eye. There was a hint of amusement in his eyes, and a rakish, assured confidence in the wink he gave me. I turned away. I'd take Hugo's soft smile over a smirk like that any day.

Despite what I'd said on the Dovecote station platform about this not being about me and him, the moment the door of the flat above his parents' former grocery shop closed behind us, we fell into each other's arms. Was I using him to erase the memory of Zeyla's touch? Possibly. Was he using me as a release of tension and anxiety before rejoining his regiment? Undoubtedly. But we both knew it, that was the thing.

He lit a cigarette and laid back against the headboard, his arm around me as I rested against his shoulder.

'What do you want to do, after all of this is over?' I asked, my voice soft and quiet.

He took a long drag of his cigarette and puffed out the smoke into the small, darkened room.

'We shouldn't think too far ahead, Vi. I may not make it back and—'

I lifted my head sharply. 'No, I refuse to think of that.' I laid back down and drew lazy circles through his chest hair with my finger. 'Let's assume you survive. I can't bear to think of a world where you don't.'

'Alright, you always were a dreamer. What do I want to do?' He stroked my arm. 'I'm being trained to kill, Violet. We're at war and I'm going to have to kill other human beings. I wish it were different, but that's the reality. So, when this madness is over, I only want to grow and nurture. Maybe I could be a gardener?' He paused for a moment. 'Yes, a gardener. I'll grow roses. I'll make you a rose garden, Vi.'

A large tear rolled from my eye and landed on his skin.

'What about you, Vi? What do you want from life?'

I thought about it for a moment. 'Safety and love. And to paint. I want to be a proper artist, Hugo. I want to distil all the good there is in the world into a painting. I want to share the joy I find in a view or a place or a thing.'

Outside the window, the short day came to a grey end, but

in that little room lying safe in Hugo's embrace, I glowed with the brightness of a thousand suns.

'Don't move,' I said, getting up and wrapping a blanket around my bare shoulders. I pulled the curtains and flicked on the light. From my bag, I fetched my sketchbook and a charcoal pencil. The cigarette drooped from Hugo's lips and his eyelids were heavy. But it was the way he was looking at me that I wanted to capture. There was a sultry, smouldering look in his eyes. It would come across much better in oils, but charcoal was all I had to hand.

'Damn it, Vi,' he murmured, a soft smirk pulling at his lips. 'You looking at me like that is making me quite unnecessary.'

I smirked back from behind my sketchbook. 'You'll have to control yourself.' All I got in return was a low growl. I wouldn't keep him waiting long.

# FORTY-TWO

## EMILY

August 2016

Emily dragged her suitcase up the last stretch of steep driveway to Clifftop Cottage, her shoulder protesting as the wheels caught on the gravel. The hinges of the sage-green gate creaked slightly as she pushed it open; they needed a squirt of oil. The climbing roses trailing over the porch roof were in full bloom, the dusty pink flowers giving off a heady scent. She ran her hand over the lion's head knocker as she slipped her key into the lock. Emily left her suitcase at the bottom of the stairs and sank into her sofa with a groan. It was good be home.

'Hi, Hugo,' she said to the portraits sitting on the mantlepiece. Hugo brooded at her.

She went to the shelves on the far side of the fireplace. What must Violet have thought when she'd found Zeyla's diary just sat there amongst the novels and gardening books? Her finger came to a stop on the worn and aged orange and cream banded spine of *Orlando* by Virginia Woolf. Will flitted through her mind. Had he come back to Dovecote, or was he hiding himself away in London?

She was too tired to care. All she wanted to do was pour a glass of wine and slip into a hot bath in her own bathroom.

The beep of her mobile disturbed the peace and quiet of the cottage.

*Are you home yet? Will sent Sue a text to say he got back to London hours ago. Is everything okay? Xx*

She didn't even have the energy for Gio tonight.

*I'm fine, thanks. Just got home and I'm shattered. I'll call you tomorrow. X*

The following evening, Emily waited for Gio at Dovecote station. She sank into his embrace, letting his firm chest absorb all her mixed emotions about the long weekend in County Kerry.

'Yes, that's all very interesting, darling,' Gio said, as they sat on the empty beach, and she recounted everything Zeyla had told her about Violet. He picked up a flat stone and rubbed it between his thumb and forefinger. 'But what about you and Will?'

'It was fine,' Emily replied, staring out at the lighthouse on the headland. The setting sun was reflecting off the white paint, making it glow a brilliant orange. 'But he's so infuriating, the way he loves to show off all the time. You should have seen the car he rented. It was ridiculous, and it just sat outside the hotel all weekend. And the hotel, talk about luxury. Honestly, it was almost embarrassing.'

Gio rolled his eyes. 'I don't see a problem, Em. He booked a nice hotel, hired a nice car. So what?'

'Don't you see, Gio? He only did it to remind me how much better he considers himself to be to everyone, especially to me.'

He put down the stone and took Emily's hand in his. 'You don't think maybe you're projecting a little bit?'

'Since when did you become a psychologist?'

'Well, when you've been in therapy as long as I have, it kind of rubs off.'

Emily raised an eyebrow. A while ago, Gio had confided in her that he'd been seeing a therapist but had never said any more about it. He was looking at her intently, his dark brown eyes seeing deep into her soul.

'I know Will said a hurtful thing to you a long time ago. But you've internalised it and now you think it's true. So, when someone does something nice for you, you can't see it for what it is. You don't trust kindness because you don't think you deserve it. All the years I've known you, I've watched you push good people away and I never understood why. I do now. It's because you don't think you're good enough for kind people, or for good things. So, you choose bad people, people you know will hurt you, because that's all you think you deserve. It breaks my heart, Emily, because you deserve all the best things in life. You need to start recognising that you are worthy of love.'

Emily turned away from the sea, and from Gio, and wiped her wet eyes. What Gio said only hurt so much because there was some truth in it.

'Anyway, that's what I think. You can tell me to shut up.'

'No. Gio, if there's some home truths I need to hear, then there's no one else I'd rather hear them from.'

He placed a warm hand on her knee for a moment. 'It's all said with love. And it comes from experience. Mostly because of what happened with my father when I came out. For a long time, I felt as though I didn't deserve to be treated well. In my case, low self-esteem manifested itself in my avoidance of serious relationships. I thought if I didn't care about anyone, then I couldn't be hurt by them not caring about me.' He glanced at Emily. 'I didn't work all this out for myself. It's taken many hours, and hundreds of pounds' worth of therapy to get it worked out in my head. But do you know what's finally made me realise that I must stop running away from my feelings?'

Emily shook her head.

'Meeting Harrison. He's shown me that I can be loved, and I can also love. It's very corny and quite nauseating, but he is the best thing to ever happen to me.'

Emily put her arm around Gio's shoulders and hugged him tightly. 'I love you.'

'I love you too, darling. Come on. Sue's got the champagne on ice.'

'I didn't get the portraits, Gio. Zeyla clammed up when I asked about them. She said they didn't exist, but I could see in her eyes that she was lying. I had one job, and I failed. Terry is going to be so disappointed.'

'Oh, it doesn't matter. We'll work something out. Come and have a glass of champagne anyway. Cher is waiting to see you.'

The heaviness in Emily's body lifted enough to allow her to laugh. 'Waiting to tear strips off me, more like. Yeah alright, I suppose I have to face the music at some point. I hate to think what Will might have told his parents. I did lose my temper with him. But you know what?'

'What, darling?' Gio said, looping his arm through Emily's as they walked along the beach.

'I think I needed to say it to him, to tell him how badly he hurt me. He's far too self-centred and egotistical to feel guilty, but by telling him, I've offloaded some of the weight onto him. By letting it out of my head, it's kind of lightened it a bit. Does that make any sense?'

Gio gave her a light kiss on the forehead. 'Emily, very little of what you say and do ever makes sense to me. But as long as it makes sense to you, that is all that matters.'

'I'm so sorry, Terry,' Emily said, taking a goat's cheese and fig bruschetta from the plate Sue was handing round. Even in the golden glow of the late evening sun, Terry looked pale and gaunt. Sue looked anxious.

'Don't worry, love. You tried and that's all any of us can do.'

'We can still have the exhibition, can't we?' Sue asked, reaching for the champagne bottle and refilling everyone's glasses.

'Of course we can,' Harrison said. Margo was watching him closely, waiting for him to drop a morsel of cheese. 'Stop staring, Margo,' he chided, giving her a scratch behind her ears. Margo flopped down in the shade of the parasol. 'We have the portraits of Hugo, and you said there were some unusual paintings in the shed, Emily.'

Emily nodded. 'There are a few paintings that people will recognise as her work, beach scenes and landscapes. But there's also what look like experimental pieces. And the unfinished painting.'

'And we have the sketchbook. Could we not display some things from that too?' Harrison asked, casually slipping a sliver of cheese under the table much to Margo's delight.

'I have been thinking,' Gio said, scratching Cher under her chin. She was curled up on his lap contentedly snoozing. 'We want to make this big, right? So we can make as much money as possible, yes?'

The others around the table nodded.

'But we do not have the first clue about how to put on an art exhibition. At least, I'm presuming none of you do?'

Slightly more sombre nods.

'Well, I know an events organiser and exhibition curator at

an upmarket art gallery in London.' He glanced nervously at Harrison who raised an eyebrow. 'An old friend,' Gio added, but the blush on the back of his neck gave away his white lie. 'I was thinking maybe I could speak to him and get his advice. If we could get him on board, he'd be a useful way to spread the word.'

Emily gave Gio a smile. Getting in contact with Scott would not be an easy thing for him to do, not after the way things ended between them the previous Christmas. It was brave of him to offer.

'Are you sure, Gio?' Emily asked quietly and he nodded.

'It's ancient history now. You see, it is possible to put the past behind you and move on.'

Emily coughed and her cheeks flared. 'Touché,' she muttered.

'If you could, Gio, that would be fantastic,' Sue said, brightening a little. She did look awfully tired. 'How's the website coming along, Emily?'

'Nearly done. I'd say it'll be ready to go live sometime this week. I've created a page for ticket sales so we can turn that on once we have the exhibition details.'

'That all sounds marvellous. Doesn't it, Terry? *Terry?*' Sue nudged her husband.

'What? Oh sorry, must have dozed off. Yes, yes, marvellous.'

'Are you okay, Dad?' Harrison asked, frowning.

'Yes, fine. I might go for a little lie down, if no one minds?'

They all shook their heads again, except Sue who was chewing on her thumbnail.

Harrison leant across the table and took his mum's hand once Terry had gone inside. 'He needs to see the doctor, Mum.'

Sue sighed. 'I know. But you try telling him that.'

. . .

That night Emily settled herself into the big double bed and pulled Violet's old patchwork quilt up to her chin. She smiled to herself. Meeting Zeyla had been quite the experience. But she still had questions. Where had Hugo come from? Did he know about Zeyla? Did Violet have any other romantic liaisons between the end of her love affair with Zeyla, and taking up with Hugo? And if she had, who had they been with? Did Janice know more than she'd admitted?

# FORTY-THREE
## VIOLET

February 1944

The week passed in a haze of sketching and talking and drinking. We ate at the nearby newly opened 'British Restaurant', the Ministry of Food's communal kitchen, where for ninepence we got a three-course dinner every day. Seeing as neither of us had valid ration books for Brighton, it was ideal. Of course, in his uniform, Hugo managed to get hold of a few essentials for us, as well as enough bottles of beer to keep us going for the week. For our last evening, Hugo insisted we go out with a bang.

We picked our way carefully along roads marked with deep craters and mounds of rubble. Brighton had taken a horrific pounding. And yet each person we encountered met us with a cheery hello and a smile. The bombings may have destroyed buildings, but it hadn't changed the people. Hugo had offered to walk with me over to Hereford Street, but I declined. There wasn't anything or anyone there for me to see.

'Oh heavens. Look.' I pulled Hugo to a stop in front of a two-storey red-brick building. There was no glass in any of the windows and a large part of the roof was missing. A pile of bricks and some slates were all that remained of a smaller building which had once stood to the side. 'Our old school.' A cold shiver ran through me.

'They must have been aiming for the gasometer behind,' Hugo said, his forehead creased in a deep frown. 'I wonder if—'

'Don't say it,' I said, my stomach churning. I couldn't bear to think of how many children might have been injured, or worse.

He squeezed my hand. 'Come on, let's not spoil my last night of freedom before I'm back to being shouted at as I wade through freezing water holding my rifle above my head.'

'Where are we going, anyway?' I asked, banishing the terrifying images of Hugo at war from my mind.

'Somewhere I think you'll like,' was his enigmatic reply. I punched his arm.


The pub was not much bigger than an average front parlour and was decorated like one too. My jaw dropped as I looked around at the small tables and cosy nooks. By the window, two women were openly holding hands across a table and two men in a booth in the corner were sat far too close together to just be chums.

'Hugo?' I asked quietly.

He smirked back at me. 'Yes?'

'Nothing,' I said with a grin. He ordered us a couple of beers and we sat at a table by the door. I had never believed that such a place could be possible, that there was somewhere one could go where two women holding hands or two men engaged in intimate conversation would be permitted. Four women wearing full-length blue coats with red Ambulance Service badges sown onto the upper lapels, entered the bar laughing. One of them, a stunning redhead with sapphire eyes, was wearing slacks. I must have been blushing as Hugo nudged me, one eyebrow raised.

'You're staring,' he said.

'No, I'm not,' I replied, looking down at the table. I chanced a quick glance at the women, but they were busy ordering drinks. Of course, I knew there had to be other women like me and Zeyla out there, but I'd never given any thought as to how I might meet them. Trust Hugo to be the one to show me, in his own special way, that I wasn't alone.

'That red-headed ambulance driver couldn't take her eyes off you,' Hugo laughed, taking my hand and leading me down the dark streets.

'Don't be ridiculous,' I said, blushing. 'She was looking at *you*.'

'Violet, you daft thing. She was most certainly *not* interested in me.'

In the dim glow of a shielded streetlamp, I wrapped my arms around his waist and looked up at him. 'I'm going to miss you so much,' I said, my voice wobbly, and not solely from the beer. 'This week has been wonderful. And I don't just mean because of the you-know-what.'

He chuckled and kissed me gently on the forehead. 'Will you promise me something?'

'Anything.'

'Don't wait for me.'

I raised my head from where I had laid it on his shoulder. 'What?'

'I mean it, Vi.' He drew a deep breath. 'I don't know what's going to happen in the next few months, but there's something brewing. Things can't stay as they are for much longer, we're going to have to go on the offensive sometime soon and when we do, well, it's going to be rough. I don't want to be marching my way across Europe thinking of you sitting at home alone. I'd much rather think of you having fun and enjoying yourself. I want you to do all the things I shan't be able to. I want you to go dancing. I want you to kiss anyone and everyone you can. I want you to be the reason I keep going. I want you to live, *really* live. Otherwise, I can't see what the hell we're fighting for. Will you do that? For me?'

I sniffed loudly and drew the back of my hand across my wet cheeks. 'Alright.'

'Promise?'

'If you promise me you'll come home.'

Hugo sighed. 'I wish I could.'


He was gone when I woke the following morning. He'd left ten bob and a note on the kitchen table.

*Her name is Peggy, and you'll find her at the ambulance station at Brighton Municipal Hospital. Live, Violet. Live, in case I die.*

# FORTY-FOUR

## EMILY

September 2016

The glorious weather was stretching into September and, although the holidaymakers and day trippers had left, Dovecote still had the feeling of summer about it. Emily walked slowly down the High Street smiling to herself at the posters in every shop window. Molly had stuck a poster right in the middle of Harrington's biggest window. What had started as a simple exhibition of Violet's paintings, had morphed into a town-wide festival celebrating her work and her life. Everyone from Molly in the bookshop, to Declan at the pub, and even Aoife at her salon, were getting stuck in. The only person who didn't seem to be getting involved was Will. He'd barely been seen in Dovecote in the month since their long weekend in Glencaragh. Emily was totally fine with that. Of course, that would all change later that evening. It was too much to hope he wouldn't turn up to his own birthday party.

As she crossed the High Street onto The Promenade, her phone rang.

'Hi Sue. Everything alright?'

'Yes, all fine. I just wanted to let you know that Scott has called to say he's on his way with his team to oversee the setting up and kitting out of the temporary exhibition hall. The driveway might be blocked for a while. It was inspired of Gio to get a professional art exhibition organiser involved. We'd have been lost without Scott.'

'Yes, I know.' She was rather proud of Gio. A few months ago, he would have fallen apart at the mere thought of being anywhere near Scott, but it hadn't fazed him at all. If only she could bring herself to be the same around Will. She turned her attention back to Sue on the other end of the phone. 'I can't wait to see it. From what I've heard, it's going to be amazing. And no worries about the driveway. Did Janice get back to you about catering for the opening night?'

Emily could hear Sue shuffling papers. 'Yes, she did. Not a problem, she can get everything ready at the café or in the kitchen here. We did wonder whether we should maybe get some waiting staff in. What do you think?'

'If there's budget for it, then I think that would be a great idea.'

More paper shuffling. 'I think we can factor it in. Leave it with me, I know a few people.'

Emily laughed. 'Thank goodness you and Terry have so much experience in hosting big events, Sue. We'd be sunk without you, and without the Dovecote estate grounds.' The original plan to hold the exhibition at Dovecote Museum had been shelved when the demand for tickets exceeded their expectations. This was all thanks to Scott and his network of London art lovers spreading the news that Violet Cooper's never-before-seen work was going on display. According to Gio, Scott had said there was a huge buzz about it.

'To think we nearly sold off the west lawn when we first bought the manor. And we're not doing much. Gio has been a godsend.'

'In so many ways, Sue.'

'You are coming tonight, aren't you?' Sue asked, and Emily's stomach did a somersault. What had Will told her?

'I should think so.'

'Lovely. I'll see you later, then.'

'Bye, Sue.'

'Bye, love.'

Emily took a deep breath and pushed open the door of The Seaside Café. It was a touch cooler indoors, out of the bright sun. Typical that the weather would be perfect for Will's birthday. Why was she giving him so much space in her head? Maybe Gio was right, and she needed to move on. But that wasn't easy when everything around her made her think of him.

'Morning, Janice. You're quiet today.' Emily glanced around the café as she approached the counter. The Seaside Café was deserted.

'It'll pick up. How are you doing, love?'

'I'll be better after a cuppa and a sticky bun.'

'So, you met Zeyla, then?' Janice asked, as she filled a teapot and took a sticky bun off the pile under the glass dome on the counter. 'Sue told me,' she added, in response to Emily's raised eyebrow. 'What's she like?'

'Fascinating. You'd never know she's over ninety by looking at her.'

'Hmm.' Janice avoided making eye contact as Emily paid for her breakfast.

'Janice, how close were you and Violet?'

Janice rolled her eyes and leant against the counter. 'I should have known you wouldn't let it rest. Alright, Violet and I were close, despite her being quite a bit older than me.'

'How did you get to know her?'

'When I came back to Dovecote in the mid-seventies after some time travelling around, and restored The Seaside Café, Violet was the only person who believed I could do it. The café had been derelict for years, since the end of the war, but she remembered what it had been like in the forties. She told me how she used to come in because it was the only place you could get proper sugar in your tea. Violet was in her fifties by then, but she got stuck in, helping with cleaning and redecorating. I couldn't have done it without her.

'We spent hours together in this café, getting it ready. And we talked, a lot. By then, she'd given up trying to sell her paintings. The new styles she was experimenting with at the time hadn't been that well received, which discouraged her a bit. Her students at the art college in Brighton where she taught from 1965 became her focus when she slipped quietly out of the public eye.' She fixed a searching stare on Emily. 'There's more you need to know, isn't there?'

Emily nodded and Janice sighed.

'Alright, because if you're anything like her, you won't let it drop. So, I may as well tell you.'

They sat down at the table closest to the counter. 'Go on then, what do you want to know?'

'What I want to know is how she came to meet Hugo. Where did he come from and how does he fit into her relationship with Zeyla?' Emily sliced a chunk off her sticky bun and popped it in her mouth. It was incredibly delicious.

'Good old Hugo. He was such a lovely man. He was one of those people that everyone loved. Violet and Hugo were friends from when they were children in Brighton. He lied about his age and joined up at seventeen in 1940, just before Violet, her mother, and brothers were bombed out of their house. He got sent to the army and was involved in D-Day. As he'd have everyone believe, he single-handedly liberated Belgium in 1944. I think it was in early 1944, before D-Day, that he came to Dovecote on leave. Violet was living in Clifftop Cottage by then, having lost her home again in the 1943 bombing of Blythe Avenue that killed her mother. She didn't tell me all the details, but it was around the time that things weren't going well with Zeyla and, reading between the lines, something happened between Violet and Hugo. But it wasn't anything serious and he went back to the front. When he came home for good after the end of the war they got married.'

'Did he know about Zeyla?'

'Oh yes. In fact, it had been quite a surprise to him that she'd fallen for him. Before then, he believed she was only interested in girls. I think that was quite hard for him because he'd been in love with her since they were kids. Anyway, he was hired by the Wythenshawes, where he worked on the gardens at Dovecote Manor. Violet and Hugo had, gosh, it must have been nearly fifty years together before he died in the early nineties.'

'I wish I'd known about all of this when Violet was still alive. I'd have loved to have heard her tell her story.'

'I think there's a fair bit of it in her paintings, love. If you look closely.'

Emily sipped her tea. Thanks to Scott and his good eye the exhibition would tell that story. Her mobile beeped and she glanced quickly at Harrison's message.

*You could have warned me how hot Scott is.*

She groaned. She'd deal with Harrison later.

'Can I get you another pot of tea?' Janice's question brought Emily back to the café.

'I won't say no,' Emily replied.

'Zeyla told me that she and Violet's relationship ended in January 1944, when Zeyla got engaged to Rupert,' Emily said when Janice brought over the refilled teapot.

'Yes, she told me that too. Broke her heart, that did. But she got over it. I think Hugo helped. With everything Violet went through, Hugo was the one constant. He was always there for her, and she for him.'

'Did she have any other love affairs after Zeyla, but before she and Hugo got married?'

'I don't know what happened in the time between things ending with Zeyla and the end of the war when Hugo came home. She didn't say much about that. I think she might have gone back to Brighton for a short while.'

Emily put down her cup and scratched her temple.

Janice twisted the cord of her reading glasses around her finger. 'There is one more thing you should know about your great-aunt,' Janice said, glancing out of the window at some people walking by the café towards Victoria Park. Emily had seen the auburn-haired man and dark-haired woman around town a few times, mostly in The Royal Oak. The woman worked at Crawford's Opticians on the High Street. They had James Rutherford's son with them, and a chocolate-brown labradoodle who seemed intent on catching one of the fat seagulls that loitered on the railings outside the café. It would seem Janice's sticky buns were as popular with the birds as with the human population of Dovecote.

'Michael and Thomas?' Emily asked, tentatively.

'How do you know about them?'

'I asked Reverend Clive to have a look through the parish records to see if there was anything about Zeyla.' She reached into her bag and carefully unfolded the piece of paper Clive had given her, smoothing it out on the table. It was the first time she'd looked at it since that day in the church and the words brought a lump to her throat once again. 'While he was looking, he found the baptismal records of Michael Cooper born in 1947 and of Thomas Cooper born in 1949. And he also found these.' Emily leant over and read from the pages, blinking to clear her vision. '*Michael Cooper, died April 1947, aged ten days. Thomas Cooper, died September 1949, aged seven months.*'

'Funeral records,' said Janice drawing a shaky breath. 'It all happened when I was a small child, so I don't remember first-hand. But Violet talked about her sons quite a lot. It was so sad. To lose both babies like that. I can't even begin to comprehend how heartbreaking that must have been for her, and for Hugo of course.'

'What happened to them?'

'Michael, who was named after Violet's father, was premature and quite sickly. Of course, there wasn't the medical science then that we have now, so things went undiagnosed. As you can see, he only survived a few days.' Her voice cracked and Emily placed a hand over Janice's where she'd rested it on the paper.

'And Thomas?' Emily's own voice was shaky.

'Thomas's death was even more tragic. He was a healthy baby, named after Hugo's father, and then died one night. We call it sudden infant death syndrome these days, but back then it was put down to unknown causes.' There was a sheen to Janice's eyes, and she looked away. Clearly talking about it was hard, even for her. Janice gave Emily a weak smile. 'After Thomas, Violet and Hugo reluctantly decided they couldn't risk it happening again, as much as they wanted to be parents.' She gripped Emily's hand. 'That's another reason why she was so happy when you were born. She used to travel up and down to London to see you all the time when you were little.'

'I wish I could remember.' Emily gave Janice a rueful smile. 'I never realised how much I meant to her.' She blinked again. She'd go and find Michael and Thomas's graves, and she'd let the tears out then.

'I know, pet. But you have the memories of the summers you spent with her.' Janice held up her hand when Emily opened her mouth to speak again. 'Don't say it. It wasn't your fault that you lost touch with her. It's hard when there's a falling-out after a split. It's always the children who miss out. I suppose you lost contact with your grandparents and your great-uncle John, too?'

'Yes, I did. It's not Mum's fault either though. I think Dad made it awkward for everyone.'

'Hmm, yes. Violet certainly had some thoughts about her nephew.'

'She wasn't the only one.' Emily let out a short, sharp laugh. That was a whole other thing that she should probably deal with. She hadn't spoken to her dad in years. If there was anything she could learn from what Zeyla had told her about losing touch with her sons, it was that hatchets should be buried while there is still time. Reluctantly, Emily got up from the table. 'Thank you again, Janice, for everything. I feel as though I know Violet so much better now. I'd better go. It's Will's birthday party tonight and I promised Harrison I'd go.'

'That will be fun, love. Have a good time.'

Emily couldn't think of a polite reply. But she could guarantee that an evening in the presence of Will and his no doubt equally annoying friends would not be fun. The only redeeming factor was that, presumably, Tabitha wouldn't be there.

# FORTY-FIVE
## VIOLET

June 1944

By early June, I'd had enough of all the people, noise, and hustle and bustle. Brighton had become overrun with servicemen of various allied nationalities: Polish, Canadian, and American. Every inch of space was taken up with army encampments, supply dumps, and stores. Even the ambulance crews at the hospital had been squashed into one room at the ambulance station to make space for a munitions store. My dispatcher's desk had been reduced to a telephone and a radio precariously propped on a box of first aid equipment. Was this the big thing Hugo had warned me about?

On top of it all, after four intense months, my relationship with Peggy had become strained. We were living in each other's pockets, between working together on the ambulances, her as a driver and me as a dispatcher, and sharing her small room. It would have been too much for two people in love, and we were far from that. With both of us in possession of bruised hearts, we were never destined to fall in love, only lust.

Early one Tuesday morning, before the sun was up, I kissed

Peggy's sleeping cheek, silently gathered my belongings, and walked up the hill to the train station. Brighton was curiously quiet, the pre-dawn loaded and expectant somehow. Without a backwards glance, I boarded a train bound for sleepy Dovecote. I missed my tired little cottage with its battered furniture and mended curtains. I couldn't lie to myself. I had been hiding in Brighton, and now it was time to go back. All I could hope was that in the intervening months the ghost of Zeyla would have moved out of Clifftop Cottage.

To her credit, Zeyla had kept her word. Clifftop Cottage was as I left it. The hinges of the sage-green gate still creaked softly, the lion's head knocker still welcomed me, and my key still fitted the lock. I stooped to pick up a pile of envelopes and dropped them on the writing desk. The house needed a good airing. With all the windows and doors flung open, the rooms were soon filled with warm summer air and the familiar, comforting tang of salty sea and heady scent of rhododendron.

I was reduced to making do with a cup of Camp Coffee with powdered milk. I would have to resupply my kitchen as best I could. I had become used to my rations being supplemented with items pilfered from the Dovecote Manor kitchens by Zeyla, but no more. I was on my own, but I would, as I had thus far, survive. When I'd called Mrs Harrington from Brighton, she'd said my job at the bookshop would be waiting when I came back. But maybe I could do something different. The farms in the hills up behind Dovecote were crying out for more land girls, and at least then I might get proper milk.

I stepped out into the sun in my little courtyard. The honeysuckle was in full bloom, and I pinched off a flower and gently squeezed the nectar into my coffee. It wasn't sugar but it took the bitter edge off somewhat. Breathing in the salty air, I looked out over the sea and nearly dropped my cup. The horizon was filled with boats, hundreds of them, thousands maybe. All different shapes and sizes. An armada. The sky was filled with droning and a squadron of aircraft whizzed overhead. I hurried back inside and flicked on the wireless in time for the ten o'clock news. My mouth hung open as I listened. The invasion, long rumoured, had begun. Hugo was probably out there at sea that very moment. My hands began to tremble. He had to come home, he just had to.

I tried to keep my mind off what was happening across the English Channel by busying myself with Clifftop Cottage's much-overdue spring clean. I ventured into the potting shed and cleared out all the old gardening equipment and swept the cobwebs from the ceiling. The morning sun coming in through the window cast such a lovely light that an idea suddenly occurred to me – the room would be perfect as an art studio.

I sanded down the kitchen cupboards, determined to replace the hideous brown with a nice light blue. Then I turned my attention to the sitting room. I stood, hands on hips, for a long while before deciding that the threadbare rug in front of the fire had to go, as much for the memories it held as for its dilapidation. I rolled it and dragged it down the driveway, where I added it to the pile of junk by the gate. The salvage squad would come along and take it if it were deemed of any use.

As I turned to head back up the driveway, a car trundled down from Dovecote Manor and slowed as it approached the gate. Zeyla, in the back seat, looked radiant, draped in antique white lace. No doubt a Wythenshawe family heirloom. Trust Zeyla to pick the most important day of the war for her wedding day. Everything always had to be about her. Her dainty mouth formed a silent 'O' as she glanced out of the car window and our eyes met. I raised my hand in a wave, but she had already looked away.

'Good luck, my darling,' I whispered, as the car turned out of the gate and across the road to St. John's Church. I laughed to myself as a vision of Zeyla running out of the church, leaving Rupert standing at the altar, and back into my arms sprang into my head. I didn't wish for it. As much as I loved her, and I did, ours was not a healthy relationship for me. I'd meant what I said to her, that I never wanted to be someone's secret. But more than that, I never wanted to be in someone else's shadow. And I would have always been in hers.

Back at the cottage, I sat down at my writing desk and leafed through the pile of post. There was one letter with a Yorkshire postmark, dated February. The writing on the front was not Beryl Carmichael's familiar scribble. With a coil of dread unwinding in my stomach, I gingerly opened the envelope. The letter inside had been typed on an official-looking letterhead, with a crest imprinted at the top of the paper.

*Dear Miss Saunders,*

*I write to notify you of the application by Mr Arthur and Mrs Beryl Carmichael of Foxdale Farm, Hunmanby, East Riding of Yorkshire, to formally adopt John Saunders (aged 9 years, 5 months) and Oliver Saunders (aged 8 years, 3 months).*

*John and Oliver have been in the care of Mr and Mrs Carmichael since their evacuation from Dovecote, East Sussex, in September 1940. The young boys arrived in a state of malnutrition and without any of their own possessions, their home having been recently bombed. In the intervening years, the boys have thrived, and they are healthy and well settled in Hunmanby. The Education Committee of East Riding of York-*

shire have confirmed that John and Oliver both regularly attend school and are performing satisfactorily within expectations for children of their respective ages. Mr and Mrs Carmichael have also confirmed that both children have made friends and have developed close relationships with other children within the wider Carmichael family. Mr and Mrs Carmichael do not have any children of their own. Both John and Oliver have been interviewed and independently stated that they are happy and enjoying living on Foxdale Farm.

The death of Mr Michael Saunders, their father, in 1939, and the subsequent death of Mrs Rebecca Saunders, their mother, in May 1943 rendered the children orphaned. It is therefore the opinion of the adoption board that it is in the best interests of John and Oliver that they remain in Hunmanby and be formally adopted by Mr and Mrs Carmichael.

Mrs Carmichael has asked that I relay to you that she and her husband do not wish to cause you any distress, and that their request is made purely out of their devotion to, and love for, Oliver and John, with whom they have developed a parental bond.

If you wish to object to the decision of the adoption board, please do so in writing within sixty days of receipt of this letter to the address above. If no such objection is received, the adoption will be formalised with effect from 3 May 1944.

Yours sincerely,

Ms A Bates

Secretary to Mr H. Illingworth, Director of Child Welfare, East Riding County Council

I wiped the tears from my cheeks with a shaking hand. Would I have written an objection if I'd been here to open the letter in time? The infrequent letters that had come down from Yorkshire painted such a picture of love and happiness, I doubt I would have. This news and seeing my beloved parents' deaths described so coldly and officiously was like a shard of glass in my chest. But I had to acknowledge that John and Oliver *were* better off where they were. They were loved, well cared for, being educated, healthy, and happy. There was no sense in causing upset for them, and for Beryl and Arthur. And what was one more assault on my already fractured heart.

# FORTY-SIX

## EMILY

September 2016

As Emily approached Dovecote Manor, wobbling slightly across the gravel in her heels, Margo bounded towards her, her tail going nineteen to the dozen. The front door had been decorated with fairy lights and bunches of black and gold balloons. Even from outside, Emily could hear plummy voices and shrill laughter. Someone opened a bottle of champagne with a pop.

*We're out on the terrace x*

'Thank you, Gio,' Emily said to her phone. She took the narrow path leading around the house, past the sitting room bay window, to avoid having to walk through rooms full of Will's friends. Margo trotted obediently next to her. A sheepdog without a flock.

She released a tense breath as she hopped over the little wall around the terrace and saw, not only Gio and Harrison and Terry and Sue, but Molly and Jez. She'd not seen them since their wedding.

'Evening all,' Emily said, smoothing out the folds of her navy knee-length dress. 'Thanks, Gio.' He pressed a glass of champagne into her hand.

'You're going to need this,' he said, raising an eyebrow.

'That bad?'

He nodded. She swallowed a large mouthful of bubbles.

'No Aoife?' Emily asked, sidling up to Molly.

'No. She couldn't make it,' Molly said.

'Is she alright?'

Molly leant in a bit closer. 'To be honest, she's a bit embarrassed about the whole one-night stand with Will. She opted to mind the kids for us instead.'

Emily snorted. 'I don't think she needs to worry.' She nodded towards the French doors. The ballroom was packed with handsome men in expensive suits and beautiful women in designer dresses. Jewels sparkled in the light of the chandelier. 'I'd say she's not the only one.' Her stomach knotted. She had to count herself in that number too.

There was a tense atmosphere as the group huddled together outside. Sue looked as though she was on the brink of tears.

'What's going on, Harrison?' Emily whispered. 'Is it me, or is everyone a bit on edge?'

'I think you're about to find out.'

They turned towards the ballroom as Will made his big entrance to whoops and whistles from his pals. How dare he look so good? It irked more than it should have, and Emily was transported to Loughnacran House. Will smiled and looked around the room. When his brown-gold eyes met Emily's for a split second she was back in the cosy lounge of the hotel. She fought against the same inexplicable, and entirely unwanted, desire that had bubbled in her that evening, and looked away. Emily's jaw dropped nearly as much as her stomach as Tabitha walked into the room and took hold of Will's hand.

'Seriously?' she breathed.

Gio's hand touched her arm. 'It gets worse,' he muttered.

'I can think of an Elton John song that fits this,' Emily sniped, waspishly.

'Indeed,' Harrison said out of the corner of his mouth. 'She's back. And she's here to stay.'

Emily glanced over at Sue. She was clinging to Terry's arm and the smile on her lips didn't reach her eyes. Will and Tabitha moved through the room, swapping air kisses and back slaps. Eventually they reached the terrace and Emily spotted the ring. It was an obscenely large rock. Sue and Tabitha regarded each other with matching false smiles. It was Terry who broke the silence, kissing Tabitha on the cheek.

'Welcome to the family, love,' he said. Sue squeezed his arm a little tighter. Bless him, he was trying his best.

'Hi, Emily. Long time no see.' There was a sardonic tone to Will's voice and Emily flashed him a smile.

'No, indeed. You've not graced us with your presence in a while.' She turned to Tabitha. 'Congratulations.'

'Oh, like, yeah, thanks,' Tabitha drawled.

'You'll be having your wedding reception here, I presume?' Molly asked, exchanging a sparkly-eyed look with Jez. Will shifted from one foot to the other and looked at Tabitha. She rolled her eyes a fraction.

'Oh, well, we've not decided. Give us a chance, she only said yes an hour ago.' His laugh fell a little flat. 'But, um, it will probably be in London. Most of our friends and all of Tabby's family are there, so...'

Emily snuck a peek at Harrison who was, in turn, looking at his mother. There was worry in his blue eyes. Tabitha had Will right where she wanted.

'We might be coming to see you, Gio. I hear you're one of the best wedding planners around,' Will added.

Gio looked at him for a moment before glancing at Tabitha

and raising one eyebrow a miniscule fraction. 'We're fully booked up with weddings at the hotel for the next three years, but I can add you to the waiting list,' he said, with a dismissive sniff. Emily nearly cheered. Harrison coughed to disguise a snort. Tabitha pulled on Will's arm.

'I'd better go and mingle,' Will said, flashing one of his charming smiles. It faltered a fraction when he caught Emily's eye, and his gaze lingered a heartbeat longer than was natural. Emily turned away, her heart pounding. Damn him. What had happened to his epiphany that day at the piano? Tabitha must have talked him round. Well, as long as it was what he wanted, and he was happy. But why did seeing him with Tabitha make her lungs constrict?

'It will be fine, Sue,' Molly said, giving Sue's shoulder a reassuring squeeze.

'Thanks, Molly. I'm afraid we're hardly going to see him now. She's got him wrapped around her little finger.'

'Come on, love, Molly is right. It will all work out. We have to let go eventually,' Terry sighed. 'Sorry,' he added, with a slow shake of his head. 'I'm going to have to call it a night.'

Harrison wrapped his arms around his mum. 'I'm not going anywhere, Mum,' he said. Sue sniffed and nodded. Emily could see her watching Terry shuffle away.

'You'd better not.' She looked up at Gio. 'No stealing him away.'

Gio grinned and gave her a kiss on the cheek. 'I couldn't even I wanted to.'

Emily caught a look that passed between Harrison and Gio. There was something unsettling in it, a touch of frostiness maybe. Her biggest fear about them getting together had been what would happen if they broke up. That was too horrendous to consider. A round of peeling laughter floated out of the ballroom over the terrace.

'I think we're going to call it a night too,' Jez said, quietly.

'The kids have to be up in the morning for football and ballet, and I know they won't go to bed until we get home. Aoife will have let them stay up eating sweets and watching something unsuitable.'

'The last time she babysat, they watched *Ghostbusters*. Zoe didn't sleep for a week,' Molly added, shaking her head.

'We're stopping by The Royal Oak for a quick one, if you want to come along,' Jez whispered in Emily's ear. 'I can't be doing with that sort,' he added, with a small nod towards the crowd inside. Emily considered the empty champagne flute in her hand. It wasn't hitting the spot.

'Sounds like a plan. Do you mind if we stop by the cottage so I can change my shoes? I've no chance of getting into town in these without breaking an ankle.'

Jez winked and Molly smirked. It was like being a naughty teenager, sneaking out with your mates, all over again.

There was a good crowd in The Royal Oak, and Emily squeezed her way to the bar.

'Ah, Emily,' Declan greeted her with a smile. 'Thought you'd be up at the manor with Will and all his mates?'

Emily rolled her eyes. 'I showed my face. I don't think Will would have noticed if I hadn't. Did you hear he and Tabitha got engaged?'

'That stuck-up miserable little blonde cow? A fella like Will must have girls throwing themselves at him. Why'd he pick that one?'

'God knows, Declan. Can I have a pint of ale for Jez, a gin and tonic for Molly, and a double vodka and coke for me? Cheers.'

'Coming right up.'

Emily's phone buzzed in her bag.

*Where did you go? X*

She typed a quick reply.

*Sorry, Gio. I'm down at The Royal Oak with Molly and Jez. Why don't you and Harrison come down once Will and his mates go on to wherever they're going? Xx*

The party at Dovecote Manor was only a pre-party drinks reception. Will had hired out a hotel somewhere further along the coast where they were all staying for the main party. More proof that he loved to show off.

*I'll suggest it. They should be leaving in about an hour. X*

'Here you go.' Declan placed the last of the drinks on the bar and Emily gathered them in a triangle between her fingers. Jez and Molly had snapped up the last available table, right by the fireplace.

'Ah cheers,' Jez said, taking his pint from her. He downed a quarter of it. 'That's better. Not a fan of champagne.'

'I'm not either,' Molly said.

'I quite like it. The other people at the party, not so much.'

'I have to agree with you there, Emily.' Jez nodded.

'So, Emily, you never told us how your trip to Ireland went?'

Emily smiled, remembering her afternoon with Zeyla. 'It was very... um... memorable, that's for sure.' Her smile faded at the recollection of her tirade at Will on the beach. She would not be telling Molly and Jez about that.

# FORTY-SEVEN

## EMILY

September 2016

Bright sunlight filtering through the thin curtains at the small window in the room above The Royal Oak caused a spike of pain in Emily's head when she woke up. She cautiously opened one eye. Declan was snoring beside her. She opened the other eye and raised her head a fraction, instantly regretting moving when the room started to spin. Molly and Jez had been as good as their word and gone home after one drink. Then Gio and Harrison arrived, which was when it all got a bit messy. Aoife, relieved of babysitting duties, turned up a bit later. After Gio and Harrison left, Emily and Aoife started downing shots. When one of Aoife's exes offered to take her home, Emily started flirting unashamedly with Declan. The last thing she remembered was catching Declan's eye as he began to close up, agreeing to join him for a nightcap. The bit between leaving the bar and ending up in his flat above the pub was a little hazy.

She slipped as quietly as she could out of the bed, although judging by the snores coming from Declan, an earthquake couldn't wake him. Having scrabbled around for her hastily discarded clothes, she made her way down the stairs and out the front door. She shivered in the sharp wind that funnelled up the High Street from the sea, trying to decide which route to take home. Up the High Street and over the railway line was longer but a gentler climb. The shorter way along Beachfront Road meant dealing with the steps up the cliff. The way her head was spinning, it was probably best if she stayed away from steep drops.

There was a light on in Clifftop Cottage that pulled her home as she dragged herself up the driveway. The promise of a strong coffee eased the pounding in her head and spurred her on up the slope. She still hadn't put any oil on the gate hinges and the creak was getting worse. The roses had yet to open their petals, but a bee optimistically buzzed from flower to flower looking for breakfast.

'Gio?' she asked, pushing open the door and coming to an abrupt halt seeing him slumped on the sofa. 'What are you doing here?'

He looked as rough as she felt, and she went into the kitchen and put a pot of coffee on to brew without waiting for his reply. He followed her and sat down heavily at the table. A few minutes later, she pushed a mug of black coffee into Gio's hands.

'Where have you been all night?' he asked. Emily's cheeks burned and Gio's right eyebrow twitched. 'Emily!'

'What?' she shrugged. 'Don't pretend to be shocked.'

'I'm not. Are you okay?'

'Apart from being disgustingly hungover, I'm fine.' She gave him a cheeky smile as she sat down next to him. 'Nice, simple one-night stand. No strings. No expectations. It's been a while and was just what I needed. But what's more worrying is what you're doing here. Where's Harrison?'

'I don't know, and I don't care.' There was fury in his dark eyes and Emily let out a low whistle.

'Do you want to talk about it?'

Gio put down his mug and rubbed his face. 'No.'

Emily drank her coffee, gradually becoming something close to human again.

'I can't believe he's jealous about Scott.'

'Oh.'

'I told him what happened between me and Scott, and how it ended. He was a bit shocked that I'd been involved with a married man, but I explained how it happened. That might have been a mistake because now he's convinced that Scott still holds that power over me and thinks I'm going to go running back to him.'

'Did you tell Harrison how you feel about him?'

'I said he was being stupid. It didn't help. We started shouting at each other.'

'Oh, Gio. Scott is a very good-looking man that you have history with. I can kind of understand where Harrison is coming from. The only way to allay his fears is to tell him how much you care about him, how much you love him. Because you *do* love him.'

'I do, Emily. But I can't deal with this. Maybe it's better if I walk away now, before I get more involved. Because otherwise when we break up it's going to be far too painful.'

Emily rested her head on Gio's shoulder. 'Don't be daft. Stick with it. You and Harrison are great together. If it does go wrong in the future, yes it will hurt. But what if it goes right? As you know, I've let the chance for happiness pass me by. Please don't make the same mistake. Is being with Harrison worth the risk of being hurt?'

'Yes.'

'Well then you know what you have to do.'

'What?'

'Talk to him. *Tell* him.'

Gio drew a deep breath and shook himself down. 'Okay.'

They sat together in silence for a bit, Emily gazing into her empty mug.

Gio nudged her. 'Your turn, while we're talking about love. What's going on with you and Will? We are all disappointed that he and Tabitha are getting married, because she's such a nasty piece of work, but there was something else in your reaction. If I were to take a guess, I'd say you like him.'

'Don't be ridiculous, Gio. Of course I don't. I can't stand him. The way he throws his money around, his ludicrous sports car, and designer clothes. And don't forget, he's the one who is responsible for every bad dating decision I ever made, as you so observantly pointed out.'

'What about the way he came to check on you when you had your car accident? Or how worried he was about Terry that day at the fair? And there's the fact that he arranged and paid for everything so you could meet Zeyla? And that he's paying for Violet's exhibition building and all the staff for the opening night? Would it be out of order for me to point out that you're the only person in Dovecote that doesn't like him?'

Emily got up from the table and grabbed the two empty mugs. She shot Gio a glare as she crossed the kitchen.

'I suggest you get your own relationship sorted before trying to tell other people how to feel.'

Keeping her back to him, she put the mugs into the sink and leant over the counter. Her bottom lip started to wobble and her chin dropped. She lifted her head as Gio came over and stood next to her, his hand on her shoulder.

'I'm sorry. You're right, I should keep my thoughts to myself.'

Emily turned and Gio gathered her into his arms. 'No, the problem is, Gio,' she mumbled into his shirt, 'I think you might be right.' She pulled out of his hold a fraction, wiped her sleeve across her wet cheeks, and sniffed. 'As much as I don't want to, and I've tried not to,' she sniffed again before blurting out, 'I think I might like him quite a lot.'

A knock at the front door made them break apart.

'That's either your one-night stand, the man you fancy, or my boyfriend,' Gio said warily.

'I doubt very much it's Declan,' Emily said, dragging herself out of the kitchen towards the door.

'Hold on. *Declan?* How drunk were you?'

'Declan's alright.'

'I didn't think perma-tanned pretty boys were your type.'

Emily shrugged. 'He has a nice smile.' She opened the door and Harrison looked at her with wide eyes.

'Is Gio...?'

Emily stepped to one side, revealing Gio standing behind her. 'I'm going to have a long bath,' she said, giving Gio an encouraging smile.

An hour later, Emily emerged from her bath, rested and relaxed. She got dressed and was brushing her teeth when she caught the faint sound of a siren. It was such an unusual occurrence in Dovecote that it took her a moment to realise what it was. She leant out of the bathroom window as the siren got louder and then stopped. An ominous blue strobing light was coming through the forest. She slammed the window shut and ran down the stairs.

'Sorry to interrupt.' Harrison and Gio were mid-kiss. 'But I think something's happening at the manor, Harrison. There are blue flashing lights in that direction.'

# FORTY-EIGHT

## EMILY

September 2016

They reached Dovecote Manor as an ashen-faced Sue was climbing into the back of an ambulance. Harrison ran over while Emily and Gio hung back. The look on Harrison's face told them all they needed to know.

'I'll drive,' Emily said, as Harrison frantically searched his pockets for his car keys. 'Then you can call Will on the way. And Gio and I can come back to look after the dogs.'

Harrison disappeared to find Terry and Sue, so Emily and Gio sat down in Brighton General Hospital's waiting area. Emily glanced at Gio; from his face, he wasn't in the mood to chat either. Since that day at the fair, Terry had been looking increasingly unwell and now here he was being rushed to A&E. It was the thing that everyone feared but hadn't wanted to say.

Out of the corner of her eye, Emily spotted Will rushing through the doors, all trace of his usual cool suaveness replaced by wide-eyed panic. He didn't see Emily and Gio, focusing only on getting to the reception desk.

Gio dug Emily in the ribs. 'No sign of Tabitha.'

'I suppose she wanted to stay with their party guests,' Emily said with a shrug. 'No skin off my nose.' Considering Tabitha's behaviour at the fair, Will was probably relieved not to have to babysit her; he had enough on his plate.

A few moments later, Harrison emerged from behind the double doors and came over, rubbing his eyes.

'He's stable,' he said, his brow furrowed and his mouth in a tight, thin line. 'There's talk about surgery. It's probably over-due, to be honest.'

'Did Will find you?'

Harrison nodded and then turned to Gio. 'I could do with a coffee.'

Emily smiled to herself when Gio slipped his hand into Harrison's and led him out of A&E.

A little while later, Emily was reading the information notices dotted around the walls of the waiting area for the second time, when she locked eyes with Will. His eyes looked a little red around the edges.

'Hi,' he said. 'Do you mind?' He indicated the empty chair next to her. Emily gave him a small smile.

'How's Terry?'

Will glanced back at the double doors. 'Stable. Conscious and talking, which is good.'

'Was it another heart attack?'

'Yeah, but thanks to Mum watching him like a hawk, they got him here in good time. They're doing an angiogram now, but as this was a big one they're probably going to do a bypass. The cocktail of drugs he's on doesn't seem to be doing the job.'

'I'm sure he's in good hands.'

They lapsed into a mildly uncomfortable silence. What Emily said to Gio in the kitchen that morning bounced around her head. Had she meant it? Was that what the mess of her conflicting emotions about Will meant? There were so many reasons to fight it, if she was falling for him. Their history only being one part of it. There was also the matter of Tabitha.

'I'm guessing Tabitha had to stay with your party guests?'

Will jolted as though she'd interrupted a deep thought. 'Huh? Oh. Yeah. Well, most of them said she should come with me, but she doesn't like hospitals.'

'Neither does Gio. But he's here. He and Harrison have gone for a coffee.'

'You don't like her, do you?'

'It's irrelevant if I do or not. I'm surprised, that's all, considering what you told me in the ballroom the morning after Molly and Jez's wedding.' The morning after Aoife. But after what she'd done the night before with Declan, she was in no position to judge on that score.

Will shrugged. 'I may have been a bit harsh. She's not as bad as I made out. She's not perfect, but then who is?'

'She talked you round, then?'

'*We* talked.' There was a warning tone in his voice.

Emily held up her hands. 'Alright, alright.' Clearly it was a touchy subject. Did that mean he was having doubts? The butterflies did a lap around her stomach again.

Will fidgeted in the chair and drew a deep breath. 'Times like these make you think about stuff,' he said.

'Such as?'

'Such as how I owe you an apology. My memory of fifteen years ago is a bit hazy, and I honestly don't remember being so cruel to you. That probably doesn't reflect well on me, that I didn't feel guilty about it enough to even remember. What I do remember is the way I felt about you.' His small smile was almost shy. The dimple was back, as were Emily's butterflies. 'I'm not using this as an excuse, but I had some particularly obnoxious mates who chose you to be picked on that summer.

And, in my teenage insecurity, I was too much of a coward to stand up to them. Instead, I went along with them. Until *that* evening. Suddenly I found myself alone with you and, well, I didn't have to hide that I liked you.

'But the next day, the others started up again and I found myself choosing them over you. I had to hide what had happened between us, otherwise they'd turn their derision on me. That's the thing with popularity, it breeds the fear of losing it.' He paused and drew another deep breath. 'It's fifteen years too late, but I am sorry for hurting you, and for being a complete and utter...' he glanced around the room, populated with a smattering of families with small children, 'idiot.' He'd clearly wanted to use a stronger word, possibly one of the many that Emily had used to describe him over the years. 'For what it's worth, after all this time, I am sorry for what I said.'

Emily stared at him for a moment, gobsmacked. She searched his face for any trace of sarcasm or mockery but all she could find was sincerity. There was a lump in her throat but also a lightness in her limbs. Could a simple, but seemingly heartfelt, apology heal fifteen years of hurt? Before she had a chance to say anything, Harrison and Gio returned.

'Mum's messaged me,' Harrison said, putting a hand on Will's shoulder. 'Dad's back from his angiogram and the consultant is coming to discuss the next steps soon. We should get back in there.'

Will stood up. He gave Emily a quick smile which she returned. Thankfully, the urge to throw herself into his arms abated before she could act on it.

'We'll head back and let the dogs out,' Gio said. 'Cher will be screaming for attention.'

'Call us if there's any news, or if you need us to do anything,' Emily added.

'What about the exhibition? It's only three weeks away,'

Will said. Emily's eyebrows launched themselves up her forehead. He was thinking about the exhibition? At a time like this?

'Leave it with us,' Gio said. 'It's all under control.'

'Don't spend too much time with Scott,' Harrison said, but there was a grin on his face.

Gio leant closely into Harrison. 'I love you,' he whispered.

Harrison bit his bottom lip. 'I love you too.'

Emily was still smiling when she and Gio got into her car. She drove out of the car park and headed towards home.

'Did you say earlier that Will is paying for the exhibition buildings?' she asked.

'Yes. And quite a lot more besides. Did you think he hadn't done anything to help?'

Emily's cheeks flared and she kept her eyes firmly on the road.

'Hmm,' Gio added. 'I keep telling you he's a far better person than you appear to give him credit for.'

Now *there* was something for Emily to think about. But even if her opinions of Will Prentice were dangerously close to changing, it was too late. He was still going to marry Tabitha.


Margo and Bernie were delighted to see Emily and Gio, greeting them with wagging tails. Gerry had to be coaxed away from Terry's armchair in the sitting room with a piece of roast chicken, and Cher bared her teeth at Emily even more menacingly than usual. It took intensive fussing and a sliver of smoked salmon from Gio to calm her down. Out on the terrace, with the dogs sniffing and rolling around the lawn, Emily turned to Gio.

'So, everything's sorted with Harrison, then?'

'Thanks to you. Everything with Harrison is new to me. I've not had to navigate the ups and downs of a serious relationship before. I'm a little scared that I'm going to mess it all up.'

'You're doing fine. I'm no expert either, don't forget. People aren't psychic and we can't expect people to know how we feel unless we tell them.'

Gio blew out a long breath. 'Why do we do this to ourselves?'

Emily laughed. 'Because it's worth it.' Her mobile phone rang, interrupting anything else she was going to say. She looked at it and frowned, nausea churning her stomach. She waited until the caller rang off and put her phone back in her pocket.

'Is everything alright?' Gio was looking at her with concern in his brown eyes.

Emily forced her jaw to relax. 'Fine.' She chewed at a loose piece of skin on her thumb. 'Are you okay looking after the dogs if I go back to the cottage for a bit?'

'Of course. Is something wrong?'

Emily avoided his look. 'No, I just need to do some work.' Lying to Gio was not something she relished. But if she told him who had called her, she'd get an earful.


Max had left a voicemail message and Emily made herself a cup of tea before she listened to it. She'd have preferred something a little stronger, but she still might have to drive back to the hospital, depending on what news came through about Terry. She steeled herself and hit the play button.

'Missing you. Call me.'

It was good to hear her voice again. But the message left Emily cold. She ventured into Violet's art studio.

With three weeks to go until the exhibition, the canvases in the studio had been divided into three stacks: those that were not going to be displayed, those that were for display only, and those that Emily and Scott had decided would be a good idea to sell.

Scott had done a lot of research into Violet's work in the two weeks between Gio asking him to be involved and visiting

Clifftop Cottage. He'd had the time of his life rifling through the studio. His expert eye was able to distinguish her early work of the late 1950s through to the mid-seventies from the later paintings she did after she retired from teaching in the mid-eighties. Even though the subjects and themes were the same, apparently there was a difference in the brush strokes. At that point in their meeting, Emily's eyes, and brain, glazed over and she'd nodded dumbly and let him get on with sorting the paintings.

Initially, Emily hadn't wanted to let any of Violet's work go, but she couldn't display it all. And if some pieces could find appreciative homes while simultaneously raising money for the museum, then it was selfish to hold on to them. Of course, the portraits of Hugo were not for sale, neither was the unfinished painting of Dovecote beach from the top of the cliff. It was still on the easel, and Emily stood in front of it, her mind wandering. Violet had perfectly captured the colour of the sea on a sunny day – the mix of silvery-blue and watery-green with scattered whitecaps. Her phone beeped with a message that made her stomach twist.

> *Sorry for the rubbish voicemail. What I meant to say is that I'm really missing you. Life is not the same without you. Is there any chance we could give it another go? Anyway, it would be great to hear your voice so maybe you could call me? M x*

Emily leant against the workbench under the window. A few months ago, Max's message would have had her reaching for her suitcase and car keys without a second thought. But now? The idea of returning to London was almost as discombobulating as the idea of coming to Dovecote had been back in June.

'Alright, Aunt Violet, I get it. I understand why you arranged for me to end up here. There are things I've learnt about you that I need to apply to my own life. You win, you got me.'

And what had she learnt? That love could be deep and intense, but not eternal. That friendship was a solid basis for a romantic relationship. That the past should be left behind sometimes. That a genuine and sincere apology could stitch the fractured pieces of a heart back together. What did all that mean when it came to Max?

There was no apology in Max's words; she hadn't even acknowledged that she'd done anything hurtful. Even Will had managed that. If the romantic relationship was taken out of it, could she call Max a friend? Not really. And what state was her heart in anyway? Was it available to be given to Max, or had someone else claimed it? But if she had lost it to Will, he was in no position to accept it, so that was a dead end. Was that a reason to run back to Max? She unfolded her arms and picked up her phone.

*Hi. While it's nice to hear from you, I don't think you are good for me. So, no, I'm not going to come running back to you. Wishing you all the best for whatever life gives you.*

Emily ran her fingers through her hair and wiped away a solitary tear that dripped down her cheek. But a smile spread across her lips. She was worth more than what Max would give her, and it swelled her heart to know that she was strong enough to show that to the world.

# FORTY-NINE
## VIOLET

October 1944

The frustrating thing about war is the relentless monotony. Days, weeks, and months of doing nothing except surviving. The nights were drawing in again, stockings still needed darning, rations still needed to be eked out. It was all so much of the same, over and over again.

I had flirted with the idea of getting work on a nearby farm but Mrs Harrington, at the bookshop, tripped and broke her ankle in the blackout not long after I got back to Dovecote from Brighton. So, I went back to the bookshop to help her.

A brief dalliance in August with Alf Crawford, the optician's son, provided a pleasant respite from my tedious routine. Poor Alf had been invalided out of Burma. It had taken six months to get him home. Mr Crawford played matchmaker and wasn't best pleased when I ended it. I shall probably have to go elsewhere for any glasses I might need in the future. But it wasn't fair to string Alf along, not when my heart wasn't in it. He hadn't seemed that upset and was courting Betty Jones within a week.

I'd received several letters from Zeyla. The one light in her life seemed to be that now she was expecting, Rupert had ceased his unwelcome night-time visits to her bedroom. Poor thing, my heart did go out to her. It was a rotten situation to be in, but one of her own making to my mind. And what could I do about it? Well, if writing all her woes down and sending them to me helped her get through it, then she could carry on. I wasn't about to reply. Largely because I didn't want to give her the impression that I was pining for her. I missed her. I missed what we'd had for those delightful months. But I didn't miss the feelings of inadequacy she unintentionally drew up in me. I missed Hugo more.

Thinking about Zeyla took me out of Clifftop Cottage and into the painting studio I'd created out of the old potting shed. I propped up my sketchbook against the window and placed a newly stretched canvas on the easel. With the help of the ten bob Hugo had left me, I'd finally managed to save up enough to kit out the studio with all my favourite oil paints and bits and bobs. I also started experimenting with watercolours, but oils were still where I was most comfortable.

I flicked through my sketchbook, pausing momentarily on the drawings of Hugo in the small room above the grocer's shop. The one of him by the window, looking over his shoulder at me while pulling the curtain, was a particular favourite. It took a few goes to get the shape of his buttocks right. I giggled at the memories. That had been quite a week. But I wasn't ready to convert my rough sketches into a portrait yet. Not while I didn't know where he was. The last I'd heard from him, his regiment had fought through Normandy and the Ardennes and had reached Brussels. That had been back at the beginning of September, and there'd been no more news since. The very thought of something dreadful happening to him dried my mouth. But I had promised him that I wouldn't mope or wallow. I had promised him that I would live, and so I would.

I turned over one more page and inhaled sharply at Zeyla's lithe and slinky body draped seductively across the page. I tried to imagine her with a belly swollen with her unborn child, but the image wouldn't come. My mind could only see her as she had lain on the threadbare rug in front of the fire, or propped up in my bed surrounded by our hastily discarded dresses like she was in my sketch. With a chuckle, I picked up a light charcoal and began sketching out a few guidelines.

'Alright, Zeyla darling. Let's see if I can remember the texture and shade of your skin.'

# FIFTY

## EMILY

September 2016

It had taken Scott and his team two weeks to get the exhibition hall up and ready, and they would be back to finish any last-minute tweaks in a few days. With only a week to go until the big opening night Emily's nerves had been keeping her awake. Tickets had sold out via the museum's website for the whole of the exhibition. But there was still a creeping dread that no one would come, that all the effort and money spent would be in vain. Terry was home and looking better by the day and that was what kept Emily going.

She was on her second coffee of the morning, reviewing the exhibition brochure one last time before it went to print, when the loud knock of the lion's head on the cottage door made her jump.

Tim Jackson, the Dovecote postman with knobbly knees, handed her a large, thin rectangular package, wrapped with brown paper and tied with string. The postmark was Irish. Her hands trembled as she carefully untied the string and peeled off the brown paper to reveal something wrapped in bubble wrap.

A small blue envelope slid onto the floor and Emily picked it up, placing the package down on the sofa.

*Cois Farraige, Glencaragh*

*14 September 2016*

*Dearest Emily,*

*You have been on my mind since your all too short visit last month. Thank you for bringing my darling Violet back into my life. Although she has resided in my heart for many years, I had not allowed myself to let her into my mind. I have put many ghosts to bed since speaking with you. With Caroline's help, I have spoken to Philip, and we are working on contacting George. Talking about it all with you made me realise how ridiculous it is that I have lost contact with them, and how much I would regret not making amends before my life comes to an end. That event cannot be far off – I am too old as it is.*

*I am under no illusion that I did not fool you for a second when I said that I did not know if Violet had ever transformed her sketches of me into paintings. I do hope you will forgive me my small lie.*

*I wish you every success with the exhibition, and I hope it goes some way to gaining Violet the recognition she deserved. I am only sorry that at my age it would be foolhardy of me to attempt to visit to see it for myself. I only ask that these be returned to me as soon as is convenient after the exhibition. Should the exhibition outlast me, then I leave them in your possession.*

*Yours,*

*Zeyla*

Emily gathered the portraits up in her arms, still encased in bubble wrap, and bolted for Dovecote Manor, her heart pounding in time with her steps on the path. There was no time to lose.

Everyone gathered around Emily in the kitchen of Dovecote Manor as she carefully unwrapped Zeyla's parcel.

'Oh, my,' Sue exclaimed, as the bubble wrap fell to the floor.

'Let's see,' chorused Harrison and Gio, and Emily laid the two portraits down on the table. In the first, Zeyla was lounging on a sofa, one arm flung casually over her head, one leg slightly drawn up and crossed over the other at the knees, her eyes closed. In the second, she was sitting up surrounded by pillows, her bright-green eyes looking directly outwards, her cheeks flushed pink, her hair dishevelled. Beside her on the bed, a green dress lay in a pile tangled with a sky-blue dress with white dots. In both paintings, she was completely nude.

'Those eyes will follow you around the room,' Harrison said.

'It's a very intense stare,' Gio added. 'Hugo has a similar look in his portrait.'

'Clearly Violet had that effect on people,' Emily said. 'Well, on two particular people, anyway.'

'Emily, is that the dress you wore to Molly's wedding?' Sue looked at her with wide eyes and Emily leant closer to the painting. It *was* the dress.

'Wow. I think you're right, Sue.' Emily straightened up and folded her arms. 'That's going to take some getting my head around.'

'We should put the dress on display next to the portrait,' Gio said clapping his hands together. Emily gawped at him.

'No, Emily, he's right. It would be amazing. Just think, we have the dress either Violet or Zeyla wore, which Violet then captured in the portrait. How incredible is that?' Harrison's excitement was infectious.

'That must have been the day of the tea dance. Zeyla wrote in her diary that she lent Violet a blue and white tea dress, while she wore a long green one.'

'Right,' Sue said. 'Gio, you get on to Scott, we don't have much time to get this added to the exhibition. Emily, we need the dress and a photocopy of the diary entry. Oh, and any sketches that match the portrait. I have an old dressmaker's mannequin in the loft we can use for the dress. Harrison you'll have to go up and get it.'

Gio chewed his lip for a moment. 'It's probably going to cost to get these changes made at such a late stage.'

Sue glanced at Terry, who gave her a weak thumbs up from the armchair that had been moved into the kitchen so he could sit and chat with Sue while she cooked. 'Leave that to me,' she said. 'There's a bit left in the budget but, if necessary, I can give Will a call. I'll run it past Gordon and James too, although they have said the exhibition is our baby. They're just grateful we're doing this for the museum's benefit.'

'When you speak to Will, can you ask him to call Caroline, Zeyla's granddaughter, and get Zeyla's permission to display a portion of her diary? Zeyla was quite unnerved by me having read it. I don't know what she'd think of hundreds of strangers reading her most intimate thoughts.'

'Of course. Yes, indeed. Good thinking,' Sue said, tapping her phone against her thigh. 'Okay, team, let's get to it.'

Back at the cottage, Emily flicked through Zeyla's diary, stopping when she came to the right page.

*18 December 1943*

*V has been griping that we don't go out anywhere together, and I can't entirely blame her. But we made up for it today by venturing into Brighton (it's quite a mess after all the bombings) and going to a tea dance. Ladies only. Gosh it was thrilling. To be able to hold V in public and dance with her somewhere other than the sitting room of Clifftop Cottage was utterly intoxicating. I wore my long green taffeta; it's a little on the dated side, but I do love it. V, of course, had nothing to wear, so I gave her an old tea dress of mine, the blue one with the tiny daisies on it. It looked far better on her than it ever did on me. Of course, I spent most of the day thinking about getting her out of it, which I did with unseeming haste the moment we got back. She wouldn't let me fix my hair before she sketched me afterwards.*

Emily smiled to herself. She had done it, she'd found Violet's missing portraits, and what a story they told.

# FIFTY-ONE

## EMILY

September 2016

There was an unseasonable warmth in the sea breeze that blew up the cliff and embraced Clifftop Cottage a week later, as Emily closed the French doors behind her. She drew a deep breath of salty air to settle her nerves and slipped into Violet's studio and switched on the light. The room seemed much emptier with so many of the canvases up in the exhibition hall. As much as Clifftop Cottage was now her home, the potting shed was still, and would always be, Violet's.

'So, Aunt Violet,' Emily whispered to the still air in the room. 'Here we are. People are coming from all over to see your paintings. And all for a good cause, too. I hope, wherever you are, that you're happy with what we've done.'

Emily was about to turn off the light when there was a tap on the door. Gio was looking as elegant and suave as always. He kissed her cheek.

'Are you nervous?' he asked. 'Because I am.'

'It's all going to be fine, Gio,' Emily said, giving his hand a quick squeeze. 'You've done a fabulous job.'

Harrison appeared at the door, looking as uncomfortable in his suit as he'd been at Molly and Jez's wedding.

'Hey, Emily. Looking good.'

Emily glanced down at her new knee-length burgundy velvet dress. Not her usual colour choice but it seemed right for the occasion, and the cute sweetheart neckline had swayed her.

'You're sure it doesn't clash with my red hair?'

The two men shook their heads in unison.

'Trust me, darling. You look gorgeous.'

The three of them stood in the studio for a minute as if in silent tribute to Violet. It was Emily who broke the stillness.

'Is all of this okay?' she asked. Gio and Harrison gave her quizzical looks. 'I mean, as far as we know there's only us, Sue and Terry, Will, Janice, Caroline, and Zeyla who know that Violet was bisexual. In a few hours, pretty much the whole of Dovecote will know, as well as the press and some of London's top art critics. Is it right that we're outing her, even though she's gone?'

Harrison drew a deep breath and Gio rubbed his left eyebrow.

'Bit late to be worrying about that now, Emily,' Harrison said.

'I know. I guess I needed to put it out there.'

Gio took her hand in his. 'When you spoke to Janice, she said Violet never deliberately hid who she was. And people not knowing was because they made assumptions, right?'

Emily nodded.

'I think she would be quite comfortable that you, as one of her only surviving relatives, are setting the record straight. Or not straight, if you get what I mean.'

'Yeah, I get it.' Emily chuckled. 'Thanks, Gio.'

The look of love and pride Harrison gave Gio made Emily's heart swell to bursting point.

'Alright, let's do this,' she beamed.

'You two go ahead,' Harrison said, heading back towards Dovecote Manor. 'I promised I'd help Mum get Dad's wheelchair down the driveway.'

'How is he?' Emily asked.

Harrison grinned. 'Like a new man.'

Gio offered Emily his arm. 'Shall we?'

'No sign of Will, then?' Emily asked as they made their way down the driveway from Clifftop Cottage. The entrance to the west lawn was at the bottom of the main driveway. 'Surely, he's going to come. Won't he want to see what we've spent his money on?'

'Maybe. No one has heard from him for a week. Not since Sue got a text from him to say not to worry about the extra cost, and that Zeyla had given permission for her diary to be displayed.'

'I guess Tabitha has got her hooks well and truly into him.'

'You almost sound sorry for him.'

Emily looked up sharply at Gio. 'I don't feel sorry for him, as such. I hope he's happy, that's all. And that he's back with her for the right reasons, and she's not going to hurt him.'

'Uh-huh. Now you sound like you care about him,' Gio teased. Emily elbowed him in the ribs. 'Anyway, while I have you alone, I have some news.'

Emily dropped her hand from around Gio's arm and stopped walking. 'Should I be worried?'

'Darling no, this is all good news. As long as me being around more is good news. Since Terry's operation, he and Sue have admitted they can't keep running the events business themselves. They've offered me a job. It's not as much money as being a London wedding planner, but I've said yes.'

Emily squealed and flung her arms around his neck. 'That is brilliant news, Gio. Oh my goodness. How exciting. Congratulations!'

'Thank you. It has worked out quite well, considering my other news.'

'Spit it out.' Emily laughed as Gio chewed his bottom lip.

'Harrison has bought Seaglass Cottage. And he's asked me to move in with him.'

Emily shrieked. 'That's so cute. You have said yes, right?'

Gio laughed. 'Do I look like an idiot? Of course I said yes. Although I did mention that I've never lived with anyone, in that way, before.'

'I'm sure it will all be fine. I'm so happy for you. My bestie is all settled down. I can't believe it. I never would have thought I'd see the day someone finally tamed you.'

'It was about time I grew up.'

Emily hugged him tightly and blinked back the tears pricking her eyes. For once, they were happy tears.

The path from the Dovecote estate gate, through the rhododendrons and across the west lawn, to the exhibition hall was bathed in the glow of fairy lights threaded through the trees. It would be magical in the full dark. Scott was waiting at the end of the path.

'We're all ready for you,' he said, with a flourish.

'Oh my goodness, it's so beautiful,' Sue cried from behind them. 'I can't believe how good it looks. Scott, you are a miracle worker.'

Emily could feel the heat coming off Scott's cheek as he ran his fingers through his short, blond hair, and air-kissed her. 'I had a good team. And the events people Gio hired are brilliant,' he said, flashing a smile at Gio. Harrison took Gio's hand and shot Scott a look, but then smiled and Emily breathed a little easier.

'After you,' Harrison said, nudging Emily forward. 'This was your idea.'

Emily stepped into the hall and gasped. From the outside, the temporary building looked like a log cabin but inside it was pure, cool white. The floor was as smooth and shiny as a dance-floor, with a red-carpet path around the sides, guiding visitors from painting to painting. Spotlights highlighted the artworks, bringing them to life. The paintings were arranged in groups depending on style and subject. The seascapes were hung on blue walls, the landscapes on green. And the experimental canvases covered in bright splodges were stunningly hung on a pure white background. In the middle, in their own pool of light, arranged on opposite sides of a square pillar were the portraits. Each one was accompanied by a notice explaining who the person in the portrait was, and how they were connected to Violet.

'I can't believe we've pulled off something this incredible,' Emily exclaimed, walking over to the portrait of Zeyla and the dresses. 'You were right, Gio, having the dress here brings it all to life. I wonder if Violet would have loved this.'

'I think she would have been very proud of you, darling. For lots of reasons.'

'Thank you.' Emily sniffled, trying to casually wipe away a tear. She turned back towards the door as a rumble of noise turned into the excited chatter of voices. 'Well, time to see what our invited guests think.'

Emily was doing her second circuit of the room, and was on her second glass of champagne, when she found Janice looking at one of the beach scenes.

'The two boys?' Janice whispered, not turning away from the painting.

'Yes, they're always there. At first, I presumed they were her brothers, but—'

'They could be her sons, Michael and Thomas.'

'Yes, they could,' Emily said, haltingly.

Janice drew a deep breath. 'We'll never know, but I'd like to think they're all of her boys and all of the children who didn't get to grow up. I know Violet often considered how lucky they were that they'd all survived the first time they got bombed out. So many didn't.'

'There's such a delightful innocence to them, too. She's painted these children in a happy scene, without a care in the world. As children should be,' Sue said, coming up behind them and taking in the picture. 'They could even be my two when they were little, mucking about on the beach.'

'Or my girls. Or my grandchildren.' There was a curious edge to Janice's voice, but Emily didn't get a chance to probe any further as Molly came up and grabbed her elbow.

'Emily, oh my goodness. Your dress.' She pulled Emily towards the display in the middle of the room again. That seemed to be the way the night was going. Whenever she drifted away from the portraits someone, or something, pulled her back.

'Violet's dress. I know, isn't it amazing?'

'What's amazing is how young I looked. How young I was.'

Emily spun on her heels at the voice behind her.

'Zeyla,' she cried, enveloping her in a hug. 'You came. You said it would be foolhardy of you to attempt the journey.' Emily narrowed her eyes slightly. Zeyla looked fantastic in a sea-green kaftan covered in swirls of blue and white. She was like a living sea.

'Well, I've been a coward far too long, Emily. It was about time I did something brave and come back to Dovecote at last. And I had some help.'

Emily followed Zeyla's gaze to where Will was greeting his parents.

'Will?'

'He drove all the way to Glencaragh and back so I wouldn't have the upheaval of getting on a plane. But I'll let him explain it to you.' Zeyla moved around the square display. 'That's quite enough of looking at my own naked body, although I hardly recognise myself. I don't look like that now; I can tell you that for nothing.'

'Your eyes are the same,' Emily said, smiling at her.

'You're too kind. But let's have a look at this Hugo chap. Let me see the man who made the love of my life happy.' She stood looking at the portrait of Hugo at the window for a long moment before letting out a light peal of laughter. 'Oh, I like him.' She clapped her hands together. 'He looks like he could handle our Violet alright. He's got a cheekiness about him and a bit of mischief in his eyes. Oh yes, I like him very much.'

# FIFTY-TWO

## EMILY

September 2016

The evening passed in a whirl of conversation, champagne, and canapés. There was lots of interest from people with deep pockets over the paintings that were for sale, and by the end of the night, quite a few little red dots had been stuck to the walls. Once everyone had gone and the events team had set up for the following day when the exhibition opened to the public, Emily made her way back up the driveway to Dovecote Manor with Gio, Sue, and Harrison. Terry having given in to Will's insistence on driving him up the hill.

'I think we all deserve a little drink,' Sue said, grabbing Emily's hand and pulling her towards the house. 'Come on in everyone and let's celebrate a job well done.'

Emily glanced over her shoulder as Will pulled up on the gravel. A pair of emerald-green eyes peered out cautiously from the passenger seat.

Emily caught Sue's eye. 'It's her first time back here in seventy-two years. Goodness knows what she's thinking.'

Sue drew a breath. 'Indeed. I hope she likes what we've done with the place.'

Harrison gave Terry a hand as he extracted himself from back seat of the car while Will helped Zeyla out of the front. She stood, leaning on him slightly, looking up at the house she once called home. She raised a bony finger and pointed at the window on the far right of the upstairs floor.

'That was my bedroom,' she said. 'The morning after Violet's mother was killed, I was woken up by her throwing bits of gravel at the window. So many memories...' Zeyla's voice trailed off. Her green eyes glistened.

Sue reached out a hand and Zeyla took it. 'Welcome, Zeyla. Come on in, we'd love to hear your stories about the manor.'

Emily caught Will's eye. As her heart was close to bursting, she could only nod at him.

Harrison had insisted on making some of Violet's famous martinis and Emily was a little lightheaded as she wandered into the library. She'd been looking for Will, meaning to thank him for bringing Zeyla back to Dovecote, but instead she found Zeyla herself, sitting in the chair by Terry's desk looking up at a portrait of a severe-looking man.

'Who is he?' Emily asked, almost in a whisper.

'That, my dear, is Randolph Wythenshawe. My father. It's quite fitting that he had a huge portrait of himself on the wall of his own study.'

'He does look rather frightening.'

'He was.' There was a glimmer of a tear in Zeyla's eye. 'And if he hadn't been so intimidating, then maybe I could have stood up to him. If it hadn't been for him, and Mother of course, I never would have married Rupert.' She wiped her wet cheek and let out a short, sharp huff. 'Who am I kidding? It wasn't them; it was me. I was the one who made the choice to take the easy route and marry Rupert.'

Emily knelt on the rug beside the chair and put her hand on Zeyla's knee. 'It wasn't the easy route, Zeyla. You had to hide who you really were and do things you didn't want to.'

'Which is why, looking back, it makes no sense. I was so blinded by the promise of a few nice dresses and a comfortable lifestyle, that I threw away the chance for true happiness and erased my own identity. What on earth was I thinking?'

'It was a different time.'

'And it was all for nothing. Because when I left Rupert, Mother and Father disowned and disinherited me anyway. I could have saved myself a whole load of heartache by upsetting them twenty years earlier.'

They sat in silence for a moment.

'It's quite odd, being back in the room where it all went wrong.' Zeyla inclined her head towards the middle of the room, where Gerry was curled up on the rug having a snooze. 'That was where Rupert proposed. And I, the damned fool, accepted. There were nights when I imagined what would have happened if Violet had barged in and dragged me away with her. But I betrayed her, and I can't blame her for what she said or did afterwards. I deserved it. I wrote to her for a couple of years, but she never replied. Then, not long after the end of the war, the portraits arrived, wrapped in brown paper and tied with string. I knew it was her way of telling me that we were finished. Almost as if she was sending me the last reminder of me, and of us, she had. I didn't write to her again after that.'

'I can't believe you never came back to Dovecote, in all those years. Didn't you miss it?'

'I missed Violet, and that is what kept me away. Mother and Father preferred to visit Rupert and me and the boys in Oxford. I did come back, once. In 1968, or thereabouts. I'd settled in Glencaragh by then but had come back to London for something or other. I found myself at Waterloo station and decided, in the spur of the moment, to come home. I figured enough time had elapsed that Violet might have forgiven me. I stepped out of Dovecote station and saw her. She was on The Promenade, with a man. Hugo, probably, but I didn't know about him at the time. They were laughing about something. They might even have been sharing an ice cream. I knew I had to let her go. I turned around and got right back on the train.

'I loved her all my life, you know. When I read in *The Times* that she'd died, I cried for hours. I didn't think I still had it in me. It was only because the obituary mentioned her maiden name that I realised it was her. I'd heard of Violet Cooper but had never put two and two together which was unspeakably dense of me. Perhaps I didn't want to. I've spent decades hardening myself against heartache, running away from love, isolating myself to prevent pain. It's been lonely.'

Emily sniffed and wiped her eyes with her sleeve.

'Oh, look, now I've made you cry. I'm sorry, my dear,' Zeyla said, with a light laugh through her own tears. 'Don't go spoiling your make-up over an old fool like me.'

'Thank goodness for waterproof mascara,' Emily said with a weak smile.

'Oh Emily, you are so young. You have your whole life ahead of you. Promise me something, would you?'

'What?'

'Promise me you'll never erase your identity. Promise me you'll always be true to yourself and never let anyone destroy who you are.'

Emily looked up and Zeyla's green eyes were flashing. 'I promise.'

Zeyla took her hand and gave it a squeeze. 'And be brave. If you love someone, tell them. Do everything you can to make sure love doesn't slip through your fingers, like it did mine. If the chance comes your way, grab it with both hands and hold on tight. Do you hear?'

'Yes.'

'So, what are you waiting for? Off you go.'

'Sorry?'

Zeyla gave her a knowing smile. 'Will. Go on, tell him. Right now.'

'I don't...'

'I could see it in your eyes that day in Glencaragh. I could see how much Caroline flirting with him the day we met in the pub pained you. And no, nothing happened between them. Goodness, Caroline is a lovely woman, but she's flighty. Not the right sort of woman for Will at all. He needs someone steady and dependable. Someone who's not afraid to tell him when he's being an idiot. And I could see something else, you were fighting your feelings, for some reason.'

'It's a long story, Zeyla.'

'And how does it end?'

'From where we are now, it ends with Will marrying Tabitha and me growing old in Clifftop Cottage.'

'I see a different ending, but it requires you to be brave. I can't promise you anything. All I can tell you is that you will regret it if you don't do something about it. Trust me, life is a very long journey to carry that kind of regret.'

Emily got to her feet and Zeyla nodded at her. At the door, Emily turned back.

'Maybe we should ask Terry to replace the portrait of your father with one of you? The one of you on the bed would look fantastic up there.'

Zeyla laughed. 'Oh goodness. I both love that idea and hate it. But you're right about one thing, the portraits should stay in Dovecote, with the ones of Hugo. They're only stuffed in the back of the wardrobe at home anyway.'

'I'll put them up in the cottage.'

'It's where I was the happiest I've ever been in my life, dear. I think that's a very good idea.'

Will wasn't in the ballroom, or the sitting room, where Harrison tried to convince Emily that a second martini would be a good idea. Terry, rather sensibly, had retired to bed.

'If you're looking for Will, he went for a walk. Silly boy out traipsing around at this time of night,' Sue giggled. She was already halfway through her second martini.

'He said he needed a bit of air. I think he was headed for the beach,' Gio added with a knowing glint in his eye.

'Thanks,' Emily said.

She stood at the top of the cliff steps, peering into the darkness. The beam from the lighthouse in the distance swept out over the waves. Was that someone down on the beach? There was only one way to find out. Thankful for the solar lights Terry had installed along the path, and for her flat shoes, Emily gingerly made her way down the steps. The tide was in, and waves gently splashed the rocks beneath the wall along Beachfront Road. In the glow of the lights on The Promenade, she could make out the shape of someone on the stone bench. Will looked up as her footsteps crunched the pebbles.

'Hey.'

'Hi.'

'What are you doing down here in the middle of the night?' Will asked.

'I could ask you the same thing.'

A momentary silence, filled only with the fizz of water on pebble. Even the seagulls had called it a night.

'I wanted to thank you for everything you've done to get the exhibition off the ground.'

'I didn't do much, but like I said to you that day we found Zeyla's diary, I'm more of a "pay someone else to do it" person.'

'You've been very generous. We literally couldn't have done it without you. You could have just donated directly to the museum.'

'But if I had, then Violet wouldn't be getting the time in the spotlight she deserves, and that you wanted for her.'

'Oh. Thank you.' He'd done it for her, as much as for Terry. Emily's skin crawled with the memory of the mean things she'd thought and said about him. How had she not seen him for who he really was? And why had she let something from so long ago cloud her judgement? 'Also, thank you for bringing Zeyla tonight. It was so lovely to have her there, and for her to see Violet's paintings. Did you really drive all the way to Glencaragh?'

He leant forward, resting his elbows on his knees. 'Yeah. I needed some headspace. And when Mum told me the portraits had arrived, I figured I may as well go and speak to Zeyla.'

'I mean, driving all that way. How far is it?'

'About five hundred miles from London. Turns out I'm not great on a ferry though.'

'You're nuts.'

Will laughed. 'Maybe.'

Emily looked down at her hands. 'So, how come you needed some headspace? All the wedding planning getting a bit much?'

'The wedding's off.' He said it so quietly Emily wasn't sure at first what he'd said. 'I called it off.'

'You called off your wedding? Why?' Emily could barely hear her own thoughts above the pounding of her pulse in her ears.

'For all the reasons I gave you that day in the ballroom, and more besides.' He leant back against the bench. 'No, that's not true. This time it wasn't about Tabitha. It was about me. I don't want that life any more. I've had enough. I'm burning out. And when you see your dad nearly die of a heart attack, it puts things into perspective. It's not the fast-paced life, or the stressful job, it's that it's all so fake. Any one of the people that are supposed to be my friends would stab me in the back if it meant getting a step ahead of me. I can't do it any more. I can't deal with not being able to trust anyone. And that includes Tabitha.'

'Oh Will, I'm sorry.'

He grimaced. 'Don't be. I'm pretty sure I'm not.'

'Oh. So, what are you going to do?'

Will let out a long breath and ran his fingers through his hair. Emily's nerves fired a jolt of electricity that made her fingers tingle.

'Jez's dad has a financial advice firm here in Dovecote. He's looking to retire, and I think I might buy him out. I'll have to take some exams and get re-licensed and certified. It's been a few years since I moved away from the advice side of things and into fund management.'

'Wouldn't you be bored within a month?'

'Probably, but maybe a bit of boredom might be good for me. And I think it's time I came home to the people I love.'

'Have you told your mum and dad?'

'Not yet. The only person I've told so far is Zeyla. And now you.'

'Did Zeyla tell you to be brave?'

'Yeah. How did you know?'

'I think it's her stock piece of advice.'

'What did she tell you to be brave about?' He was looking at her with an intensity in his brown eyes and Emily very nearly lost her nerve. But Zeyla was right, she had to take the chance. And now that things were over with Tabitha, the end of the story that she had mapped out had been unwritten. There was nothing but a blank page.

'She made me promise that I wouldn't let the chance of happiness slip through my fingers. And she told me to be brave about telling someone how I feel about them.'

'And how is that?'

'That I forgive them. That, thanks in part to their sincere apology, I've been able to grow and heal and realise that maybe I don't deserve to be hurt or treated badly. But you don't get to claim all the credit for that, Gio's been giving me a talking-to as well.'

'Does that mean you don't hate me?'

'I don't think I ever did. I think I hated myself.'

'You mustn't. Because you're brilliant and amazing. You were glorious tonight at the exhibition. The way you talk to everyone so easily, and the genuine love and affection you have for Violet and Zeyla, and everyone, shines out of you. You've always been incredible. I was so, so wrong when I called you a nobody. You're a very special somebody.'

'Thank you.' Her heart fluttered as the church clock chimed midnight.

'It's getting a bit chilly, and a bit late. We should probably head back.'

'Yeah, you might need to rescue your mum. Harrison's been making Violet's martinis again.'

Will laughed and offered Emily his arm. 'Shall we?'

Emily took it and they walked up the beach. At the top of the steps, Emily drew Will to a halt.

'Actually Will, there's something else I want to say.'

He raised an eyebrow. Emily looked down at the pavement, there was a little bird's footprint in the concrete. She drew a steadying breath. It was now or never. And if he was going to be staying around Dovecote, never would be a very long time.

'I don't know how to say this, because I've only just allowed myself to believe it.' Will was looking at her with a mixture of curiosity and confusion. The gold flecks in his eyes sparkled in the light from the streetlamp. 'But the thing is. Oh hell, I'm just going to say it. I love you. Despite my best attempts not to, I do.'

He blinked at her a few times and then shook his head. 'I, um... I wasn't expecting that.'

'I'm sorry. Forget I said anything.' Emily began to walk away but Will placed a gentle hand on her shoulder. Firm enough to let her know he wanted her to stay but light enough that she could keep walking if she wanted to.

'Emily.'

She turned back to him.

'What I meant was I wasn't expecting that because I thought you were a lesbian.'

Emily sighed. 'I'm not. Didn't Harrison tell you? I'm bi. Just like Great-Aunt Violet.'

'He failed to mention that. Emily, for months I've been fighting my feelings for you because I thought I had no chance. I am so sorry for making an assumption about your identity. Oh my God, seriously. You don't know how many times I've had to stop myself from saying something or doing something. That evening in the lounge at the hotel, I was so close to... and then you started flirting with the woman behind the bar the next night.' He put his arms around Emily's waist and pulled her in close. He rested his forehead against hers. 'The main reason I ended it with Tabitha was because I'm not in love with her. I'm in love with you.'

It was a kiss that had been fifteen years in the making, and it was worth waiting for.

# FIFTY-THREE
## VIOLET

December 1944

I don't know how I missed it, sitting there in plain sight on the bookshelf beside the fireplace. The brown leather of the book was worn and soft. I traced the gold embossed Z on the top corner of the cover as I recalled the morning after her party in January. I'd come home after spending the night in Hugo's bed to find Zeyla at Clifftop Cottage. She'd been standing by the bookshelf when I walked in. I fanned the pages and the book, her diary from 1943, fell open on a random page.

*23 June 1943*

*I must learn to do some basic household chores, or I shall be utterly useless to V when we set up our love nest together. She said tonight, as we laid under her bedsheets, that she'd give anything for a soft-boiled egg with buttered soldiers to dip in the runny yolk. I will learn how to boil an egg so I can give her this simple pleasure. Listen to me, promising to actually do something useful. I must be in love.*

I flicked a few pages over, the words blurring slightly.

*10 July 1943*

*V wanted to draw me again last night. More than happy to lie on the couch, or her bed, with a summer evening breeze coming through the window. The way her eyes sweep across my body and then linger over some part of me, sends electric shivers across my skin. Quite the turn on. She never lets me see what she's drawn though. I don't want this to ever end. When I am old and I get asked how I survived the war, I shall reply 'because I was in love.'*

'And yet you gave it up so easily,' I whispered, tracing her words with my finger. Something made me flick to the pages towards the back. Was I looking for mention of him, of Rupert? Why was I torturing myself? I shoved the diary into the top drawer of my writing bureau and my memories of those days to the back of my mind. Why didn't I pack up and go? I had nothing tying me to Dovecote. Except Hugo. If he came back and I wasn't here, how would he know where to find me? No, I would stay put, living with the shadows of the heady days of 1943 until he was safely home. Then I'd begin my life.

The loud thud of the lion's head door knocker roused me from my daydream. It was rare I received visitors. I was grateful neither Randolph nor Venetia Wythenshawe ever had the urge to call upon their tenant. I'm not sure I could have coped with having to make polite enquiries into the wellbeing of their daughter. In Zeyla's most recent letter, she'd begged me to come and see her. I tore it up and threw it in the fire.

I let out a squeal of delight when I opened the door. Without a word, Hugo gathered me in his arms, squeezing me so tight I nearly burst and lifting me clean off my feet. He carried me into the sitting room.

'Hugo, goodness. How wonderful to see you.' I kissed his cheek.

'Violet, listen. I don't have much time. I've only got forty-eight hours' shore leave before I have to be back in Brussels, and I've spent twenty of them running around looking for an open jeweller.' He rummaged around in his coat.

'Hugo... I...' My voice faltered as he drew a small box out of his pocket and knelt down on one knee.

'Violet, I know this is going to come totally out of the blue, but you have been on my mind every day since I left you in Brighton. There have been long days, and even longer nights, as we battled our way through France and into Belgium, when thoughts of you have been the only thing that's got me through. Violet Saunders, I love you, and I can only hope you feel the same way. Will you marry me?'

The ticking of the clock and the thudding of my heart marked the seconds that hung in the air.

'Hugo, I...' He looked up at me with such intense longing and deep affection that I was quite swept away. Could this, could he, be my future? Why not? Yes, why not? Zeyla was gone, there was no going back to what we had. My brief affairs with Peggy and Alf had been fun but I hadn't been in love with either of them. My mind fired snapshots of the happy times I'd had with Hugo: long summers before the war, that night at The Royal Oak, the week in Brighton. I also remembered how much I'd missed him, and worried about him. It hit me like a runaway train. I loved him. I truly, deeply loved him.

'Yes,' I eventually said. 'Yes!'

The ring slipped effortlessly onto my finger, immediately becoming a part of me.

'How long do you have?' I asked when he released me from a long, lingering kiss that lit a fire deep in my bones.

'Long enough,' he said, his voice low and soft.

I nearly dislocated his shoulder pulling him towards the

stairs. I wasn't about to let him disappear off again without something to remember me by.

# EPILOGUE

## EMILY

June 2017

A cheer went up from the crowd gathered around the large scale-model of 1940s Dovecote in the main hall of Dovecote Museum as Zeyla, with James and Gordon Rutherford's help, snipped through the ceremonial ribbon across a set of new glass double doors. The doors led into the brand new extension, complete with a full-size replica of the air raid shelter that had been under The Royal Oak. James gave Zeyla a reassuring nod as he handed her the microphone. She cleared her throat and glanced at Emily, standing at the edge of the crowd with Will.

'Oh, hello. Apparently as the only person here ancient enough to have been in the original shelter in the basement of The Royal Oak, it falls to me to say a few words. Where do I start? It is quite surreal to stand here next to a replica of a place I haven't seen since I was a young woman. This facility is incredibly important. There are fewer and fewer of us still around who remember the war, and therefore a place like this where today's children can experience what it was like, is a tremendous resource.

'If you will indulge me, I'd like to tell you a little story that involves the shelter. It was April 1943. I was eighteen and on my way to the cinema in Brighton with a friend when the siren went off. We dived for the shelter at The Royal Oak. And it's a blinking good job we did. In that shelter, I found the love of my life. I hurried down the steps and saw the most beautiful woman in the world sitting on the bench in the corner. Her name was Violet Saunders. Most of you will have known her as Violet Cooper, which she became after she married. It was love at first sight. It took me a while to convince her, but we got there in the end.'

The gathered group laughed. Emily reached for Will's hand.

'Violet was a wonderful artist, and an exhibition of her work last year raised money for this building. Thank you to all who came and supported. No doubt she would have been humbled to think that her work still has the power to do good in the world. It's not a bad legacy, is it?

'It is also quite poignant to be standing on this spot today. In May 1943 a German bomber, aiming for Brighton, dropped a bomb on a square of houses right here, between Blythe Avenue and The Promenade. Violet and her mother lived in one of the houses – number 24, which would have been where the back of the museum is now. Violet was with me at the time, but her mother was fatally injured in the blast and died in Bayview a few hours later. It is fitting that we remember Rebecca Saunders and all those killed that night.'

A respectful hush fell over the crowd for a moment.

'I want to say one more thing. It is Pride Month, and it is very fitting that an exhibition of work by a bisexual artist has helped bring this project to fruition. We have come a long way since love between people of the same sex had to be hidden out of fear and shame. And it's wonderful.'

Emily winked at Gio who was standing with his arm around Harrison's shoulders. He smiled back.

'But there is still work to do and as long as I have breath in my lungs I shall do whatever I can. Love blossomed in the original air raid shelter, and the project to get the replica built has also been a fertile hunting ground for Cupid. Let this air raid shelter remind you all to never let love slip through your fingers.'

The gathered Dovecote residents erupted in applause. Will wiped the tears from Emily's cheeks and kissed her lightly on the forehead.

'Are you going to take a look? I think you and Zeyla should go in together.'

'Yes,' Emily sniffed. 'I think I will.'

Emily made her way through the crowd to where James and Gordon were talking rather animatedly to Zeyla.

'What you said about it being Pride Month really hit a chord, Zeyla,' James was saying. 'There's a story there. And it's not one that's been told enough.' He glanced at his father who was nodding, but in a way that made it clear he had no idea what was going to come out of his son's mouth next. 'Queer Dovecote. What do you think, Zeyla?'

'About?'

Emily grinned. Zeyla looked as lost as Gordon.

'About helping us tell the story of the LGBTQIA+ history of our town?'

'Oh,' Zeyla gasped, clapping her hands together. 'What a marvellous idea. You're more than welcome to start with my diary. If Emily can bear to let it out of her hands.'

'I was thinking I should give it back to you, Zeyla. It is yours, after all. Your speech was beautiful.'

At that moment, Caroline appeared at Zeyla's shoulder with Freddie, clutching her hand while devouring a bar of chocolate.

'Grandma, what a wonderful speech. I got a bit choked up. Hey, Emily.'

'Hi, Caroline. Thanks for coming, and for bringing Zeyla over. It's good to see you again.'

'I couldn't miss out on a trip to Dovecote now, could I? I mean, it's my heritage, right? And I'm in no hurry to go back to the States.' She took hold of Zeyla's hand. 'Come over here for a second, Grandma. Have you met Declan? He runs The Royal Oak.' There was a look in Caroline's eyes that Emily recognised from the way she'd looked at Will. Caroline and Declan? Not the most obvious match, but love was a strange thing.

Zeyla put her hand on Emily's arm. 'Sorry, dear, did you want me for something?'

Emily shook her head. 'No, don't worry. Nothing urgent.'

They could visit the shelter another day, especially as Zeyla had hinted that she might return home to Dovecote for good. Her house in Glencaragh was already up for sale and she'd enquired about room availability at Bayview Care Home. But if that didn't work out, Sue had said that with Harrison now living at Seaglass Cottage with Gio, and Will living in Clifftop Cottage with Emily, there was plenty of room at Dovecote Manor.

Zeyla blew Emily a kiss as Caroline dragged her and Freddie to where Declan was manning a makeshift bar in the far corner.

Emily scanned the room looking for Will, but she couldn't see him. He'd probably ducked outside for a moment. It was a glorious summer's day. She snuck towards the door of the museum, catching only Gio's eye.

'He's in Victoria Park,' Gio mouthed.

Emily found Will near the bandstand, sitting on the bench that overlooked The Promenade and the beach.

'I think this is where Zeyla first kissed Violet,' Emily said, sitting down next to him. She laid her head on his shoulder. 'And Violet panicked and ran away. It's a good job Zeyla was persistent.'

'Yes, otherwise Violet might have been at home the night 24 Blythe Avenue was bombed. Even if she'd survived, she might never have moved into Clifftop Cottage, and you would never have come bursting into my life, completely derailing it. Not once, but twice.'

'Isn't it funny how a million different things have had to take place, good and bad, to bring us both to this exact place and time?'

'And how the choices people make affect so many lives for generations?'

Emily gazed out over the low stone wall around the park and the turquoise railings of The Promenade. Beyond, the beach was dotted with families and people enjoying the sunshine. Down near the shore, a pair of small boys were building a miniature fort out of stones. They could have stepped right out of one of Violet's paintings. She was aware of Will fidgeting beside her. When she turned to look at him, he had a curious look on his face, and something hidden in his hands. He shuffled off the bench and bent down on one knee. Tears were already brewing in Emily's eyes.

'Emily Carmichael, you are the best thing that has ever happened to me. These past nine months have been the happiest of my life. You've made me want to be a better person, to change from who I was. I can't even count the number of ways you have made my life complete. I love you. Will you marry me?'

Emily could barely speak through the tears pouring down her cheeks.

'Yes,' she eventually managed to say. 'Yes!'

He slipped the most beautiful ring on her finger. It fitted as though it had been made for her. The modest diamond was exactly the right size for her hand. Will stood up, pulled her to her feet, and kissed her.

Emily glanced over her shoulder. Everyone was still inside the museum. She took Will by the hand and led him out of the park and along The Promenade towards Beachfront Road and the steps up to Clifftop Cottage. No one would miss them for a while.

# A LETTER FROM LAURA

Dearest Reader,

Thank you so much for choosing to read *My Great-Aunt's Diary*. I really hoped you enjoyed meeting Emily and Violet and being immersed in their stories. If you enjoyed *My Great-Aunt's Diary* and would like to find out about all of my latest releases, you can sign up at the following link. Your email address will never be shared, and you can unsubscribe at any time.

*www.bookouture.com/laura-sweeney*

As a lot of the story in this book takes place in Brighton during the war, I visited the Brighton Museum and Art Gallery, which is in the grounds of the stunning Brighton Pavilion. There I fell in love with a desk from 1903 designed by E A Taylor and made by Wylie & Lockhead, Glasgow. The ebonised oak desk with leaded glass panels and silvered metal handles became the inspiration for Violet's much loved and cherished writing bureau. Also at the museum, I came across a collection of personal items belonging to Myra Violet Thomas and Betty S. Hakesley who both served in the Sussex Royal Battalion Women's Royal Army Corps. They were together more than fifty years. Theirs is just one of the many LGBTQIA+ stories from the war period that are only now being uncovered and told. I hope many more such stories are given the reverence and limelight they deserve.

I really love hearing from readers, so please get in touch via social media.

Thank you so much for your support.

Laura

www.laurasweeneyauthor.co.uk

 x.com/laura_c_sweeney

 instagram.com/laura_c_sweeney

 bsky.app/profile/lauracsweeney.bsky.social

# ACKNOWLEDGEMENTS

Here we are, book two. Wow! Getting to have one book published is an immense thrill, two is mind-blowing. My first thank you must go, again, to you, dear reader. Readers are why writers write; we would literally be nothing without you.

Thank you again Imogen, for your support, patience, and encouragement, and for putting up with my random comments throughout the editing process. Thank you to the whole Bookouture team for all your hard work. You are all amazing, and I am very lucky to have you on my team.

As always, I couldn't have got through this strange, and often lonesome, journey of writing a book without my writing community. Thank you to the BookCamp mentees, the Primadonna gang, my RNA friends, and the Devon Bananas (who were there right at the early stages of this book's existence).

Thanks to the wonderful authors I've met, either in person or online, who have encouraged, supported, and inspired me. And thank you to AJ West and Vic at The Book Party, for making me feel like a proper author.

I don't remember how I first came to discover Duncan Grant's incredible art, but I suspect the wonderful Damian Barr had something to do with it. So thank you, Damian. Thanks also for the voice message and for the hug in Edinburgh.

I promised I'd give a mention to Alex, Michael, Pedro, and Sally at Bert's Books. Thanks for all the chats, encouragement, book recommendations, and for providing a safe space for me to vent.

*Go raibh maith agat* to Jamie Uí Chormaic for checking my Gaeilge. I really should have paid more attention in school.

A very special thank you to Jo for sharing your dad's story. I hope I have done his bravery and spirit justice.

And of course, love and hugs to all my family, friends, and colleagues who have looked after me, cared for me, poured me drinks, bought me chocolate, and made me laugh. You're the best x

# PUBLISHING TEAM

Turning a manuscript into a book requires the efforts of many people. The publishing team at Bookouture would like to acknowledge everyone who contributed to this publication.

## Commercial
Lauren Morrissette
Hannah Richmond
Imogen Allport

## Cover design
Debbie Clement

## Data and analysis
Mark Alder
Mohamed Bussuri

## Editorial
Imogen Allport

## Copyeditor
Deborah Blake

## Proofreader
Liz Hurst

# RAISING READERS
Books Build Bright Futures

Dear Reader,

We'd love your attention for one more page to tell you about the crisis in children's reading, and what we can all do.

Studies have shown that reading for fun is the **single biggest predictor of a child's future success** – more than family circumstance, parents' educational background or income. It improves academic results, mental health, wealth, communication skills, and ambition.

The number of children reading for fun is in rapid decline. Young people have a lot of competition for their time, and a worryingly high number do not have a single book at home.

Our business works extensively with schools, libraries and literacy charities, but here are some ways we can all raise more readers:

- Reading to children for just 10 minutes a day makes a difference
- Don't give up if children aren't regular readers – there will be books for them!

- Visit bookshops and libraries to get recommendations
- Encourage them to listen to audiobooks
- Support school libraries
- Give books as gifts

Thank you for reading: there's a lot more information about how to encourage children to read on our website.

www.JoinRaisingReaders.com

Made in the USA
Monee, IL
01 August 2025

22361683R00204